In her spellbinding romance *The Prisoner*, Karyn
Monk introduced beautiful Genevieve MacPhail
Kent and her spirited brood of rescued urchins.
Now, from the glittering ballrooms of London to
the Scottish Highlands, secrets and passions collide
as the saga of Genevieve's orphans continues....

The
WEDDING
ESCAPE

KARYN MONK

Bantam Books

THE WEDDING ESCAPE
A Bantam Book / March 2003

Published by
Bantam Dell
A Division of Random House, Inc.
New York, New York

ISBN-13: 978-0-553-58440-0

ISBN-10: 0-553-58440-5

Manufactured in the United States of America
Published simultaneously in Canada

OPM 10 9 8 7 6 5 4 3 2

For

Carson

With all my love

The
WEDDING ESCAPE

Chapter One

IF THERE WAS A HELL, THEN SURELY HE WAS IN IT.

"Do sit still, Jack," whispered Annabelle, nudging him hard in the ribs.

Jack regarded his sister sullenly, struggling to reposition his enormous frame within the confines of the ancient pew. "We've been trapped in this godforsaken mausoleum for over an hour and the bloody wedding hasn't even started yet. The stench from these flowers is choking me, I'm ready to strangle the choir, and I've lost all feeling in my backside."

"That old man over there looks like he's dead." His brother Simon frowned.

Charlotte gave her siblings a mildly reproachful look. "I think the flowers are lovely," she countered softly. "Genevieve said the bride's mother, Mrs. John Henry Belford, designed the arrangements herself, stripping bare nearly every conservatory in England in the process. It must have cost a fortune."

"Roses and orange leaves were a good choice for the Gothic arches." Her sister Grace studied the four extraordinary floral arches that soared over the aisle, creating a magnificent canopy of blossoms beneath which the bride was to make her much-anticipated appearance. "And the fence of lily of the valley and mums at the altar rail is stunning."

"Jamie, go over to that old man and make certain he has a pulse," said Simon, still concerned for the elderly gentleman a few rows across who sat frozen with his eyes closed. "He may need a doctor."

"He's just asleep," his brother assured him. "I saw him scratch himself."

"Lucky bastard," muttered Jack.

"Jack!" Annabelle regarded him with exasperation, while Charlotte and Grace giggled beneath the brims of their enormous hats.

"Perhaps you should step outside for a moment and stretch your legs, Jack."

Haydon Kent, Marquess of Redmond, regarded his son from the next pew with equal measures of empathy and amusement. At sixty-one he had learned to endure the tedious social ordeals that his status demanded of him, but Jack could see he would have dearly loved to escape the suffocating church as well. "Given the funereal pace with which things have progressed, I'm sure you've got a few minutes before we get started here."

"Just make certain you return before the bridal party begins to walk down the aisle," added Genevieve. His mother smiled fondly at him. "No bride wants a wayward guest stumbling over her train as she enters the church."

The colossal organ above blasted the cavernous space once again as the sixty-member choir wearily rose.

"I'll just be outside." Not waiting for the protest that was sure to come from Annabelle, Jack escaped down the aisle, ignoring the disapproving glances of the women in the church and the mournfully envious stares of the men sweating profusely beside them.

The overwhelming stench of the thousands of blossoms within had seeped beyond the church doors and saturated the hot summer air outside, forcing Jack to seek refuge at the side of the ancient stone building. He loosened his necktie and inhaled a deep breath, ridding his lungs of the cloying sweetness.

What madness had possessed him to let his family persuade him to attend this ridiculous wedding? he wondered irritably. He scarcely knew the Duke of Whitcliffe, and he had never met Amelia Belford, the fabulously wealthy American heiress the aging duke had finally deigned to make his wife. If not for the fact that Jack was so anxious to see his family after having been away at sea for three months, he would never have agreed to endure what was turning out to be the most excruciating social torture of his thirty-six years. The lavishness with which the church had been decorated did not bode well for the festivities to come. Five hundred guests were invited to the duke's estate following the ceremony for three interminable days of entertainment. That had to be at the expense of the bride's parents, Jack decided, for it was well known that old Whitcliffe had been struggling to maintain his decrepit family estate for years. Today His Grace would gain a handsome fortune through his blushing bride's dowry. What the sweating guests inside were about to witness was purely a business transaction, with Miss Belford gaining the dubious prestige of an archaic title and Whitcliffe reaping riches that far surpassed any he might otherwise have hoped for in this lifetime or the next.

Jack withdrew a silver flask from inside his morning coat and swallowed a mouthful of whiskey. He didn't care how many spoiled, social-climbing heiresses elected to race across the ocean to set their hooks into some doughy, impoverished aristocrat with yellowing teeth and a pitifully receding hairline.

All that he asked was that they show up for their own goddamn wedding before he died of asphyxiation and boredom.

"Dear God," a small voice suddenly whispered urgently from somewhere above him, "please don't let me be killed."

He looked up in astonishment to see a slender, ivory-stockinged leg hoisted over the gray stone balustrade of the balcony that ran along the side of the church. A snowy cloud of fabric followed it, wadded into such an enormous profusion of petticoats and skirts and lace that it entirely obliterated the wearer. The shapely leg fumbled about with the toe of its delicately fashioned shoe, frantically searching for a hold in the thick, woody vine that grew in a twisted green lattice up the gray stone wall. Having found a branch that seemed to suffice, the small foot tested it once, bending the dangerously makeshift step as it applied more weight. Then another leg swung over to join it, and a veritable snowstorm of bridal finery began to awkwardly creep down the leafy trellis.

All at once the vine began to give way. The frothy confection yelped with fright and crashed into the bushes below in an explosion of silk and leaves. His heart pounding, Jack sprinted toward the tangle of vines and lace, certain the foolish girl had snapped her neck.

"Mercy!" she exclaimed, sounding more breathless than broken. "That was a real cropper!" Her head bobbed up and she began to quickly extricate herself from the crushed bushes.

Relieved that she was not gravely injured and curious to see what she would do next, Jack quietly slipped behind a tree to watch her.

Unable to free herself from the trappings of her extravagant gown, she jerked mercilessly at the hand-stitched fabric, causing it to tear broadly. Finally she had rent it sufficiently that she was able to scramble out of the bushes. She balled up the cumbersome length of her tattered train and veil, then darted as quickly as her fashionable little shoes would permit over to the edge of the church wall. Cautiously, she peered around the front.

The choir had finished its hymn and the bishop was assuring the melting assemblage that the marriage ceremony was about to commence. Jack thought that unlikely, given that the bride had just hurled herself off a balcony and was in the process of making her escape. He watched her spy the long line of handsome carriages arranged down the laneway. The first of these was the bridal carriage, a gaudy affair of ebony and gold bedecked with fat satin ribbons and gigantic white flowers. Evidently deciding that it would be unseemly to flee from her groom in his wedding carriage, the bride raced past those appointed for the wedding party and toward the next available vehicle.

"Quick, drive away!" Amelia managed breathlessly as she scrambled inside, slamming the carriage door behind her. She glanced anxiously through the window to see if she was being followed. Then, remembering her manners, she graciously added to the driver, "Please."

A wizened little man with sleepy eyes and a scraggle of snowy hair turned and regarded her incredulously. "Here now, lass, what's this about?"

"Good afternoon, Miss Belford," said Jack, casually opening the door to the carriage. "A pleasant day for a ride, is it not?"

"Forgive me, sir, but this carriage is already engaged." Amelia struggled to remain calm as she glanced nervously out the window to see if anyone else had noticed her escape. "I'm afraid you will have to find another one."

"The lass is wantin' me to drive away with her," the driver reported to Jack, sounding thoroughly rattled.

"Really, sir, I must insist that you find your own

carriage," Amelia protested, desperate to leave. "This one is already spoken for."

"Unfortunately, this is my own carriage," Jack informed her.

Amelia's heart sank. "Forgive me—I didn't know. In that case, I shall have to find another one."

She wadded up the voluminous trappings of her gown once more and scooted toward the door. Suddenly the mournful strains of the organ within the church stopped and agitated shouting rent the air.

"It would seem," Jack began, cocking his head toward the church, "someone has noticed the bride is missing."

The blood drained from her face, making her alarmingly pale. For a moment Jack feared she might actually faint.

Instead, she jerked off her emerald earrings and tossed them to him. "Will those combined with this necklace be enough for me to purchase this carriage from you?" she asked, unhooking the strand of diamonds around her neck.

Jack stared at her in astonishment.

"You may have this ring as well," she added, straining to pull an enormous ruby surrounded by a glittering halo of diamonds off her right hand. "Lord Whitcliffe said it had been in his family for generations. Of course I've been told that he has been forced to sell the most important Whitcliffe family jewels over the years to meet his debts, but I don't think he would have given it to me unless it was worth quite a bit. He is extremely concerned about appearances."

"I don't want Whitcliffe's ring," Jack protested, flustered.

Her expression fell. "You're right, of course—it doesn't really belong to me. But the necklace and earrings are mine," she vowed fervently. "My father gave them to me for my nineteenth birthday a few months ago. You may take them, sir, feeling absolutely confident that no one will ever come after you and challenge your—Quick, get in, they'll see you!" She grabbed him by his coat sleeve as people began to pour from the church shouting her name. "Hurry!"

Jack reluctantly climbed onto the seat opposite her and closed the door.

"Miss Belford," he began, adopting what he believed was his most reasonable tone, "you are clearly distraught and overcome with emotion. I'm sure that if you take a moment—"

"What is your name, sir?"

He regarded her in exasperation, aware that it would be scant minutes before someone decided to orchestrate a search of the carriages. "It's Jack," he told her. "Jack Kent."

"Tell me, Mr. Kent, have you ever been utterly, hopelessly trapped?"

Her eyes were wide and filled with emotion. They were the color of the sea, Jack realized as he studied her, the dark, unfathomable blue of the ocean when the sun sparkled like fallen stars upon its softly rippling waves. Long, smoky lashes veiled her upper lids, which on closer inspection were puffy and rimmed with scarlet, and crescent-shaped bruises of sleeplessness stained the delicate skin below. Her features were small and beautifully rendered, her complexion as fine as creamy silk, save for a playful splash of freckles that slipped across her nose, which Jack found disconcertingly charming. Her once artfully arranged hair was spilling in pale gold around her shoulders, a hopeless tangle of wayward pins, tattered veil, and bits of leaf. His runaway bride was tall, and her escapade down the wall suggested that she was fairly strong, but in that moment she seemed achingly small and fragile amidst the copious layers of her ruined bridal finery.

"Have you ever felt that you were about to be

sentenced to a horrible existence you knew you could not bear," Amelia continued earnestly, "because the world wanted to imprison you simply because of who you were?"

His jaw tightened. The wounds of his past were buried beneath the years of Genevieve and Haydon's gentle care, but Miss Belford's words still cut him. Some wounds could never heal, he reflected bitterly, no matter how many•years or how much money was layered in protective bandages over them.

For a moment Amelia feared she had offended him. A flash of anger had heated his gray gaze, and she noticed an almost imperceptible clenching of his jaw. There was a harsh wariness to the man before her that she had not encountered in any of the other scores of preening men she had met since arriving in England. His features were handsome but ruggedly cut, his tall physique lean and muscular, which was unlike the indulged softness she had come to expect from most of his peers. A jagged scar marred the darkly stubbled skin of his left cheek, and it seemed to have grown whiter as he considered her question.

"Perhaps you have never known what it is to feel absolutely desperate," she continued, shrinking back from the window as dozens more people flowed from the church to join the search for her. Her maid was now standing on the balcony from which she had made her escape, and a crowd had gathered to point excitedly at the telltale broken vine and crushed bushes below. "So desperate that you would risk anything, and everything, just for the faint chance that maybe there was another life waiting for you somewhere, if only you could break free and find it."

Her eyes were luminous with a haunting mixture of frail hope and overwhelming fear. Jack cursed silently. He was not in the habit of rescuing runaway heiresses.

He had only agreed to attend Whitcliffe's nuptials as a way of having some brief time with his family before heading back to Scotland. There he would spend a quick day or two getting updated on the status of his shipping business before departing for Ceylon. He did not have time to get involved in Miss Belford's romantic dilemma, however unfortunate or compelling it might be. The only rational thing to do was to open the door at once and escort her out of the carriage and into the welcoming arms of her betrothed, who was no doubt currently overcome with concern for her welfare.

He stole a glance out the window. Amidst the crowd he now saw the imposing figure of Mr. John Henry Belford, her father, bellowing her name, whether with alarm or profound irritation Jack could not be sure. A heavily jeweled woman draped in pale peach silk trimmed with sable, which was utterly inappropriate given the blistering heat of the day, stood at his side, her face twisted into a mask of tightly affected calm. The bride's charming mother, he decided. And standing off to one side was pompous old Whitcliffe, his bulky, sagging form sweating in an ill-fitting wine-colored morning coat and trousers, his flaccid face nearly purple with apoplectic rage.

Perhaps her betrothed's arms were not so welcoming after all.

"I take it then, Miss Belford, that this match was not of your own choosing?" Jack ventured, not quite ready to abandon her to her fate.

Amelia shook her head miserably. "My mother was very determined that I marry an aristocrat of no lesser rank than a duke. But unfortunately there aren't that many dukes running about, and fewer still who are actually available for marriage. Lord Whitcliffe was the best she could find, and he was willing to take me on, despite the fact that he believes me to be common and foolish."

"He told you that?" Jack felt a sudden overwhelming urge to grab Whitcliffe by his almost nonexistent neck and choke an apology from him.

"I overheard him telling my father. At first I thought he was only saying it because he was trying to get my father to pay him more for the privilege of my marrying him. It may surprise you to learn, Mr. Kent, that for an American girl to marry an English lord costs quite a bit of money. But then Lord Whitcliffe cited some examples of what he called my 'crass and unseemly behavior,' and I knew he really did think that I was frightfully uncouth." She lowered her gaze and made a halfhearted attempt to straighten the torn cocoon of satin and silk surrounding her.

Jack thought of her scuttling down the side of the church in her wedding gown. Whitcliffe would have probably had a heart attack had he been witness to that particular escapade. He repressed the impulse to smile.

"If you won't sell your carriage to me, Mr. Kent, would you consider permitting me to hire it for a day or two?" Amelia persisted hopefully. "I promise that I shall take very good care of it, and will send it back to you directly."

Jack avoided her imploring gaze. His family had exited the church and was standing in a cluster, searching the crowd for him. His three sisters looked extremely pretty in their elegant outfits, which had been designed by Grace. Each of his sisters was happily married to a man of her own choosing. Although Jack was familiar with the practice of arranged marriages, particularly amongst the nobility, Genevieve's gentle upbringing had always stressed the principles of independent thought and freedom of choice, and she had instilled those values in her children. The idea of Annabelle or Grace or his beloved Charlotte being offered up like prized lambs to be purchased by the highest bidder was utterly abhorrent.

"Mr. Kent?" Amelia's voice was strained.

A party of men was fanning out to search the carriages. Jack noticed Simon and Jamie making their way toward his vehicle. Genevieve had probably asked them to take a look inside, not to search for the missing bride, but to see if their wayward brother had taken refuge within and fallen asleep. The minute they discovered Miss Belford, the carriage would be swarmed. His determined little heiress would be hastily extracted and marched into the church to meet her fate with Whitcliffe, willing or not.

And there wouldn't be a damn thing he could do about it.

"Please, Mr. Kent," Amelia whispered.

She reached out and laid her hand upon his, beseeching him with her touch.

He stared at her hand in surprise. It felt cool and soft upon his skin, despite the sweltering heat of the day and the sudden closeness of the carriage. It was a small hand, made even slighter by the enormity of the ostentatious ring Whitcliffe had elected to bestow upon it. The fingers were slender and immaculately manicured, as one might have expected of a bride on her wedding day, and the skin was pale and silky smooth, indicating that it had spent much of its existence safely swaddled in expensive gloves. But it was the profusion of thin, scarlet scratches hatched across it that captivated his attention. They must have occurred during her fall, Jack realized, as she desperately struggled to cling to the vine before plummeting helplessly into the bushes below. He took her hand and slowly turned it over, only to discover a deeper cut slashed into the tender flesh of her palm. It oozed a thin stream of blood, which had smeared his own skin.

She had asked him if he had ever known what it was

to be hopelessly trapped. The bitter truth was, he did know all too well. Until he saw that ruby stain of blood marring his own skin, he had not understood how desperate she was.

And suddenly he remembered with piercing clarity how it felt to be alone and terrified.

"Oliver," he began, the steady calm of his voice belying the enormity of what he was about to do, "turn the carriage around and slowly drive away."

The driver's aged eyes widened in disbelief. "With her?"

Jack nodded.

"But—she's the bride!" Oliver protested, as if he thought that Jack must have overlooked that particular detail.

"I realize that."

"They'll come after us!"

"Only if they think that Miss Belford is hiding in the carriage," Jack countered. "As long as we drive slowly and give no cause for suspicion, I believe they will continue to search the surrounding area and the remaining carriages." His body tensed as Simon and Jamie drew near. "We have to go *now*, Oliver."

The old man hesitated barely a second, then obligingly snapped his whip lightly over the glossy black hindquarters of his horses. Jack leaned out the window as the carriage rolled forward, blocking his brothers' view of the distraught, rumpled bride hidden within.

"Too bad no one had the wit to check upon the bride earlier," he complained irritably. "I could have left for Scotland an hour ago." He pretended to stifle a yawn.

"You're not going home now, are you?" Simon looked disappointed.

"Miss Belford is certain to be found shortly," Jamie added. "She's probably just having an attack of nerves."

"I don't really give a damn," Jack replied, looking thoroughly bored. "I don't have time to stay for the celebrations anyway. I'm heading back to Inverness, and then I'm sailing for Ceylon. If you don't stay in England too long, I might see you before I leave. Tell Whitcliffe I'm sorry he lost his heiress," he added, waving to the rest of his family. "Maybe next time he should try to find a bride who isn't American—I understand they can be trouble."

With that he slouched wearily against his seat, folded his arms across his chest and closed his eyes. He didn't so much as look out the window as the carriage ambled down the shaded laneway, leaving the others to frantically continue their search for the elusive Miss Amelia Belford.

Chapter Two

"To London," Amelia directed Oliver, nervously clutching at the tatters of her ruined gown. "Please."

"To the train station, Oliver. We're going to Inverness."

Amelia regarded Jack in confusion. "Isn't Inverness in Scotland?"

"Unless they have recently moved it."

"But I can't go to Scotland," she protested. "I must get to London at once—that is where my betrothed is!"

"Your betrothed is standing by the church seething with rage about a half mile back." Jack suddenly wondered if perhaps Miss Belford was mentally unstable. "I am happy to have Oliver turn the carriage around and reunite you with him if you wish."

"Not Whitcliffe," Amelia amended. "He was only my betrothed in the eyes of my mother and father, but he was never my true love. The truth of the matter is, Mr. Kent, I was secretly engaged at the time my parents arranged my betrothal to Lord Whitcliffe. Of course, he wasn't a duke," she quickly added.

"Of course not." He felt a stab of disappointment.

Somehow he had thought there was more to Miss Belford's gloriously capricious escape than the mundane desire to be with another man. For a brief moment he had imagined he had caught a glimpse of something wild and free within her, a flash of spirit and independence that set her apart from all the other sheltered, gently bred women he had known. She had talked of finding another life. He had assumed she meant breaking free of the fetters of her womanhood and forging a new existence entirely on her own. Instead she merely wanted to exchange one keeper for another. He should have suspected as much, he told himself, suddenly annoyed at having become involved in her romantic escapade. Few women would flee from a life of extraordinary affluence and status unless they knew they were falling into a gilded nest of comparable luxury. The only woman he had ever known to do such a thing was Genevieve, and he had always understood that she was unique.

"His name is Percy Baring," Amelia continued, her cheeks now flushed with excitement. "He is the fifth Viscount Philmore. No doubt you have heard of him?"

"No."

She blinked in astonishment. "You haven't? How peculiar. Lord Philmore knows everyone in London, or so it seemed every time we met. He belongs to the Marbury Club, which is terribly exclusive, and was at all the important balls and parties of the season."

I'm sure he was, Jack thought irritably. "I'm from Scotland, Miss Belford. I don't go to London much."

"I see," said Amelia. "I suppose that accounts for your accent, then. I couldn't help but notice that it was different—but then, everyone sounds strange to me over here," she quickly added, not wanting to offend him, "just as I know I sound strange to them. Lord Whitcliffe told me that I would have to work on that, once we were married. He said my accent was atrocious, and that he couldn't have a duchess of his walking around sounding as if she didn't know how to speak proper English." Her pale brows twisted together in a frown. "He actually said that I butchered words. I thought that rather funny, because I always thought that it was he who was mispronouncing words, not me—but I never would have dreamed of saying anything to him about it, for fear of injuring his feelings."

The idea of old Whitcliffe having his feelings hurt by Miss Belford struck Jack as highly improbable. "Lord Philmore doesn't mind your accent?"

"He finds it charming."

Of course he does, Jack reflected wryly. With the potential of millions of pounds in dowry payments dangling over his head, Lord Philmore would undoubtedly claim to find everything about Miss Belford charming. After all, a viscount could not afford to be nearly as discriminating as a duke. "But a viscount wasn't high enough on your parents' ranking of aristocrats?" His voice was edged with contempt.

"It sounds awful when you put it like that," Amelia acknowledged. "But it isn't what you think. Both my mother and my father come from simple beginnings, and my father has worked his entire life to achieve his financial success. While he has been absorbed with his business, my mother has struggled to elevate our family's place in society. Money doesn't buy respectability, Mr. Kent, and there are many society gatherings in New York from which my parents are still excluded."

"And if you married a duke, that would change."

"I don't think my mother is naive enough to believe that it would change how society looks at her and my father," Amelia replied. "She is thinking about me and my brothers, and any children I might have. Marrying Lord Whitcliffe would have guaranteed their place in society."

"She didn't care that you wanted to marry someone else?"

"She thinks I'm too young to understand what will make me happy," she explained. "When I told her about Percy, she forbade me to ever see him again or even to write to him to tell him that my parents had learned of our relationship. She denied that we were engaged, saying that since my father hadn't given his permission, it was not a proper betrothal. I told her that we had sworn ourselves to each other, and that a union of the souls can never be separated." Her blue eyes sparkled with steely defiance. "Don't you agree, Mr. Kent?"

Jack shrugged. Genevieve had spent over twenty years trying to break him of that unrefined habit, among many others, with only limited success. "I suppose." He didn't have much experience with unions of the souls. "What did your mother say to that?"

"She said that I was just a child, and couldn't possibly know what was best for me, but that one day I would thank her for arranging my marriage to Lord Whitcliffe. And then she never permitted me to be alone, and ordered the servants to intercept all of my correspondence, so that I would not be able to get word to Percy of what had happened, and would not have knowledge of any notes he tried to send to me."

"So you don't know how your viscount reacted when he heard that you were now officially engaged to marry Lord Whitcliffe?"

"I know in my heart that he was devastated," Amelia told him, "and that he would have realized that it was not by my choice."

Jack arched a skeptical brow. "What makes you think that he hasn't just gone and gotten himself betrothed to someone else?"

"Percy swore to me that there would never be anyone else for him, ever. I'm positive he has been heartbroken these past few months, as I have. He will be thrilled to discover I have returned to him, and that we are now free to marry as we planned."

His deeply rooted cynicism made Jack wonder if this viscount's first concern might not be that by publicly defying her parents' wishes and running away on the day of her marriage, Miss Belford had effectively destroyed her relationship with them, thereby severing any possibility of either a dowry or inheritance in the process. Lord Philmore might have originally hoped that with a secret engagement and marriage, Mr. and Mrs. Belford would eventually come to accept their daughter's union, and would have been willing to help the newly wedded couple get settled in a manner comparable to the lavish lifestyle in which their precious daughter had been raised. But there was a marked difference between quietly eloping with an unattached heiress and marrying a runaway bride who was now at the center of a mortifying scandal.

"Does Philmore have any money of his own?"

Amelia was taken aback by the question.

"Forgive me." Jack realized Miss Belford had probably never been exposed to the tawdry business of personal finance, and might not realize that the men who had courted her so enthusiastically would have been attracted to more than her uncommon beauty. "What I meant was—"

"I know exactly what you meant, Mr. Kent," Amelia assured him tautly. "Despite what you may think of me, I'm not a fool. I have spent the last year on the marriage market in London and Paris, and I'm painfully aware of the fact that most men—Lord Whitcliffe included—look at me first and foremost as a prodigious source of income. London town houses and country estates are expensive to maintain, and many English lords currently find themselves in a position where they don't have sufficient income to keep a roof over their heads that isn't about to fall down about their ears. Marriage to an American heiress, even one with an atrocious accent like myself, provides them with the means to instantly eradicate their debts and support their lavish lifestyles, all while pouring new money into their precious, decrepit ancestral homes."

Her cheeks were heated with indignation. It was clear he had insulted her.

"I can assure you that Viscount Philmore is different," she continued emphatically. "Although I do not know the precise nature of his financial affairs, I can tell you that he is a man of honorable means and he doesn't care about the wealth of my family. Each time we were together, Percy swore that my fortune meant nothing to him—it was only I who had captured his heart." Her eyes flashed with challenge. "Do you find that so impossible to believe, Mr. Kent?"

She was an enigma, Jack realized. One moment she seemed as forlorn as an abandoned child, huddled amidst the ragged remains of her gown with her scratched hands and her red-rimmed eyes. And the next she was like an outraged angel, filling the carriage with her strength and her passion as she defended the man to whom she believed she had united her soul. If this Philmore had any inkling of the woman breathing beneath the shimmering trappings of wealth and cultivation in which her family had swaddled her, he would have been a fool not to want her.

Unfortunately, in Jack's experience, most men born to a life of privilege were utter morons.

He didn't have time for this nonsense, he reminded himself impatiently. He was scheduled to meet with the manager of his shipping company to review its finances and finalize the details of the shipments scheduled for the next four months. He planned to remain in Inverness for no more than three days before boarding his ship for Ceylon. He didn't have time to go traipsing off to London to deliver Miss Belford into the arms of her paramour. But what the devil was he to do with her? He could hardly drag her all the way back to Inverness against her will and then abandon her. By helping her escape her marriage to Whitcliffe, he had inadvertently assumed responsibility for her, at least temporarily.

The most logical course of action was to see Miss Belford safely deposited into someone else's trust. While that would inconveniently delay his business dealings by a day or two, it would absolve Jack of any further responsibility regarding her welfare. If Philmore was as happy to see her as Miss Belford claimed he would be, then Jack could leave her in his tender charge to marry or do whatever she bloody well pleased while he got on with his own affairs.

"Oliver," he called, "we're going to London after all."

Oliver abruptly halted the horses and turned to scowl at him, his white brows knotted in exasperation. "Are ye sure, lad? I can always just stop for a bit at the side of the road while the two of ye make up yer minds. After all, I've nae better to do on this blisterin' afternoon."

"I'm quite sure, Oliver," Jack replied, wholly untroubled by the old man's churlish attitude. "Just get us there as quickly as you can."

"Fine. London it is." He grumbled something more under his breath that Jack couldn't quite hear as he snapped the reins smartly over the horses' hindquarters.

"Is he always quite so—discourteous?" wondered Amelia, amazed by the rude tone the driver had taken with Jack.

"Frequently."

"Then why don't you discharge him?"

"Because he has been part of my family for years."

Amelia didn't know what to make of that. Her mother had discharged scores of servants for far less serious infractions than the impertinent manner Oliver had taken with Jack. Certainly none of them were ever thought of as part of the family.

"Was he always a coachman?" She couldn't imagine another employer tolerating the old man's insolence.

"Actually, he was a thief." Jack was amused by the look of incredulity on her face. "And quite a good one, too."

Amelia stared in fascination at the back of Oliver's snowy head. She had never met a criminal of any kind before—at least, not knowingly. "Didn't you check his references?"

"Actually, I didn't hire him," Jack told her. "My mother employed him years ago. She took him straight from the Inveraray jail to her home, and certainly wasn't expecting him to have any references."

"Wasn't she concerned about having a dangerous criminal in her employ?"

He shrugged his shoulders. "Other than his sharp tongue, Oliver isn't dangerous. My mother likes to help people who find themselves in unfortunate circumstances."

"Then it seems you and she have something in common. You both have very kind hearts."

Jack said nothing. It wasn't often that anyone accused him of being kind.

"Forgive me," Amelia apologized, stifling a yawn. "I'm afraid I didn't sleep very much last night—or the last few nights, for that matter."

"It is several hours to London. You should try to get some sleep."

"I don't think I could possibly sleep in this crowded coach. Not that you are making it crowded," she quickly amended, although in truth Jack's immense frame and long legs were taking up much of the available space. "It's this ridiculous gown that is making it impossible for me to get comfortable. My mother ordered it from Charles Worth, the famous designer in Paris." She valiantly began to beat down the expensive silk and satin exploding around her so that she might have more room. "I don't suppose you have heard of him," she added, remembering that he had never heard of Viscount Philmore.

"Actually, I am familiar with the name. Although I don't take much notice of women's fashions, my sister Grace has a small dress shop in Inverness. She designs the gowns herself, and I have heard her mention Mr. Worth."

Amelia stopped pummeling her gown for a moment, intrigued. "Your sister designs gowns? Would I have heard of her?"

"I doubt it. She only has the one shop, although her husband has been trying to convince her to open another in Edinburgh or London."

"Her husband permits her to work even though she is married?" Amelia was astonished.

"Grace is very independent, and has always loved to design clothes. Her husband wants her to be happy, so he is supportive of her career."

"I would love to meet them. Perhaps once Lord Philmore and I are married we will travel to Scotland."

Jack thought it far more likely that Miss Belford's new husband would immediately shut her up in some faded, velvet-draped home and expect her to play hostess at an endless array of spectacularly dull teas and dinners and accompany him to every tedious social event imaginable. Until he got her pregnant, at which point he would banish her from society completely.

Jack turned to study the shifting ribbons of afternoon light from his window, wondering why he was determined to find her prospects with this unknown viscount so bleak.

"Forgive me, Mr. Kent, but would you mind helping me with the pins securing my veil to my hair?" She leaned into him and bent her head.

Jack hesitated.

And then, not knowing what else to do, he began to clumsily pluck the dark wire hooks from the tangled mass of blonde before him.

Her veil was a gossamer shroud of the finest silk he had ever seen, held in place by a sparkling diamond tiara. The dozens of pins used to anchor the piece had kept it from flying off when she tumbled from the vine and crashed into the bushes. Jack worked in silence, carelessly dropping the pins on the floor of the carriage, watching in fascination as her hair unraveled from the elegant configuration some lady's maid had spent hours fussing over. Finally the glittering tiara slipped heavily into his hand, trailing no less than nine feet of veil.

Amelia sighed, massaging her aching scalp. "You can't imagine how dreadfully uncomfortable it is to have all those wire pins poking into your head, and that tiara was insufferably heavy." She dragged her fingers through the length of her hair until it poured like liquid honey over her shoulders and down to her waist.

"Here," said Jack thickly, offering her the tiara.

"Just put it on the floor," she instructed, now working on wadding up the train of her gown and stuffing it into the corner for a pillow. "I'll get it later."

Instead Jack placed the diamond necklace and emerald earrings Miss Belford had given him earlier into the center of the tiara, then wound the veil protectively around the valuable cache of jewelry before placing it on the seat beside him.

Amelia settled wearily against the lumpy satin cushion

she had created. "I do hope you'll forgive me, Mr. Kent, if I close my eyes for a moment."

"Go ahead." Jack leaned back against his seat and stretched his legs out as much as the carriage would allow. "I'll wake you before we reach—"

He stopped suddenly and regarded her in confusion.

And then the corners of his mouth twitched with amusement as he realized the lovely, elegant Miss Amelia Belford was snoring.

JACK KNEW THEY HAD REACHED LONDON LONG BEFORE he drew back the maroon curtain to see the ghostly forms of Mayfair's sleeping houses standing in endless neat rows before him. The stench of the city assailed his nostrils, a caustic brew of ash and smoke spewing from the chimneys of homes and factories, combined with the stomach-churning fetor of the Thames. The sooty veil that hung in a perpetual caul over the city's crowded skies was less effusive in the summer than in winter, when tens of thousands of coal fires were lit across the city every morning to banish the chill of night and facilitate the preparation of the day's meals. Unfortunately, the serenity of the warm night air had trapped the day's smoke, blending it with the reek of the tons of horse manure that fell unceremoniously onto the streets each day and the human sewage that flowed with equal abandon into the gray, fetid waters of the Thames.

It was almost enough to make Jack wish he were back in the floral-choked confines of the church.

He stretched his neck from side to side, silently groaning as he released the tight grip of muscles corded there. Then he gingerly shifted his position, marginally alleviating the pressure that had built along the vertebrae and muscles of his back, taking care not to disturb the sleeping form of Miss Belford. She had been in a deep slumber for several hours now. As her repose wore on, her initially upright position within the carriage had gradually deteriorated, until finally Jack had been forced to reach out and catch her just before she slid off her seat entirely. Her response had been to snuggle against his chest, evidently finding him a far more comfortable mattress than the scratchy clump of embroidered satin and pearls against which she had previously been lying. Reluctant to waken her when she was so obviously exhausted, but unable to support her for any length of time while seated on the opposite bench, he had moved beside her, thereby enabling her to capsize completely, until her little stockinged feet were drawn up beneath her and her hair was spilling in a tangled river across his lap.

For a long while he sat rigid, unaccustomed to having a woman lie so trustingly against him while she slept. It occurred to him that his experience with women was somewhat limited in that regard. He had indulged in more than his share of sexual pleasure, but he preferred the company of the females he met abroad. They were inclined to view him as a pleasant but fleeting diversion, which he supposed lessened their expectations of him. Delving into the twisted roots of his past was of no interest to them. By contrast, the well-bred young ladies of Scotland and England never let him forget his despicable beginnings.

From the time he had fallen into Genevieve's care he had been obsessed with trying to make something better of himself—to carve himself into a man who bore no resemblance to the filthy, illiterate, angry little thief she had rescued from the Inveraray jail some twenty-two years earlier. It had been a long and arduous battle. Genevieve and Haydon had done everything within their power to assist him with his transformation. After teaching him herself for a time and gradually fostering an interest in learning, which had previously been buried beneath arrogant indifference, Genevieve had decided he was bright enough to attend university. His preparation involved suffering through an excruciating series of deathly dull tutors, who nearly succeeded in dousing the flame of curiosity that Genevieve had so tenderly coaxed to life. He was a fair student at best, for he had not learned to read or write until he was nearly fifteen, and his ability in both remained frustratingly slow. He had hated the study of Greek and Latin, and had not understood how these two ancient languages would ever be of any earthly use to him. But he was quick with numbers and liked history and art, which were particular passions of Genevieve's.

Eventually he was deemed fit to attend the University of St. Andrews, where both his teachers and fellow students roundly despised him. The fact that he was the ward of the Marquess and Marchioness of Redmond bore little weight amongst the imperious sons of the English and Scottish nobility, who had been raised to worship at the shrine of their own superiority, and to detest the baseness of lower class scum like him. Fortunately, his years of living on the streets had rendered him sufficiently impervious to their disdain, which he met with an equal measure of cool contempt. He was tall and strong and quick with his fists, earning him a temporary expulsion during his first year there, but that had the benefit of establishing his reputation as a street fighter with ample skills to match his temper. Few dared to bother him after that, enabling him to struggle through the remainder of his studies in relative peace.

Haydon and Genevieve were disappointed that he had not made any friends while at university, but Jack was accustomed to being despised, and had not been bothered by it. He had his loving parents and the brothers, sisters, and "servants" he had acquired when he joined Genevieve's household, each of whom boasted a background that was as extravagantly flawed as his own.

As far as he was concerned, the rest of the world could go to bloody hell.

"We're here, lad," Oliver announced as the carriage finally ambled to a stop before the elegant stone structure of Genevieve and Haydon's London town house. The old man slowly climbed down from his perch and opened the carriage door. His sharp little eyes were nearly lost in the folds of his lids as he squinted into the darkness of the vehicle. "Safe and sound and nae the worse for it—though these old bones will be needin' a wee rest an' a fair drop o' drink afore we set out again." His brows furrowed into a single white pelt as he took in the sight of Amelia curled up on Jack's lap. "Looks like yer bride is in need of a wee rest as well."

"She isn't my bride," Jack objected.

"She's more yours than old Whitcliffe's," observed Oliver, shrugging. "Lizzie and Beaton must be in their beds," he decided, removing his battered felt hat so he could give his head a thorough scratching. "They're nae expectin' anyone to return after Whitcliffe's weddin', as Miss Genevieve planned to return to Inverness after. I'll just go open up the house." He rubbed his gnarled hands together in anticipation. "I'm a bit out of practice, but I'd wager there isn't a lock in London I canna open."

"Just ring the bell, Oliver."

"Now lad, there's nae sense in wakin' poor old Lizzie and Beaton when I can get ye in quicker than a greased frog—"

"I don't want Lizzie or Beaton to think the house is being robbed and bang you over the head with a pot the minute you open the front door."

Oliver frowned. "Who said anything about goin' in the front door?"

"Oliver—" Jack began in a warning tone.

"All right, then." He crammed his hat back onto his head and stomped toward the door, clearly irritated at having his skills called into question.

"Where are we?" murmured Amelia, her voice thick with sleep.

"We're in London."

She was silent for a moment, trying to make sense of the deep, unfamiliar voice. Slowly she opened her eyes to find her head pillowed against the hard muscles of Jack's thighs while her hand lay with shocking intimacy upon his knee.

"Oh!" she gasped, bolting upright and scrambling away from him. "Please excuse me—I'm afraid I must have been very tired."

"You were." Jack was amused by her sudden sense of propriety.

"Is this your house?" she asked, desperate to shift his attention away from the fact that she had just been lying atop him. "It's very nice."

"It belongs to my parents, the Marquess and Marchioness of Redmond, but no one is here now except for a couple of servants. Come." He leapt down from the carriage and extended his hand to her. "I believe we can find a bed inside that is far more comfortable than—" He was about to say "my lap," but the heated stain on Miss Belford's cheeks suggested she might not appreciate his attempt at humor. "—this carriage."

She groped around the dark floor for her shoes and slipped them onto her feet before laying her palm lightly against his hand. It felt soft and small, like a sun-warmed petal against his callused skin.

"Perhaps you had better take your jewelry as well," he suggested, indicating the veil-wrapped bundle on the seat.

She scooped up the priceless bundle without interest, gathered her crumpled skirts into one hand, and permitted Jack to assist her from the carriage.

"Lord have mercy on us—it's Mr. Jack!" cried a startled voice.

A short dumpling of a woman with a flushed face and a frazzle of silver hair poking out from beneath her nightcap stared at them wide-eyed from the doorway. Her cheeks were fleshy but wrinkled and her little round eyes were slightly glazed, as if she had just been roused from a deep sleep. She opened her mouth to say something more, exposing a row of slightly crooked, yellowing teeth, but all that came out was an extremely loud hiccup.

"Good evening, Lizzie," said Jack as the house-keeper clapped a hand to her lips. "I hope we're not causing you too much inconvenience with our late arrival."

The syrupy smell of gin wafted from the older woman's nostrils and mouth as he escorted Amelia into the house.

"Of course not," mumbled Lizzie, struggling admirably to affect a sober demeanor. She hiccuped loudly again, then blinked, hoping no one had noticed. "We just wasn't expectin' you, is all."

"I'm sorry I wasn't able to give you notice," Jack apologized. "I had not intended to come to London, but my plans changed."

A great, round ball of a man exploded suddenly through the kitchen door, desperately trying to tie the sash of his crimson dressing gown over the generous expanse of his girth. A blue-and-white-striped nightcap drooped precariously upon his shiny bald head, and he had only managed to find one scuffed and worn bed-room slipper, leaving the stubby toes of his other foot bare. Like Lizzie's, his face was amply lined, suggesting he had seen sixty years and more, but Amelia thought there was something sweetly childlike about him as he fumbled clumsily with the fraying tie of his dressing gown.

"Good evening, Beaton," said Jack.

"Goda'mighty!" swore Beaton, his glassy eyes nearly popping from his head as he stared in bleary confusion at Amelia. "Our Mr. Jack has gone and gotten himself married!" Overcome, he stumbled forward and clamped his stout arms around Jack's waist. "Congratulations, sir," he gushed, sniffing with emotion. "If you don't mind my sayin' so, she's a real spanker." He belched.

"Drunk as wheelbarrows, the pair of them," observed Oliver in disgust. "Ye canna find decent help these days."

"I'm no such thing," protested Lizzie indignantly. "I need to take a spot of gin now and again for my poor old heart, is all." She hiccuped again, then proceeded to affect a fit of phlegmy coughing.

"An' I only took a nip to keep her company," added Beaton, still standing with his arms wrapped tightly around Jack's waist. Amelia was not certain whether the butler was clinging to Jack out of fondness or his very real need for support.

"Ye're completely wellied, both of ye," Oliver objected irritably. "Ye should be ashamed of yerselves."

"Now, Oliver, we cannot fault Lizzie and Mr. Beaton for having a little drink when the house was safely locked up for the evening and they weren't expecting our arrival—especially as Lizzie obviously needs to take gin for medicinal purposes."

The servants stared at Amelia in slack-jawed surprise. Even Jack regarded her with curiosity. He had not expected his fabulously wealthy heiress to be quite so forgiving of his servants' obvious shortcomings.

"Thank you, Mrs. Kent," said Lizzie, coming dangerously close to toppling over as she bobbed a clumsy curtsey. "You're most kind." She hiccuped.

"She's a real spanker." Beaton winked at Jack.

"Miss Belford is *not* my wife," Jack said, prying Beaton's arms off his waist. He held the butler's wrist for a moment, making sure the fellow was steady on his feet before actually letting go. "She is my guest, and she will be staying with us for a day or so while I make arrangements to—"

"Miss Belford?" Lizzie's withered brow puckered in confusion. "Miss Amelia Belford, the American heiress?"

Amelia regarded Jack uncertainly.

"Bless my soul, you are her, aren't you?" Lizzie leaned closer to Amelia to take a better look, overwhelming Amelia with the stench of gin. "I've seen your picture in the shops, and of course the society pages have been filled with talk of your upcoming weddin' to that fat old codger, Whitcliffe."

"Here now, we'll have none o' that talk," interjected Oliver, concerned that Amelia might take offense at having her betrothed described in such unflattering terms. "Old Whitcliffe is nae fat—he's just a wee bit beefy. All dukes are," he added with uncharacteristic charity. "That's what comes of bein' well stuffed from cradle to grave."

"I'm sure it's you," Lizzie insisted, as if Amelia needed convincing of her own identity. "Your picture has been in all the shops."

Like most heiresses who traveled to London to find an English lord, Amelia's mother had arranged for her to be photographed by one of the city's leading photographers. Her portrait had been for sale in numerous shops, enabling a fascinated public to purchase her picture. Beyond the popularity of her portrait, Amelia's wedding had received extensive coverage in both the

English and American newspapers during the previous weeks, a fact that distressed her but pleased her mother immensely.

"Goda'mighty—she is her—isn't she?" Beaton's eyes bulged from his shiny round head.

"Yes," said Jack. Lizzie and Beaton had been in his parents' employ for more than ten years, and although they clearly liked to indulge in a drink now and again, Jack knew that in matters of importance they could be absolutely trusted. "She is."

"Oh, my, you're even prettier in the flesh!" gushed Lizzie, studying Amelia with fresh rapture. "Even if your hair is a mess and your gown looks like you've been crawlin' about the coal bin."

"But you were to marry Lord Whitcliffe today," pointed out Beaton. "It's been in the paper for weeks—with sketches of you and His Grace, and the gifts and flowers and lists of food—"

"They said your garters had gold clasps with diamonds on them," interrupted Lizzie excitedly. "Is that true?"

"No." Amelia was horrified that the London papers had gone so far as to falsely describe her undergarments. Did people really believe she could be so idiotically frivolous as to wear lingerie studded with diamonds?

"Oh, but look at what's happened to your lovely gown," Lizzie moaned, "and your hands too, you poor lamb." She took Amelia's badly scratched hands into her own and clucked her tongue sympathetically. "Did you have an accident?"

"I fell," Amelia replied. "Into a bush."

"Miss Belford had a change of heart at the last minute," explained Jack.

"But your betrothed was a bleedin' duke!" burst out Lizzie. "Whitcliffe lives in one of the grandest castles in all England!"

"Aye, and the lass decided she didna want him," interjected Oliver, coming to Amelia's defense.

"Surely she must have known he was beefy before she agreed to marry him," argued Beaton, still focused on the matter of Whitcliffe's size.

"I've heard of cases amongst the rich where the bride is not permitted to see the groom till she rubs elbows with him at the altar," Lizzie said, "out of fear she might change her mind and call the whole weddin' off."

"If t'were me bein' forced to marry old Whitcliffe, I know which direction I'd have run." Oliver chuckled, forgetting that but a moment earlier he had been defending Amelia's choice for a husband.

"Miss Belford is very tired, Lizzie." Jack thought Amelia had endured enough questions for one night. "Do you think you and Beaton could prepare a bath for her and find her something suitable to wear? I'm sure there must be something appropriate in my mother's wardrobe. See that she is given whatever she needs in terms of clothes. She will sleep in the blue guest bedroom tonight."

"Of course you're tired, you poor lost lamb." Lizzie clucked her tongue sympathetically. "Follow me, dearie, and I'll get you settled in as cozy as a kitten in a basket."

"You're very kind." Amelia suddenly felt as if she were about to collapse from exhaustion. "I apologize for interrupting your sleep by arriving here unannounced. I hope you won't have to go to too much trouble on my behalf."

Beaton and Lizzie blinked in confusion. Neither had ever met an American heiress before, but everything they had heard about these fantastically indulged beauties suggested that they would be just as haughty and condescending toward their class as the English aristocracy generally was.

" 'Tis no trouble at all, miss," Lizzie assured her.

"We weren't doing anything before you came," added Beaton.

"Except for gettin' soaked," Oliver muttered.

"Up we go then," said Lizzie, ignoring Oliver's insult as she shepherded Amelia toward the stairs, holding her mangled train behind her. "Beaton will set to heatin' some water for your bath while we see about gettin' you out of this gown."

Jack watched as the servants set to work to provide for Miss Belford's comfort.

Then he jerked off his necktie and headed toward the drawing room, very much in need of a drink.

THE WHISKEY WAS WELL AGED AND FULL-BODIED, with just enough of a smoky finish to remind him of the sweet burning peat of the Highlands. Jack sipped it slowly, taking time to appreciate its carefully cultivated scent, body, and flavor.

There had been a time when he had not been quite so discerning.

He'd started drinking at the tender age of eight, when he used to sneak a fiery swig from a chipped brown jug hidden beneath a filthy crate in the kitchen. That was where the old bastard his mother paid to look after him used to hide it. Jack was never sure whether he was concealing the foul-tasting brew from Jack or from his own wife, a nasty-tempered woman who also enjoyed a good solid drunk now and again. After Jack ran away from them at the age of nine and began living on the streets, he found his taste for alcohol grew. By the time he was fourteen he was arrogantly proud of the fact that he could consume nearly an entire bottle of spirits without vomiting it back up again. He had done just that the night before he was arrested for stealing some cheese, a bottle of cheap whiskey, and a pair of worn shoes. He sobered up quick enough when he found himself sentenced to thirty-six stripes of the lash, forty days imprisonment, and two years at a reformatory school. At the time he had believed he had reached the end of his short, miserable life, for he did not expect to survive the brutality of the judicial system.

Then Genevieve had appeared in his cell, and everything he was destined to become was changed forever.

It was strange, he mused, how some facets of life could be irrevocably altered in an instant, while others remained infuriatingly fixed. He had struggled for years to cast off the filthy mantle of his sordid beginnings. He was the unwanted progeny of a drunken whore and some base customer whose identity he had never known, which was just as well. As a lad he had been a scrawny thief who survived on little more than his sharp wits and his bloodstained fists. His existence had been pitted with desperation and violence, and he had done what he had to in order to survive. And then he was suddenly the ward of the Marquess and Marchioness of Redmond, who made him part of a loving family while helping him to rise above the dark sludge of his origins.

When he was a callow lad of fifteen, he had told himself that he was a born survivor and that he would have managed well enough, regardless of whether Genevieve had come into his life or not. As he matured, the harsh reality of the world took on a different cast. He had only to look at the rough, half-starved young men hanging about the streets of Edinburgh and Glasgow to see what he would have become but for Genevieve: illiterate, angry, and contemptuous of the world around him. Most of these aimless fellows scrabbled out a miserable living slaving in the factories or stealing, both professions that were better performed sober, which they rarely were. Trapped by poverty and ignorance, they hoped for little more than to still be alive the following week, and not jailed or killed by alcohol or a brawl or some ungodly piece of factory machinery.

It was scarcely a life worth surviving for.

How different were the travails of Miss Amelia Belford. For her, hunger was an entirely abstract concept, based upon the vaguely empty sensation one felt between the hours of luncheon and teatime. Jack could not imagine that she had ever been permitted to want for anything—save perhaps a gown so extravagant even her father had been forced to question its necessity, or perhaps those ludicrous diamond-studded garters Lizzie had gone on about. For Amelia, life was a glorious pageant of everything she could ever have possibly imagined, and more.

Yet she had risked all of it to scale down a church wall and run away.

She was naive in the extreme if she thought for a moment that her Viscount Philmore could provide her with anything resembling the affluent life she might have enjoyed with Whitcliffe, Jack decided, albeit at her father's expense. Jack didn't know Philmore, but if he was at all typical of his class, Jack knew his type. Spoiled, arrogant, and lazy. Jack supposed he should not judge him for being tediously representative of his class. After all, even Haydon had once borne these very same traits. But if this Philmore cared for Miss Belford as much as she evidently believed he did, why hadn't he married her? Had it been Jack, he would never have let Amelia's subsequent betrothal to Whitcliffe and her parents' refusal to let him see her stand in his way. If he had suspected for an instant that she was being forced into a marriage she did not want, he would have bloody well charged through her home and knocked aside anyone who got in his way as he took her out.

He extricated himself from his chair, too weary to think about the matter anymore. He blew out the lamp in the library and slowly mounted the stairs, unfastening the buttons of his shirt.

Upon reaching the upstairs floor he noticed a spill of lamplight seeping onto the richly woven Persian carpet from the ajar door of the guest bedroom. Frowning, he walked toward it, wondering if something was amiss with Miss Belford.

Asleep, she lay tucked in a tiny ball upon the bed, her honey-gold hair trickling in soft swells across the expansive white ocean of her pillow and sheets. Her hapless wedding gown and veil rested in a discarded froth upon a chair, and there was a tray of tea, toast, and cold beef sitting untouched upon a table. She had kicked off her woolen blankets, but the air gusting through the open window was cool, and it was clear to Jack as he moved toward her that she was chilled and needed to be covered.

She was wearing a nightgown of ivory cotton, delicately embroidered with a scattering of tiny pink rosebuds at the neckline and trimmed with a cascade of filmy lace. It was void of all the shimmering ornamentation that had rendered her wedding gown so ostentatious, and Jack felt it suited her much better. The scalloped neckline draped loosely over her shoulder and across her breasts, exposing an expanse of silky skin, and the lacy hem had shifted up her calves as she kicked away her blankets, revealing her small, perfectly formed feet. He leaned upon the bedpost and studied her a long moment.

And then he frowned at the sparkle of tears upon her lashes.

He should have asked Lizzie to stay with her, he realized. Despite the confident, determined composure she had maintained during their ride to London, it was clear Miss Belford's wedding day had been filled with extreme emotions, which obviously had taken their toll when she finally rested her head against her pillow. But for his agreeing to spirit her away, the young woman before him would have been a prisoner in Whitcliffe's bed tonight, a terrified, unwilling bride with no choice but to endure whatever her new husband wanted of her. And Whitcliffe would have wanted as much of her as he could consume. Despite the duke's advanced age and substantial weight, Jack did not believe any man could have resisted such exquisite beauty.

Outrage unfurled within him. No man had the right to force himself on an unwilling woman, regardless of whether the law, the church, and her parents conspired to give him that right. Jack did not know whether Amelia had wept out of fear of her future or sheer relief at having escaped her bondage to Whitcliffe. Whatever the reason, the trail of tears staining her cheek cut him to the core. He lifted the disheveled blankets at the foot of the bed and clumsily draped them over her.

Then he blew out the lamp and quit the room, too angry to wonder at the unfamiliar flame of protectiveness burgeoning within his chest.

Chapter Three

AMELIA SHRANK FURTHER INTO THE DARK RECESSES
of her father's wardrobe, her sweaty hand gripping the frayed
string she had tied to a nail on one of the doors to keep them
closed. She liked the big, shadowy cupboard, with its familiar
scent of oiled wood, polished leather, and the spicy linen sachets
that were carefully placed amongst her papa's meticulously
laundered shirts and coats. The stillness of the place soothed
her, as did the orderly arrangement of her father's attire. She
settled herself against her makeshift bed of folded trousers,
imagining she was in a tent in Morocco or Egypt, with nothing
but a flimsy canvas barrier protecting her from the raging winds
and the ferocious animals prowling outside. Or perhaps she had
stowed away on a pirate ship bound for the wilds of Africa, and
was forced to hide in this tiny cupboard, only venturing forth at
night to steal scraps so she wouldn't starve to death.

Suddenly hungry, she pulled a crumpled napkin out of her
pocket and buried her finger into the squashed piece of coconut
cake within. Sighing with pleasure, she licked the dense treat
off her finger, relishing every morsel. If she was very careful,
perhaps she could make it last for the duration of the six-week
journey. A more difficult problem was water. For that she

would have to venture onto the deck, which meant creeping over the murderous pirates as they slept. If one of them wakened, she would have to fight for her life with her sword. Her fingers gripped the fine stick Freddy had found for her in the garden. She thought she could probably overtake a dozen or so of them, but how many cutthroats were aboard this terrible ship? Thirty? Sixty? A hundred?

"Miss Amelia, you come out at once, do you hear?"

Her heart pounding, she stuffed her precious food back into her pocket and pulled the string tighter. It was only a matter of time before they discovered her, she realized desperately. What foul punishment would they inflict upon her? Would they lash her? Cut her throat? Make her walk the plank? The string was biting into her flesh now, straining against her grip as someone pulled with fierce determination upon the door of her hiding place. Amelia held fast, but she was no match for the steely strength of her captor.

The string snapped suddenly, causing the wardrobe door to fly open with such force it slammed against the nursery maid's forehead. The poor girl shrieked with outrage and went running from the bedchamber, wailing that Amelia had tried to kill her.

Amelia sighed.

It would be days before she was permitted to leave the upstairs nursery again.

THERE WAS A CLOCK DILIGENTLY TAPPING AWAY SOMEwhere in the room. It was this that her mind fastened upon first—the steady, rhythmic cadence of time. It chipped insistently at her senses, eroding the filmy layers of exhaustion. She burrowed her face deeper into the pillow and squeezed her eyes tight, fighting it. She did not want to waken. She had not wanted to waken for months now, not since her life had been taken from her and pressed firmly into the damp, fleshy palm of Lord

Whitcliffe. Every morning she was overcome with the same paralyzing despair, which she fought by trying to retreat back into the warm waters of sleep. But as the days pushed her ever closer to her union with the repellent old duke, even sleep had lost its ability to grant respite. The memories of her childhood antics had become bittersweet, the endings invariably bleak. She was always trapped at the conclusion, a prisoner of her family, her servants, herself. Soon she would be a prisoner of Lord Whitcliffe's, in body, at least, if not in soul.

A wave of nausea coursed through her. She threw back the covers and staggered from the bed, desperate to find the wash basin. It wasn't where it was supposed to be. She stared in confusion at the unfamiliar furnishings surrounding her in the darkened chamber, suddenly stricken with dread.

"Good mornin', my lamb—how are we feelin' this morning?"

A tray banged down on a table and the drapes were wrenched open, flooding the chamber with a blaze of light. "Half starved, I'd wager, an' no wonder, since you hadn't the strength last night to even touch your tea and toast, you poor duck."

A plump, gray-haired woman clucked with dismay over the untouched tray of the previous evening. Amelia's memory came rushing back in a sudden burst of clarity, eradicating her nausea and replacing it with a kind of mesmerized awe.

Oh, my God, she thought, feeling a dizzying infusion of both elation and fear. *What on earth have I done?*

"Did you sleep all right?" asked Lizzie.

She nodded.

Lizzie regarded her doubtfully. "Well, those circles under your eyes are bound to plague you for a while, what with all the excitement. Tonight I'll fix you a nice cup of warm milk and brandy, to calm your nerves and make you sleep. If that doesn't work, we'll try a conserve of red roses and rotten apple wrapped in linen, and see if it won't fade that black."

Despite the woman's concern, Amelia hoped she wouldn't be staying another night. If Jack was able to find Percy, then it was vital she be united with him immediately. Only then would she be safe from Lord Whitcliffe and her family, who were undoubtedly doing everything they could to find her. Her father in particular would be distressed by her sudden disappearance. Although he was undoubtedly infuriated by her actions, Amelia knew he would also be desperate to know if his little girl was safe.

She swallowed thickly, fighting the tears that blurred her eyes.

"Here now, dearie, it's all right," Lizzie cooed, alarmed by her despair. "You're safe now; me and Beaton and Mr. Jack will make sure of that. If anyone comes round lookin' for you, I'll send them runnin' with a whack of my broom against their backside."

"Thank you, Lizzie," said Amelia, moved by the woman's unexpected protectiveness. "You're most kind."

"Seems to me you need a little kindness." Lizzie went to the tray and dumped a generous amount of sugar and milk into a teacup. "Mr. Jack said you was so set on escapin' old Whitcliffe, you climbed down the church wall and crashed into some bushes. What kind of parents would force their daughter into a marriage where she'd rather risk breakin' her neck than goin' through with it?" She clucked her tongue with disapproval.

"My marrying a duke has been my mother's dearest wish from the time I was a little girl," Amelia told her. "But for years I also thought it was a wonderfully romantic idea—until I arrived in England and actually met the dukes who were available for marriage."

Lizzie filled what little space remained in the cup with a splash of tea and handed it to her. "A miserable lot, were they?"

"They were old and brusque and arrogant, and they made me feel as if they were lowering themselves by having anything to do with me. It was clear they were only interested in my fortune."

The elderly housekeeper sighed as she pulled out a chair for Amelia, indicating for her to sit. "I know just what you mean."

"For months everyone tried to convince me of how fortunate I was that Lord Whitcliffe had agreed to marry me—even though he only did so after weeks of negotiation with my father's barristers," Amelia continued, seating herself. "And I kept trying to tell them that even if it was fortunate, I didn't want to marry him. When I finally got the courage to run away yesterday, I knew I wasn't just abandoning Lord Whitcliffe—I was abandoning my family as well." Her voice was hollow as she finished despondently, "That is the part I cannot bear."

"There, now," Lizzie soothed, patting her hand. "Your family is sure to forgive and forget—time has a way of healin' even the deepest cuts." She spread a thick layer of butter and jam onto a piece of toast. "I suppose your parents thought that even if you didn't love Whitcliffe, you'd at least learn to tolerate him. That's the way of it in most marriages, and the couples seem to get on fair enough." Frowning at the toast, she added a hefty slice of cheese to it.

"That was their hope," Amelia agreed. "Unfortunately, I had met someone I wanted to marry, but my parents refused to grant their permission, saying he wasn't good enough for me." She set her tea down, untouched. "Mr. Kent is going to find him, and when we are married my parents won't be able to force me to do anything. I'll finally have control over my life."

"Bein' married doesn't mean havin' control, at least where ladies are concerned," Lizzie reflected. "Still, if he's fine enough to have won your heart, I'm sure he's a good man and he'll make you happy. Mr. Jack and Oliver left early this mornin' without a word, so they must have gone to fetch him." She moved a plate heaped with fried eggs, ham, bacon, and a thick wedge of meat pie in front of Amelia. "Eat your breakfast, and then we'll see what we can do about fitting you into some of Miss Genevieve's clothes. After all, when your betrothed arrives we want you ready to receive him."

"Do you think Mr. Kent's mother will mind if I borrow some of her things?" Amelia wondered.

"Miss Genevieve would be pleased to help you," Lizzie assured her, "just the same as Mr. Jack and Oliver was." Her voice was filled with warmth as she finished emphatically, "That's the way of it in this family."

LIONEL HOBSON PEERED ENQUIRINGLY OVER THE WORN gold rims of his spectacles, the lenses of which were badly scratched and in dire need of replacement. "Forgive me, Mr. Kent," he asked hesitantly, "did you hear me?"

Jack jerked his gaze away from the strip of azure sky he could just make out beyond the soot-crusted rooftop of the warehouse across the street and regarded his earnest young employee blankly. "What?" Realizing his error before the word had even left his lips, he quickly amended, "Pardon?"

"I'm wondering how you want me to deal with the losses we have incurred this month and last, due to the damage the *Shooting Star* suffered two weeks ago," his London manager repeated, pushing his glasses up the considerable length of his nose for the hundredth time.

He raked a fan of ink-stained fingers through his limp hair and squinted at the black columns of figures scripted with painstaking neatness into the ledger upon his desk, wondering at his employer's uncharacteristic lack of attention. "As I mentioned, the repairs on her are taking longer than we projected, with the result that we have had two of our contracts canceled. According to the shipyard, they have every man available working on her, but it will still be at least another ten days before she is seaworthy again. If she takes that long, we shall be forced to renegotiate our contract with Reynolds and Sons. Should they decide not to grant us another extension, then we shall lose that contract as well." He nibbled anxiously upon a blackened thumb.

A dull throbbing pounded at the base of Jack's skull. Until Lionel had wrenched him from his reverie, he had been lost in contemplation of Amelia Belford's enormous eyes, which were the same intense blue as the slender ribbon of sky winking teasingly at him from above the crumbling rooftops across the street. He had left the house before she awakened that morning, anxious to take advantage of his unexpected expedition into London by meeting quickly with Hobson. Once Jack was updated and had made a perusal of his ledgers, he planned to go straight to the Marbury Club, which Miss Belford had mentioned when describing the vague accomplishments of her betrothed, Lord Philmore.

"Mr. Kent?"

Jack straightened in his chair to demonstrate that he was now truly paying attention. "Could you repeat that, Hobson?"

"If Reynolds and Sons cancels its contract with us, it will be the fifth contract we have lost in the past six months." Lionel enunciated the words slowly, as if he thought his employer was having difficulty with his hearing.

Jack frowned. Each contract represented thousands of pounds, and it was money badly needed to meet his payments to the bank and his employees. If the sabotage upon his ships continued at this rate, North Star Shipping would be bankrupt before the year was out.

And all the money that Haydon and his associates had so generously invested in Jack's fledgling shipping business would be lost.

"Any word from the police on who the hell is vandalizing my ships?"

Lionel shook his head. "Police Inspector Sanger, who is in charge of the case in London, says he is working on several leads, but has nothing concrete as yet."

Of course not, Jack reflected bitterly.

When he had initially reported the vandalism of his ships in London and Inverness, the police in both cities had reacted with infuriating disinterest. They reluctantly agreed to investigate, which entailed questioning some drunken sailors at the docks to see if they had noticed anything unusual on the nights of the wreckage, then filing a report concluding nothing was amiss. Haydon had tried to convince Jack that this was merely the normal ineptitude of the justice system at work, but Jack believed the police's indifference was rooted deeper. As one of the "urchin wards" of the Marquess of Redmond, as he and his brothers and sisters had come to be known, his criminal background was renowned. The authorities' nonchalance toward his problems made it clear they had no interest in assisting a former criminal—regardless of who had taken him in, how much money he now enjoyed, or how many years had passed since his last offense.

Respectability was a quality he could not earn, regardless of how bloody hard he tried.

"What about Quinn and the men he hired to guard my ships against further vandalism?"

"They claim to have been carefully watching the ships docked in London. They say no one boarded the *Shooting Star* or left her on the night she was vandalized except for the members of her own crew—each of whom swears he knows nothing about how the damage to her hull happened."

Somehow Jack refrained from cursing. "Then fire them," he instructed tautly.

Lionel knotted his brow in confusion. "The crew?"

"No, not the crew," Jack snapped, although in his current dark mood he wasn't sure that firing the crew was a bad idea. "Fire Quinn and his men. I'm not paying them to watch my ships only to have the vessels vandalized while they are supposedly under their guard. The *Viking* has already left for Karachi, has she not?"

"She set sail yesterday," Lionel confirmed.

"Which means only the *Charlotte* and the *Liberty* remain docked here."

"The *Liberty* is due to sail for Jamaica in two days, and the *Charlotte* is not booked for sail at the moment." Lionel was silent a moment, gauging Jack's mood before hesitantly adding, "The steamships can travel faster, through almost any kind of weather, therefore they generate more business for us. The *Charlotte* being a clipper ship, businesses are less apt to use her for transporting goods, unless it is a relatively short run. At the moment we are paying just to keep her maintained and keep a small crew aboard."

Jack gazed out the window and said nothing. He knew it made no business sense for him to keep the *Charlotte*. She was slowly bleeding his company of money that she wasn't earning back. Given the current trend toward steamship use, she wasn't likely to ever earn it back.

Even so, he could not bear the thought of parting with her.

The *Charlotte* had been his first ship; he had named her in honor of his gentlest, quietest sister, with whom he shared a special bond. The ship was not large and her reliance on the wind rendered her hopelessly quaint in this new age of the steamship, but Jack refused to sell her all the same. After he had graduated from university he had worked and sailed for years on other vessels before he finally had enough money to make the *Charlotte* his own. Once he stood with his hands on her wheel and her deck shifting comfortably beneath his legs he had done what Genevieve had always told him he would do, from the time he was fourteen and she had first shown him pictures from a magnificent old volume about ships. He had broken free from the boundaries of Scotland and set out to see the world of which he had only dreamed.

"Mr. Kent?" Lionel's voice was timorous, as if he were reluctant to interrupt his employer's reverie yet again.

"I'm keeping the *Charlotte*." Jack's tone was final. "As for Quinn and his men—keep them only until you have managed to secure the services of someone else. Then fire them. Tell the shipyard we need the *Shooting Star*'s repairs to be completed in seven days, not ten. Have them hire extra men to labor throughout the night, if necessary. If they can have her ready in a week, we will pay them an additional twenty percent. That should give them the incentive they need to get things moving.

"Contact Thomas Reynolds and tell him we apologize for the delay in moving their goods, but if they will just bear with us for a few more days, we will give them a discount of ten percent. If he rejects that, you may go as high as twenty percent. Just be sure to make him feel as if he is the one who has driven a hard bargain. Can you do that, Hobson?"

Lionel looked up from his ink-smudged paper and nodded. "How do you want me to deal with our reduced income versus our expenditures for this month and last?"

Jack picked the ledger up from the desk and studied it, swiftly adding, subtracting and forecasting the lengthy columns of numbers in his head. Learning to read had been a challenge, but mathematics had come quite naturally.

"The sailors have to be paid or they will quit, so see that they are compensated first," Jack began. "Secondly, tell our suppliers that if they extend our terms another sixty days, we will pay them an additional eight percent. Then contact all our clients and propose that if they are willing to pay fifty percent up front instead of the normal thirty, we will grant them a discount of five percent. If we can defer our expenses and recover our costs on our shipments sooner, this will immediately improve our cash position."

Lionel nodded as his hand scratched feverishly across a yellowed sheet of paper. "What about our bank payment?"

Jack frowned at the ledger, considering. "When I am back in Inverness I will meet with the bank and let them know our payment is forthcoming, but that it will be in two installments. Once the *Viking* has returned and we collect the balance of her fee for this delivery, we can pay the bank the first installment. By then the *Shooting Star* will be seaworthy again and we will have her deposit in hand. In the meantime, I shall be leaving for Ceylon in a few days to finalize our contracts there, which will also mean a substantial infusion of funds within the next month or so." He mentally ran through his calculations one last time, then laid the ledger back on Lionel's desk, satisfied that he had addressed everything for the moment. "Is there anything else?"

Lionel scribbled away at his notes, anxious to record every detail accurately. "No, sir, Mr. Kent."

"If you need to reach me, I shall be staying in London at my father's house tonight. Tomorrow I am returning to Inverness, and then I'm off to Ceylon. Should anything urgent come up this afternoon, you can reach me at the Marbury Club."

Lionel's pen froze in mid-scrawl. "The Marbury Club?" He knew his employer detested that particular bastion of elitism.

"I'm going there because I'm trying to find a Lord Philmore." Jack was not sure why he felt he needed to justify his actions to his employee. Maybe because Lionel, like himself, had come from inauspicious beginnings. While his employee had never lived on the streets, or been thrown in jail for stealing, or been subject to vicious beatings, Lionel Hobson had lived a life utterly void of luxury or privilege. It had only been through considerable discipline and struggle that the young man had managed to secure for himself a respectable job as an office manager, for which he earned the sum of one hundred and forty pounds per year. If he continued to work for Jack without the business going bankrupt, he might eventually be able to lease a small house and take on the burden of a wife and children.

The idea of dining at a place like the Marbury Club was as inconceivable to Lionel Hobson as going for tea at Buckingham Palace.

"Do you mean Viscount Philmore?" Lionel wondered.

"Do you know him?"

"I've read about him in the newspaper—he attends almost every important ball and social event in London."

Because he is a fatuous fool with nothing more important to do, Jack reflected acidly.

"He was mentioned in the *Morning Post* just this morning," Lionel continued, clearly excited by the prospect that Jack was going to see someone of such recent notoriety. "I've got it here." He struggled to pull open a warped drawer in his desk.

"And just what glorious thing did the viscount do to merit being in the *Morning Post* today?" Jack enquired sarcastically.

"He is going to marry one of the richest American heiresses in London," Lionel reported, finally freeing the recalcitrant drawer. He cleared a space on his desk and spread out the wrinkled sheets of his newspaper. "Here it is." He pointed a blackened finger at the headline.

VISCOUNT PHILMORE TO MARRY AMERICAN BEAUTY.

Jack frowned, confused. Although it was possible the papers were aware that Miss Belford had deserted Whitcliffe at the altar the previous afternoon, how in the name of God could they have known that she had returned to London with the intention of marrying Lord Philmore? He quickly scanned the paragraph below.

And realized the newspaper was not referring to the American beauty he had left curled in bed but a few hours earlier, her tearstained cheeks luminous in the leaden morning light.

THE MARBURY CLUB WAS SITUATED IN THE HEART of the supremely fashionable district of London known as Mayfair. Its entrance was evocative of a Greek temple, boasting a stately row of Corinthian columns capped by an enormous pediment, which housed a violent frieze of the Roman army conquering some helpless enemy. Once one summoned the self-assurance needed to walk through the building's heavily carved oak doors, one was overwhelmed by the oppressive sumptuousness of the Grand Hall. Beyond this were the elegantly appointed rooms in which the club's members cocooned themselves each day. The windows were shrouded in plum velvet curtains, which custom dictated must never be opened more than a handsbreadth; the walls were paneled in somber English oak; and the floors were buried beneath acres of worn, musty carpets. It was here that the feckless gentlemen of London society gathered, closeting themselves from the rest of humanity so they could smoke, drink, eat, read their newspapers and gossip amongst themselves in the drearily oppressive and rarefied atmosphere of the privileged few.

Jack had not been inside more than a minute before he felt as if he were suffocating.

"Good God, Jack Kent, is that really you?"

A barrel-shaped man with a cigar in one hand and a brandy in the other reeled out of a leather chair and lumbered toward him, obliviously dropping a gray chunk of ash onto the carpet as he went. A thick swath of coarse white hair covered his head, and he sported a massive mustache that looked like two curling rodent tails pinned beneath his spider-veined nose.

"Good afternoon, Lord Sullivan," said Jack. The man was a friend of Haydon's and amiable enough, when taken in small doses. "How are you?"

"Still alive and still bloody thirsty." He took a swig from his crystal glass, then smacked his liver-colored lips with satisfaction. "Damn doctor has told me I have to cut back. The man's a perfect half-wit, I say. Drinking and smoking are the only things keeping me here. If he had any bloody sense, he'd tell me to drink more. Here, everyone, look who has decided to grace us with his presence," he blared drunkenly, seizing the attention of every man in the room. "Redmond's ward—the one who likes ships. Just come back from India, if I'm not mistaken."

It was a fascinating aspect of Jack's notoriety that despite the fact that he so rarely frequented the club, once he was there most of the members took great pains to speak to him and feign their welcome. The bitter furor that had erupted when Haydon first fought to have his wards made members of the club had been a dark chapter in the Marbury Club's otherwise deadly staid two-hundred-year history. On the exceptional occasion of Jack's attendance, there was a perverse curiosity to find out just what Lord Redmond's wild and reckless eldest ward had been up to. The news of the sabotage and financial difficulties his shipping business was encountering would have provided much fodder for the Marbury Club's otherwise stultifyingly vapid afternoon discussions.

"Good to see you, Kent." A dried-up little husk of a man with a fringe of straw-colored hair skirting his otherwise shiny pink head approached and extended a scaly hand. "How was India? Damned hot, I would imagine." He looked about the room and guffawed.

"It was, Lord Chesley." Jack accepted the glass of brandy a footman offered him on a silver tray and took a deep swallow. He would need ample fortification if he was to play this game of strained civility for long. "But I enjoy the heat."

"Of course you do." Lord Farnham, the Earl of Palgrave, studied him with supercilious amusement as he fingered the ends of his short, dark beard into a perfect point. "And I'd wager you enjoyed the special charms of the native women there as well, did you not?"

The entire room broke into a chorus of raucous male laughter, much of it half drunk, although it was barely midday.

"I enjoy the charms of women wherever they are

offered—as I'm sure every man in this room does, including you, Lord Chesley." Jack raised his glass at the hunched little bird of a man and winked, causing the assemblage to roar with laughter once again.

"So, Kent, what brings you to London?" asked Lord Farnham. "I hear you've been having some trouble with ruffians vandalizing your ships." His expression was mild. "That's all been straightened out, I hope?"

"The matter is under investigation," Jack replied impassively. "Fortunately, the damage has been minimal and has not affected my shipping schedules."

It was vital to maintain the impression that his business was thoroughly sound. Any rumors suggesting otherwise would make his investors and clients uneasy, which could result in loans being called and contracts being canceled, either of which would be disastrous for him.

"Really? I had heard otherwise." Lord Spalding regarded him intently over the rim of his glass, his bloated face drawn into a mask of barely veiled disdain. "One never can be sure of the accuracy of information these days," he added, absently twirling the gold crest ring on his left hand.

His inference that Jack was lying was unmistakable. Aware that everyone was waiting for his reaction, Jack forced an amused smile to his lips. "You're absolutely right, Spalding," he agreed amiably. "That's why I have always preferred to rely on facts and figures. They bring a remarkable clarity to matters of business—as no doubt you have also found. One day I'll take you through my plans for the expansion of North Star Shipping over the next five years. I'm sure you'll find it most intriguing."

His expression dubious, Lord Spalding took a swallow of his drink. "Indeed."

"Actually, I came to England to visit my family, who were attending the Duke of Whitcliffe's wedding yesterday," Jack continued, casually steering the conversation toward the subject of Miss Belford and, by association, Viscount Philmore. "I'm only here to check on my London office before heading back to Scotland."

"Now there's a catastrophe if ever I heard of one." Lord Beardsley rested his drink on the mound of his enormous belly, which rose like the hump of a whale over the arms of his chair. "Poor Whitcliffe must be stumbling about in a daze, wondering how the hell he could have come so close to that fortune, only to have it snatched away before the papers were signed."

"It's his own damn fault for not keeping the girl on a tight leash." Lord Dunlop thumped his cane for effect. "I've met Miss Belford, and she is just as outspoken and uncouth as the rest of these wealthy American girls are. If Whitcliffe couldn't take measures to control her, he bloody well deserves to have her run off on her wedding day." He banged his cane against the floor to underscore the point.

"I heard Whitcliffe boasting that Miss Belford's dowry and allowance amounted to well over half a million pounds," said Lord Farnham. "For that amount of money, a man could learn to endure her impertinence— and that perfectly hideous accent!"

Jack took a swallow of brandy. But for his need to find out more about Viscount Philmore, he would have cheerfully wrapped his hands around Farnham's throat.

"The newspapers say Miss Belford was abducted," said Lord Beardsley. "There is a ten-thousand-pound reward for any information leading to her being found and reunited with her family."

"I don't believe the girl was abducted for a minute," Lord Sullivan scoffed. "How could someone abduct a bride on her own wedding day, with hundreds of guests milling about? Wouldn't she have screamed? Wouldn't someone have heard her?"

"Maybe not." Lord Chesley's dark little eyes narrowed with intrigue. "Perhaps whoever took her gagged her—or drugged her."

"Then where is the ransom note?" Lord Dunlop demanded, pounding his cane furiously.

"It's possible the family had not yet received it at the time that the newspapers were printed," suggested Lord Beardsley.

"They haven't received it because there is no ransom note." Lord Sullivan took a long draw upon his cigar, wreathing his white head in smoke. "The silly girl has run away, and the family is too bloody embarrassed to admit it."

"That's the trouble with these ridiculous American girls," Lord Farnham fumed. "They flounce about over here, giving themselves airs and trying to buy titles to which they have no earthly right, and then they do nothing but whine the minute they're married and realize that a husband is part of the bargain. Lord Kemble's American wife spent the first two months of their marriage locked in her room weeping, for God's sake. Nearly drove the poor chap mad. Thank God he had his French mistress to keep him sane."

"It seems the American heiresses' reputation for being difficult has not kept Lord Philmore from getting himself engaged to one," Jack observed offhandedly. "Didn't I read about his betrothal in the *Morning Post*?"

"Ah, yes, and I expect we'll hear all about it shortly when he arrives for lunch," said Lord Chesley. "He usually appears at one o'clock."

"Fortuitous that he was finally able to snare one of those girls," observed Beardsley. "God knows, he's been working at it long enough."

"Edith Fanshaw seems a quiet, sensible kind of girl," Farnham added. "If she never opened her mouth and revealed that horrid accent, you'd think she was English."

"She has a face like a squashed cabbage," objected Lord Sullivan with drunken candor. "And no neck whatsoever. The children she will breed will look like trolls."

"She may not be as comely as Miss Belford," conceded Lord Farnham, "but she won't cause Philmore any headaches, either. At any rate, I'm sure he's relieved. He couldn't have gone on much longer if Miss Fanshaw's father hadn't agreed to let him have her."

Jack was careful to appear only mildly interested. "What do you mean?"

"Philmore has been teetering on the brink of financial ruin for years," supplied Lord Sullivan. "Well, everyone knows it," he snapped, scowling at the disapproving glances of the other members. "It's no great secret."

"Sullivan is right," agreed Lord Chesley. "Until he signed the papers with Miss Fanshaw's father yesterday, Philmore couldn't begin to cover the expenses of running his estate."

"Or his gambling debts," added Lord Beardsley.

"Or his taste for expensive women," observed Lord Dunlop.

Lord Sullivan snorted with disgust. "Or expensive men."

A strained silence fell upon the room.

"Oh, for God's sake, all of London knows about that." He glared at the other members as if they were all imbeciles. "You can't think Kent here will be shocked by Philmore's appetite for stupid, brawny young men. He pays to bed them, then pays them again to keep their mouths shut."

Lord Chesley scratched his nose with his little claw hand. "Obviously he hasn't been paying them enough."

"Very little has the power to shock me anymore—except for Lord Sullivan's remarkable ability to hold his liquor." Jack smiled and raised his glass to him, as if he thought Lord Sullivan's remarks must have been a drunken joke.

"Damned right." Lord Sullivan clamped his cigar between his yellowing teeth and held out his glass so it could be filled once more.

"At any rate, it's good that Philmore finally caught himself an heiress," said Lord Beardsley, trying to revive the conversation. "He needs the money desperately."

Jack signaled for his own glass to be filled again. "But surely he inherited some wealth along with his title?"

"Any money he inherited he lost to gambling years ago," replied Lord Farnham. "He's terrible at it, yet he can't stop himself."

"Don't forget about those dreadful investments," added Lord Dunlop, thumping his cane. "The fall in Great Atlantic's stock has nearly destroyed him."

"Didn't he inherit some land?" persisted Jack. "Some sort of ancestral holding?"

"He inherited the family's country estate, with a house in dire need of repairs. But the days of living off the land are gone—as we all know."

"Bloody agricultural depression," growled Lord Sullivan. "Ten years and it's still got us landowners by the throat."

"There won't be any end to it," predicted Lord Beardsley, morosely staring into his drink. "Foreign produce floods our shores every day. Damned American wheat has practically killed English wheat farming."

"I've reduced the rents of my tenant farmers so many times, I might as well pay them to live on my lands," grumbled Lord Chesley.

"It's either reduce their rents or lose them altogether," Lord Beardsley pointed out, "and there's no one to take their place."

"Young men go to the cities now," reflected Lord Dunlop. "Can't make money as a farmer."

"In the meantime, the costs of running our estates keep escalating. Every time it rains I think my roof is going to come crashing down." Lord Sullivan huffed with annoyance. "It takes over forty pots just to catch the drips."

Although Haydon had managed to elude the financial strain of the current agricultural depression by making shrewd investments in industry years earlier, Jack was not unfamiliar with the economic difficulties of the landed gentry. Repairs and maintenance for their ancestral homes were exorbitant, and could only be contemplated once the countless daily expenses of upkeep had been addressed.

Obviously whatever Viscount Philmore was collecting on his rents could not begin to address the constant hemorrhage of his crumbling estate. If one combined that with his gambling debts, failed investments, and assorted vices, it was no wonder he had scurried to find another heiress the minute his seduction of Amelia had failed. God forbid he might actually try to find himself a job, Jack reflected contemptuously. Not even the threat of financial ruin could rouse these aristocrats to join the ranks of the working class. They believed it was far easier to marry wealth than to earn it—even if that meant enduring a bride for whom they harbored nothing but disdain. Marriage to an heiress would enable Philmore to settle his debts and restore his estate.

All while he indulged in his taste for men.

Abruptly, Jack set down his glass.

"You're not leaving?" Lord Sullivan's expression was genuinely mournful.

"Come, Kent," said Lord Chesley, "you've only just arrived."

"Lunch will be served shortly." Lord Beardsley tried to entice him. "I understand larded guinea fowl is on the menu."

"I'm afraid my visit to London is too brief to permit me to stay," Jack explained. "I have some business matters to attend to, and then must leave for Inverness. Perhaps another time."

He thought he detected a flash of envy, as if they wished that they had somewhere of consequence to go, where they would be called upon to make decisions of import. But in the next moment their expressions were resigned and blank once more. They sank into their deeply padded chairs and signaled for the footman to bring them another round of drinks, preparing to get more inebriated before they had to rouse themselves for the serving of their six-course lunch.

To THE HOUSE, OLIVER." JACK SLAMMED THE DOOR of his carriage shut.

Oliver regarded him curiously from his driver's seat. "Did ye find him, then?"

"He wasn't there."

"Did ye get his address?"

"No."

Oliver folded his arms across his skeletal chest and waited.

"Are ye fixin' to tell me what's made yer temper so black, or are we goin' to sit here awhile an' enjoy the sights?" he asked finally.

"My temper isn't black." In truth Jack felt dangerously close to smashing something. "Lord Philmore wasn't there, but he is due to make an appearance shortly for lunch." His voice was dripping with acrimony. "I learned enough about him to realize that he is not a suitable match for Miss Belford. I intend to tell her so."

Oliver raised a quizzical brow. "Do ye now? And just what is it, exactly, about his lordship has brought ye to this decision?"

"Lord Philmore has found himself another heiress to wed."

"So?"

"So Miss Belford can't very well expect him to marry her when it was announced in the newspapers today that he intends to marry someone else."

"Seems to me that's nae your decision to make, lad," Oliver argued. "The lass didna ask ye to decide for her whether ye thought the match was good or no. All she asked was that ye find her precious viscount an' take her to him, plain and simple. An' that's what ye agreed to do."

"That was before."

"Afore what?"

Jack hesitated. "Before I discovered that her precious viscount is a man who is apparently without funds or honor." He decided to spare Oliver the more sordid details of Philmore's character.

Oliver chuckled. "Ye've been away at sea too long, lad. There's more honor amongst thieves than amongst those rich nobs, an' that's the sad truth o' the matter."

"Haydon is honorable."

"Aye, he is. But his lordship is nae like the others. That's always been plain enough, I think."

"I don't like the fact that Philmore was so quick to bag himself another heiress the moment he realized Miss Belford was no longer available. If he actually cared for her, he would have at least had the decency to wait before chasing after another rich woman."

Oliver cocked a white brow with amusement. "So 'tis his timin' that's stuck like a bone in yer gorge, and nae else."

Jack stared out the carriage window and said nothing.

"Think for a moment, lad," Oliver urged. "If ye return to Miss Amelia now an' tell her ye didna meet with her betrothed because ye've found that he's gone and gotten himself another bride, how do ye suppose she's goin' to react? Do ye think she's goin' to thank ye for decidin' she best not see him?"

"Yes."

Oliver snorted, exasperated. "Ye're nae thinkin' clear. 'Tis more like she'll tell ye ye're wrong, and demand ye take her to him straightaway. If ye refuse, she'll find him herself. An' how do ye suppose he'll react if the lass just shows up on his doorstep with nae warnin'—maybe while his bonny new bride-to-be is there?"

That would be disastrous, Jack realized. Not just because Philmore would be caught unawares and might react unpleasantly, but also because there would be others present—servants, or even one of Philmore's lovers—who might be tempted to turn Amelia in. With ten thousand pounds being offered for information leading to her whereabouts, her situation was extremely precarious.

"Whatever blather ye've heard, ye've nae way of knowin' for certain whether this Philmore cares for Miss Amelia or not. Who knows? He might break his betrothal and marry Miss Amelia instead."

"He was only interested in Amelia for her money," Jack told him with absolute certainty. "Since she no longer has any, Philmore won't marry her. If those men in there are even half right about his financial situation, he can't afford to marry her."

"Seems to me ye're nae considerin' he might actually care for her," Oliver argued. "Surely ye can see how rare bonny she is. Even old Beaton could see that, an' he was completely stewed."

Jack said nothing.

"Ye'd best hope Philmore does decide to marry her," Oliver continued. "If he doesna, then just what, exactly, are ye plannin' to do with her?"

Jack shifted restlessly against his seat. He could

hardly leave Amelia alone at Haydon and Genevieve's home. But he couldn't hang about London looking after her, and he certainly couldn't take her back to Scotland with him. Reluctant reason began to temper his disgust with Philmore.

"Fine. I'll meet Philmore and tell him Amelia is in London, and I'll arrange for him to see her. But he mustn't know who I am. I can't risk having him or someone else track her back to Haydon and Genevieve's house. No one must know where she is staying."

"Surely ye dinna think Philmore would betray her?"

"There is a ten-thousand-pound reward being offered for information leading to her discovery. While Philmore won't care about that now that he has another heiress to support him, he might let it slip that I know where she is to someone who finds her reward tempting. I can't take that chance. Also, I don't want Haydon or Genevieve associated in any way with Amelia's disappearance."

"So it's a disguise ye're needin', is it?"

Jack nodded. "Philmore is due to arrive shortly for lunch, which gives us a couple of hours to prepare. Do you think that is enough time?"

The old man's mouth split into a grin. "I've just the place, lad."

He KNOWS." LORD FARNHAM NERVOUSLY TWISTED the tip of his beard. "We have to call it off."

"No."

"For God's sake, Spalding, are you mad?" Farnham's gaze darted anxiously around the dining room before he hissed fiercely, *"He knows."*

"Kent doesn't know a goddamn thing."

Lord Spalding paused as a footman filled his wineglass, moodily contemplating Jack's unexpected arrival at the club. Spalding had been startled to see him, but quickly decided Kent was merely there to assure the members that all was well with his precious shipping company.

Appearances, as Spalding understood only too well, were half the battle.

"He may be suspicious, but he doesn't know anything for certain," Spalding continued once the servant was gone. "The plan goes ahead as scheduled." He sawed vigorously at a thick slab of gray beef.

"At least call off tonight—let's wait until he has left London," urged Lord Farnham.

"If we wait for him to leave, we may lose our chance to strike. I won't do that. This is a war, Farnham, and in war you have to hit your enemy hard and fast, again and again, until he is destroyed." Spalding shoveled a forkful of fatty meat into his mouth, then cringed. Why the hell did that bloody French chef cook beef until it had the taste and texture of boot leather?

"It doesn't seem that we're having any effect," objected Lord Farnham, shifting restlessly in his chair. "We're taking enormous risks, yet North Star Shipping continues to do well."

"Of course Kent claims it is doing well—he doesn't want anyone to know how badly his company has been hit," Spalding countered impatiently. "The fact is he has already lost several contracts, and he cannot afford to lose any more. If word of that gets out, his investors will become nervous." He swallowed a mouthful of wine before finishing darkly, "After tonight, the filthy little upstart will have difficulty convincing anyone that their goods are safe on one of his goddamn tramp ships."

BRILLIANT GARLANDS OF MELON AND COPPER SUNlight flickered upon the stone façade of the Marbury Club as Jack and Oliver sat sweating within the dark heat of the carriage.

"By the toes of Saint Andrew, if he doesna come out soon, I swear I'm marchin' in there and draggin' him out myself," grumbled Oliver, shifting against his seat. "How long does it take a man to eat?"

"I imagine he is celebrating his newfound fortune with his fellow members by buying them drinks with his bride's money." Jack twisted his rough woolen cap in his hands and continued to wait impatiently for Lord Philmore to emerge.

The ill-fitting clothes he had purchased from a shabby little shop far from the elegant enclave of Mayfair were cheap and poorly made, which was exactly what he had wanted. The loose brown trousers and coat were of crudely stitched wool, and the coarse cotton shirt beneath was thin and turning yellow. His polished leather boots had been replaced with an ugly pair of shoes that pinched his feet, but they were the largest the shop had. To complete his appearance Jack had rubbed his hands, face and outfit with a liberal application of dirt and grease. If Philmore was the kind of man Jack suspected he was, he would look no further than Jack's clothes to judge and dismiss him in one swift glance.

"He could be in there hours yet," Oliver muttered irritably. "Why don't ye just march in there an' tell his lordship ye've another bride waitin' for him, an' if he wants her ye can have her delivered to him safe an' sound by tonight?"

"There he is." Jack watched as a slender man of modest height emerged from the heavy doors of the Marbury Club. He wore a tailored charcoal coat over a crisply starched shirt and cravat, from which an enormous ruby pin winked in the sunshine. A silver-capped walking stick was tucked jauntily under one arm, and he was pulling on a cream-colored pair of leather gloves as he trotted down the stone staircase to his carriage, his buffed shoes tapping lightly beneath his graceful movements, his face set in the same self-satisfied expression Jack had seen in the newspaper that morning.

"What are ye waitin' for?" demanded Oliver impatiently. "Go talk to him afore he leaves—an' dinna forget to take the polish off yer tongue!"

Cramming his cap onto his head, Jack leapt down and raced over to Philmore's carriage.

"What the devil do you think you're doing?" demanded Viscount Philmore as Jack jerked open his carriage door and climbed inside. "Here now—get out at once!"

"Shut yer gob and listen," Jack growled.

"Help!" cried Philmore, rapping the wall that separated him from his sleepy driver.

Misinterpreting the meaning of the agitated rap, the driver snapped the reins over the horses and the carriage lurched forward.

"What do you want?" asked Viscount Philmore nervously, scooting like a frightened bug away from Jack.

His cheeks and forehead were barely lined, indicating he was younger than Jack had initially thought, perhaps thirty-five or so, but no more. Yet there was a priggishness to him that made him seem older. It was as if all the whimsy and daring of his youth had been either frightened or beaten out of him at an early age, replacing it with a fussy, supercilious demeanor that Jack found patently ridiculous. Of course it was possible Philmore had always been that way, but Jack couldn't imagine any self-respecting lad being quite so timid. How could this frightened little mannequin be the man with whom Amelia fancied herself in love? He supposed Philmore was handsome enough, with his neatly clipped red hair peering from beneath the shiny black of his hat and his fastidiously maintained mustache curled ever so slightly at the ends. Jack was no authority on what women found appealing in a man, but he was not so blinded by contempt that he could not concede that Philmore was not unattractive.

Even so, the cowering little dandy was hardly the kind of man that Jack would have chosen for a highly spirited, independent-minded woman like Amelia.

"I'll give you everything I have in my billfold," Lord Philmore bleated, slipping a gloved hand into his coat pocket. "Will that satisfy you?"

"I don't want yer money," Jack replied tersely. "I've a message for you."

Panic rounded Lord Philmore's eyes into two tea saucers. "I told Hawkins I would pay him as soon as I'm able," he blurted out desperately. "He just has to be patient a little longer—"

"I'm not here about that," Jack snarled. "I'm here about Amelia Belford."

Lord Philmore's expression puckered with confusion. "Amelia? I haven't seen her in months. Of course I read in the paper that she was abducted yesterday—surely you don't think that I had anything to do with that!" His expression grew agitated. "I swear to you, I know nothing whatsoever about—"

"I'm here to give ye a message from her."

Lord Philmore withdrew a white linen kerchief from his pocket and dabbed at the moisture beading on his brow. "What message?"

Everything about Lord Philmore disgusted Jack, from his twitching mustache to his sexual inclinations to his frantic protestations of ignorance. No wonder Amelia's parents had been appalled when she informed them that she was betrothed to the quivering squirrel. At least Whitcliffe's arrogance gave him some small measure of backbone.

Lord Philmore momentarily paused in his ministrations to his forehead. "Did Amelia send you to me?"

Jack hesitated. And then, remembering it was

Amelia's wish to be reunited with her viscount, he reluctantly answered, "Yes."

A flicker of something lit Philmore's eyes. "Where is she?"

The fact that his first enquiry wasn't regarding her immediate welfare bothered Jack. Shouldn't his initial concern be whether or not she had been harmed?

"She's in London," Jack replied vaguely. "She wants to see you."

There it was again. Something was bubbling in Lord Philmore's mind, but whatever it was, he was clever enough to try to mask it in Jack's presence.

"When?"

"Tonight."

"Where shall I go to see her?"

"I'll bring her to yer home. Make sure there's no one else there, an' wait 'til we come."

"I'm afraid that won't do," Lord Philmore protested. "I have an engagement."

Jack regarded him incredulously. "Cancel it."

"Unfortunately, that is impossible." His forehead sufficiently dabbed, Philmore carefully folded the linen square and replaced it in his pocket. "I am the guest of honor, you see. But that does not mean I am not most anxious to see Miss Belford," he quickly assured Jack. "It just means we shall have to make alternate arrangements." He pulled a small card from his coat pocket and began to write upon it with a gold pencil. "If you would be so kind as to give this note to Miss Belford," he continued, slipping the card into an envelope, "it will tell her exactly where we should meet."

Jack took the creamy stationery in his grimy hand, smearing it with grease in the process.

"Here is something for your trouble." Lord Philmore dropped a half crown in Jack's hand, taking care not to mar the pristine finger of his glove as he did so, then rapped twice on the carriage floor, signaling for the driver to stop.

Jack stared at the silver coin resting against his grubby, callused palm. He had done everything he said he would. He had found Amelia's betrothed and arranged for them to meet. If all went well, she would be back in her soul mate's arms that very evening, leaving Jack free to return to Inverness and get on with directing the affairs of his shipping business. He should have felt profoundly relieved.

Instead he climbed down from the carriage filled with self-loathing, as if he had just betrayed his runaway heiress.

Chapter Four

M AKE WAY—COMIN' THROUGH!"

Blinded by a tower of boxes, Beaton barreled through the doorway and crashed directly into Jack. The impact had little effect on Jack other than to further irritate him. Poor Beaton, however, fell unceremoniously on his backside while trying to shield himself from a shower of gaily colored packages.

"Bloody hell!" he yelped. "Them boxes is sharp!"

"Beaton, quit your dawdling and bring them new things up here," ordered Lizzie impatiently from the top of the staircase. "Oh, hello, Mr. Jack," she added, seeing Jack staring at her in astonishment. "Pardon the mess, we wasn't expectin' you home quite so soon—here now, what's happened to you? You look as if you've been slatherin' grease in the shipyards!"

"What the devil is going on here, Lizzie?" Jack demanded.

"Me and Beaton are tryin' to fix up Miss Belford with a nice new wardrobe, just like you said." Looking frazzled, Lizzie scooped up four more gowns, two velvet cloaks and a beaded shawl that were draped carelessly upon the banister and disappeared back into Amelia's bedroom.

"Looks more like ye're fixin' her up with ten new wardrobes," chortled Oliver, eyeing the boxes and parcels strewn throughout the entrance hall, library, and dining room of the main floor.

Most of the packages were open, revealing what Jack felt certain was enough feminine attire to clothe the entire city of London. Expensive gowns, cloaks, and crinolines were haphazardly draped over chairs and doorways, while the floors were choked with elegantly fashioned shoes, boots, gloves and reticules in every shade of leather, silk, satin and linen imaginable.

"I told you to get Miss Belford a wardrobe?" he demanded, turning to Beaton.

"Well, of course you did." Beaton pulled himself awkwardly up from the scattered packages. "Miss Belford told us so. She said you didn't want her goin' off to meet her betrothed in rags, and as there was nothing suitable in Lady Redmond's wardrobe, she asked me and Lizzie to go out and collect a few things for her. She made a list and told us which shops to visit, so as to be sure to bring back things to her likin'." He fished a crumpled ball of paper from his coat pocket with a long list written in delicate handwriting upon it. "I've been driving back and forth all day, pickin' things up and takin' things back."

"And just how, exactly, did you pay for them?"

"Why, I put them on your account, just like Miss Belford told me to." Beaton fumbled through his pockets and produced a half dozen more wrinkled slips of paper. "There's a few receipts there, and of course there's more in the boxes, and Lizzie's got a stack of them upstairs in Miss Belford's room. You needn't worry though," he quickly added as Jack's eyes widened at the exorbitant sums at the bottom of each bill. "I told the shopkeepers the items were for Lady Redmond, so they wouldn't be suspicious." He gave Jack a conspiratorial wink.

"Canna imagine Miss Genevieve ever buyin' a houseful of clothes like this," mused Oliver, gazing around at the explosion of garments. "Once ye've learned to measure every purchase by how many meals ye might have made from it, ye can nae spend on some-thin' fine without feelin' a wee bit o' guilt first."

"Genevieve would never buy all these clothes—first because she would be incensed by their excessiveness, and second because she and Haydon couldn't bloody well afford them." Jack stalked angrily up the stairs, nearly tripping over the waterfall of boxes as he went.

"This one won't do either, I'm afraid." Amelia frowned at the gown she was holding up to the mirror. "The sleeves are too tight, the hem is too long, and these tiers of roses are entirely too large. Also, it is far too bright a pink; I'm afraid my complexion calls for a rosier shade." She tossed the offending garment onto the enor-mous pile of equally objectionable fashions upon the bed, then went to take the next gown Lizzie held out to her.

"Good afternoon, Miss Belford." Jack fought to re-main calm as he scanned the litter of expensive garments scattered about the room. "I see you've had no trouble keeping yourself occupied during my absence."

"Oh, thank goodness you're back!" Amelia cried, rushing toward him.

She was clad only in a dressing gown of pale peach silk, which was loosely cinched about her tiny waist and gaping just enough to reveal a hint of creamy bosom and the ivory corset laced tight beneath it. Her pale blond hair had been pinned into a loose arrangement atop her head, but the exertion of trying on dozens of gowns had left numerous tendrils dangling in wispy spirals around her face, giving her a charmingly disheveled look. She wore stockings but no shoes, despite the fact that there must have been over a hundred pairs in the house, and Jack found her unadorned little feet strangely entrancing as they peeked out from the hem of her robe.

"I was worried when I awakened and realized you were gone," Amelia confessed softly. "I didn't know whether you would come back."

He stared at her in bewilderment. Had she honestly believed that he would simply abandon her? The delicate scent of her was flooding his senses, a light fragrance of sunlight and soap touched with a hint of orange and some tangy clean flower he could not identify. The violet shadows beneath her eyes had faded slightly, and the dozens of scratches on her hands looked less raw. Her spirit was clearly stronger than it had been the previous night when he had found her lying curled upon the bed with tears sparkling upon her lashes. And yet there was an aching vulnerability to her, which pierced his anger with the efficacy of an arrow.

"Did you find Percy?"

Disappointment sliced through him.

"Yes." His tone was unaccountably brusque.

"I knew you would!" she exclaimed, ecstatic. She reached out as if she meant to hug him, then frowned. "Why are you dressed like that—and how did you get so dirty?"

"I thought it best that your precious Percy not know who I was."

"Why not?"

"I take it, Miss Belford, that you have not read today's newspaper."

"I've been much too busy to read the paper." Amelia gestured in frustration at the heaps of garments strewn around her. "I've been trying to put together an adequate wardrobe for myself since early this morning, and I'm afraid it has not been easy."

"So I see. And just how, may I ask, do you expect to pay for all of this?"

"Is that what has made you so angry?" She looked genuinely taken aback. "The fact that I sent out for a few outfits?"

"This is not a few outfits," Jack observed tautly. "This is the annual production of some two hundred or more seamstresses, hatters, leather-goods manufacturers, and cobblers, which could easily outfit the entire city of London for the next five years!"

"I'll just be seein' what's happened to Beaton." Lizzie hastily snatched up a few discarded gowns and bustled out the door.

Amelia's gaze remained riveted on Jack, but the color of her eyes had cooled, like the ocean darkening before a storm. "I had nothing to wear." Her voice was deliberately measured, making it clear he did not intimidate her in the least. "I could scarcely present myself to my betrothed in rags, wearing a ruined wedding gown that was designed for my marriage to another man. Did you expect me to go to Viscount Philmore looking like this?" She skimmed the tips of her fingers over the loose dressing gown she wore, which was now tantalizingly close to falling open.

The idea of her idiot viscount, or any other man for that matter, seeing her in her current state of undress only inflamed Jack's anger.

"I told you that you could help yourself to any of my mother's clothes," he returned evenly. "Surely there were enough outfits there from which you could choose that you did not have to empty every shop in London in your quest to find a suitable gown."

"Lady Redmond and I are not the same size," Amelia pointed out, "and her wardrobe is not—"

"Not what?" Jack interrupted. "Expensive enough to suit a spoiled American heiress, because most of the clothes have been designed by my sister instead of some pretentious French fool, and sewn in a modest little shop in Inverness instead of in some salon in Paris?"

"No, Mr. Kent." Amelia tilted her head up so she could meet his glare with her own. "Your mother has excellent taste, and your sister is obviously a very talented designer. I could not wear her clothes because they did not fit. As for the cost of my wardrobe, I assure you that I intend to pay for it myself. As soon as I am reunited with Lord Philmore, I will make certain you are generously compensated for all the trouble you have gone to on my behalf. My Percy is a gentleman, and would never permit either a kindness or a debt to go unpaid."

"You're wrong," Jack snarled, infuriated by the veiled inference that he was somehow less of a gentleman than her simpering little betrothed. "Your precious Percy is bloody well up to his eyeballs in debt, and would gladly let anyone pay them on his behalf—even a naive young girl who is nothing more to him than a quick and easy way to flood his bank account with money he could never have dreamed of getting his hands on otherwise, short of gambling for it, which he does rather badly, or stealing it."

"How dare you!" Amelia balled up her fists as if she meant to strike him. "First of all, Mr. Kent, I am not the naive young girl you seem to think I am, and secondly, Percy doesn't care about money—and neither do I!"

"That's because you have never known what it is not to have any."

"And neither, apparently, have you!" she retaliated, sweeping her arms around the elegantly appointed bedchamber.

Jack stared at her in surprise. She didn't know about

him, he realized. Didn't know about his childhood, which forever branded him as a filthy, ignorant thief, no matter how hard he tried to wrest himself above the stench and the squalor. She had no concept of the things he had been forced to do to survive—of the brutal beatings he had endured and later inflicted, of the stealing and lies, of the constant need to fight for food and clothing and shelter, all while desperately scrambling to keep from being killed and out of jail.

She didn't know anything about him at all.

"Forgive me," he murmured, feeling as if he had momentarily lost his bearings. He raked his hand through his hair, feeling hopelessly ill-equipped to handle the situation. "Sometimes I say things without thinking." He shrugged helplessly.

Amelia frowned, studying him. She was not terribly familiar with the garb of the lower-class people in London, but she was amazed at how convincing Jack looked in his shabby coat and trousers. Most men she knew would have appeared ridiculously out of place in the coarse, poorly sewn attire. Certainly Percy was too finely boned and softly fleshed to ever play the part of a man who earned his living through physical exertion.

With his powerful frame straining against the poorly tailored shirt and coat and his rough-cut jaw smeared with grime, Jack Kent seemed every inch the contemptuous laborer he was pretending to be. His hands were huge and bronzed by the sun, the calluses upon his palms making it clear he was a man well accustomed to hard physical labor. His eyes were filled with scorn as he spoke of her betrothed, and she sensed that it was not just Percy whom he despised, but all those of his class. This was bewildering, given that her host was obviously accustomed to a life of privilege. She continued to stare at him, intrigued by the paradox of his emotions, and the lengths to which he had gone to ensure that Percy would not learn of his identity. She suspected Jack had done this to protect her, although she believed his efforts to be misguided, Percy would never permit her to come to harm. But there was a constant wariness to the man standing before her, a cool distrust that shadowed the hard gray of his eyes. Her gaze fell upon the thin white scar snaking along his left cheek. Somehow that pale streak touched a chord within her. She found herself wanting to touch him, to lay her hand upon his cheek and feel its roughness beneath her palm, to soothe his anger and contempt with the coolness of her fingers, and know the pulsing heat of him against her skin.

She turned away abruptly, self-consciously tightening the sash of her robe.

"What did you mean when you asked if I had read today's paper?" she asked stiffly.

Jack hesitated. It would be painful for her to hear, he realized. "Viscount Philmore has found himself another bride. This morning's paper announced his engagement to a Miss Edith Fanshaw."

She whirled about, her expression outraged. "You are mistaken." Her voice was brittle.

"I can send Beaton out to buy a copy of the *Morning Post* if you doubt me. The members of the Marbury Club were discussing the news when I went there. They were under the impression that Philmore is suffering from severe financial strain, and that his engagement to Miss Fanshaw comes at a most opportune time. It seems she is also an heiress from America."

"I know Edith Fanshaw," Amelia informed him in a tight voice. "Her father is Arthur Fanshaw of Baltimore, and although he has some holdings of import in Chicago real estate, the Fanshaws do not possess any great wealth."

"Evidently they possess enough to make a marriage

to their daughter palatable," Jack observed. "Philmore has agreed to marry her."

"He cannot be doing it of his own free will," Amelia decided. "Something has happened—some dreadful calamity has forced him to do this."

"He's doing it because he hasn't got any money, and when he marries Miss Fanshaw that little problem will be instantly solved."

"I don't believe that Percy hasn't any money, but even if he doesn't, I don't care. He loves me, and I love him. Once he knows that I have run away from Lord Whitcliffe to be with him, he will break his betrothal to Miss Fanshaw and marry me instead."

"I think you should be prepared for the possibility that he may not be quite so willing to give her up. After all, Miss Belford, at the moment you are an heiress without means, having run away from your marriage and estranged yourself from your family's considerable fortune."

Her eyes flashed with fury. "Tell me, Mr. Kent, do you believe no man could possibly want me just for the woman I am?"

"No—"

"Then kindly refrain from insulting me by questioning Lord Philmore's motives for wanting to marry me. Did you actually meet with him, or did you merely listen to idle gossip being bandied about by his associates at the Marbury Club?"

"I met with him," Jack replied. "He gave me this note for you." He produced Lord Philmore's envelope from inside his coat and handed it to her.

"I knew it!" she cried, freshly elated as she read the card within. "He says he is counting the moments until we are to be reunited. I am to meet him at the Wilkinsons' ball tonight, at precisely nine o'clock. There he will declare his intention to marry me before the hundreds of guests in attendance, and shall make arrangements for our marriage shortly thereafter."

Jack stared at her incredulously. "Why in the name of God would he put you in such a public place when all of England is looking for you?"

"It's very clever, don't you see? My parents will not want to endure any further scandal by trying to stop a marriage that has been formally announced in a public setting. It's brilliant."

"It's madness," Jack countered furiously. "You may be interested to learn, Miss Belford, that there is a ten-thousand-pound reward being offered for any information leading to your being found. That means anyone at that ball could grab you and claim that reward—or, if they prefer a less sensational route to your father's wealth, they could merely contact the authorities and let them know where you are."

"Percy would never let that happen."

"Percy wouldn't have any goddamn choice," Jack snapped. "Only a fool would let you walk in there alone. You're not going."

"Forgive me, Mr. Kent, but I was not aware that you were my keeper."

"I'm not your bloody keeper, but I am your—" He stopped, unsure how to finish.

"I asked you to help me get to London and find Viscount Philmore, and I am indebted to you for having done both," Amelia assured him. "I do not, however, expect you to dictate to me how or where I am to reunite with him. Percy believes this is the best way for us to make our intentions public. If he suspected there was any risk involved, he would never suggest it."

"He may not have thought the matter through." Either that or Lord Philmore was a goddamn idiot, which was entirely possible. "Or he may not be aware of the reward. Either way, Miss Belford, I'm asking you to trust me." He moved closer to her, narrowing the gulf between them. "Stay here tonight, and let me go to the ball and meet with Lord Philmore instead. I will make him understand the ball is not safe for you, and arrange another meeting for tomorrow night. If he cares about you as much as you claim, he won't mind a delay of one day. If anything, he will appreciate my concern."

Amelia wanted to say no, to tell him that she refused to be separated from her Percy even a day longer, for every moment was like torture to two tragically separated lovers. But something in the powerful intensity of Jack's gaze made her pause. Somehow she did not think he would be moved by her declarations of love. Jack Kent did not strike her as a man who had ever known what it was to surrender himself to that glorious emotion. He would also not share her confidence that Percy would do everything within his means to see that she was safe. Jack had already made it abundantly clear that he despised Lord Philmore, although she didn't understand why. All she knew was that he believed he was protecting her, while she was quite certain she needed no such protection.

He was staring at her intently, waiting for her response. It confused her that the man who had so reluctantly spirited her away from her own wedding now felt that he held some sort of responsibility for her. She certainly didn't want Mr. Kent to think she was ungrateful for all that he had done for her. But she also didn't want to be separated from Percy even a moment longer—not when he was so close and their life together was finally about to begin.

"Very well, Mr. Kent," she said. "I will remain here while you make alternate arrangements for our reconciliation. Will that satisfy you?"

Jack regarded her warily. "Yes."

"Now if you will excuse me, I still have a number of

outfits to try on before I send Beaton to return the clothes I will not be keeping." She scooped up an elaborate gown of amethyst silk and a delicate pair of matching evening shoes.

Jack's jaw tightened as she raised the gown to her shoulders and turned to study herself in the mirror. Should Lord Philmore decide to break his betrothal to Miss Fanshaw, he would not be in any position to pay for the extravagant clothes to which Miss Belford was evidently accustomed. Somehow Jack forced himself to turn away from her, denying himself the pleasure of her loveliness as she cast the gown aside and rifled through the mound on the bed, searching for another.

If Miss Belford's precious viscount did decide to marry her, then she would learn the harsh reality of Philmore's finances and sexual preferences soon enough.

Chapter Five

WE LOST HIM."

The old man scowled with impatience. "What do you mean, you lost him?"

Neil Dempsey swallowed nervously and stared down at his notes, wondering how much this recent failure was going to cost him. It was difficult to predict the mercurial moods of his volatile employer, who could be unaccountably enraged by the most innocuous of details, and then moved to the brink of tears by some other equally insipid observation. Cursing his associate for losing Kent, he consulted the brief telegraph message he had received earlier that day.

"He was last seen yesterday leavin' Lord Whitcliffe's wedding in his rented carriage, with his old servant, Oliver, driving. Mr. Potter, my associate, was under the impression that Mr. Kent was plannin' to return to Inverness by train. Unfortunately, it seems he never reached the station. There's nae record of him purchasin' a fare, and no one saw either him or his servant boarding the coach. My associate continued to watch the station until the last train left last night. He then went to Whitcliffe's estate, where some of the guests were stayin', but Mr. Kent was nae there, either." He closed his journal. "I'm afraid that's all I have, yer lordship."

The earl sat upright suddenly, which provoked a violent fit of phlegmy coughing.

"Get out!" he snapped furiously at the sausage-shaped woman who opened the door. "Get out, I say!"

"Ye should save yer breath for them that's willin' to listen to ye," the woman retorted, marching purposefully into the room. She poured some water from a jug into a glass, added a few drops of laudanum from a small brown bottle, then slipped a strong arm behind his back and held the glass to his papery lips. "Drink this."

The once formidable Earl of Hutton reluctantly choked down a few sips of the foul-tasting brew. "Enough!" Edward barked when his coughing had subsided. "I'll not drink a sip more—I swear you're trying to poison me!"

"If I were, I'd use something that'd finish ye in one tidy gulp," his nurse assured him brusquely. "That way I'd nae have to listen to ye chokin' and rantin' as ye went." She eased him back against his pillows and briskly adjusted the covers over his frail form before turning to give Neil a stern look. "I've told ye to nae excite him."

"And I've told you to mind your own bloody business!" snapped Lord Hutton, only to start hacking once more.

"I'm sorry, Mrs. Quigley," said Neil. "Perhaps I should come back tomorrow—"

"Stay where you are." Lord Hutton cast his investigator as menacing a look as he could muster, given his state of undress and feeble condition. "And you," he added, turning to glare at his nurse, "get the hell out."

"Ye've but five minutes," Mrs. Quigley informed Neil, ignoring Lord Hutton. "Not a second more."

"I'll be finished." Neil did not know which of the two he found more intimidating.

"I'll decide how much longer he has," Lord Hutton objected fiercely.

"Aye, ye will," she agreed. "Because if I hear ye spewin' up yer lungs again, he's out on his ear, and never mind the five minutes I promised." She banged the bedroom door shut behind her.

"I'd like to throw her out on her backside," Edward muttered irritably. "How the hell did Potter lose him?" he demanded, turning his attention back to the twitching little mouse before him.

Neil stared morosely at his closed journal. "His telegraph didn't say, yer lordship. I imagine he must have looked away for a bit, or let too much distance grow between Kent's carriage and his own. Ye have to do that, sometimes, so them that ye're watchin' doesna get wind of the fact that he's bein' followed—"

"Spare me your inane excuses," Edward snarled. "Tell Potter his services are no longer needed."

Neil nodded glumly. "Do ye want me to find someone to watch for Kent in Edinburgh or Glasgow, or maybe London? He may have gone there to do some business—"

"Or he may be on his way to bloody Bangkok." Edward steepled his hands together, thinking. "Go down to the docks and see if you can quietly find out whether or not they are still expecting him to sail on the *Lightning*. If something happened to change his plans, it's possible he sent word. If they haven't heard anything, plant yourself outside his house and don't bloody well move. He may show up there yet."

"Aye, yer lordship," said Neil hastily, relieved to have another assignment. Lord Hutton paid him a handsome salary for simple, regular work that so far had required no risk whatsoever. He did not want to lose his employment with him.

"If you've nothing more for me, then get the hell out."

"Aye, sir."

Edward watched as the skinny, flat-faced young man fled the room, no doubt afraid that his crotchety old employer might suddenly decide to sack him anyway, in a fit of pique. It was certainly within the realm of possibility. As it was, however, he was too bloody tired to do any more sacking. He lowered his hands and closed his eyes, trying to ignore the grindingly incessant pain that radiated now throughout his bones and organs and flesh, and fighting to stifle the cough that threatened to burst from his chest. If he permitted himself to cough, Mrs. Quigley would come running with her insufferable nattering and bossiness and foul-tasting medicines, which she would force past his lips as if he were some helpless, stupid child who didn't know what was good for him.

It was pathetic and degrading, this condition to which he had been so cruelly reduced at the age of sixty-nine. In his mind he was still a robust young man, while his pitifully failing body had transformed him into a quivering, coughing, aching husk. Cancer, the doctors had told him some six months earlier—an evil tumor swelling within his abdomen or bowel or some such foul place. They could try to cut it out, they told him, as a handful of surgeons had been attempting such drastic measures, but his chances of surviving the surgery were remote. At best they could assure him that if he did submit to the surgery, he could take comfort in the knowledge that he was helping to advance the science of medicine, and others might benefit from his sacrifice. Never one to choose the more difficult path, Edward had opted to endure the cancer and live whatever time he had left on his terms.

Had he known he was going to be reduced to this helpless, pain-wracked, bedridden state, he would have told them to hack him open and be done with it.

He opened his eyes and stared at the portrait of himself hanging over the fireplace on the opposite side of the room. His mother had commissioned it when he was a young man of twenty-eight, and his life had stretched before him like a spool of golden ribbon spilling across a sun-soaked lawn. He had been arrogant and pompous and lazy—he realized that now—but at the time he had thought himself to be a fine example of his class, and he had genuinely believed that he was going to actually do something of significance with his life. And why not? God knows, he had the means to do almost anything he wanted. A first-rate university education, a respectable title, a beautiful home and accompanying lands that simply fell to him for having the good luck to be born male, and first. There was also the fact that he was blessed with a sufficiently handsome face and hardened physique that could loosen both the morals and thighs of almost every woman he ever pursued. It was clear to him now that his money and his title were a significant part of his appeal, but at the time he was callow enough to believe that his conquests were thoroughly enraptured by his personal charm.

He had been an idiot.

He reached under his mattress and withdrew a small silver flask. Unscrewing the top proved to be a challenge for his severely weakened fingers. Finally he put the damn thing between his teeth while twisting the flask in his hands. His persistence was rewarded with the fiery heat of fine French brandy bathing his mouth—a gift from the scrawny little chambermaid who changed his sweat-soaked bed linens every day. Of course he had to bribe her in exchange for it, but that scarcely mattered. Money was the only allure he had left now, but at least he had enough of it that it wasn't an obstacle. He rolled the liquid around his tongue for a moment before swallowing, then sighed as the liquor burned a slow path of flames down his throat and chest. There were so few pleasures left that he could enjoy, he'd be damned if he'd let Mrs. Quigley or any of those mutton-headed doctors keep him from at least having a bloody drink. What the hell were they worried about, he wondered darkly—that the liquor was going to kill him? If so, that was an unexpected benefit. He took another long swallow, enjoying it even more because he knew it wasn't permitted.

Strange, he mused, suddenly melancholy. After so many years of indulging in anything that gave him pleasure, he now employed doctors and nurses and servants whose sole function, apparently, was to deny him whatever pleasure he might have left. He should discharge the lot of them, and fill his house with young, rosy-fleshed strumpets who would be only too eager to do whatever he asked of them, whether that meant serving him the entire contents of his wine cellar or dancing naked for him upon his bed.

He felt a vague stirring in his loins—a faint, fleeting memory of what it was to have his prick harden. He concentrated on it for a moment, straining to recapture the sensation of being aroused.

Ultimately he gave up and took another swallow of brandy.

Even if he had a woman straddling him all hot and wet and willing, he would not have been able to service her. Between his flaccid cock and his swollen, cancer-ridden belly, he hardly made a very desirable lover. He could accept that. What pained him more was that after sixty-nine years he had no one but servants surrounding him, who cared that he go on living only because their livelihoods depended upon him. His wife had died some

eight years earlier, thank God. He had married her because his mother had insisted upon it, and as the daughter of a marquess, she had come with a reasonably
attractive dowry. *Marry her to run your household and bear
your children,* his mother had commanded. *You can always
amuse yourself with mistresses, as long as they're clean and
reasonably discreet.*

A fiercely pragmatic woman, his mother. No romantic illusions clung to her steely breast. He supposed
his father had cured her of any she might have had as a
young bride. Just as he had cured his own wife.

A fist of guilt tightened in his chest, causing him to
take another drink. In fairness, he reflected, he had not
understood at first what his wife had expected of him.
He had thought that she went into the marriage as he
had, looking for a sensible, practical union that would
enhance their social status and produce reasonably intelligent children, one of which absolutely had to be a boy.
He had sincerely believed that when one tossed in the
title of countess and all the social niceties and servants
and jewels she received as a result of their union, that
she was actually getting the better part of the bargain—
despite the fact that her dowry was helping to pay for it.

He had been genuinely taken aback the night she
wept so wretchedly when she discovered he had slept
regularly with other women since their marriage. He
had not understood what she wanted—did she really expect him to forfeit all the amusement in his life merely
because he was now married? She was being a silly little
nitwit, which he told her in no uncertain terms. They
did not love each other, he reminded her briskly, nor
had they ever lied and said that they did. And she had
confessed to him, through a haze of tears he had thought
pitiful and irritating, that she had hoped that eventually
they might have come to love each other. That she had
spent the year since they had married trying to love him,

and that despite his efforts to maintain his distance, there were actually moments where she felt she did. She was eight months pregnant with their first child at the time, and he had imagined he was being a considerate husband by seeking his carnal pleasures elsewhere. The idea of actually loving her was completely ridiculous. He had no need to love her. And more, he didn't want the burden of her love, and he told her so.

She had cried so violently her birthing pains started. The screams that filled his home that night and into the next were unlike anything he had ever imagined.

Late the next evening she finally gave birth to their first child. A girl. When it was finally over the doctor had told him that his wife had nearly died, and that there could never be any more children. Overcome with shock and remorse, Edward had gone into her bedroom to see his young bride lying pale and broken, too weak to even hold the tiny child she had labored so hard to deliver safely from her body. He had sat beside her, hollow and ashamed, struggling to find some words. Finally, not knowing what he could possibly say, he had reached out to caress her cheek.

And she had closed her eyes and withdrawn from him, forever severing whatever tenderness they might have sifted from the ashes of their relationship.

Regret pulsed through him, as dark and ragged and painful as it had been that terrible night. He took another swallow of brandy, but it had lost its power to comfort him. With effort he managed to secure the cap once more, then bury the flask beneath his mattress, where Mrs. Quigley wouldn't find it. Too tired to blow out the lamp beside his bed, he lay back and closed his eyes, almost as weak as his poor Katherine had been the night she put up a wall between them to save herself. He swallowed thickly, feeling the hot lick of tears pooling beneath his eyelids.

There was so much for which he was sorry, he scarcely knew where to start.

Percy Baring, fifth viscount philmore, slipped a gloved hand into his exquisitely tailored waistcoat and withdrew a finely wrought gold watch. It had belonged to his great-grandfather, and bore two small enameled blue birds surrounded by diamonds on its polished cover. Opening it, he studied the time, then frowned. Seven minutes past nine o'clock. He twisted the tip of his carefully waxed mustache with annoyance and snapped the watch closed before dropping it back into its satin-lined pocket.

American heiresses, he had discovered, were rarely punctual.

Edith Fanshaw was different, of course. Her offense was that she was always unfashionably early for any event she attended, due to her parents' misguided conviction that it was essential for their daughter to be seen for the entire duration of each social occasion to which they had managed to garner an invitation. This unfortunate misconception meant that painfully shy Edith had been dreadfully overexposed to English society. Had they been clever, her parents would have had her arrive late, leave early, and keep her mouth invariably shut, cultivating at least some faint air of mystery.

Unfortunately, Percy's bride-to-be always looked hopelessly miserable, like a rabbit caught in a snare. When one attempted to engage her in conversation, a kind of desperate panic spread across her face, as though she were about to vomit. Her timorous disposition had caused her to languish on the marriage market too long without a single proposal, which was the death knell for a woman hoping to secure a marquess or better. By the time Percy's financial situation had become so tenuous that he was forced to swallow his pride and approach her father about marriage, Edith's parents had reluctantly concluded that they had no choice but to lower their expectations for their daughter. Lacking in beauty, charm, or wit, utterly graceless in social situations, and without a monumental fortune gilding her otherwise inadequate pedigree, Edith Fanshaw was damned lucky to have him ask for her quaking little hand.

Of course the Fanshaw wealth could not compare to the vast railway empire of John Henry Belford, but at the time Percy had been desperate. His debt had grown to staggering proportions, and the enormous investment he had made in Great Atlantic Steamship stock, which was supposed to save him from destitution, had instead dropped by a third of its value, nearly wiping him out. He and a few other investors were taking steps to address that, but the stock could take months to recover, and time was a luxury Percy no longer enjoyed.

Then there was the unpleasant matter of Dick Hawkins.

The young brute had been eager enough when Percy invited him to share his bed for a few days. But he had seduced Hawkins too well, for the ruffian enjoyed not only their rough play but also the fine wine and expensive accoutrements that went with it, which Hawkins was loath to forfeit. The filthy thug had vowed to smash Percy's legs and reveal every detail of their fucking to his peers, unless Percy paid him a generous monthly allowance. That final pressure had sent him rushing to seduce Amelia Belford, who had eagerly lapped up his charms—until her parents intervened and put an end to his courtship. Then he had no option but to settle for Edith Fanshaw, resigned that the key to the Belford coffer had escaped his grasp.

As it turned out, he mused, fastidiously brushing his mustache with his knuckles, he had been mistaken.

"Champagne, milord?"

A shriveled old footman appeared beside him, his arms trembling as he struggled to balance an enormous silver tray filled with glasses of champagne. An unkempt nest of white hair shot out in all directions from his head, and wiry white brows and a poorly clipped beard covered much of his chalky, wrinkled face. His dark coat and trousers were threadbare and ridiculously short on his stooped frame, suggesting the garments had originally been fitted for someone else. Lord and Lady Wilkinson must be watching their expenses, Percy decided as he helped himself to a glass of champagne. No cost had been spared on the dozens of potted orange and lemon trees, thousands of aromatic flowers and candles, and miles of gauzy draped fabrics that had transformed the ballroom into a tented tropical paradise, and the food and drink being served were exceptional. Nevertheless, one could always tell much about one's hosts by the caliber and attire of their servants. Once he was married and his financial situation had been resolved, he would see to it that his entire staff was completely outfitted with new uniforms and footwear.

"A fine party—don't you think, Lord Philmore?"

Percy arched a brow at the doddering old servant as he sipped his champagne. It was not so peculiar that the aged fellow knew his name, for Lord or Lady Wilkinson had probably identified him from some corner of the congested ballroom and instructed the man to offer him a drink. He was, after all, an honored guest, who was expected to formally announce his betrothal to Edith Fanshaw at exactly ten o'clock. It was not precisely the match of the decade, Percy realized acidly. It certainly could not compete with the Duke of Whitcliffe's announcement months earlier that he was to wed the stupendously wealthy Amelia Belford. Nevertheless, any pairing between an English lord and an American heiress aroused excitement amongst English society, which meant that Lady Wilkinson could safely count on her ball's being written up in the next day's society pages.

What was incomprehensible to Percy was that this badly attired servant was engaging him in casual conversation, as if he were an acquaintance or peer.

"Perhaps you should see if there is anyone else wanting refreshment," Percy suggested crisply. He tilted his head toward the crush of elegantly dressed ladies and gentlemen swirling about the dance floor.

"No one here looks like they are about to die of thirst." The old man's clear gray gaze bored into him with unnerving intensity. "Miss Belford is not coming," he said in a low voice.

Percy's pale features crumpled as he realized the man before him was no mere servant. "But she must!"

"Your eagerness to see her is most touching. Unfortunately, your choice of venue was not wise." Jack's expression was hard beneath the layers of his artfully applied disguise. "Surely you must know there is a substantial reward for finding Miss Belford? Did you not realize she would be instantly recognized here, and in danger of being seized?"

"Nonsense," protested Percy, salvaging his composure. "Miss Belford would be among friends. I would not let anything happen to her."

Jack studied him, unsure whether he was being sincere or not. His gut instinct told him that Lord Philmore was not to be trusted. But he could not be sure that he didn't feel that way simply because he despised the preening fool.

He had slipped into the house some two hours earlier, shielded amidst the wave of temporary footmen, maids, cooks, and page boys who had been hired for that evening to assist with the ball. No one had taken any notice of him as he shuffled along the corridors of the grandly appointed home. He had found no sign of either Whitcliffe or Amelia's parents, nor were there any police constables milling about ready to grab her and deliver her into the arms of her family.

As for Philmore, other than his being dressed like a fatuous dandy and his irritating tendency to consult his pocket watch every few minutes, Jack could not see any indication of anything amiss.

"She won't be coming to you tonight," Jack told him flatly. "It's too dangerous. She will meet you tomorrow."

Percy's mustache twitched with exasperation, reminding Jack of a disgruntled rodent. "But that is not what I arranged!"

Jack fought the urge to turn and walk away. "Listen carefully. Tomorrow at two o'clock you'll be picked up in front of the Marbury Club. Once the driver is certain that you are not being followed, you will be taken to a safe place where you can see her."

"Where?" Percy demanded.

"You don't need to know that."

"I'm not about to just get into some carriage and let a stranger drive off with me," he objected huffily.

"Fine." Jack turned to leave.

"Wait!"

He hesitated.

"Once I am taken to her, what then?"

"That's up to you. She has nothing now," Jack told him bluntly. "She left it all behind the minute she ran away from Whitcliffe. So if you plan to marry her, understand that you are getting only her, and not her family's fortune." Jack regarded him intently. "Do you still want to make her your wife, Philmore? Or was it only the lure of her money that enticed you to court her against her parents' wishes?"

"Get out," Percy snapped, banging his empty glass on Jack's tray, "before I have you thrown out." He gave each side of his mustache another exacting adjustment with his gloved knuckle and walked away.

Infuriated, Jack turned.

And stared in stunned disbelief at the sight of Amelia gracefully descending the vast marble staircase leading into the ballroom.

Even if she hadn't been the famously missing Miss Amelia Belford, she still would have seized the attention of every man and woman in the room. The gown she had chosen to wear to meet her viscount was the amethyst confection she had been examining as he left her. It had looked attractive enough just casually draped about her shoulders, but wrapped around her slender curves the effect was nothing short of exquisite. Silver and gold embroidery shimmered across the narrow contours of the tightly fitted bodice and full skirt, and a satin train spilled behind her upon the stairs like a glittering pool of starlit water. Her hair had been swept up into a loose arrangement studded with a scattering of delicate amethyst flowers, and the expanse of creamy bosom rising in a soft swell above the low dip of her gown's neckline was sparkling with diamonds. It was the same necklace she had worn on her wedding day, Jack realized, which she had tried to give to him as she bartered so desperately for her freedom.

A startled hush rippled through the crowded ballroom. The orchestra continued to play despite the fact that no one was dancing any longer, but even the musicians could not help but glance at the magnificent young woman floating down the stairs with such apparent serenity.

In that moment Jack saw the Amelia Belford he had heard about, but not yet met. Gone was the terrified young bride who had recklessly scuttled down a vine-covered wall in her priceless wedding gown before crashing unceremoniously into the bushes below. The girl who had curled herself into a ball upon her bed and cried herself to sleep the previous night had vanished. In her place was this glorious woman, radiating confidence and triumph as she peacefully endured the relentless scrutiny of some eight hundred discerning aristocrats, each of whom would have enjoyed nothing more than to find some aspect of her hopelessly lacking.

He gripped his tray, furious that she had defied him. Philmore was walking slowly toward her, his arms extended. Jack's gaze raked the room, searching for some indication that something was wrong, that someone was going to suddenly spring forward and grab her. The members of the Marbury Club were clustered together looking contentedly drunk in one corner of the ballroom beside an enormous ice sculpture of a giant fish. Lord Sullivan appeared to be dangerously on the brink of falling headfirst into the punch bowl. Other than that, nothing seemed amiss.

A lifetime of surviving on instinct would not permit Jack to believe that Amelia was safe, despite Lord Philmore's assurances.

Amelia paused upon the second step above the floor, waiting for her betrothed to come to her. Her heart was pounding wildly against the constricted cage of her ribs, which Lizzie had laced so tightly into her corset she scarcely found the room to draw a breath. Her expression was deliberately calm despite the churning of her stomach, her stature straight and graceful, just as she knew it should be. Her gaze was riveted upon Percy, who seemed to be moving with leaden speed, his expression contained. Of course she had not exactly expected him to race across the packed ballroom and swoop her up in his arms, but somehow she found his carefully controlled reaction disappointing. Percy was a man for whom appearances were supremely important, she reminded herself, from his meticulously maintained mustache to the perfectly manicured tips of his milky fingers.

An image of Jack slouching opposite her in the carriage flashed into her mind, his necktie undone and his shirt and coat hopelessly wrinkled from the heat, somehow even more handsome because it was so obvious he didn't care. Jack's hands were large and bronzed by the sun, with palms roughened from years of hard physical labor. A shiver rippled through her. She did not know whether it was from the memory of Jack's touch or the fact that the man to whom she had pledged her eternal devotion was now reaching out to her with a single, immaculately gloved hand.

"Amelia," Percy murmured, the corners of his mouth barely curved, "I am pleased to see you look well."

She laid her gloved palm against the damp heat of his, vaguely irritated by the formality of his greeting. What on earth was the matter with her? she wondered. Did she expect him to crush his lips to hers and profess his love for her in front of all these people?

Clearly she was thinking like an idiot.

"Come," he said, leading her through the parting crowd and into the center of the dance floor. "Let us dance."

One hand resting against his, the other carefully holding the heavy weight of her train, Amelia obediently circled the ballroom. The other couples began to dance again, but their attention remained focused upon her and Percy. Of course they were waiting for Percy to formally declare his intention to marry her.

She frowned, suddenly wondering why she had never noticed that her betrothed was actually rather short.

"I have missed you terribly, Percy," she declared fervently, pushing the thought aside. "When my parents told me I would never see you again and that I had to marry Lord Whitcliffe, I was certain that I would die."

"It was unfortunate your parents could not be made to understand how much we cared for one another," Percy remarked, gazing dispassionately around the room. "However, I am certain they believed that they were only doing what was best for you."

Amelia looked into his eyes. They were not the deep, piercing blue she had remembered. They actually struck her as small and rather watery. They also seemed vaguely preoccupied—almost as if he were concealing something from her. That was ridiculous, she told herself. She moved a little closer into him, seeking to minimize the distance that seemed to have grown between them.

His brow puckered with displeasure, Percy stepped away.

"Is something wrong?" she asked, surprised and slightly hurt.

"Everyone is watching us, Amelia. There is an appropriate distance that must be maintained when one is dancing. You were moving beyond it."

"I suppose I no longer care much what others think is appropriate," Amelia replied, telling herself that her betrothed's preoccupation with what was socially correct was part of what she adored about him. "After all, just yesterday I crawled down a church wall and ran away from my own wedding. Somehow I don't think that fits in with most aristocrats' idea of proper etiquette." She gave him a mischievous smile.

"You're right. It doesn't." His tone was disapproving.

"I did it for you, Percy." She disliked intensely the way his mustache was twitching. And why did he insist upon waxing those feathery tips into those ridiculous little curls? "I ran away from Lord Whitcliffe, my family, and everything I have known, at great risk to my own well-being, just so we could be together. You might be somewhat more sympathetic to what I have endured, instead of acting as if you are embarrassed."

"Forgive me, my dear. I did not mean to insult you." He managed a small but contrite smile.

She regarded him blankly, thoroughly distracted by the jumbled crookedness of his bottom teeth. They were yellow and stained, no doubt from the vast amounts of wine and tea he consumed.

When on earth had that happened? she wondered, slightly disgusted.

"In fact I have been most worried about you." Percy's gaze was sorrowful as he tentatively added, "As have your parents."

She stiffened. "How would you know whether my parents have been worried or not?"

"Amelia, my darling, your parents have been utterly sick with concern from the moment you disappeared yesterday. After all, they had no way of knowing whether you had run away of your own accord, or if you had been abducted. Surely you can appreciate their suffering."

"If they were truly concerned for my well-being, then they never would have tried to destroy my relationship with you while forcing me into a marriage I could not bear," Amelia countered passionately. "All they care about is marrying their daughter to a duke, to gain prestige for the family and ensure that their grandchildren are born and raised as aristocracy. I am but a means to an end for them, nothing more."

"You judge them too harshly. Your parents only want what is best for you." He hesitated a moment before cautiously pointing out, "Lord Whitcliffe can offer you a life that I cannot, Amelia."

Prickles of anxiety rose along her spine. "I don't want a life with Lord Whitcliffe. I want to spend my life with you."

"And I with you," Percy assured her, still gliding her in elegant circles around the ballroom. His expression grew wistful. "Unfortunately, my love, it was not to be."

Her anxiety hardened into alarm. "What do you mean?"

"The flame of our love burned brightly for a moment, sweet Amelia." Percy paused, giving her time to appreciate what he felt certain was an enviable poeticism. "Unfortunately, my love, that time has now passed. We must accept our respective fates, however tragic and painful that may be."

She nearly tripped over the train of her gown. "Are you trying to tell me that you intend to go ahead and marry Edith Fanshaw?"

"I have pledged my troth to Miss Fanshaw." Percy regarded her mournfully, as if the matter was far more distressing for him than for her. "I cannot break my word." His eyes grew even more watery. For a moment he looked as if he might actually shed a tear.

"You pledged your troth to me also," Amelia pointed out, her emotions swinging between outrage and hurt disbelief. "Or does the love you professed for me count for less than that which you have experienced in the arms of Miss Fanshaw?"

"Amelia—"

"Tell me, Percy, did you hold her close and tell her she was like a beautiful orchid that you wanted to protect forever from the world?" she demanded. "Or did you skip that part and go straight into assuring her that you had never known a woman who could touch your heart as she could? Did you kiss her on the mouth and tell her that the press of her lips set your world afire? Or have you not managed to pry her away from the constant guard of her parents?"

"Now you're being common." His weepy eyes had dried with annoyance. "I expect you to handle this with more dignity."

"But I don't have any dignity, Percy. I'm American, remember? We don't know the first thing about restraining our emotions. That was part of what you said you found so refreshing in me—the fact that I was honest and open."

"There is a time to be open, and there is a time to behave with appropriate decorum," Percy informed her curtly. "When eight hundred people have their eyes upon you, that is a time to exercise correctness and control. You wouldn't want to embarrass yourself and your family in front of the finest of London society, would you?"

Amelia's breath froze. "What do you mean, my family?"

He tilted his head toward a corner of the ballroom. Amelia followed his gaze.

And was horrified to see her parents and her two brothers, William and Freddy, flanking Lord Whitcliffe. Her bridegroom glared at her, looking only marginally less enraged than he had the previous afternoon when she had peered at him through the window of Jack's carriage.

It was impossible, she told herself frantically. How could they have known she was in London, and that she would be attending the Wilkinsons' ball that evening?

Understanding cut through her in a swift, agonizing stroke.

"I did it for you, Amelia," Percy said, watching as her expression shifted from disbelief to sick dismay. "I knew that you did not want really to be estranged from your family, and that once you understood that it is now impossible for us to marry, your best course of action would be to reunite with your parents and accept your betrothal to Lord Whitcliffe—"

"You did this so you could collect the reward." Amelia's voice was hollow. "That's why you wanted me to come here tonight—to meet you in front of all these people. You believed that I would be forced to go quietly with my family, that I would not be common enough to make an embarrassing scene for you."

"I arranged for you to come here because I felt it was the best way for you to make amends with your family and Lord Whitcliffe," Percy retorted, sounding thoroughly offended by her accusation, "and to demonstrate to everyone that you are prepared to accept your responsibility and take your place in society as the Duchess of Whitcliffe. I was only thinking of you, Amelia."

She stared at him a long, anguished moment.

And then she slapped his pompous, lying little face as hard as she could.

"Mind if I cut in?" Jack shoved the heavy tray he was carrying at Percy, who stood paralyzed with shock. "Shall we, Miss Belford?" Without waiting for a response, Jack pulled Amelia into his arms and began to swirl her around the dance floor away from Lord Philmore.

"How dare you!" Amelia protested, struggling to get away from him. "Let go of me at once!"

"For God's sake, Amelia, stop thrashing about," Jack ground out, holding her firm. "I hate dancing as it is, and you're not making it any easier."

Amelia looked at the aged face of the man holding her in astonishment. The wig and makeup were ingeniously applied, and the threadbare gloves he wore effectively hid the strong hands that were now gripping her. But there was no mistaking the hard silver-gray of those eyes.

"Jack!"

"I think you will agree that this is a trap," Jack said, swiftly scanning the perimeters of the room. "Your parents are over in that corner with Whitcliffe, and two other men whom I recognize from your wedding."

"They are my brothers," Amelia informed him miserably. "William and Freddy."

"How nice that they all came to welcome you home together," Jack observed dryly. "In addition, there are at least four footmen standing guard at every exit leading from the ballroom. They may or may not have been instructed to keep you from leaving. Regardless, if you try to charge past them I'm certain they will decide to be heroic and stop you once your parents sound the alarm."

She regarded him mournfully, her eyes sparkling with tears. "I'm sorry." She bit her lower lip to keep it from trembling.

"Amelia, if you want to get out of here I need you to stay strong and keep your wits about you," Jack said brusquely. "But if you've changed your mind and want to go to your parents and Whitcliffe, tell me now."

"There is no way out." She felt as if her world was collapsing. "I'm trapped."

"Do you want to stay here and marry Whitcliffe?"

"I have no choice." She felt as if she could barely breathe. "I've nothing now—nowhere to go—"

"Amelia!" He gave her a hard shake. "Do you want to marry Whitcliffe—yes or no?"

He was holding her tight against the wall of his body, shielding her with his powerful strength as he continued to guide her around the room. His carriage was tall and straight and sure, forcing her to tilt her head back to meet his silvery gaze. It was obvious he didn't give a damn about what was an appropriate distance between a man and a woman. His eyes were darkly intense, searching beneath the layers of her panic and despair. It was as if he were trying to see deep into her soul, to understand the essential truth of who she was and what she really wanted. And in that awful, frozen moment, as she felt fear well up inside her with such ferocity that she thought she would suffocate, she was awed that this man she scarcely knew was holding her in his arms and asking her what she wanted.

As if he actually believed he might be able to give it to her.

"There is no shame in going back to Whitcliffe," Jack assured her, watching as she struggled with her decision. "He will be more than happy to have you. In time, the scandal of your having run away will be almost forgotten. You can live the rest of your life amidst the wealth and privilege to which you are accustomed—as a duchess."

Amelia glanced over at her family. Her mother was dressed in a garish fuchsia gown of French silk, heavily brocaded with a lavish pattern of an enormous sunburst outlined in pearls. The neckline was trimmed with diamonds and rubies, sewn onto it just for that evening, and a tall black ostrich plume waved about her painstakingly coiffured head. Rosalind Belford's face was a mask of firmly screwed composure, as if she dared not give so much as a hint of a smile or frown, for fear of what gossip might arise from it. A lifetime spent trying to rise above the poverty of her childhood had left her mother obsessed with maintaining appearances.

Her father, by contrast, looked openly grumpy and uncomfortable. Amelia knew he loathed these formal affairs, and was much happier back in New York, either in his office or, better yet, inspecting the railway yards himself, barking orders at everyone. He had intended to sail back to America the day after her wedding, with or without his wife, to escape what he called the damned idiocy of English society and get on with running his business. Amelia felt sorry for him as he stood glaring about the crowded ballroom. But for her, he would be on his way home right now.

Her brother William stood beside him. At twenty-four William was much like his father, from his prematurely graying hair to his substantial frame that betrayed his fondness for fine drink and rich foods. He looked thoroughly annoyed by the drama playing out before him. Her brother Freddy was slouched casually against a pillar, cheerfully sipping champagne as he curiously studied her and the strange old man with whom she was dancing. Freddy was only twenty-two and had been blessed with the same honey blond hair and blue eyes that she had, set against boyishly handsome features. He was an easygoing young man, who had inherited neither his mother's social ambition nor his father's work ethic. Freddy spent most of his time happily pursuing pleasure, which wasn't difficult, given his looks and the vast amount of money at his disposal.

Sandwiched in the center of the Belfords was old Lord Whitcliffe, his chalky, spider-veined face twisted into a hopelessly pained expression as he watched his runaway bride waltzing with a lowly servant. He was probably wondering if she was touched in the head, Amelia speculated, and worrying that her madness would be passed on to their children. His pudding-shaped form had been cinched into an evening coat and trousers that strained ominously against his girth, making it look as though the fabric might suddenly explode at any moment, revealing the sagging physique of the hoary ninth Duke of Whitcliffe. She was a virgin, but she had not been so sheltered that she didn't understand completely what was expected of her as a wife. Old Whitcliffe

would want her to give him heirs? And that meant lying
dutifully beneath him at night while he grunted and
sweated and crushed her beneath his massive weight, trying to fill her body with the next duke.

"Amelia, do you want to marry Whitcliffe?"

She blinked and looked up at Jack, feeling sick. "I
would rather die."

Jack studied her, wondering if she understood the
enormity of what she was saying. There was fear in the
glittering sapphire of her eyes. He did not know
whether it was fear of the unknown path she was choosing, or the possibility that she might be caught and
forced to marry Whitcliffe after all.

He swore silently. His life would be far less compli-
cated if Amelia would just capitulate to her family's
wishes and marry the old duke. Whitcliffe didn't deserve
her, but he struck Jack as marginally less contemptible
than Philmore. At any rate, Whitcliffe was less apt to humiliate her with a parade of male lovers. He might indulge in a mistress or two, but that was considered
entirely acceptable among his peers. Amelia could
marry him and take her place in society, with both her
wealth and her reputation safely intact.

And Jack could get on with his own damn life, free
of any further responsibility for her.

"Please, Jack." Amelia regarded him in desperation,
sensing his reluctance to become further involved in her
situation. "Please."

Her grip upon him tightened, as if she were afraid
that he might suddenly release her, abandoning her to
whatever fate her parents had decided upon for her. And
in that moment he remembered once again what it was
to be desperate. The sensation washed over him in a
dark, nauseating wave, stripping away his reticence, and
leaving only the cold, sharp focus that had enabled him
to survive.

"We can't get out by the main staircase, so we'll head toward the west hallway that leads to the kitchen," he told her, swiftly evaluating their limited options for escape. "Once we get there, stay close to me."

He began to lead her in a subtle, sweeping arc toward the exit he had decided on, thankful for the first time in his life that Genevieve had insisted he take dancing lessons. He wasn't good at it, but at least he knew how to move a woman around a ballroom without falling on his face. At that particular moment, the skill was proving invaluable.

His peripheral vision told him he and Amelia were quickly being surrounded. Having disposed of his tray, a highly aggravated Philmore was cutting through the crowd of dancers. John Belford was also striding toward Amelia with grim purpose, no doubt thinking that all his daughter needed was a good, stiff reminder that he was in charge of her life. Her two brothers, William and Freddy, had each taken a position at the bottom of the massive marble staircase, erroneously assuming that their sister would attempt to flee the same way she had come in.

Lord Whitcliffe remained with Amelia's mother, looking thoroughly disgruntled as he finished the remains of his drink.

Just one more minute of music, thought Jack, broadening his steps as he led Amelia toward the corner of the ballroom. *That's all I need...*

"That will do, Amelia." Percy laid his gloved hand firmly upon her shoulder. "You've embarrassed both yourself and your family quite enough for one night. You will come with me quietly over to Whitcliffe so that you may apologize and make amends."

"Take your hand off her." Jack's voice was dangerously low. "Before I break it."

"Look, old man, I don't know who you are, but this is a family matter—"

Jack jerked Percy's hand off Amelia's shoulder and twisted back the viscount's thumb just to the point before it would snap from its joint.

Percy howled with pain and collapsed on his knees to the floor. "My hand!" he wailed, cradling the gloved appendage. "You've broken it!"

"What in Sam Hill is going on in here?" demanded Arthur Fanshaw, who stood at the top of the stairs with his wife and cowering daughter.

"Move!" Jack pushed Amelia through the crowd of horrified couples ahead of him.

"Here now, stop!" John Belford thundered, not quite sure whether his daughter was in the process of running away or being abducted. "Stop them!"

The ballroom exploded into a crush of surging bodies as people fought to get closer to Jack and Amelia, while others, terrified that Jack was dangerously violent, scrambled away.

A high-pitched scream split the air. Amelia turned and saw her mother with her black ostrich plume fluttering wildly, shrieking with uncharacteristic abandon. Not to be outdone, other women joined the chorus. Some elected to swoon instead, forcing their partners to catch them and drag them off the dance floor.

"He's stealing my daughter—stop them!" bellowed Amelia's father, still trying to fight his way through the crowd.

Having reached the hallway leading to the kitchen, Jack and Amelia were suddenly confronted with a parade of servants bearing towering silver platters of food and refreshment.

Jack grabbed a tray of champagne and hurled it at the advancing throng behind him.

A shower of wine and crystal stemware rained upon

the exquisitely attired mob, halting them in their tracks more efficiently than any firearm might have done. The sound of shattering crystal was followed by shrieks and shouts as people slipped and fell on the precariously wet floor.

"That old chap is plenty quick," commented Lord Sullivan drunkenly, helping himself to another glass of whiskey. "Reminds me of myself when I was sixty. Never surrender, I say!" He raised his glass to Jack.

Following Jack's lead, Amelia grabbed a tray from the next footman and sent it flying through the air behind her, bombarding her pursuers with a colorful hailstorm of fruit.

"Doesn't look to me like that Belford girl is being abducted," Lord Chesley observed, perilously close to toppling over. "Not with the way she's flinging food about."

"Five hundred pounds says she and the old chap are successful," proposed Lord Beardsley.

"A thousand pounds says they haven't a prayer," Lord Dunlop countered, banging the floor with his cane. "It's just the two of them, and they're completely surrounded."

"I'll take that wager and double it." Lord Sullivan watched Amelia with admiration. "The odds may be against them, but that girl has got real spirit."

"Let me go!" raged Amelia, kicking her feet wildly as someone wrapped their arms about her waist and plucked her off the floor.

Jack turned to see a footman had grabbed Amelia and was now valiantly fighting to save her. Jack heaved another tray onto the hapless fellow's head, burying him in an avalanche of coconut cake with whipped-cream topping.

Suddenly finding herself free, Amelia raced down the narrow corridor. She burst through the doors to the kitchen, where two dozen cooks and kitchen maids were frantically stirring, carving, ladling, and arranging, oblivious to the pandemonium exploding just beyond their steamy sanctuary.

"This way!" Jack led Amelia through the crowded maze of tables, sinks, and stoves toward the kitchen's back door, knocking bowls, pans, and trays of food onto the floor behind them as he went.

"Oliver!" he shouted, crashing through the back door, "Let's go!"

"Ye said ye'd come out nice and quiet," Oliver complained, scowling as he drove the carriage out from the shadows, "an' instead ye barrel out shoutin' at the top o' yer lungs like a wild—"

"Amelia!" roared William, hurtling out of the kitchen, "Stop!" His hand snaked with bruising strength around her arm. "Have you gone completely mad?"

"Take your hand off her," Jack commanded harshly, "or I'll—"

"No, Jack!" Despite her determination to escape, she would not permit her brother to be harmed. "You mustn't hurt him."

"Let go of her, William." Her brother Freddy appeared through the doorway, still holding his glass of champagne. "It's clear she wants to get away."

"I don't give a damn what she wants," William snapped. "She's made us all look like fools. It's time she thought about the family, for God's sake, instead of herself. You should be ashamed," he told Amelia furiously, "humiliating Mother and Father this way!"

"Please, William, let me go." Amelia regarded her brother earnestly. "I know it's hard for you to understand—no one can force you to do anything you don't want to do—"

"We all have to do things we don't like, Amelia," William informed her flatly. "Even me. It's part of life."

"More like it's part of being a Belford." A thread of rancor darkened Freddy's tone. "Rather ironic, given that the rest of the world thinks having money means having freedom." He downed the rest of his champagne.

"It's different for both of you," Amelia objected. "Maybe you haven't always been able to make your own choices, but at least you both have some control regarding with whom you will live the rest of your life!"

"Mother is only trying to protect you, Amelia, the same way she always has." William's voice grew marginally gentler. "Do you honestly believe you can choose just any suitor? Surely you must realize that it was your wealth that drew Philmore to you. At least with Whitcliffe you're getting something substantial in return."

"I don't care about being a duchess," Amelia told him. "Not if it means marrying an old man who doesn't even like me."

"He'll like you once he gets to know you," William assured her. "He won't be able to help himself. You'll see." He turned toward the door, pulling her behind him.

Jack hesitated, wondering if any of William's arguments might eventually influence Amelia. He was reluctant to interfere now that her brothers had come after her.

"No, William." Amelia jerked her wrist away from him. "I'm not going in with you. I'm leaving."

"If you run away, you'll have nothing, Amy." Freddy's expression was troubled. "Do you understand that?"

"I'll have my freedom," she retaliated fiercely. "And I'd rather die than marry Whitcliffe."

"This nonsense has gone on long enough," William growled, taking hold of her wrist once again. "I'm taking you back into that ballroom, so stop behaving like a child and start acting like a duchess!"

"Let her go, William." Freddy grabbed Amelia's other arm. "This is Amelia's decision to make, not yours."

"Seem to me ye're goin' to have to decide if ye're helpin' the lass or no," observed Oliver to Jack. "Or are ye hopin' she'll suddenly change her mind and go back to Whitcliffe all meek and quiet?"

"It would be damned simpler for me if she did," Jack muttered.

"Aye, there's nae denyin' that," Oliver agreed. "But it looks to me like the lass's mind is set, an' if ye dither much longer, there'll be nae ye can do to help her." He tilted his head toward the growing rumble of agitated voices coming from the house.

Jack cursed.

"Let go of me, William!" Amelia commanded, fighting to break free from her brother's powerful grip. "Now!"

"I think you should do as she asks."

William glowered at Jack. "I don't know who the hell you are, old man, but unless you want to find your-self sleeping behind the bars of a prison tonight, I sug-gest you get into your carriage and drive away." He turned, hauling Amelia behind him.

Seizing the moment, Jack hoisted the back of William's evening coat over his head, imprisoning him within its black fabric.

"Get in the carriage!" Jack directed Amelia.

"You'd best drive fast." Freddy advised Oliver. "I can hear more people coming." He regarded his sister fondly. "Don't worry about Mother and Father, Amy," he added cheerfully. "They'll calm down after a while."

"Thank you, Freddy." She could not imagine her parents ever forgiving her for the dreadful scene she had just caused.

"Go, Oliver." Jack climbed into the carriage beside Amelia and slammed the door shut.

"Hang on!" Oliver snapped his whip against the horses and the carriage tore into the night.

"Stop!" raged Percy, stumbling out the kitchen door with John Belford, Lord Whitcliffe, and a shouting mob behind him. "Come back!"

"They went that way," Freddy declared, blithely pointing in the wrong direction.

"Don't listen to him!" William's voice was muffled beneath his coat. "Whatever he says, he's lying!"

"Really, William, you shouldn't drink so much," Freddy scolded. "It makes you say the most ridiculous things. I'm absolutely certain that the carriage went that way." He pointed in the opposite route he had just indicated.

Lord Whitcliffe looked as if he were about to explode in frustration. "Which is it, you damn fool?"

"That way." Freddy again gestured in the wrong direction. "I'm positive."

"You're drunk," observed John Belford in disgust.

"Not nearly as drunk as I would like to be." Freddy hiccuped loudly, then turned and threaded his way through the curious crowd of onlookers back toward the ballroom, leaving Amelia's father, brother, and suitors staring in helpless fury into the darkness.

Chapter Six

THE CARRIAGE RACED THROUGH THE SILKY NIGHT, leaving the brilliantly lit mansions of Mayfair and Belgrave Square, with the strains of Mozart and the scent of blossoms and richly spiced food wafting upon the still summer air. After a time the glittering manors gave way to tenement buildings, their crumbling walls oozing the harsh sound and stench of human misery. Children cried while men and women brawled drunkenly, the ugly din resonating through the stink of sewage, boiled cabbage, and spoiled meat, and the smoky pall of thousands of braziers and grease lamps.

Amelia sat hunched within the folds of her evening gown. She could not bring herself to look at Jack, who sat opposite her in grim silence, stripping away the white tufts of hair that covered his head, brows and cheeks before rubbing at the chalky mask of his wrinkled face with a damp cloth. Instead she stared out her carriage window, overwhelmed by the ramifications of what she had just done, and the crude, unfamiliar world now unraveling before her.

Despite the late hour, the streets in which Oliver

steered the carriage were teeming with activity. Drunken men and women stumbled from the taverns with heavy, dripping bottles pressed against their rotting mouths. Roars of laughter and outrage filled the night as the men clumsily groped their heavily painted female companions, who tolerated the mauling of their breasts and slobbering against their lips with weary enthusiasm.

Prostitutes, Amelia realized, shocked.

She swallowed thickly. Just the previous day she had been destined to marry Lord Whitcliffe. Had she gone through with it, she would have been required to lie in his bed that very night—in exchange for the title and privileges she would have gained as his wife. She had railed and wept bitterly over her betrothal, but until the moment she decided to scramble out the window and down the church wall, she had all but accepted her fate. As hopeless as she had believed her situation to be, it could not compare to the desperate circumstances of the ragged, half-starved women on the streets before her.

She stared at her exquisite gown, feeling small and ashamed. She had never known what it was to be hungry to the point of pain, or shivering without any hope of finding shelter, or ill without the comfort of a soft, clean bed and the attention of servants and a reputable doctor. She knew nothing whatsoever about the dreadful lives these women were forced to endure. Even when she had dared to run away from her marriage, she had done so expecting to marry Percy and live a life of comfort as the esteemed wife of an English lord.

How could she possibly judge these women for what they did when she had no comprehension of the wretched nature of their lives?

"Turn down that alley, Oliver." Jack's expression was hard as he stared out the back window at the street behind them.

"'Tis best to keep goin', lad," Oliver barked over

the clatter of the carriage wheels. "They couldna have started too quick after us, an' they're nae expectin' us to take Miss Amelia through a nasty puddle o' scum like this. They're still prowlin' about Mayfair, most like, thinkin' to find her hidin' in one of their mansions."

"If no one is following us, then it won't matter if we lose a few minutes," Jack insisted. "Stop the carriage over there."

His tongue clacking with exasperation, Oliver reluctantly turned the horses down the alley Jack indicated.

"There now, ye see?" The old man scowled. "We're beggin' to have our throats cut sittin' here, with Miss Amelia flashin' all those bleedin' diamonds. We should just keep—"

He stopped, startled by the elegant black carriage that suddenly tore down the very street from which they had just turned. A stinging torrent of foul words erupted as drunken men and women scrambled out of the way to avoid being crushed beneath the expensive vehicle's heavy wheels.

"Percy!" Amelia gasped.

"I believe he's with your devoted brother William," observed Jack dryly.

"But how would they know to look for me here?"

He shrugged. "He and Percy probably set out as quickly as they could and asked people if they had seen a carriage matching this description hurrying down the streets. Once they established which direction we were headed, they likely concluded the quickest way for you to get out of London is by ship. That's why they're going toward the docks."

"And where are we going?"

"That depends. Do you have any relatives here beyond your immediate family, Amelia? Someone who would be willing to take you in?"

She shook her head. "I have no family here, other than my parents and brothers. They are all in America."

Jack had suspected as much. "If I got you back to America, is there anyone there with whom you might stay? An aunt or uncle, perhaps, or even a close cousin?"

"None of my relatives would ever incur my father's wrath by letting me stay with them against his wishes. It isn't that they wouldn't wish to help me," she quickly qualified. "It's just that my father has been very generous to all of them over the years—he bought many of them their homes, or gave them jobs in his company. They have a deep sense of loyalty to him. . . ."

"They would be afraid that if they took you in he would cut them off," Jack finished succinctly.

"Yes."

"Fine. What about friends? Do you have any friends whose parents didn't have their homes purchased by your father, and who don't happen to also work for him? Someone who would be willing to give you shelter for a while, until you sort out what it is you want to do?"

Amelia thought for a moment. "I don't think so. The only friends I've ever made have been through social affairs that my parents have either planned or taken me to—and that generally means that their fathers have some business connection with mine. Of course they might be willing to put that at stake, but I have no way of knowing for certain. I might turn to one of them for help, only to discover they felt compelled to contact my parents and let them know where I am. Then my mother would simply pack me onto the next steamship back to London."

Jack sank back in his seat. A dull throbbing had started at the base of his skull.

"Couldn't I just stay for a while at your parents' house here in London?" Amelia regarded him hopefully. At least London was familiar to her, and she felt at ease around Beaton and Lizzie, who had been so kind in helping her to prepare for her ill-fated meeting with Percy. "I promise I won't be any trouble—"

"It's too dangerous for you to remain in London, Amelia," Jack said flatly. "Your face will be on the front page of every newspaper by tomorrow morning—or evening at the very latest—along with the details of the enormous reward your family is sure to offer for your return. You won't be able to so much as stick your head out a carriage window or open your mouth and reveal your American accent without someone chasing after you. We have to get you out of here."

"Why don't we just take the lass home with us?" asked Oliver.

"No."

He frowned. "Why not? Ye've just said yerself she canna stay here, and she's nae kin to go to in America. I'm sure Miss Genevieve would be pleased to have her."

"She is not going to Genevieve's, Oliver. I don't want her or Haydon involved in this."

"Right, then. She can stay at your house. Ye're scarcely there anyway." Oliver winked at Amelia, pleased that he had solved the problem.

"Where do you live?" asked Amelia.

"I have a very small house in Inverness," Jack admitted reluctantly, "but it isn't suitable . . ."

" 'Tis warm and dry and pleasin' enough, if ye dinna mind the sight of a lot o' ships an' swords an' strange lookin' masks all around ye," Oliver interjected. "Once we get a fire goin' an' brush some o' the dust out, I'm sure ye'll find it cozy."

"I'm sure I will, Oliver," she said with forced cheer. "It sounds lovely."

She didn't want to go to Inverness. She had never been to Scotland, but everyone in London spoke of how bleak and gray and cold it was there, and how the people were rough and unrefined. All she wanted in that moment was to go home. To her father's beautifully ap-pointed mansion on Fifth Avenue in New York, which boasted acres of polished marble and soft velvet and was fitted with all the latest amenities in hot-water plumbing and electric light. Or to the sunny estate her family owned in Newport, where she and her brothers had played every summer for as long as she could remember. The weather was gloriously warm and breezy there in August, and there were all kinds of splendid picnics and boating parties and lively balls to attend. She shivered, despite the warmth of the night and the heavy mantle of her gown. She had foolishly believed she was gaining her freedom when she tore out of that ballroom with Jack.

Without money, she was swiftly discovering, there was no freedom.

"I won't impose upon your hospitality for very long," she assured Jack, aware that he was not pleased that she was going to be his guest. "I shall try to make other arrangements for my lodging as soon as I can."

Jack said nothing. In truth, he had no idea what was to become of her. Amelia was suddenly in an extremely untenable position. She no longer had any marriage prospects. Given her sheltered existence and lack of marketable skills, he couldn't imagine that she would ever be able to find a job and support herself. By tomor-row all of England and Scotland would be looking for her because of the enormous reward her capture repre-sented. Amelia Belford's life had been turned completely upside down, and he had helped her to heave it over.

Now what the hell was she supposed to do?

"You can stay at my house, for as long as you need to," he told her. "It's not fancy, but it's comfortable enough."

"Thank you."

He rubbed his temples, fighting the pain pounding across his skull. "Your father will undoubtedly have the police monitoring every road from London and searching every train," he reflected grimly, "so the only safe way to get you out is to put you on one of my ships."

She regarded him in surprise. "Do you own a fleet, then?"

"The lad has his very own shipping line." Oliver's aged face beamed with pride. "No doubt ye've heard of the North Star Shipping Company?"

Amelia shook her head. "I don't think so."

"Really?" The old man looked disappointed. "Oh, well—'tis just a matter of time. Our Jack here has loved the sea since he was but a stripling, and is makin' quite a name for himself in the British shippin' industry."

"Really?" Amelia regarded Jack with genuine admiration. "You didn't mention that."

Jack shrugged, disliking the way Oliver was exaggerating. He owned a grand total of five ships, one of which was currently undergoing extensive repairs and was therefore not seaworthy, and one of which was a clipper ship and in little demand. "You never asked me what I did."

"When I asked Lord Whitcliffe about how his family made their fortune, he was shocked," Amelia explained. "He told me that in England a lady doesn't enquire about business affairs. It's considered vulgar. It's different in America, of course. At home men love to talk about their businesses and their investments with anyone who will listen. My father adores regaling people with his story about how he started as an impoverished farm boy and then went to the city and started his own railway line, which is now one of the biggest in the country." She smiled fondly. "The toes of his feet are bent from having to squeeze them into the worn-out shoes of his older brother. With nine children to feed and clothe, there were no new shoes to be had. If he has too much to drink, Papa removes his shoes to show people, much to their horror. My mother has to run over and stop him. Mother hates it when he tells that story. She likes to pretend that she and my father came from very wealthy families—which isn't true. She was the daughter of a poor greengrocer, but she'd rather die than admit that to anyone."

"There's nae shame in bein' poor," observed Oliver. "There's oft more shame in bein' rich."

"I thought things were different in America," Jack remarked. "That people didn't measure you by whether you were born poor, but only by what you made of yourself in your lifetime."

"It is different there," Amelia assured him. "But people still take notice of how old one's wealth is—not by hundreds of years, of course, but whether it's first- or second- or third-generation. Here the men tell you about their ancient estates and illustrious pedigrees. They even boast about some illegitimate ancestor who was supposedly sired by royalty. But ask them about their business affairs and they act as if you were trying to uncover some dreadful family secret."

"That's because so many of them are suffering financially," explained Jack. "And few of them are willing to work and try to make a new fortune on their own. They would rather sit around the Marbury Club drinking themselves into a stupor, hoping some wealth falls into their laps."

"Like marrying an heiress." Amelia shook her head ruefully. "You must think I'm a terrible idiot, for having believed in Percy."

Jack said nothing.

"I was an idiot," she admitted with painful candor. "But my father always says, there's no shame in making mistakes, as long as you learn from them."

"A stumble helps ye to right yer fall," added Oliver philosophically. "An' if ye ne'er stumbled, how would ye learn to walk?" He chuckled. "Our Jack here stumbled so often, Miss Genevieve was always frettin' he would end up in jail—or worse. 'Twas only by luck and her fierce will that the lad managed to stay a step ahead of the law—that an' his uncommonly fast feet. One time, when he was about fifteen, he and the other children decided to fleece a wee shop in Inveraray—"

"It's time we headed out," Jack interrupted brusquely. "Lord Philmore and your brother have probably figured out by now that we didn't go to the river, and are looking for us elsewhere."

Amelia bit her lip. "But what if they're still there?"

"Dinna worry, lass—I can turn this old carriage around and slip ye into the shadows quick as a whip," Oliver assured her. "Did I nae just tuck ye nice an' safe into this alley?"

"You did." Amelia smiled. "That was very clever of you, Oliver."

"Why, thank ye, lass," he said, beaming. "When we reach Inverness, I'll show ye how ye can slip away from trouble with trouble nae the wiser. 'Tis a skill I'm fairly good at, if I do say so myself. Who do ye suppose taught the lad here about wearin' such a fine disguise?"

"It was thoroughly convincing," Amelia told him. "When Jack took my hand and started to dance, I thought one of Lord Wilkinson's servants had gone completely mad!"

"She won't be going anywhere where she needs to slip away," Jack said firmly.

Oliver scratched his head. "Well, that's fine then. But if the lass learns a trick or two from me, where's the harm in that?" He winked conspiratorially at Amelia, then snapped the reins, setting the carriage in motion before Jack could answer.

THE THAMES RIVER WAS A BROAD BLACK RIBBON OF choppy cold water, its edges littered with ships groaning and straining against thick, brine-soaked ropes that tethered them to the docks. The river was a forbidding abyss of dark secrets, a churning reservoir of murky water and sea life fighting to survive amidst the fetid flow of the sewers that leeched the filth of London's population through a decaying maze of rotting brick and clogged drains. Several of Amelia's suitors had treated her to carriage rides along the Thames on bright afternoons, where the sun had glinted upon its smoky blue waters like a golden shower. She had thought it beautiful then. Tonight she found it ominous and forbidding, its brackish stench filling her nose and throat until she thought she would gag with revulsion.

"Here we are, then," said Oliver, easing the carriage to a halt. "Nae amiss—only the dredgers at work." He indicated a small, battered boat bobbing slowly across the rough surface of the water. Two men stood at the back of the craft, feeding a trawling net into the inky depths.

Jack leapt down from the carriage and raked the darkness with his gaze. Huddled about the docks between massive walls of barrels and crates were the sleeping, snoring men, women, and children who had not secured shelter in one of the city's thousands of common lodging houses, or "padding-kens." The night was warm, which made sleeping in the open with the relatively fresh air of the docks preferable to being crammed into a squalid room of thirty or more unwashed bodies. There one paid for the privilege of sharing a vermin-infested bed with as many strangers as could be squeezed in it, or collapsing onto a "shakedown," a greasy, bug-ridden bundle of rags on the floor crammed into the narrow spaces between the beds. In each room there was a single rusted tub overflowing with an unspeakably foul sludge of urine, vomit and feces in which the nightly tenants relieved themselves.

During the long years Jack had lived upon the streets of Inveraray, the lodging houses of Devil's Den had been much the same. He had always elected to sleep outside during the summer—unless he could find shelter in a stable or shed. The smell of animal manure was preferable to the appalling stenches that a filthy, cloistered assemblage of human beings created when trapped in one small room.

"Why are those men fishing at this late hour?" Amelia wondered.

Jack glanced at the men dropping their net into the river. "They aren't fishing. They're dredging."

"Dredging?"

"Dragging the riverbed."

Amelia frowned, confused. "What are they looking for?"

"Anythin' that might be unlucky enough to be down there," supplied Oliver, climbing awkwardly down from his driver's seat.

"What could they possibly be hoping to pull up from the river?"

"Corpses, mostly," Oliver answered cheerfully. "Some nights the river is fair burstin' with them."

Amelia's eyes widened. "Do people just fall in?"

"If they're stewed enough, they do," Oliver replied, untroubled. "'Course some poor souls jump in of their own accord, while others are given a wee push. The dredgers pull them up and see if there's a reward to be paid for findin' the poor buggers. There's always pockets to be emptied first. They believe there's nae wrong with takin' what's left on a dead man—especially seein' as how the police will only do the same, given the chance."

"They steal from dead bodies?" Amelia found the idea atrocious.

"They dinna see it as stealin'," Oliver explained,

trying to help her understand. "'Tis more like a fee, for findin' them and bringin' them to the attention of the authorities. An' since the poor sods themselves won't be needin' what the dredgers find on 'em, they see nae harm in helpin' themselves. 'Tis a business, an' they expect to be paid for their work."

"Watch your step." Jack extended his hand to Amelia to help her down from the carriage. He wanted to get her safely onto his ship and inside a cabin before the dredgers pulled up a body, should they be fortunate enough to find one.

"Is this your ship?" Amelia stared in bewilderment at the dilapidated steam cargo ship tethered at the end of the wharf. Paint was peeling in fist-sized clumps off its rusting hull, and a black plume of oily smoke was belching erratically from its single battered smokestack. "It looks terribly old."

"The *Liberty* has taken cargo to and from Singapore, Hong Kong, India, and the West Indies," Jack informed her crisply. "She may not be what you're accustomed to traveling on, Miss Belford, but she will have to suffice." He strode toward the ship, leaving Amelia behind.

"Forgive me—I meant no insult," Amelia swiftly apologized, realizing she had offended him. "I'm sure she's a fine vessel," she added lamely as she struggled to keep up with him.

"She seems to be throwin' off an awful lot of smoke." Oliver frowned at the acrid haze spewing in ever-thicker plumes from the ship.

Jack did not slow down as he studied the sooty shroud building against the star-pricked sky. "She's not due to sail until the day after tomorrow. The trip to Inverness will interrupt her loading, but after she drops us off she can head back to—"

An explosive ball of fire suddenly tore from the ship, lighting the darkness in a fiery storm of copper and gold.

The intense heat from the blast hit the threesome in a scorching blow. Jack grabbed Amelia and threw himself to the ground, shielding her from the searing explosion with his body.

"Get down!" he roared at Oliver.

Oliver collapsed against the dock and buried his head beneath his hands as another blast ripped from the *Liberty,* then another. A glorious shower of glittering sparks filled the sky before raining onto the ebony ripples of the river below.

"Sweet Saint Columba," swore Oliver, hazarding a peek.

Amelia lay with her face buried against the hard wall of Jack's chest. She was acutely aware of everything around her, from the acrid sting of the smoke-laden air to the rough graze of Jack's cheap woolen coat against her cheek. He was lying sprawled atop her, his legs entwined with hers, his powerful arms and chest pinning her to the ground. For a long moment she lay frozen, feeling his heart pound against her chest and the steady gust of his breath in her hair.

"Are you all right?" Jack raised himself onto his elbows, lifting his weight off of Amelia, but still shielding her in case there was another blast.

"I'm fine, lad," said Oliver, awkwardly pulling himself to his feet. "Dinna worry about me."

"I'm fine, too." Amelia's voice trembled slightly.

Jack studied her a moment, as if he did not quite believe her. Her hair was scattered in golden strands against the rough planks of the dock, her breasts falling softly back from the neckline of her gown. She made no attempt to break free from his embrace, even though his leg was pressing intimately between her thighs and his hands were clutching the satin of her shoulders. Shadows and light were playing against her creamy skin, illuminating it in flickers of amber and coral. The *Liberty* was ablaze, Jack realized, not bothering to turn and look at it. His ship was destroyed, yet that realization seemed strangely distant against the extraordinary sensations coursing through him. All he could think of was how small and soft Amelia was as she lay so trustingly beneath him, her slender body pressing into the hard edges of him, filling him, caressing him, stirring his blood and heating his flesh until he wanted nothing more than to taste her lips while his hands roamed the sweet lushness of her.

Appalled, he rolled off her and sprang to his feet. His crew. He began to run toward his burning ship.

"Here now, lass, let me help ye," said Oliver, offering his hand to Amelia.

"Oh, no," she gasped. "Look!"

Some two dozen men were pouring onto the deck of the *Liberty* from the levels below. They stared at the blaze uncertainly, wondering if they should try to put it out.

"Get off the ship!" roared Jack, standing on the wharf below them. "Now!"

The men ran toward the stern of the ship, where the gangplank joined the *Liberty* to the dock. A scorching wall of fire and smoke blocked their path.

"Jump into the water!" he shouted, realizing they could never get through the blaze.

The blasts had awakened the men, women, and children who had been sleeping peacefully on the docks moments earlier. They raced toward the burning ship, anxious to help. The dredgers had also abandoned their miserable work and were rowing toward the ship, anxious to pull live bodies from the river instead of dead ones.

The crew aboard the *Liberty* began clambering over the railing at the front of the vessel, hesitating barely a second before hurling themselves into the frigid black water below. The drop would be bruising, Jack realized, but not deadly.

"Throw them something to hold onto!" he commanded, directing the ragged men, women, and children who had come to offer assistance. "Rope, barrels, crates—whatever you can find!"

Everyone immediately set to work hauling heavy lengths of rope and barrels and hoisting them off the dock into the water. Amelia and Oliver struggled to turn a barrel on its side before rolling it over the wharf's edge. One thrashing sailor swam over to it and grabbed hold, while others reached for the secured ropes that were being tossed down to them.

"You two, come with me." Jack motioned to a couple of strong-looking young men. "We'll take that skiff and pull them out of the water."

"Jack—look!" cried Amelia, pointing.

A young boy of about thirteen stood alone upon the deck of the *Liberty,* desperately trying to summon the courage to throw himself off the ship.

"Jump!" Jack ran to the edge of the wharf so the boy could see him. "Don't think about it—just jump!"

The boy hesitantly climbed over the railing, then stared in terror at the rough waves below.

"Let go, Charlie!" yelled one of the sailors from the water, trying to encourage him.

"It ain't that far!" shouted another.

"We'll grab you the moment you hit the water!" added a third.

Whimpering, the boy closed his eyes.

Another explosion suddenly tore from the ship, violently rocking the vessel. The boy screamed as he fell forward, his legs kicking wildly as he fought to regain his hold. One hand still gripped the railing. With colossal effort he pulled himself up and scrambled back onto the deck.

"I can't swim!" His voice was terrified.

"It doesn't matter!" Jack told him. "We'll pull you from the water—I promise!"

Charlie stared at the churning depths below, then shook his head. "I can't," he sobbed.

"Oh, God." Amelia's heart clenched with fear.

"The lad's got to jump," Oliver said grimly. "If he doesna, he'll burn to death."

"Row that skiff over and start pulling men from the water," Jack ordered the two men he had chosen as he loosened his neck cloth. "I'll be back in a minute."

Amelia watched as Jack swiftly wrapped his neck cloth around his nose and mouth. "What are you doing?"

"I'm going to get that boy."

"Surely you're not thinking of trying to run through the fire!"

"If I don't get him, he'll die," he said simply.

He sprinted up the gangplank and onto the deck of his burning ship, tearing off his jacket. A terrible heat seared his lungs as he approached the smoky inferno at the center of the *Liberty*. He studied the fire a few seconds, trying to determine where there might be a gap in the flames, or at least a place where it was burning with less ferocity. Inhaling a gasp of hot, heavy air, he raised the thin shield of his jacket to protect his face, then charged blindly into the smoke and flames.

"He's bleedin' mad," said a man standing on the dock, watching.

"He won't make it," predicted another. "If the fire doesn't get him, the smoke surely will."

Amelia stood with her hands fisted at her sides, waiting for Jack to emerge. Her heart was ramming painfully against her chest and her breath was trapped, making it impossible to speak, or cry, or do anything except watch with agonizing dread as huge pillars of flame wavered with grotesque beauty upon the ship.

And then, just when she was certain that Jack was dead, he burst through the valley of fire.

Throwing down his burning jacket, Jack doubled over and coughed heavily, trying to expel the smoke and heat from his lungs. He tore his neck cloth from his face and inhaled a few marginally cooler breaths. Then he ran toward the boy huddled upon the deck at the bow of the ship.

"Hello, Charlie," he said, the calmness of his voice belying the gravity of their situation. "I think it's time we got off this ship, don't you?"

"I ain't goin' into that fire!"

"Me, neither. I just ran through it, and I didn't find it a particularly pleasant experience."

"I ain't jumpin' neither! I can't swim!"

"I won't let you drown, Charlie. I give you my word."

Charlie regarded him helplessly, his eyes wide with fear.

"Take my hand." Jack's voice was gentle but firm as he extended his hand to the shivering boy. "That's all I want you to do. Just take my hand."

"You'll try to push me off," he said accusingly.

"I won't," Jack promised. "You're a young man, Charlie, not a child. You have the right to choose to die if you want to. And if you want to stay here and be burned alive, I'll respect your wishes. Is that what you want?"

He frantically shook his head.

"Then take my hand."

Charlie whimpered, then reached out and grabbed Jack's hand.

"Good." Jack held him tightly. "Now we're going to climb over the railing together, and then we're going to just step off the ship. There's really nothing more to it than that."

Dazed with terror, Charlie allowed Jack to guide him over the railing. Suddenly he froze, clinging to the rail with one hand, holding fast to Jack with the other.

"I'll drown," Charlie whispered, staring at the inky depths below.

"No, you won't. For a few seconds you'll fly through the air, and then you'll hit the water. Hold your breath and keep your mouth and eyes closed. I'll grab you and pull you up. Ready?"

Charlie looked terrified, but he nodded.

"All right then, let's go."

Amelia watched in awe as Jack and the boy stepped off the ship, holding hands. Charlie's scream split the air, and then was obliterated by the splash of the water. Both disappeared for a few interminable seconds, rendering the night grimly silent.

Then Jack exploded from the water, holding a gasping, choking Charlie in his arms.

A resounding cheer burst from the men and women crowded upon the docks and clinging to barrels and crates in the water. Holding fast to the boy, Jack swam over to the skiff that was rowing out to meet them, and helped the men on it pull Charlie safely aboard. Then he climbed into the boat himself and set to work helping the rest of his ship's crew out of the river.

"'Tis a fine thing ye did, lad," Oliver said gruffly when Jack finally stood, cold and dripping, upon the wharf. "Ye made me right proud."

Amelia hurried over from where she had been helping the men and women distribute their ragged shawls and blankets to the shivering crew members. She studied Jack anxiously. "Are you all right?"

Her once artfully arranged hair was falling in tangled disarray around her shoulders, her cheeks and hands were smudged with dirt, and her elegant evening gown was badly torn. Jack thought she looked unbelievably beautiful. "I'm fine."

"The crew is all accounted for, Mr. Kent, sir," said a lean, gray-haired man of about forty-five. "For a while we thought Evans, Lewis, and Ritchie were missing, but we've just found them—they were visitin' the taverns when the *Liberty* caught fire."

"Where was everyone when the fire broke out, Captain MacIntosh?" asked Jack.

"Most of the crew had retired for the night," the captain replied. "With the *Liberty* due to sail the day after tomorrow, we've been breakin' our backs these past few days getting our cargo and supplies stowed and ready. Most of the men were just too tired to go lookin' for—" He glanced uneasily at Amelia, taking note of her elaborate jewels and expensive gown. "Entertainment," he finished delicately.

"Who was on watch?"

"Davis and Patterson. I've already talked to them. They said a carriage came round about an hour ago, with two fancy gents in it. They asked Davis if he'd seen another carriage before them. He told them he hadn't, and they moved on down the wharf. Other than that, nothin' was amiss."

Jack saw Amelia's face pale. He had to get her out of there soon, he realized. While he doubted either his sailors or the men and women who had been sleeping on the docks could read a newspaper, it was possible someone had seen her picture and knew of the reward being offered for her capture. Standing on the docks in a ball gown with her jewels sparkling against her skin, she was certainly arousing their curiosity, especially now that the crew from the *Liberty* was safe.

"The fire probably began in the engine room," suggested Captain MacIntosh. "The boiler must have exploded."

"It seems unlikely that the boiler would explode when the ship was docked," Jack observed.

"Then it had to be the coal cargo," the captain decided. "That's a tricky one to stow. It lets off dangerous gases when it's all piled up in a hold. Sometimes they smolder, and suddenly—boom."

"Or maybe a lantern caught a whiff of the gases and set it off," suggested Oliver.

Jack said nothing. He was well aware that coal fires accounted for a high number of British ships being lost each year—sometimes as many as a hundred. He did not particularly like transporting coal for that very reason. But it was a major British export, and as the owner of a struggling shipping company, he could not afford to be overly discriminating about his cargoes. Even so, he didn't believe that the boiler or its coal had caused the fire on the *Liberty*.

Someone was trying to destroy his company, and with the loss of the *Liberty*, they had come very close to succeeding.

"She'll burn the better part of the night," reflected Oliver. "Nothin' we can do for her."

"A shame." Captain MacIntosh regarded the ship mournfully. "She wasn't much to look at, but she was a tough old thing. She had at least another ten years in her."

Jack scanned the crowd of people clustered around the docks, wondering if any of them had played a part in the destruction of his ship. It was even possible the vandals were amongst his crew. He searched for some sign of Quinn or his men, but didn't see them. He had instructed Lionel Hobson to fire Quinn, but only after he had found a replacement. It seemed unlikely that he would have been able to do so in such a short period of time. It didn't matter. Watched or not, the *Liberty* had been destroyed, along with her cargo.

It was a terrible blow.

"What do ye want to do now, lad?" asked Oliver.

"Perhaps we should return to your parents' house," Amelia suggested hopefully.

Jack shook his head. "The *Charlotte* is moored not far from here. We'll take her instead. Captain MacIntosh, I need you to select a crew member who can be trusted and knows how to drive a carriage to come with us and take my carriage back to my parents' house," he continued. "The rest of the crew can go home. You will visit my office tomorrow morning and tell Hobson what has happened. He should contact our client and advise them that our insurance company will cover the loss of their cargo. The authorities will also have to be notified so they can make a report." Which, Jack reflected, would uncover nothing. "Advise Hobson that I have taken the *Charlotte*. I will contact him when she becomes available again, should anyone be interested in hiring her."

"Yes, sir." Captain MacIntosh stared at his burning ship a long moment. "I'm sorry, sir," he apologized gravely. "The *Liberty* was my responsibility. I failed both you and her."

"We'll get past this, Captain," Jack said briskly, trying to diminish the seriousness of the situation. Captain MacIntosh was a good man and an excellent sailor, and Jack did not believe he had anything to do with the destruction of the *Liberty*. "None of the crew was lost or injured, and that is the most important thing. Unfortunately, I've no openings on any of my remaining ships for a captain. But as soon as I find a vessel to replace the *Liberty*, I'll be contacting you."

"Thank you, sir."

Of course he couldn't even remotely afford another ship, and the insurance he had on the *Liberty* would not be nearly enough to replace her. But Jack did not want anyone to think that her loss was significant enough to

ruin him. If word of that got out, then he would be ruined for certain.

"Here is some money." He pulled some wet notes
from his billfold. "If any of the men don't have a place to
go tonight, see that they have shelter and a hot meal. I
will make sure they are reasonably compensated for their
loss of work, but in the meantime they will have to look
for other employment. Unfortunately, I don't have another ship to put them on."

"The men will understand, sir. Thank you."

Jack turned and offered his arm to Amelia. "Come."

She looked at the ragged men, women, and children
still crowded around the rescued crew, sharing their
filthy, torn blankets and sips from their precious bottles
of cheap spirits.

She removed one of her emerald earrings and
pressed it into Captain MacIntosh's hand. "Do you
think if you sold this you would have enough to give
these people some decent food and blankets?"

Captain MacIntosh regarded her in astonishment.

"That isn't necessary—" Jack began.

"I'm not leaving until Captain MacIntosh assures
me that tomorrow night these people will have blankets
and bread," Amelia insisted. "If he won't do it, then I
shall stay here and see to it myself."

Oliver's mouth twitched with amusement. "I
wouldna bother to argue, lad. Ye know how the lass is
once she sets her mind on something."

Jack sighed. "Take the earring to Hobson and tell
him that I want him to come down here tomorrow
night and distribute blankets, bread, cheese, and dried
beef to everyone." He specifically failed to mention
what Hobson should actually do with the earring. He
recalled that they had been a gift from Amelia's father,
and he did not want her to lose one of the few precious

items that remained from her former life. Instead, he would pay for the supplies himself.

"And fruit," Amelia added. "The children need to have fruit."

"And fruit," repeated Jack.

"And all the children must be fitted for new shoes," Amelia continued. "And new stockings too, so they don't get blisters."

Jack regarded her incredulously. There had to be at least fifty children crowded on the docks. Outfitting each of them with new shoes and stockings would cost a fortune.

"Here." Amelia realized that everything she was asking for probably cost more than one earring. "You will get more for them if you sell them as a set." She dropped the other sparkling gem into the captain's palm. "The stones are quite clear and their color is excellent—and it would really please me to know that they had been used to help feed and clothe these people." She regarded him hopefully. "Perhaps you will have enough to also buy the women new shawls?"

"Thank you, your ladyship," said Captain MacIntosh, stunned. "I'm sure the people here will be most appreciative of your generosity. Who shall I say is their benefactress?"

"Her ladyship prefers to remain anonymous," Jack swiftly interjected. He took Amelia's arm and began to steer her toward the carriage before she completely bankrupted him.

"Just tell them an angel crossed their path tonight," said Oliver, chuckling. "A bonny wee angel."

He turned to follow Jack and Amelia, leaving everyone else silhouetted against the glare of the brilliantly burning ship.

Chapter Seven

ONE STEP CLOSER AND I'LL BLAST YE SO FULL OF bloody holes the rats'll be lickin' ye off the dock."

Jack looked up to see an elfin man with a wild bush of red hair pointing a rifle at him.

"Good evening, Henry. I've come to take the *Charlotte* out for a run."

The scrawny sprite squinted at him through the darkness, still clutching his enormous firearm. "Saint Ninian's ballocks!" he roared. "Drummond! Finlay! Get yer fat, hairy arses over here and drop the gangplank—Captain Kent has come—and Oliver, too, by the look of it!"

"Here now, we'll have none o' that kind of talk, Henry," scolded Oliver, frowning as he climbed from the carriage. "There's a lady present."

"A lady?" Henry seemed dumbfounded by the idea. "Ye're nae thinkin' of bringin' her aboard, are ye?"

"Actually, yes," said Jack.

Henry stared in awe at Amelia as she emerged from the carriage, taking in her uncommon beauty and the extravagance of her gown and jewels. "Saint Ninian's ball—"

"Stop!" barked Oliver. "One more curse and I'll scour yer filthy tongue with soap!"

"Yer pardon, yer ladyship," Henry apologized, chastened. "I fear I've been away at sea too long to remember to hold my tongue when a lady is near."

"Have no fear, sir." Amelia smiled at the diminutive, middle-aged man, amused. "I have heard colorful language before, and am not bothered by it."

Jack regarded her curiously. "Where would you have heard 'colorful language'?"

"You forget, my father's beginnings were extremely simple," Amelia reminded him. "He has been known to utter a blasphemous word or two when his patience is sorely tried."

"Judgin' by the way you two came crashin' out of that ball, I'd wager he fairly spewed foul words this evening," said Oliver, chuckling.

"Good evening, yer ladyship." Henry managed an awkward bow as Jack led Amelia onto the deck. "I'm Henry, and this here's Drummond, and that's Finlay." He gestured at the two rough-looking men who were practically folded over beside him, staring solemnly at their knees.

"Good evening, gentlemen," said Amelia, speaking as if she had just been introduced to three lords at a ball. "I'm so sorry if we have inconvenienced you in any way with our unexpected arrival."

"'Tis nae bother," Finlay assured her cheerfully, springing up again. He was a tall, gangly-looking fellow of about twenty-five, with scraggly black hair that he wore tied back with an oily scrap of leather.

"We wasn't doin' much." Shorter in stature and five times wider, Drummond made a formidable impression with his muscled arms, enormous shaved head, and the thick gold hoop that dangled from one fleshy ear. "We was just watchin' the fire down the river."

"Went off like a firecracker, she did." Henry shook his head mournfully. "A terrible thing to lose a ship to a fire."

"Unfortunately, that's the *Liberty* burning," Jack told them.

"No!" Finlay's eyes rounded with shock. "What happened?"

"It isn't clear how the fire started, but I suspect it was another attack by vandals."

"Filthy devils!" spat Henry, gripping his towering rifle. "They'd best nae try anythin' round the *Charlotte,* by God, or I'll blast their scurvy arses from here to China!" His expression brightened suddenly. "Would ye like me to go over and shoot them?"

"I'm afraid they're probably gone, Henry," Jack replied.

The little man looked disappointed. "How about I fire a few shots into the air, then, just as a warnin'?"

"That won't be necessary."

"Are ye sure?"

"I'm sure."

Henry muttered something under his breath.

"Was anyone hurt?" wondered Drummond.

"Everyone made it off safely, but the ship is destroyed," Jack told him. "Consequently we are going to be sailing the *Charlotte* to Inverness tonight. I trust we have enough crew aboard to make the trip?"

"Aye, we do," Henry assured him excitedly. "An' they've been itchin' to sail for weeks now."

"They're down below snorin' like bairns, but when I ring that bell they'll come runnin'!" Finlay hurried toward an enormous brass bell.

"I'd prefer it if you rouse them quietly, Finlay," Jack said. "I don't want to attract any attention as we leave."

Henry cocked a fiery eyebrow, instantly intrigued. "Sneakin' away, are we now?"

"Are ye bein' followed, then?" asked Drummond.

"The lass is," Oliver affirmed. "There's some nasty scoundrels searchin' for her as we speak, and she doesna want to be found."

"Have no fear, yer ladyship." Henry raised his rifle once more. "If they dare show their ugly faces when I'm about, I'll shoot the buggers from here to—"

"No!" Amelia gasped.

He stared at her in confusion. "Ye don't want them dead?"

"Actually, no. But thank you so much for offering," she added politely, not wanting him to think she didn't appreciate his concern. "It was most kind."

Henry reluctantly lowered his weapon once more. "Ye'll let me know if ye change yer mind?"

"I certainly will."

"Finlay, wake the rest of the crew and tell them to take their positions," commanded Jack. Although he didn't think Percy and William would return to the docks, it was possible that by now Amelia's father had the authorities searching the city for her. The last thing he needed was for Henry to shoot at some startled constable. "Drummond, release the ropes. We're leaving."

"Aye, Captain!"

The sleepy crew of the *Charlotte* hurried onto the deck and set to work. Jack gave them their orders from the ship's wheel, skillfully guiding his vessel through the dark passage of the Thames while most of London slept. Amelia found a place to stand where she wasn't in anyone's way, and watched him in silence from the shadows.

He stood with his long legs braced apart and his hands gripping the wheel, oblivious to the chill of the wind gusting against his wet clothes. All that remained of the ill-fitting servant's uniform he had donned to sneak his way into the Wilkinsons' ball was his thin white shirt and dark trousers. He had rolled up his sleeves and his shirt had opened, revealing heavily muscled arms and a powerful expanse of sun-bronzed chest. His damp hair was dark and curling against his neck, and more hair grew upon his chest and down the flat plane of his belly before disappearing beneath the narrow waistband of his trousers. There was a fierce intensity to him as he stood there, expertly easing his magnificent ship along the moon-kissed ribbon of black, shifting the wheel with a sure, steady rhythm that demonstrated both his proficiency as a captain and his love for his craft.

He was a man who was capable of masquerading as a common worker or an ancient servant, adopting with apparent ease the mannerisms and the speech of the characters he chose to emulate. He had lived a life of privilege as the son of the Marquess of Redmond, yet he was strangely contemptuous of those who were of noble rank, a dichotomy that she was not able to comprehend. He owned a shipping line, which Amelia had assumed meant that he directed the contracts and negotiations involved in managing a fleet of ships. But it was evident that he also occasionally sailed those ships himself, and judging by the respect his crew accorded him as they hurried to do his bidding, he did so with skill and confidence. More, he was a man who despite his brusque manner cared deeply about the welfare of others—even those he barely knew. Amelia had understood that from the moment he agreed to help her escape.

But she had not understood the depths of Jack's compassion until that night, when he charged through fire to take a boy's hand and leap from the deck of an exploding ship.

"Have you eaten anything this evening?" Jack asked, suddenly noticing Amelia.

"I'm not hungry."

He frowned. "Have you eaten anything today?"

"I had tea and toast this morning."

"That's all?"

"That's enough," she assured him.

"Do you have anything to offer our guest, Henry?" Jack wondered, turning to the little man.

"There's boiled pig's trotters with cabbage and dumplings. Finlay and Drummond said it was the best they'd ever tasted," he boasted.

Amelia's stomach lurched. "I'm sure it's wonderful," she managed politely, "but I'm really not hungry."

"Take some to our guest once she has been settled in my cabin," Jack instructed, ignoring Amelia's protest. "There's a chest in there with some clothes in it," he told her. "They aren't women's garments, but you can help yourself to anything you like."

"Thank you."

"Right this way, yer ladyship." Henry bowed and pointed his rifle toward the cabins.

Amelia took a last look at Jack standing tall on the deck of his ship, appearing more at ease than he had the entire time she had known him.

And then she turned and wearily followed Henry below deck.

SMOKY STRIPS OF PEACH UNRAVELED ACROSS THE leaden sky, pressing against the night with a slow seepage of glorious color and light. Jack flexed his arms and shifted his neck from side to side, groaning at the cracking of his spine and the taut pull of his aching muscles. He had remained at the wheel of the *Charlotte* throughout the night, easing her along her inky path toward the English Channel and the North Sea. It had been too long since he had experienced the pleasure of sailing her, for his business dictated that he travel aboard one of his faster steamships now. Even though he could have relinquished the wheel to Henry long ago, he had stayed where he was, enjoying the warmth of her polished wood against his callused palms and the slow shifting of her deck beneath his legs. He knew that if his shipping line were to grow and be successful, he would have to stay abreast of new technology and invest in more steamships, particularly now that the *Liberty* had been destroyed. But no steamship could ever compare to the sweet creaks and rolls of his beautiful, aging clipper, and the sensation of her cleaving a path across the ocean with nothing but clean sea air swelling her sails.

"Ye've nae been to bed, have ye?" Oliver scowled as he emerged from the cabins below.

Jack shrugged. "I'm not tired."

"Ye look bloody awful. Ye'd best find yerself a place to catch a wink or two afore ye stumble over yer feet and fall smack into the sea."

"I'm fine, Oliver."

"Fine or no, ye've been at that wheel long enough," Oliver retaliated. "If Miss Genevieve knew ye'd been sailin' all night in soppin' wet clothes with nae to eat or drink, ye'd nae hear the end of it. Unless ye want yer ears blistered when ye get home, ye'd best get yerself below and get some sleep."

"That's blackmail."

"Aye—and if ye think an old thief like myself doesna enjoy a wee bit o' blackmail now an' again, then it's plain ye've been away from the life too long."

Jack sighed. For Oliver, Jack would always be a lad of fourteen, which meant there was no peace when the old servant was about. "Very well. You can take over now, Henry." He motioned to the little sailor, who was sitting on a barrel lovingly polishing his rifle. "Call me if there are any problems."

"I'm sure Henry can handle the *Charlotte* for a few hours while ye sleep," said Oliver, making it clear that

Henry was not to disturb Jack over any trifling matter. "Can't ye?"

"'Course I can." Henry looked insulted. "I've been sailin' since the captain here was pissin' in his nappies."

"There, ye see, lad?" said Oliver. "Nae to worry about."

"Try not to shoot anyone while I'm gone," Jack said, relinquishing the wheel to Henry.

"I'll only shoot someone if I have to," Henry promised. "Ye know, if pirates try to take over the ship, for instance, or if those rogues come lookin' for her ladyship."

"Call me first."

"I will for sure," Henry promised solemnly, watching as Jack went below.

"If there's time," he added, smiling to himself.

THE CORRIDOR OF THE DECK BELOW WAS QUIET EXcept for the sighing of the ship and the peaceful snores of the crew who had returned to their cabins to sleep. The *Charlotte* was not full, so Jack was certain he would find an empty bed somewhere. He stripped off his damp shirt as he walked down the narrow hallway, weary and stiff, looking forward to lying down and being rocked to sleep by the gentle movements of his ship.

As he passed the door of his cabin there was a muffled sound. He paused, unsure whether or not he had actually heard anything. For a long moment there was silence.

And then the weeping began again, soft and thin and achingly sad.

He rapped upon the door. "Amelia."

There was an abrupt silence. He waited a moment, listening. He knew she had deliberately quieted herself. He stood there, torn. Should he stay and insist she see him, or leave and grant her the privacy she obviously wanted? After a long moment, he started to walk away. Before he reached the end of the corridor the thready sound of crying began again.

Damning the rules of appropriate behavior to hell, he strode down the hall and opened the door.

The cabin was shrouded in gray gloom, with only the palest of light filtering weakly through the porthole. It took him a moment to adjust to the darkness. When he did, he saw Amelia lying huddled upon the bed, co-cooned in blankets, and perfectly still. It was clear she was hoping that her feigned sleep would convince him that he had been mistaken and send him from the chamber.

Instead he stepped inside and closed the door.

"What's wrong?" he demanded.

She lay frozen another long moment. And then she sat up and looked at him, her eyes sparkling with tears.

"I'm sorry," she apologized in a small, soft voice. "I didn't mean to disturb you."

"You didn't disturb me. What's wrong?"

"Nothing."

He made no move to leave.

"Everything is fine. I'm just a little tired, that's all."

He said nothing.

"I think it's just that so much has happened in these last few days," Amelia ventured, realizing he wasn't satisfied with her answer. "One minute I'm a wealthy heiress getting married to the Duke of Whitcliffe in the most spectacular wedding of the decade, and the next I'm a nobody on an old cargo ship sailing to Inverness, with a price on my head and no idea what is to become of me. I suppose I just suddenly found it all rather over-whelming."

Her chin was up and her tone was artificially bright, as if she were making light of it. But her eyes were wide and silvered with pain, and Jack knew she was merely trying to deflect his concern.

"You're hardly a nobody, Amelia."

A small, strangled laugh escaped her throat. "Ah, yes—I'm the famous American heiress, Amelia Belford, wayward daughter of John Henry Belford, newly expelled from the family fold. I haven't any money. I have no family I can turn to. I have no home, no career, no plans, and no prospects. The only things I thought I did have were my appearance and my charm, which Lord Philmore falsely claimed had caused him to fall in love with me, and Lord Whitcliffe endlessly pointed out were severely lacking. I was 'too American,' in his opinion, which meant that my skin was too freckled, my teeth were too big, I dared to have an opinion on matters of consequence, and couldn't understand all the rules that shackle every move one makes in English society. Oh, yes, and let's not forget my atrocious accent," she finished bitterly.

"Philmore and Whitcliffe are both idiots," Jack observed with irritation, moving closer to the bed. "You're better off without either of them."

"Am I?" She bit her lip and stared at the dusky veil of light seeping in from the porthole. "I don't know. I don't know who I am anymore. I ran away from Lord Whitcliffe thinking that I was being terribly daring and brave, but all the while I believed I was running to a life with Percy. But Percy didn't love me just for me, as he had claimed so often—he just wanted my money. I suppose it's inevitable, when one comes from a family of enormous wealth, that people can't see beyond that." She wrapped her arms around her knees, looking small and lost. "Tonight when I discovered that Percy had betrayed me, I felt as if something within me shriveled up and died," she confessed brokenly. "I suddenly realized that every relationship I have ever had in my life has been because of my family's wealth. That every girl who has ever befriended me, every servant who has ever assisted me, and every man who has ever spoken with me, or laughed with me, or claimed to love me, has done so not because of who I am, but because I am the daughter of one of the wealthiest men in America. Somehow everyone who meets me hopes that they will benefit from that." Her voice was ragged as she finished in a tiny, defeated whisper, "It is a cruel lesson."

"You're wrong."

She looked up at him, startled by the anger in his voice.

"I didn't help you escape from your marriage to Whitcliffe because of your wealth, Amelia," he informed her brusquely. "And I didn't try to protect you from Philmore, who is, incidentally, not worthy to shovel manure in one of your father's stables, never mind marry you, because of it. I also didn't take you away from that mob at the Wilkinsons' and hide you on one of my ships because I thought that I might benefit financially from such an escapade. I don't give a damn whether you have any money or not, and I'm certain there are others in your life who don't care about that, either."

"There are no others," she whispered with pained certainty.

"Then we'll find new friends for you. Now that you have no money, you can be sure that whoever extends you friendship is doing so because of who you are, not because of your father's wealth."

"That might have been true if my father had not offered such an enormous reward for my return. With ten thousand pounds hanging over my head, I'll never be able to trust anyone."

"You can trust me." He spoke the words with harsh finality.

Amelia stared at him in wonder. He was standing beside her, his half-naked form outlined in the waning shadows of the night and the velvety soft beams drifting through the window. He was tall and powerful against the darkness, filling the small cabin with his strength and determination, crowding the unadorned walls and spare furniture with the intensity of his anger and resolve. He was incredibly beautiful to her as he stood there, as ruggedly simple and honest as his ship and his cabin. The chiseled muscles of his chest and arms were clenched, as if he were ready to do battle for her, and his eyes held hers with unwavering determination.

In that moment, she could almost believe that he would do anything for her. She could feel his pledge across the silence, as surely as she could feel the strange sensations now heating her blood and flesh and skin, making her achingly aware of the narrow distance between her and the man who had offered his help again and again from the moment he had found her in the ridiculous process of trying to steal his carriage.

"Why?" she whispered, holding his gaze with her own. "Why do you keep helping me, Jack?"

He stared at her a moment, saying nothing. The covers around her had fallen, revealing that she was wearing one of his shirts. It was far too large upon her slender form, making her look small and soft and achingly lovely. Her champagne-colored hair was spilling over her shoulders and the ivory column of her neck was exposed through the open neckline, disappearing into shadows at the base of her throat. He had thought she looked utterly exquisite when she stood upon the marble staircase earlier that night, her elegance radiating about her like an explosion of light, easily eclipsing the beauty of every other woman in the room. But she was even more glorious to him as she was now, stripped of her gown and her jewels, her hair pouring in tangled disarray around her, her body clad in a simple linen shirt, whose only flaw was that it covered her too loosely, denying him the pleasure of seeing the curves and swells of her silky body.

He swallowed thickly and stepped away, trying to ignore the sudden hardness in his loins.

She sat huddled upon his narrow bed, waiting for his answer. What could he tell her? he wondered helplessly. That he understood with sickening clarity the desperation of being sentenced to a life one does not think one can bear? If he told her that, it would only invite more questions, and he had no desire to answer them. Once they began they would not stop, and then he would have to admit that he was not the man he appeared to be. That instead of being the coddled son of the Marquess of Redmond, as she knew him, he was also the abandoned bastard of a drunken whore. That he had spent most of his childhood being beaten to a pulp at the hands of the brute into whose tender care his hopelessly defeated mother had entrusted him, until one day he could bear no more. That he had picked up a shovel and fought back, smashing the old bastard on the head with such force that he had fallen back dead, turning Jack into a murderer at the ripe old age of nine. That he had then lived his life on the streets, scraping by on his wits and his fists, stealing from anyone stupid enough to be robbed, or even swallowing the scraps of his arrogant pride and begging when he was too weak from hunger to steal. This was his ugly legacy, and although much of it was more or less known amongst the gossiping echelons of society in Scotland and England, it was not known by the magnificent woman huddled on his bed before him. On some innocent, misinformed level, Amelia Belford believed that he was something of an equal. To her he was the son of an aristocrat, a member of her precious Percy's Marbury Club, a guest at her own wedding. What harm was there in maintaining that illusion, he wondered angrily, if only for a few more days?

"I'm helping you because I like you, Amelia," he told her simply.

"Why?"

He shrugged his shoulders. "Lots of reasons."

"Why?" she persisted.

Her expression was almost pleading. In that moment, Jack realized how very much she needed to be reassured.

"Because you would rather break your neck scrabbling down a church wall instead of going through with an obscenely lavish wedding to a man you didn't love. Because you aren't afraid to stand up to your family, even if it means causing the most incredible scene London society has witnessed in decades and running headfirst into the unknown. Because when you see people in need you actually do something to help them, whether that means rolling filthy barrels off a dock or offering your precious jewelry in exchange for food and blankets. Because you aren't afraid to admit when you are wrong. And because you aren't offended by what you so quaintly refer to as 'colorful language.' Are those enough reasons to satisfy you?"

Amelia stared at him, transfixed.

And then she leapt from the bed, flung her arms around his shoulders, and pressed an ardent, inexperienced kiss upon his lips.

"Thank you, Jack," she breathed, her face lit with pleasure as she released him and dropped back down onto his bed. "You're a good friend."

He nodded briskly, fighting the overwhelming urge to follow her onto the bed and take her mouth in his, to slip his hands beneath the loose linen of her shirt and feel her breasts against his palms, to stretch out beside her and hold her close, until there was nothing but heat and desire and the sweetness of her pulsing beneath him.

"Good night," he managed roughly, wrenching open the cabin door. He escaped through it and slammed it shut, anxious to have some barrier between them. Then he staggered down the corridor, aroused to the point of pain, and utterly certain that he would not be able to sleep.

She would learn the truth about him soon enough, he realized with bitter regret.

And when she did, he would never again know the gentle trust he had seen in her eyes as she kissed him.

Chapter Eight

A MELIA LEANED AGAINST THE HEAVY RAILING OF the *Charlotte* and inhaled deeply, filling her lungs with the salty, cold wind gusting off the Moray Firth. Waves were crashing against the ship's wooden hull, sending bracing sprays of mist into the air, wetting her skin and causing her damp hair to curl against the soft charcoal wool of the coat Jack had given to her. She sighed with pleasure and closed her eyes, washing her mind clean as she rode the invigorating rise and fall of the churning ocean.

It had taken them nearly three days to sail up the east coast of Scotland through the frigid blue waters of the North Sea. Initially Amelia had endured the journey with trepidation, for with every mile she had felt more isolated from the glittering world she once knew, and more afraid of the unknown life she faced in the barren highlands of Scotland. Everyone aboard seemed to sense her anxiety, and Henry and Oliver had done their best to distract her from it.

"Would ye like to try yer hand at shooting again?" asked Henry, who had just finished his ritual polishing of his precious rifle.

Amelia smiled. "No, thank you, Henry."

"Are ye sure?" He looked disappointed. "Ye'll nae have much of a chance to shoot once we dock in Inverness, and 'tis clear ye've a rare talent for it."

"You're being very kind, considering I was just shooting at clouds. I don't know how you could tell whether my aim is any good or not."

"When ye've been shootin' as long as I have, ye know these things," Henry declared immodestly. "I can see how ye hold the rifle straight and true, and yer eye becomes one with the barrel. Just ask the captain here to give ye a gun, and ye'll be well able to blast a hole into any rogue who gives ye trouble."

"I'm not giving her a gun, Henry," Jack repeated for the hundredth time.

"They're too clumsy and noisy," Oliver agreed. "Not at all suitable for a lass. All she needs is a wee dirk like this." He pulled a wickedly sharp silver blade from his boot. "An' she'll have nae to worry about. Here, lass," he said, handing the glinting weapon to Amelia. "Show the lad how well ye've learned to throw it."

"You taught her how to throw a dirk?" Jack was appalled.

"Aye, and she's a swift learner, too. She got a feel for it much quicker than you did. Go on, lass." He nodded at Amelia. "Show the lad what ye can do."

Amelia wrapped her fingers around the cool hilt of the dirk. Turning toward the pile of crates that she and Oliver had erected as a makeshift target, she took careful aim, lifting the dirk up beside her ear. Then she stepped forward and hurled the blade with all her might.

Oliver beamed with pride at the sight of the weapon planted straight in the heart of the middle crate. "An' that's after scarce two days. Think what the lass will be able to hit after I've had a wee bit more time with her."

"She doesn't need to know how to throw a dirk or fire a rifle," Jack said firmly.

"Why not?" Henry scratched his head, bemused. "Ye said she had scum chasin' her."

"That scum happens to be her family," he pointed out. "Somehow I don't think she'll want to shoot them or stab them if they should find her."

"It doesna hurt to be prepared," argued Oliver.

"It does if she ends up killing someone—"

"You're absolutely right, Oliver," Amelia interjected. "Although I don't think I'll shoot or stab anyone, I have enjoyed your lessons immensely. Sometimes it's good to learn something just for the sake of learning, regardless of whether or not one thinks one might actually have use for the knowledge."

Henry furrowed his brows together. "Really?"

"I've nae learned anythin' I didna have use for at one time or another," reflected Oliver.

"But you must have learned some things without knowing that one day you might have need of that skill or knowledge," Amelia argued. "For instance, when I was a girl my daily lessons included all kinds of things that I felt certain I would never have use for. Languages like German, Italian, and Latin, which seemed hardly necessary when everyone spoke English in New York, and subjects like history and literature, which were horribly tedious when taught by my governess. But worst of all were my lessons in deportment."

Oliver frowned. "Deport-what?"

"Lessons in how to sit and stand and walk," Amelia explained. "Try as I might, I just couldn't remember to keep my head high and my back straight at all times. So my mother had an awful contraption made, which I was forced to wear while I was doing my lessons. It was a long steel rod, which pressed against my spine and was strapped on at my waist and my shoulders. There was another strap that went around my forehead and pinned my head to the rod. That meant I had no choice but to keep my back perfectly straight at all times. If I had to read I had to raise the book to my eyes, and I had to learn to sit at my desk and write without bending forward. Of course it was horribly uncomfortable, and I hated wearing it. Many days I cried when my governess put it on. But now I have near-perfect carriage no matter what I'm doing. When I was little I didn't understand why that mattered, but ultimately my good posture was very important when my mother introduced me to society. People notice that sort of thing."

The men stared at her in stunned silence.

"Well, now," said Oliver, venturing into the uncomfortable quiet, "that's a rare way of lookin' at it."

"Aye," added Henry helplessly.

Jack's fists were clenched with rage. "How old were you when your mother first made you wear this device?"

"About eight years old, I think," Amelia answered. "Why?"

He stared at her with impotent fury, hating her mother for inflicting such a cruel torment on her young daughter as she groomed Amelia, even then, for her future value on the marriage market. "I was just thinking of what I might say to her if I ever have the pleasure of meeting her."

Amelia studied his hard gray gaze in confusion. It surprised her to realize that he was actually upset by her story. "You mustn't think ill of my mother, Jack," she protested. "She has always only wanted what she believes is best for me. She knew I was growing up in a world where people would constantly be evaluating me and criticizing me because of who I was and what I represented. She tried to see to it that I was well prepared to endure their scrutiny."

"And where was your father while your mother *prepared* you?"

"My father isn't interested in society and appearances. But he is also the first to admit that he doesn't know much about what to do with girls, so he left my upbringing in the care of my mother."

"If I had a daughter, and anyone dared try to put her into such an evil device, I'd damn well kill—" Jack stopped himself. "I wouldn't tolerate it," he finished with barely suppressed fury.

"Well, of course, having endured it, I would never do that to my daughter, either," agreed Amelia. "But I don't think my mother did it because she was cruel. I believe she did it because she loved me."

He shook his head, unable to comprehend how Amelia could defend her mother's actions.

"I dinna think anyone in Inverness is going to be overly concerned with how straight yer back is," Oliver speculated. "But I'm sure Miss Genevieve will be able to teach ye a thing or two about gettin' along on yer own."

"You mean Jack's mother?"

"Aye. She managed fairly well for herself afore she met his lordship, with a wee bit of help from me, of course," he added, "and she raised Annabelle, Charlotte and Grace into fine young lasses who ken how to take care of themselves. Now she's got her new brood to work on, but I'm sure she'd be happy to make time for ye."

"I'd be very pleased to meet her," Amelia declared enthusiastically.

"Amelia won't be meeting Genevieve or Haydon, or any of the family," said Jack.

Oliver looked at him in surprise. "Why not?"

"Because I don't want them dragged into this," he explained. "We've already created a scandal by running off in the middle of her wedding and causing a near riot at the

Wilkinsons' ball. We haven't seen a newspaper in days, but for all we know her parents have claimed that she's been kidnapped in order to preserve her reputation. If the police somehow decide to search for her in Inverness, I don't want my family associated with her disappearance."

"Ye know them well enough to realize they'd be glad to help. Besides, ye need another lass stayin' with her."

"They are not to be involved, Oliver."

Oliver regarded him impatiently. "Surely ye're nae thinkin' ye can keep Miss Amelia with ye alone and nae destroy her reputation in the process?"

"You'll stay there, too."

"Oh, well, that's fine, then," Oliver drawled sarcastically. "Have ye honestly been away at sea so long ye've nae sense about what's proper?"

"Fine," Jack said, exasperated. "What do you suggest?"

"We'll ask Doreen and Eunice to stay with us," Oliver decided.

"And what will we tell Genevieve?"

"Ye'll think of something."

"Who are Eunice and Doreen?" asked Amelia.

"They're part of my family," Jack explained. "Eunice was Genevieve's cook at one time, and Doreen used to help to keep the house clean, but really, they're more than that." He did not want her to think the two women were mere servants.

"Sort of like two old aunts," Oliver supplied. "Miss Genevieve took them from jail, same as she did me, and they've lived with her ever since."

Amelia's eyes widened with fascination. "Really? What were they in prison for?"

"Stealing, but they weren't professional thieves, like me," he qualified, making it sound as if he had had an illustrious career. "They were strictly amateur."

"Ye'll be able to learn a thing or two from them," Henry speculated. "Not about how to shoot, mind." It was clear that he felt he was her sole tutor for that particular skill. "But other things, I'm sure."

"We'll be docking in Inverness in less than an hour," predicted Jack, assessing the wind in the *Charlotte*'s sails. "You'd best go below and change. I've laid some clothes out for you on your bed."

Amelia regarded him in surprise. She had been wearing her evening gown during the day for the past three days, with Jack's coat overtop for warmth, because she had not been able to find anything suitable in his cabin for her to wear. "You have some women's clothes aboard?" She wondered why he hadn't offered them to her earlier.

"I have a disguise for you," Jack replied. "Since word of your disappearance and reward has probably reached the newspapers here, we have to be careful you don't stand out when you leave the ship. Your ball gown will attract too much attention—even with my coat thrown over it."

"Ye'll need to cover that hair of hers as well," Oliver reflected, frowning. "That's sure to turn a few heads afore we can hire a carriage."

"I've thought of that."

"Well, that's fine, then." Amelia found herself looking forward to wearing a fresh dress that was not as heavy and uncomfortable as her extravagant evening gown, and arranging her hair beneath a pretty hat. "I'll just go and get changed."

I F MY MOTHER COULD SEE ME NOW, SHE WOULD FAINT."

"The shirt and trousers are a wee bit large," Oliver allowed, "but other than that ye make a fine lad."

The heavy trousers and dark coat Jack had given to her were far too big, as was the white linen shirt underneath. Her hair had been stuffed into a thick woolen cap, which effectively hid it, but looked ridiculous in tandem with the rest of her apparel. She had pleaded to be allowed to keep her own shoes, arguing that with the trousers pooling around her feet no one was going to see her evening slippers anyway. That at least had spared her from the huge, clumsy boots Jack had given her, which she was certain she would have tripped over as she hurried across the dock to the carriage he had engaged.

" 'Tis nae far to the house, and then ye'll be able to change back into yer gown if ye like," Oliver promised.

"There's a carriage following us." Jack's voice was tense.

Oliver stole a cursory glance out the back window. "Aye, and there's one followin' behind it, and another after that. Ye're frettin' over nothing," he chided. "No one here is expectin' us, and there's nae way anyone could know Miss Amelia is here."

"Oliver is right, Jack," Amelia agreed. "No one knows I was on the *Charlotte*, so we must be safe for the moment."

Jack continued to watch the small, dark carriage trailing behind them, trying to get a clear view of its driver. After a moment the vehicle turned off the street they were on and disappeared. He sank back against his seat and restlessly stretched his legs. Oliver was right, he realized moodily. He was becoming paranoid.

"Inverness isn't a very big town, is it?" remarked Amelia as the carriage rattled down the narrow cobblestone streets.

"Not compared to London or New York," Jack allowed. "But it is important economically for the Highlands because of its access to the North Sea through the Moray Firth. Most of the goods entering and leaving the Highlands come through here."

"Are you from here?"

He shook his head. "I'm from Inveraray, which is further south and east."

"What brought you to Inverness?"

"Genevieve moved here after she married Haydon. He has an estate not far from here. When my brothers and sisters got older, they all settled in the area as well."

"And do you see them often?"

"When I'm not away on business. That was why I was in England. I had just arrived back from India, and was planning to leave again the following week. Since my family had made arrangements to attend your wedding, I decided to join them so I could see them briefly before I left."

"How lovely to have such a close family." Amelia sighed. "If I had married Lord Whitcliffe, my family would have returned to New York. Although I suppose my mother would have visited me occasionally, I don't think I would have seen my father or brothers much—unless I went to New York to visit them. My father doesn't like England, and couldn't wait to go home. William keeps very busy working for my father, so he wouldn't have time to travel here."

"What about Freddy?"

"Unfortunately he didn't care much for Lord Whitcliffe, and his lordship detested Freddy, so that would have made any visits a bit awkward. Lord Whitcliffe thought Freddy was a wastrel."

"Ironic, considering Whitcliffe has never worked, either."

Amelia fastened her gaze on the row of houses passing by the window. She had no idea if she would ever see Freddy again.

"We're here," announced Jack as the carriage came to a halt.

It had started to rain, veiling Inverness in a gray

gloom. Jack paid the driver, then helped Amelia down from the carriage. Once she was on the ground he released her hand.

"Can you manage from here on your own? The neighbors may be watching, and it will look strange if I escort you on my arm."

"I'm fine," Amelia assured him.

The house before her was considerably smaller than the London town house belonging to Jack's parents, but it was handsome enough and reasonably maintained. Two rows of large windows overlooked the street, and the heavy black front door sported a gleaming brass knocker in the shape of a lion's head. Amelia and Oliver huddled in the rain as Jack fumbled through his coat pocket and produced a key. The lock wouldn't move at first, forcing him to rattle the handle several times. The door remained stubbornly closed.

"It must be swollen from the humidity." He took a step back, then heaved his full weight against the door just as it swung open.

"Sweet Saint Columba!" swore Doreen, ducking aside as Jack went flying into the house. "Ye're lucky I didn't bang ye over the head with my scrub brush." Her thin, heavily lined face tightened with exasperation, as if Jack were somehow to blame for her nearly crowning him. "What are ye doin' here?" she demanded, dropping her bristly weapon into a bucket.

"I live here," Jack told her. "What are you doing here?"

"Scrubbin' the floors, same as I do every Tuesday."

"For God's sake, Doreen, I've told you that isn't necessary—"

"Ye're back!" Eunice beamed with pleasure as she squeezed her well-padded form through the door from the kitchen. "Come in quick, Ollie, afore ye catch yer death from the cold and wet—and you, too, lad," she clucked, waving a plump hand at Amelia. "Never mind the floors—we weren't expectin' ye so there's nae much in the larder, but I've just made a nice pot of tea and I've oatcakes with butter and marmalade, which should tide ye over nicely 'til we can get somethin' more."

"Ah, Eunice, ye know the way to my heart," declared Oliver.

Amelia gratefully stepped into the warm hallway. The smoky sweet scent of a fire burning in the kitchen mingled with the fragrance of lemon oil and soap. "Thank you," she said to Eunice as the white-haired woman took her coat. "That sounds lovely."

"Now there's a different accent," observed Doreen as she relieved Oliver and Jack of their wet coats. "Where are ye from, lad?"

"America," Amelia replied.

"America!" marveled Eunice. "What brings ye all the way to Inverness? Are ye workin' for Jack on one of his ships?"

"Miss Belford is going to be staying with me for a time," Jack explained. "As my guest."

The two old women looked at Amelia in surprise. She obligingly removed her cap, releasing her heavy mantle of blond hair.

"I knew it!" exclaimed Doreen triumphantly, forgetting that she had just called Amelia "lad." "These old eyes are as sharp as ever. Why are ye dressed like that, lass? Are ye runnin' from the police?" The idea seemed to appeal to her.

"Miss Belford is trying to avoid a number of people," Jack explained. "She had a change of heart at her wedding, and Oliver and I helped her to get away."

Eunice's mouth rounded with shock. "This is the lass who went missin' from old Whitcliffe's wedding?"

"Aye." Oliver chuckled. "Climbed into my carriage

in all her weddin' finery and told me to drive off, just like that!"

"I should have known you two scoundrels were involved." Doreen fisted her hands on her narrow hips. "When Miss Genevieve and the children came back without ye, sayin' ye'd driven off after the bride disappeared, I thought 'twas strange ye didna come right home like ye'd planned."

"We had to make a stop in London first," Jack explained.

"Ye should have seen the disguises the lad wore while we were there," Oliver added, chuckling. "I swear one night he looked older than me."

"Ye can tell us all about it after we've given this poor lamb a bath and some decent clothes to wear," said Eunice. "Come along, ducky," she cooed, shepherding Amelia toward the staircase. She stopped suddenly. "Whatever shall we put her in? She canna go back into this." She shook her head with disapproval at the damp, ill-fitting coat and mud-splattered trousers Amelia wore.

Doreen squinted at the mantel clock in the drawing room. "The shops are open for another hour or so. I'll go and fetch a few things for the lass while ye see to her bath."

"Oh, wonderful." Amelia was tired of wearing either Jack's clothes or her evening gown, and longed to be in something pretty and comfortable. "If you'll just bring me some paper, pen, and ink, I shall write down my measurements and make you a list of everything I require."

"Nothin' too fancy," advised Oliver, remembering the spectacular wardrobe she had ordered in London. "Remember, lass, the secret to an escape is nae how fast ye run, 'tis in walkin' slow with no one lookin' yer way."

"Do ye think old Whitcliffe will come looking for her here?" wondered Eunice.

"Whitcliffe won't, but the police or agents for her family might," Jack replied. "There is also the matter of the ten-thousand-pound reward being offered for her return, which I suspect will be reported shortly in the Inverness newspaper, if it hasn't been already."

Doreen stared at Jack, flabbergasted. "Ten thousand pounds!"

"Yer family must really want ye back," observed Eunice.

"She needs three simple outfits." Jack was determined to set limits for Amelia's wardrobe this time. "And some shoes and slippers and—whatever she needs to wear underneath. That's all."

"But what shall I wear after tomorrow?"

Jack regarded Amelia blankly.

"Three outfits will only do for one day," she pointed out. "What shall I wear after that?"

"While ye're here ye won't have to change yer gown three times a day," explained Eunice. "'Tis nae that kind of household."

"But surely you cannot expect me to wear the same gown to dinner that I have worn all day," Amelia protested. "It isn't proper."

"This isn't London, Amelia." Jack was trying to be patient. "Women here wear the same gown all day and no one thinks less of them."

"Oh." Until the night she had boarded the *Charlotte,* Amelia had been accustomed to changing at least three times a day, and that was only if there were no outings or special parties planned. Her current wardrobe consisted easily of some eighty new gowns per season and hundreds of pairs of gloves, which totaled over two hundred and forty outfits, and did not include the clothes she had left in New York. "I see."

"Three gowns will do for now," Jack insisted, sensing her confusion and disappointment. He was not about to deplete his entire bank account in order to furnish Amelia with the kind of wardrobe to which she was obviously accustomed. "If you need something more, we can always buy it later."

"Of course. Three gowns is very generous. Thank you." Summoning an extraordinary dignity, she lifted the excess length of her muddy trousers in her hands and turned, trying her best not to trip as she followed Eunice up the stairs.

"Three gowns isn't really very much," Doreen reflected after she had gone, taking pity on her.

"Ye should have seen the gown she was wearin' the other night," remarked Oliver. "I've nae seen anythin' so bonny. She looked just like a queen, she did."

"And I'll be paying for that gown when the bill comes in," Jack muttered. "Along with anything else that Beaton and Lizzie fail to return. Unfortunately, I don't have the money to buy her a new wardrobe."

"I'm sure Miss Genevieve and the girls will be willin' to give her a few things from their wardrobes," said Doreen. "When I go to Grace's shop I'll ask her if she can spare an outfit or two."

"You can't go to Grace's shop. No one can know she is here—not even my family."

Doreen frowned. "Why not?"

"It's too dangerous at the moment. Amelia has caused a great scandal by running away. I don't want my family involved. Haydon and Genevieve don't need any more scandal in their lives."

"His lordship and Miss Genevieve have known nae but scandal for as long as either of them can remember," Doreen countered. "They willna mind a wee bit more—especially when 'tis for a good reason."

"They aren't to know, Doreen." Jack's tone was final.

She huffed with impatience. "Ye canna tell me ye

plan to keep the lass here like some sort of pet, with just you and Oliver hanging about?"

"No, I need you and Eunice to stay here as well, while I figure out what I am going to do with her."

"And what am I to tell our coachman when he comes by tonight with the carriage to take me and Eunice home?"

"Tell him to explain to Haydon and Genevieve that I have returned home and need your help to get the house in order," Jack suggested.

"They're sure to think 'tis odd, since we come every Tuesday to clean and dust and see there's nae thieves nor rats livin' here while ye're gone."

"Then say there's nothing to eat in the house and you're going to stay a few days to do some shopping and cooking for me. Tell the coachman you think I'm half starved and you refuse to let me be."

"They'll have nae trouble believin' that," predicted Oliver, chortling.

Doreen snorted with annoyance. "Fine, then. We'll stay."

RAIN BLED IN DARK STREAMS DOWN THE WINDOW-panes, turning them into glistening black squares. Amelia sat huddled upon the enormous expanse of Jack's bed with her arms wrapped around her knees, contemplating her unfamiliar surroundings. Jack had insisted that she take his room, even though Amelia had assured him she would be more than happy to sleep in his guest room. Oliver pointed out that Jack didn't really have a guest room, at least not one that was properly furnished, because Jack never had guests. Amelia had not known what to say to that. She had never known anyone who didn't maintain extra bedchambers in case family or friends came to visit. Jack had muttered something about not being home very much, and the matter was dropped.

She rested her chin upon her knees and sighed. Her bed was carved of glossy mahogany, and given its large dimensions, Amelia suspected it had been constructed specifically to accommodate Jack's unusual height. The design was simple and unadorned, but within the piece's sheer simplicity was a remarkably elegant beauty. The enormous wardrobe on the opposite side of the room was similar in spirit, as was the chest of drawers by the windows. The walls were bare, save for a painting of a magnificent clipper ship in full sail upon the ocean, which hung over the fireplace. Even when he wasn't at sea, it was clear Jack liked to be reminded of it.

She blew out the oil lamp on the table beside her and lay back against the pillows. Jack's mattress was extremely hard compared to the soft feather mattresses she was accustomed to, making it impossible for her to get comfortable. The rain seemed to grow louder as it beat against the windows, and she became aware of a gnawing hunger. She had not eaten much in days. While Eunice's oatcakes and tea had seemed more than enough earlier in the evening, they could no longer quell the emptiness growing inside her. Giving up on sleep, she threw back the covers and climbed out of the enormous bed. Perhaps there were a few oatcakes left, she reflected, wrapping herself in a soft plaid blanket. She lit a candle and padded into the hallway in bare feet, determined to find something to eat.

The house was still except for the sound of the rain drumming against the roof. Amelia crept down the stairs in silence, trying to not waken anyone. When she reached the main floor she noticed a spill of light seeping from one of the rooms down the corridor. Curious, she moved toward it and peered inside.

Jack sat hunched over a desk at the far end of his study, his head buried in his arms, snoring.

She slipped quietly into the small chamber, fascinated by the artifacts he had collected from his travels. It was evident he had a passion for ancient weaponry, for one wall boasted an impressive collection of dirks and daggers, swords and sabers, shields, helmets, pikes and crossbows. Another wall reflected his appreciation for the arts in a small but magnificent exhibit of carved friezes from Egypt and Greece, coupled with polished wooden masks from Africa and colorful fragments of mosaics from the East. The third wall displayed a series of intricately drawn maps.

The wall that he viewed from his desk seemed strangely incongruous with the rest of the room. Above the fireplace hung a portrait of a pretty, auburn-haired girl of about eleven, who was seated in a chair reading a book, with an ivory rose lying on the floor by her skirts. The painting was lovely, but its gentle romanticism was inconsistent with everything else Jack had chosen to surround himself with.

The surface of his desk was littered with papers, and more lay strewn on the richly patterned carpet beneath it. He had carelessly thrown his jacket and waistcoat onto a chair and rolled up his shirtsleeves, baring the lean, muscled forearms pillowing his head. Tangled waves of dark brown hair fell across the handsome curve of his clenched jaw, and the lines of his brow had eased slightly. There was a sweet, almost boyish vulnerability to him as he slept, unaware that he was being watched. Amelia moved closer, wondering what had demanded his attention so urgently when he was clearly exhausted. She set the candle down on the desk and scanned the numerous contracts, invoices, and sheets of calculations that Jack had been working on. Frowning at his virtually illegible handwriting, she reached for one of the pages.

"Let go before I goddamn kill you," he snarled, grabbing her wrist with bruising force.

"Oh!" she gasped, startled. "Forgive me!"

Jack stared at her in bleary confusion, fighting his way out of the hazy depths of sleep. In his mind he was once again a desperate, starving youth of twelve, with nothing to call his own except his filthy, louse-ridden clothes and a blistering pair of shabby boots. It was dangerous to fall asleep. There was always someone ready to steal what little he had. But he was quick with his fists and strong for his age, and he was damned if he was going to let some shit take so much as a button from him.

"Please, Jack," Amelia pleaded, "you're hurting me."

Clarity returned with sickening force. Appalled, Jack abruptly released her.

"Jesus Christ, Amelia," he managed in a low, rough voice, "I'm sorry. I thought I was back in—" He stopped himself suddenly. "I was asleep."

His face was harshly cut in the amber light, a fierce mask of desperate remorse. Amelia studied him in bewilderment. For a moment she had been afraid. But the man before her was so obviously pained, she was now overwhelmed with a desire to comfort him. His hands were plunged into the dark tangle of his hair and his gaze was downcast, as if he could not bring himself to look at her. The thin scar that marred the chiseled plane of his left cheek was pale against a shadow of rough beard. It must have been a horrible wound. She had always assumed it had been the result of an accident. But for some reason, she suddenly wasn't so sure.

"What happened to your cheek?"

Jack lifted his head and regarded her warily. "I was in a fight."

"When?"

"A long time ago."

"When you were a man," she persisted, not knowing why it seemed so important to her, "or a boy?"

He stared at her with feigned calm. She knew, he realized, feeling defeated and sick. Not all of it, but enough. Knew that he was not what he appeared to be. In one ugly, unguarded moment he had accidentally revealed himself to her. Only a man who had endured insufferable violence in his life would lash out in his sleep the way he had. Amelia was young and inexperienced, but she was not so naive that she didn't understand cold, raw fear when she saw it.

"You were a boy," Amelia decided softly, watching as he wrestled with his answer.

He shrugged his shoulders, struggling to contrive a dispassionate air. "It was nothing." He sat up and began to straighten the papers on his desk. "Lads fight." He made it sound as if it had been nothing more than a youthful skirmish. "I barely remember how it happened."

He was lying. Amelia could feel it. And she could see it, too, in the way he avoided her gaze as he focused on the task of tidying his work. The fact that he was keeping the truth from her wounded her deeply. She could not understand why he did not trust her enough to be honest, when she had been so honest with him.

"If you don't want me to know, then say so," she said quietly. "But please don't lie to me. I need to know that you respect me enough to tell me the truth—even if you think I won't like it." Her voice began to break as she finished, "You told me I could trust you. I need to know that's true."

Jack looked up at her in surprise. She was clutching the ends of the plaid blanket over her breasts in a makeshift cape, which barely covered the fabric of her nightgown. Her budget limited, Doreen had chosen a nightgown of sturdy, serviceable cotton, without so much as a tiny bow or scrap of lace enhancing the cuffs or neckline. It was hardly the kind of apparel Amelia was accustomed to, he realized, feeling a stab of guilt. A woman of Amelia's status would have at least a dozen nightdresses or more, made of soft silk with a profusion of satin bows, intricate embroidery, and French lace. Yet here she stood, clad in plain cotton and an old blanket, her hair unbound and her feet bare.

In that moment, she was the most exquisitely beautiful woman he had ever known.

He rose from his desk and moved toward her. He wanted to say he was sorry. He wanted to tell her that he had not meant to hurt her, either with his violence or his lies, or the past that he was trying so desperately to keep from her for as long as he could. He wanted to take her in his arms and banish the hurt shimmering in her eyes, to hold her close and inhale the delicate fragrance of her, to feel her softness pressing against him, unbearably sweet and soothing. He wanted to tell her things about him, about the vile, sordid past of which he was so ashamed, and he wanted her to listen with that trusting look he had seen so often as she gazed at him. Perhaps that was what he found so compelling about her, that gentle, accepting expression that was utterly void of the contemptuous superiority he had endured from others his entire life. Of course the women he had bedded did not regard him so, at least not while he was pleasuring them. But he knew that on some perverse level they were aroused by the idea that he was forbidden to them, and perhaps even dangerous. He could see it in their contorted faces as they gasped and writhed beneath him, could hear it in their ragged whispers as they begged him to do things to them. He could feel it in the way they moved away from him afterward and began to hastily dress, as if their integrity had suddenly returned and they couldn't stand to be with him another minute. None of them had ever considered him a friend.

But Amelia did.

He reached out and wrapped his arms around her, pulling her close. "I'm sorry, Amelia," he whispered, feeling impossibly awkward and unsure as she pressed her cheek against his chest.

He didn't want to tell her about his past, he realized helplessly. Amelia had grown up in a world that was safe and sheltered and beautiful. How could she possibly understand what he had come from, the life he had endured, the shameful things he had been forced to do? How would she look at him afterward? She would turn away in revulsion and horror, and he could not blame her. She wanted him to be honest with her. But she had no idea what his honesty meant. Instead of bringing them closer, it would destroy her trust in him. It would crush the fragile foundation of their friendship. It would frighten and confuse her, and leave her suddenly stranded and alone. He would not let that happen.

He was starting to care too deeply for her to abandon her so.

"I used to fight a lot when I was a lad," he began, trying to be honest without exposing too much of himself. "And during one of those fights my opponent cut me with a blade, which left me with this scar."

"What were you fighting about?"

"I believe he was trying to take something of mine," Jack offered vaguely.

"What was it?"

"I don't really remember." That, at least, was the truth. "It may have been my boots."

"You shouldn't have risked your life over something so trivial," Amelia observed gently. "You could always have bought another pair of boots."

He said nothing.

She raised her eyes to him, her expression shadowed with regret. "Forgive me. I did not mean to judge you. I'm only sorry that he hurt you, and you were not strong enough to defend yourself."

He raised a brow in surprise. He had not meant to suggest that he had not fought back. In fact, he had smashed the older thug's nose and knocked out several of his teeth, which he suspected had been far more painful than his own cut cheek. But he did not enlighten her.

Amelia regarded Jack steadily. The sculpted planes of his face were softened against the dusky light and his gray eyes were filled with concern, making him look boyish and uncertain. She raised her hand and laid it against his cheek, tenderly covering the streak of scar tissue.

Jack stiffened. His immediate impulse was to pull away. But Amelia's caress was so pure, so completely filled with caring, he remained where he was. She was actually trying to soothe him, he realized in amazement, to ease the pain of an event that had happened over twenty years earlier. And, incredibly, she was succeeding. Not that there was any lingering pain in his cheek, or even much enduring outrage over that particular brawl itself. The event had faded in his memory, losing its shape and form as it melded with the hundreds of other battles he had fought, big and small, as he struggled each day to survive. But the softness of Amelia's hand against his cheek was calming nonetheless, as comforting as a cool cloth swept across a fevered brow. She was impossibly beautiful to him as she stood there, her slender form enclosed in his arms, filling him with a kind of fragile hope as she held her palm against him.

Unable to stop himself, he lowered his mouth to hers, pulling her tight against him as his tongue swept across the threshold of her lips and tasted the wet heat within. Just one kiss, he told himself desperately. He understood it was wrong. But she had laid her hand against his scarred cheek, and unleashed a need that he suddenly could no longer deny.

Just one kiss, and he would never touch her again.

A small, shocked gasp rose from Amelia's throat. She had thought herself relatively experienced with men, having enjoyed the attentions of an endless parade of aristocrats who were eager to whisk her into a private corner at the first opportunity and declare their undying love. She had been betrothed not once, but twice, and while old Whitcliffe had thankfully never had the inclination to put his slack, liver-colored mouth to her lips, Percy certainly had. But nothing could compare to the powerful desire now streaking through her. She did not know how to react to such an erotic assault. And so she simply stood there, clinging to Jack for support, absorbing the wonder of his mouth raking possessively over hers.

Suddenly he began to pull away.

Loss swept through her. Without thinking she looped her arms around his neck and pulled him down once more. Jack froze against her, uncertain. Amelia whimpered and tentatively traced the tip of her tongue along his lips. For a few agonizing seconds he did nothing.

And then he groaned in surrender and pulled her against him, opening his mouth to hers.

Somewhere in the recesses of his mind Jack realized what he was doing was wrong. But the reasons seemed vague and distant as he devoured the sweetness of Amelia's mouth, tasting her deeply as he held her tight against the hard wall of his body. She returned his kiss fervently, twining her tongue with his, making him feel as if he was losing his mind as his hands began to roam the lush curves of her sparingly clad body.

Her woolen cape slipped from her shoulders and pooled at her feet, leaving her in only the thin cotton of her nightgown. But even this scant barrier was excruciating to Amelia as Jack's hands skimmed across her, drawing hungry circles down her back and hips before they moved to the swell of her breasts. He cupped his hand against one breast and gently squeezed, causing her to moan with pleasure. He growled with satisfaction and grazed the soft peak with his thumb, tightening it into a nub of arousal before moving his attention to the other breast, still claiming her with his mouth. Amelia felt as if her flesh was afire, and a mysterious ache was blooming between her legs. She clawed at his back and shoulders as she pressed herself into him, wanting more, but not knowing exactly what it was that she wanted.

Jack's hand moved down and gathered up the coarse cotton fabric of her gown. Before Amelia realized his intent he was brushing against the silky, dark triangle between her thighs. And then he slipped his finger into her slick, wet heat, causing her to gasp with shock and shame and pleasure. She should stop him, she knew that, but instead she sank against him and deepened her kiss. Over and over he caressed her, his fingers circling and stroking, exploring the intimate folds of her with gentle persistence, teasing her, coaxing her, intensifying the sensations rippling through her with mounting urgency. Amelia clung to him helplessly and opened her legs more, still ravaging him with her mouth. Finally she broke away to brush ragged kisses across the rough stubble of his scarred cheek, along the rugged line of his jaw, down the corded column of his neck. She tore open his shirt to reveal the bronzed muscle of his chest, wanting to feel more of him, but her breath was coming in rapid gasps and she could no longer concentrate. Up and down and around Jack's fingers moved inside her, searching and stroking and slipping, spinning a golden web of pleasure until she was wonderfully, hopelessly trapped. She clung to him frantically as he caressed her, holding her steady with one powerful arm while he pleasured her, never breaking his patient, insistent rhythm as he rained kisses upon her temple and ear, down the ivory column of her throat, across the sensitive hollows of her collarbone. Her breath was coming in shallow, desperate little sips and her body was melting beneath her. Yet nothing mattered beyond the tightly wrought sensations escalating within her, becoming more intense and unbearable with every second. She couldn't breathe, couldn't speak, couldn't think of anything beyond Jack's touch, yet somehow it wasn't enough. She whimpered and crushed her lips to his, begging him, pleading with him, although she had no idea what it was she wanted. Suddenly she began to shatter, like a glorious burst of fire raging against the impossible darkness of night. She cried out, in ecstasy and in joy, and buried her face against his chest as she crumpled into him, feeling gloriously free as he tightened his arms around her and held her safe.

Jack laid his cheek against the tangle of Amelia's hair and closed his eyes, filling his senses with her softness and scent. He wanted to lay her on the carpet and bury himself into her, to lift the ivory cotton of her gown and sheathe himself in her silky heat, to feel the velvet skin of her pressing against him as he pulsed inside, making her his own. He had never had a woman as rare and beautiful as she, a woman whose beauty extended far beyond the façade of her face and body. He wanted Amelia more than he had ever wanted anything, and the fierceness of his desire terrified him.

She was not his, he reminded himself savagely, and she never would be. While she had somehow managed to endure her upbringing without suffering the typical afflictions of superiority and entitlement, she was nevertheless of a birthright and a quality that was, quite simply, beyond him. He could never escape the loathsome crudity of his own creation, or the repugnant life he had led before being rescued by Genevieve. He made no apology for his early years, but he was scarcely proud of them, either. He could not expect Amelia to share her life with a man such as he—a bastard and a criminal, whose legacy included countless acts of thievery and violence, and one murder. She had no inkling of who he really was. That was why she had permitted him to kiss her. That was why she had thrown herself against him when he tried to break away, eradicating what little willpower he had as she opened her mouth to his.

Appalled by his staggering lack of control, he released her and turned to look out the rain-drenched window, hating himself.

The moment Jack broke his protective hold upon her, shame welled up from the pit of Amelia's stomach, extinguishing the flames that had burned there but moments earlier. Suddenly cold, she picked up her fallen blanket and wrapped it around herself.

A horrible silence stretched between them.

"I'm sorry," she whispered finally.

Jack turned to look at her, his self-loathing complete as he stared helplessly at Amelia. "I'm the one who needs to be sorry, Amelia. I had no right to touch you."

She stared at him in silence, struggling with her emotions. No, she supposed he had no right to touch her, if having that right meant a legally signed betrothal contract followed by an opulent wedding ceremony attended by eight hundred people. They had not had that between them. There had been nothing between them at all.

Except a passion that had filled her with such magnificent desire she had thought she would certainly die from it.

"It will never happen again," Jack vowed, desperate for her to believe him. He was suddenly afraid that she would leave him. That he would wake the next morning and find she had fled, too frightened by his behavior to risk another night under his roof. "I swear it."

She should have been comforted by his assurances. Instead Amelia felt strangely betrayed. What had she expected from him? she wondered. Did she expect him to fall to his knees and profess his undying love the way Percy had? To swear to her that there would never be another for him, and that he would be honored if she would consent to become his wife? She had nothing, she reminded herself. No family, no dowry, nothing. And even if she did, she knew that Jack had little interest in the institution of marriage. He was devoted to his shipping company and the sea. What could he possibly want with a wife when he was not home enough to care if his house was properly furnished?

"I understand." She turned toward the door, unable to face him even a moment longer. And then, because she did not want him to know how deeply he had hurt her, she managed to add in a flat, polite voice, "Good night."

Jack watched as Amelia left the room, taking all its heat and joy and life with her. He poured himself a glass of whiskey and turned to the window. The light from the oil lamps burning in his study mirrored his reflection in the glistening windowpanes. He stared at himself in disgust, lifting his fingers to trace the jagged path of the scar that streaked across his cheek.

Then he drained his glass and hurled it with helpless rage against the fireplace.

Chapter Nine

FOR THE NEXT TWO DAYS AMELIA DID NOT SEE JACK. He rose at dawn and left the house before she had awakened, and returned long after she had gone to bed. Oliver told her that Jack was busy managing the affairs of North Star Shipping, which had suffered a serious blow with the destruction of the *Liberty*. Amelia supposed that the demands of Jack's company could well absorb his complete attention. She could recall many occasions when she scarcely saw her father for weeks at a time. Nevertheless, she could not help but feel that Jack was avoiding her. Given her profound humiliation after the passion that had exploded between them in his study, she should have been relieved that she was spared the awkwardness of seeing him.

Instead she felt as if she had lost her only friend.

"There, now that the meat and marrow bone have simmered, ye skim the scum off," directed Eunice, handing Amelia a skimming spoon. "Careful now, lass, ye dinna want to burn yerself on the steam."

Amelia's brow puckered in concentration as she carefully captured greasy spoonfuls of gray scum and deposited them into a dish. "Why did we put the marrow bone in if we didn't want all this fat?"

"We needed it for flavor," Eunice explained. "There's nae enough in the lamb itself because the real taste is in the bones. 'Tis the same with any meat, be it chicken or beef or hare. Ye must always boil the bones 'til they're bleached to make the broth rich and sweet."

"Eunice makes the best hotchpotch in all of Scotland," declared Oliver, who was busy pouring several pints of strong vinegar into an old black pot.

"'Tis what we call lamb and greens," Eunice explained to Amelia.

"That and her haggis are famous in Inverness," boasted Oliver.

"Well, I dinna know about that." The color in Eunice's cheeks made it clear she was pleased by his compliment. "His lordship is nae fond of haggis, so I only make it when the children come for dinner. They grew up on haggis and tatties and peas, and they're nae so fancy now that they dinna appreciate a good, simple meal when they come home."

"Where is home?" asked Amelia, still focused on her skimming.

"His lordship and Miss Genevieve have an estate some ten miles from here," said Doreen, who was aggressively grating a turnip. "We all moved there from Inveraray after they got married. 'Twas a fine time we had, with the six children thinkin' they'd all but gone to heaven to be livin' in such a grand place. It was a fair change for them, after all they'd been through. For nearly a year they still slept in but three bedchambers, even though there were more than enough for each of them to have their own."

Oliver chuckled. "They took comfort bein' close to each other."

"Except for Jack," Eunice pointed out. "He was

older than the rest, and was pleased to have his own room."

Amelia paused in her skimming, confused. She had thought that Jack and his brothers and sisters were born to Lord and Lady Redmond. Clearly that wasn't the case. "So Jack's mother was married before she met his father?"

"She almost was," Oliver replied, measuring a cup and a half each of ivory black and treacle into his pot. "But when wee Jamie came along, the spineless cur broke their betrothal. He couldna bring himself to care for another man's bastard, and thought Miss Genevieve had gone soft in the head for wantin' to keep the bairn."

Amelia's eyes rounded in shock. "Jack's mother had a child out of wedlock?"

"Jamie wasn't born to Miss Genevieve," Eunice hastily explained. "He was the bairn of her father, Viscount Brynley, and a maid. Her father died afore he knew Cora was with child, and Genevieve's stepmother threw Cora out. She died in prison while giving birth, poor lamb, and instead of lettin' her wee brother go to an orphanage, Miss Genevieve brought him home to raise him herself."

"How old was she?"

"Barely eighteen, with nae to call her own except an old house," said Doreen. "When the Earl of Linton refused to marry her, Miss Genevieve had nothin'—except wee Jamie, of course."

"I must have it wrong then," Amelia reflected, trying to sort out the order of Jack's brothers and sisters. "I thought Jamie was Jack's younger brother."

"He is," affirmed Oliver.

"But he can't be—Jamie came first."

"Aye, and then came the rest of us," Eunice explained. "First Miss Genevieve took me from prison, where I'd been jailed for stealin'—"

"Because she'd been livin' on slave's wages," Doreen interjected.

Eunice smiled at Doreen. "Well, after prison 'twas certain no one was goin' to hire me, as I had nae references and was considered a dangerous criminal. But Miss Genevieve came to me and said if I would live with her she'd keep a roof over my head and food on the table, and if I ever needed anything else I had but to ask."

"And the rest of us followed," said Oliver, mixing a half cup of oil into his pungent black brew. "Now that she'd seen the nastiness of jail and knew that lads and lasses with nae kin were sent there for stealin' a bit o' bread, Miss Genevieve decided to help. First came Grace, then Annabelle and Simon—"

"Then poor Charlotte came," Eunice interjected, "and a pitiful little creature she was, half-starved and her poor leg near crippled by her wicked beast of a father."

"And me and Doreen got taken in, too," Oliver continued. "Doreen had been in prison for stealin' from the tavern where she worked—"

"Because they paid me slave's wages," Doreen huffed angrily as she reduced another turnip to shreds.

"—and I was the best thief in the county of Argyll." His voice was filled with pride. "There's nae a lock in Scotland I canna get past, and if Jack had but given me the chance, I'd have shown you I'm skilled in England as well. I'm a fair pickpocket, too, though I dinna get to practice much." He flexed his aged hands and sighed. "Miss Genevieve doesna like it when I lift the odd thing from her guests."

"And nae wonder," scolded Eunice, tossing a few sprigs of parsley, thyme, and bay leaf into her pot. "Ever since ye took that scented hankie from Lord Healey, he's refused to visit again."

"I gave it back to him," Oliver protested.

"Aye, in front of his wife, who was sorely displeased that it wasn't her own."

"I've nae seen a woman so red," marveled Doreen. "I thought she was goin' to drop dead on the floor."

"She willna die afore he does." Oliver chuckled. "She's too mad at him to grant him any peace."

"You mean to say Lord and Lady Redmond aren't really Jack's parents—or the parents of any of his brothers or sisters?" Amelia regarded them in amazement.

"We dinna mean to say that at all," said Eunice.

"Miss Genevieve may not have borne them, but there's nae question she's their mother," Oliver added emphatically.

"And his lordship loves them and treats them exactly the same as the children that followed after he and Miss Genevieve married," finished Doreen.

"Miss Genevieve still goes to the Inverness Jail now and again, lookin' for someone to hire." Eunice smiled. "She's a great believer in seein' the good in people. That's how she came to know his lordship—he was in the same jail cell with Jack, convicted of murder."

Amelia's eyes widened.

"But eventually 'twas proven that he was just defendin' himself from ruffians who had been hired to kill him," Oliver hastily added. "If nae for Miss Genevieve believin' in him, he'd have been hanged."

"What had Jack been imprisoned for?"

"Stealin', same as the rest of the children." Eunice clucked her tongue. "Livin' on the streets, they had nae choice."

"Jack had a rare talent for it," Oliver observed proudly. "He managed to stay out of prison 'til he was fourteen."

"'Twas good Miss Genevieve found him then, or he'd have ended up dead," predicted Doreen.

"On the streets there's always those who will kill ye

for as little as a crust of bread," Oliver added. "Children suffer the most, because they're easy to lift from."

Amelia thought back to the incident two nights earlier, when she had startled Jack in his sleep and he had reacted with swift violence.

The dark days of his childhood were long past, but they had left their mark.

She turned her attention back to the puddles of fat floating in the pot, overwhelmed by the tale of Jack and his family. She wondered why Jack had not told her about any of this.

Did he believe that if she knew the truth about his beginnings, she would think less of him?

"There now, we let that simmer until the meat is tender." Eunice placed a lid on the pot. "Thank ye, lass."

"Is there anything else I can help you with?" Amelia wondered.

She had rarely been in the enormous kitchen of her mansion in New York, with its tall, glass-faced cupboards, expansive marble counters, and the most modern equipment available for cooking. The preparation of food had not been part of her education, as her mother had expected Amelia would always have servants to cook her meals for her. If her mother could have seen her at that moment, wearing a plain woolen dress and grease-spattered apron, skimming puddles of fat off a pot of hotchpotch, she likely would have fainted. But Amelia loved the warm, fragrant kitchen, which smelled of gingerbread and herbs and whatever that black mess was that Oliver was stirring.

"If ye're nae afraid of handlin' a hot iron, I can show ye how to take grease out of a shirt," offered Doreen.

"I've never ironed before," Amelia admitted. "Is it very difficult?"

"Nae if ye're careful. First ye lay the shirt out nice and flat," Doreen began, arranging the shirt on the table.

"Then we lay a scrap of brown paper over the mark and set the iron on it, liftin' and settin' it down until the grease starts to come through. Then we put another scrap of paper over the mark and keep on 'til the grease doesna come through any more."

"Does that take the spot out entirely?" asked Amelia, amazed.

"Most times it will. If it's stubborn, ye wrap a wee bit of flannel around yer finger, dip it in spirit of wine and give it a rub, and that takes the last of it out nice as ye please."

Oliver frowned. "Is someone knocking?"

" 'Tis just the wind," Eunice assured him, sifting flour into a large bowl.

"Then 'tis a wind with a fist," said Doreen. "Ye'd best go see who it is, Ollie, afore they decide to—"

"Hello, there!" called an excited voice.

"Is anybody home?"

"Jack?"

"Sweet Saint Columba," gasped Eunice, covering herself in a cloud of flour as she dropped her sifter into the bowl, " 'tis the children!"

"Where can I hide?" Amelia looked desperately around the small kitchen.

"There's nae time for that—just bow yer head and keep to yer work," Doreen instructed, handing her the iron. "And dinna open yer mouth—the minute they hear yer accent they'll know something's about." She grabbed her knife and started rechopping her carrots as the door swung open and Jack's brothers and sisters poured into the kitchen.

"Hello, everybody," said Jamie.

"Something smells wonderful," Grace exclaimed, hurrying toward the stove. "Is that beef and barley you're making, Eunice?"

"It smells like lamb." Annabelle wrinkled her nose. "It must be hotchpotch."

"I'm starving," reported Simon, gazing longingly at the stove. "Is it ready to eat?"

"We don't mean to invite ourselves to dinner." Charlotte smiled as she limped through the door. "We just came by to visit with Jack." She seated herself on a chair and stretched out her stiff leg.

"He's nae here," Oliver said, stirring his black concoction with such vigor his face was covered with dark speckles.

"We'll be sure to tell him ye dropped by," offered Doreen, savagely reducing her carrots to mush.

"If ye come back tomorrow ye might be able to catch him," Eunice finished, sifting a snowstorm of flour into the air.

"He's sure to be back soon, isn't he?" Jamie was disappointed. "After all, it's nearly five o'clock."

"He said he was goin' to be late," Doreen replied briskly. "We dinna expect him 'til the wee hours of the morning."

"If he isn't coming home, why are you preparing all this food?" wondered Grace.

"It's for tomorrow," fibbed Eunice, stirring melted butter into some treacle.

"You're making treacle scones for tomorrow?" Charlotte regarded her curiously. "Don't you always say they're only good when they're fresh from the oven?"

"Yes, well, these ones are for us," Eunice stammered.

"Wonderful—I love treacle scones." Simon went to the stove and peeked under the lid of the pot. "When will this hotchpotch be ready, Eunice?"

"I'll just put the kettle on and we can have some tea," said Annabelle, filling the kettle with water.

Jamie smiled at Amelia. "I don't believe we've met.

I'm James Kent, and this is my brother Simon, and my sisters Annabelle, Grace, and Charlotte. We're Jack's family."

"This is Miss Maisie Wilson," interjected Oliver so Amelia wouldn't have to introduce herself.

"We've hired her just for today, to help with the laundry," Doreen explained.

"The lass is a bit shy," finished Eunice.

"I'm pleased to meet you, Miss Wilson." Jamie studied Amelia with interest. "I actually need someone to come and take care of my laundry. Do you take laundry in?"

Her gaze downcast, Amelia pressed her iron hard upon Jack's shirt and shook her head.

"I'll come to help ye," offered Doreen, trying to divert Jamie's attention.

"Really, Oliver, why are you going to the trouble of making boot blacking when it's so much easier to buy it?" wondered Annabelle.

"If ye can afford to rot yer boots with store-bought blacking, that's up to you," Oliver said. "This costs little to make and polishes up so fine it makes a pair of boots look like glass."

"Something is burning," remarked Grace, sniffing the air.

Eunice glanced at the stove. "Ye must be smellin' the wood burning—"

"Blazes!" exclaimed Amelia suddenly, "will you look at that!"

Everyone turned in surprise to look at her, and the smoking black hole she had burned in Jack's shirt.

"Never mind, lass," said Doreen quickly. "That's enough ironin' for today, anyway."

"You're from America, aren't you?" asked Jamie, intrigued by Amelia's accent.

She regarded him uncertainly. "Yes."

"Whatever brought you all the way to Inverness?" wondered Simon. "It's a long way from America."

"The lass is here visitin' her family," Eunice explained.

"They live nearby," added Oliver.

Annabelle studied Amelia with new interest. "Forgive me for staring, Miss Wilson, but have we met?"

"I don't believe so." Amelia's voice was taut. "I haven't been here very long."

"I'm sure I've seen you somewhere before." Jamie was also staring at her. "Your face is very familiar."

"You must be thinking of someone who looks like me." Amelia began to awkwardly fold Jack's burned shirt.

"Sweet blessed saints!" Annabelle exclaimed. "You're Amelia Belford!"

"That's why you look so familiar," said Grace, nodding with recognition. "We didn't see you on your wedding day, of course, but your picture has been in the newspapers a great deal, both before and after you disappeared."

"No wonder Jack couldn't wait to leave from your wedding." Annabelle's eyes were sparkling with mischief. "We thought he was just being obstinate—we didn't know he was running away with the bride!"

"He wasn't actually running away with me," Amelia clarified. "He discovered me trying to take his carriage and he helped me to get away."

Jamie smiled. "That sounds like Jack."

"The newspapers are saying you have been kidnapped," Grace reflected, "but witnesses at the Wilkinsons' ball said you fought everyone who tried to save you from the old man who took you."

"Was that you, Oliver?" asked Simon.

"Here now, who are ye callin' old?" Oliver was

clearly insulted. "'Twas Jack in disguise, and he looked twice as old as me."

"Jack's disguise was superb," Amelia agreed. "When he grabbed me and started to dance, I thought an elderly servant had taken leave of his senses."

"Jack danced with you?" Annabelle looked shocked.

"Yes—why?"

The brothers and sisters exchanged bewildered glances.

"Jack doesn't care much for dancing." Charlotte regarded Amelia with new interest.

"He was only dancing with me because he was trying to get me away from Viscount Philmore," Amelia elaborated. "Things were rather confusing at that point, as no one knew who Jack actually was."

"When they came runnin' out I drove them down to the *Liberty,* but she caught fire, so we sailed here on the *Charlotte* instead," continued Oliver.

"Fortunately, me and Eunice was here when they arrived," Doreen finished. "Otherwise the poor lass would still be wanderin' around in Jack's clothes."

"Why didn't Jack tell us that he had Miss Belford staying here?" wondered Grace. "Surely he must have known we would want to help."

"The lad doesna want any of ye involved on account of the scandal," Oliver explained.

"That's ridiculous," scoffed Simon.

Jamie nodded. "We're used to scandal, Oliver."

"We've known it our entire lives," pointed out Grace.

"One more won't make any difference," Annabelle assured him.

"And Jack should know we are always eager to help." Charlotte smiled at Amelia. "We're family."

"That's why he doesna want ye mixed up in it," Oliver insisted. "Ye've all known what it is to have folk look down on ye, but now ye've made respectable lives for yerselves."

"Ye lasses are married with bairns of yer own, Jamie is a respected doctor, and Simon is makin' a name for himself as a fine inventor," added Eunice. "Jack doesna care to have ye involved."

"Now that we've met Miss Belford, I'm afraid we are involved," declared Jamie emphatically. "And we want to help you," he told Amelia. "Just tell us what your plans are, and we'll do whatever we can to assist you."

"That's very kind of you." Amelia seated herself in the chair Jamie had pulled out for her. "I had initially planned to marry Viscount Philmore, but he tried to turn me over to my family in exchange for my reward."

"The vile wretch!" Fury heated Annabelle's cheeks. "He deserves to be skinned alive, chopped up, and boiled over a fire!"

Amelia smiled. "I hadn't thought of quite so bloody a punishment."

"At the very least he deserves to suffer a perfectly miserable marriage," declared Grace.

"But then that would make his wife miserable, too," Charlotte pointed out. "I think you should be glad you discovered his true nature before you married him, Amelia, for you could never have been happy with a man like that."

"Of course you're right." Amelia immediately liked Charlotte for her quiet, gentle wisdom. "Now it's up to me to take care of myself, and I'm afraid I'm not sure how I'm going to do that. As you can see, I'm somewhat lacking in certain skills." She gestured ruefully at Jack's ruined shirt.

"Ye're hardly about to make yer livin' as a laundress," scoffed Doreen. "Anyone can see ye're much too fine for that."

"Doreen is right," Simon agreed. "We have to find some other way for you to support yourself."

"First of all, we need to evaluate your skills," suggested Annabelle. "You were taught to read and write, weren't you?"

"Of course."

"And you studied history, mathematics, and science?"

"Yes."

"Well, then, you are young, presentable, unmarried, with a solid knowledge of the primary subjects of education. You would make an absolutely wonderful governess."

"I don't think that's a very good idea, Annabelle," reflected Grace.

"Why not?"

"First of all, there is the matter of her American accent. Any family who hired her might be concerned their children would pick it up. Not that it isn't quaint," Grace quickly qualified, "but I don't think many parents here would choose to have their children imitate it."

"I'm afraid you're probably right." Amelia sighed. "Lord Whitcliffe thought my accent was awful. He also said I had no sense of what was proper behavior. I don't think those are very good traits for a governess."

"Lord Whitcliffe is an idiot," Jamie growled.

"You could become a writer," suggested Simon. "That way no one would hear your accent, or even know who you were."

Amelia was intrigued by the possibility. "What would I write about?"

"Write about your experiences," Annabelle replied. "You could write a book about a wealthy heiress who travels the world—or travel books about the wonderful places you have visited."

"That isn't terribly practical, Annabelle," objected

Jamie. "It would take a long time to write a book, and there is no guarantee she would find a publisher. You have been very fortunate with your books, but writing for publication is extremely competitive and not necessarily lucrative."

Amelia regarded Annabelle with new fascination. "What have you published?"

"Annabelle has written a wonderful series of children's mystery books called *The Orphans of Argyll.*" Simon winked at his sister. "Charlotte does the sketches for the opening page of each chapter. The books are very popular here in Scotland."

"How wonderful—I would love to read them."

"Next time I visit I'll bring you some copies," Annabelle promised.

"It must be wonderful to have some special talent like writing or painting, or designing fashions," Amelia remarked. "I'm afraid my abilities lie more in the direction of running a large household and arranging grand dinners and parties."

"That's it!" exclaimed Grace. "Amelia, how many balls and dinners and teas did you attend in London and Paris while you were being introduced to society?"

"I've no idea. Hundreds."

"And before you came to England, did your mother organize similar affairs in New York?"

"Of course. For years my mother has made it her mission to be accepted by every level of New York society, which snubbed her and my father when they first acquired their wealth. She is renowned for throwing the most lavish affairs in New York and Long Island. Invitations to her parties are highly coveted."

"Could you organize an event like a formal dinner or a wedding?"

"I know how to arrange dinners or balls for anywhere from five to five hundred. Not how to actually cook the dinners," she qualified, smiling at Eunice, "but how to organize them, right down to the forks and finger bowls."

"That's perfect! There is a lovely old hotel in Inverness where one of my client's daughters is having her wedding reception next month," Grace explained. "I'm designing the gowns for the bridal party and the mother. There are three hundred guests invited, and Mrs. Mac-Culloch is determined that the event must be utterly grand and fashionable. Unfortunately, she doesn't have the first idea what actually is fashionable these days, and apparently neither does anyone at the hotel."

"Oh, Grace, that's brilliant!" marveled Annabelle. "No one knows more about what's fashionable than Amelia—her wedding was going to be the most spectacular event of the decade!"

"Exactly. The Royal Hotel has been serving the same food and setting the same tables and decorating with the same flowers for more than fifty years. But Inverness has grown a great deal in that time, and so have the tastes of the people who live here."

"Amelia could help the hotel organize receptions that match those in London for style and grandeur, which would increase their business," concluded Charlotte. "It's a wonderful idea."

"I know Walter Sweeney, the manager of the Royal Hotel," said Jamie. "I'll drop by there tomorrow morning and speak to him about Amelia, and arrange an interview for tomorrow afternoon."

"There's just one problem."

Grace regarded Amelia in confusion. "What's that?"

"My face and my accent. All of you felt that you had seen me somewhere, but you couldn't quite place where—until you heard my American accent. Then you were able to piece it together."

"Actually, it was your hands that gave you away,"

Annabelle told her. "They're far too soft to be the hands of a housemaid, and the scratches on them reminded me that you had fallen into the bushes at the side of the church."

"You can wear gloves until the scratches heal," suggested Grace.

"But surely someone will recognize me," Amelia insisted. "My picture is in the newspapers."

"Dinna mind about how ye look, lass." Oliver's eyes narrowed as he studied her. "I can make ye look so old and haggard yer own mother wouldn't recognize ye."

"We don't want her to look too old and ugly, Oliver," objected Grace. "After all, she is supposed to be selling a more youthful, fresher way of doing things."

"Fine then," Oliver relented, impatient. "I won't make her look any older than, say, forty."

"I have some gowns in my shop that would suit you perfectly," said Grace. "If you're going to convince them that you can bring style and flair to the hotel, you can't go to an interview wearing a plain dress like that."

"Not too fancy, though, Grace," Annabelle advised. "If she's going to play the role of a woman looking for a job, she shouldn't appear to be wealthier than the manager."

"What about my accent?" wondered Amelia.

"If we had time, I'm sure I could teach you to master a Scottish accent," Annabelle reflected. "I was an actress for a time when I was younger, and I loved doing accents. But it would take a few weeks of practice for it to be really convincing."

"We don't have a few weeks," said Grace. "If we want her to get the job of arranging Mrs. MacCulloch's daughter's wedding, we have to get her an interview immediately."

"Could ye flatten yer way of speakin' a wee bit?"

wondered Doreen. "Ye know—try not to sound quite so American?"

"I don't think so." Amelia regarded the group helplessly. "This is the way I speak."

"How about tryin' an English accent, then?" Oliver suggested. "Ye know, like the way they talked at the balls ye went to."

Amelia thought for a moment. "Wonderful weather we've been having lately, isn't it?" she chirped, affecting her best English accent.

"Well, that won't do." Simon shook his head. "She sounds ridiculous."

Oliver shrugged. "So do the English."

"Maybe we don't need to hide the fact that she is American," reflected Annabelle. "I mean, lots of families here have relatives living in America."

"Perhaps we just need to say that she comes from somewhere other than New York," Charlotte suggested. "So people don't assume that she knows Amelia Belford."

"Fine, let's say she is Mrs. Marshall Chamberlain, our widowed cousin from Boston," said Annabelle. "We'll tell Mr. Sweeney she is the daughter of Genevieve's aunt."

"Does Genevieve have an aunt?" asked Charlotte.

"No, but Mr. Sweeney won't know that."

"Why does she have to be widowed?" wondered Jamie.

"Being widowed gives her a degree of respectability and dignity," Annabelle explained. "Also, it will make gentlemen at the hotel less apt to bother her."

"Dinna worry—by the time I'm finished with her, no lad will care to clap eyes on her more than once," Oliver promised.

"She can't be hideous, Oliver," Grace reminded him. "If she looks horrible, no one will want to take her advice."

"Do ye want me to disguise her or not?" he demanded irritably.

"The first thing we need to do is change her hair." Jamie frowned at Amelia, evaluating her. "Every description of Amelia Belford mentions that she is blond."

Eunice took a silky skein of Amelia's hair between her plump fingers. "I can make a special pomade that will leave it brown till we wash it out again."

"And we can darken her eyebrows with burnt cloves," added Annabelle, critically examining the pale arches above Amelia's eyes. "I used to do that when I was performing on stage."

"A wee bit o' powder will cover those freckles and make her seem older," advised Oliver.

"Spectacles are what she needs," Doreen decided. "Make those big eyes of hers smaller and closer set."

"And I will bring her some outfits that aren't overly fitted, so no one will be distracted by her figure." Grace pulled a measuring tape out of her reticule. "If you'll just stand for me, Amelia, I'll take a few measurements—here, Annabelle, you hold the end of this to her waist, and Simon, you write down what I say—"

"What the hell is going on?"

Everyone in the kitchen turned to see Jack standing in the doorway, his expression hovering between outrage and astonishment.

"We're helping Amelia get a job," Simon told him cheerfully.

"Really, Jack, how long did you think you could keep poor Amelia hidden here and not have us find out about it?" chided Annabelle.

"You must have known we would descend upon you at some point," Grace added.

"Especially after you bolted from Lord Whitcliffe's wedding." Jamie laughed. "None of us dreamed you were actually running away with the bride."

Jack raked his hand through his hair, totally disconcerted. "It isn't what you think—"

"All we think is that you befriended Amelia and are trying to protect her from being forced into a marriage she does not want," interjected Charlotte quietly. "Isn't that right?"

Jack's expression became guarded. Of all his family, his sister Charlotte was the one who understood him best.

"Yes," he said, steadily meeting her gaze. "That's all I'm doing."

Charlotte studied him a moment, as if something about him puzzled her. Suddenly self-conscious, Jack looked away.

"Amelia cannot get a job," he informed the rest of the assemblage in the kitchen.

"Why not?" wondered Amelia. "I want to work."

"Ambition's a great seed." Eunice nodded with approval.

"First of all, it's too dangerous," Jack argued. "There is an enormous reward being offered for your return, which puts you at risk any time you step out of this house."

"She's nae goin' to be recognized, lad," Oliver assured him. "Not when I've finished with her."

"Of course she can't go out of the house as herself," agreed Simon. "That's why we're transforming her into Mrs. Marshall Chamberlain, our recently widowed second cousin from Boston."

"That way she won't have to hide her accent," Jamie explained.

"And making her a widow will make men more apt to keep their distance and respect her privacy," added Grace.

"It's a brilliant characterization," finished Annabelle happily.

"Amelia has never worked a day in her entire life." Jack's tone was brusque. "Just what the hell is it that you think she is fit to do? Do you think there is a job out there where she can sit and be waited upon while she finds ways to spend vast amounts of money?"

His brothers and sisters stared at him in shock, startled by his rudeness.

"Actually, your family believes I have some abilities beyond my talent for sitting around spending money." Amelia raised her chin and glared at him, masking her hurt beneath a shield of frigid anger. "And since I have no intention of remaining here and burdening you with my presence a moment longer than is necessary, it seems best that I find employment at the earliest opportunity. If you will forgive me, ladies, I think it would be best if we finished my measurements in my chamber."

Without waiting for her new friends to respond she swept regally from the kitchen, fearful that if she stayed a moment longer the tears blurring her eyes might begin to fall.

"Really, Jack, how could you be so mean?" Annabelle gave him a look of pure exasperation as she swished past him.

"I'm sure you didn't intend for it to sound as harsh as it did," Grace allowed, following her sister.

Charlotte rose from her chair and gently laid her hand upon his arm. "Tell her you're sorry, Jack," she advised softly. "She needs to know that." She gave him an encouraging smile, then turned and limped out of the kitchen.

"Well, 'tis plain to see ye've been away at sea too long." Eunice gave him a disapproving look as she pummeled the dough for her scones.

"There was a time when ye didna like to speak very much." Doreen glared at him. "A pity ye couldna hold yer tongue just now."

"What in the name of Saint Andrew is the matter with ye?" demanded Oliver furiously. "The lass is ready and willin' to work, and instead of encouragin' her, ye're all torn-faced because 'til now she's had the good fortune to not need to. Where's the logic in that?"

"I was only trying to protect her," Jack explained, defensive. "Amelia can't work. It's too dangerous."

"Surely you don't expect her to stay hidden in your house forever," objected Simon. "Unless you're willing to support her indefinitely, Jack, she needs to learn to support herself."

"Either that or we have to find her a husband." Jamie watched with amusement as a scowl creased Jack's brow. "Which wouldn't be too difficult," he continued blithely, "given how incredibly beautiful she is."

"She doesn't want a husband," Jack snapped. "She just ran away from one marriage, only to find the man she believed she was in love with was only too willing to deliver her back to her family and collect their reward. I don't think marriage strikes her as very appealing at the moment."

"If she canna marry and ye dinna want her to work, just what, exactly, do ye expect her to do?" Doreen folded her arms and regarded him expectantly.

"I can take care of her," Jack insisted.

"I'm sure you can," agreed Simon. "But I don't think Amelia expects you to, or even wants you to. And she can't stay in this house forever, burning holes in your shirts and making hotchpotch."

"If the lass doesna want to go back and marry old Whitcliffe, then she has to make a new life for herself," rationalized Eunice.

"And for that she'll need to find a job and learn what she's made of so she can take care of herself," Oliver finished. "'Tis nae less important for her than it was for Miss Genevieve."

Why the hell couldn't they all just stay out of it? Jack wondered furiously. Why couldn't they see that he would take care of her?

"Fine—help her to find a job—or ten jobs, if it makes you so bloody happy. But if someone recognizes her and steals her away, you've only yourselves to blame. At least here, she was safe. I would have made goddamn sure of it."

He strode angrily out of the kitchen, unaware that he had revealed far more than he had intended as he slammed the door behind him.

Chapter Ten

WALTER SWEENEY GRIPPED THE EDGE OF HIS DESK, feeling a desperate need to hold on to something as he endured the whirlwind assault of the four excited women twittering like birds on the edge of their seats before him.

The Kent sisters, as they continued to be known despite their matrimonial status, had burst into his office in a chattering blast of feathered hats, glossy pearls, and tastefully tailored outfits, escorting their somewhat more understated looking cousin, Mrs. Marshall Chamberlain. Their brother, Dr. James Kent, had dropped by earlier and asked Walter if he would kindly grant an interview to his charming American cousin from Boston, who was recently widowed and now seeking a new life and employment in Inverness. Dr. Kent had explained that Mrs. Chamberlain was intimately acquainted with what was currently deemed fashionable in Boston, New York, Paris, and London, suggesting that this was an area of expertise which the Royal Hotel might find beneficial.

Walter had tactfully agreed to conduct the interview,

but purely in the interest of maintaining cordial relations with the Kent family, who comprised a vital force in the local economy. The Marquess and Marchioness of Redmond and their children were well known for their support of local business and industry, including his hotel, which had hosted numerous dinners and parties for them over the years. While Walter wanted to be accommodating to the family, he did not, quite frankly, see any need to hire someone to advise him on matters of service or presentation. He had managed those aspects of his hotel quite successfully for some thirty years now. He might not have the time or the inclination to travel to fast places like Paris or London to see what foolish nonsense other hotels were up to, nor did he have to. He knew good, plain, old-fashioned Scottish food and service when he saw it, and that was the foundation on which his hotel had built its proud and long-standing reputation. He had intended to listen attentively to whatever Mrs. Chamberlain had to say and then politely inform her that he did not have a suitable opening at the Royal Hotel which would fit her admirable qualifications. His obligation to the Kent family thus met, he would have then continued with his daily agenda.

What he had not anticipated was that Mrs. Chamberlain would arrive with her three female cousins in tow, thereby subjecting him to a dizzying assault of feminine charm. He clutched his desk with the desperation of a drowning man, struggling to keep up with the dozens of criticisms and suggestions that were being volleyed back and forth between the four women. He had begun the meeting confident that his hotel's performance and reputation were above censure. After nearly an hour of the women's exhausting offensive, however, he was suddenly not so sure.

"Mrs. MacCulloch was adamant at her daughter's last fitting that she expected her upcoming wedding to be an affair of great elegance from the moment the guests entered the reception room," Grace was saying emphatically. "She mentioned some of the items that you have proposed for the wedding dinner menu, Mr. Sweeney. While they are admirable choices, I'm sure my dear cousin, Mrs. Chamberlain, could arrange a menu that would have every wedding guest talking about the food at the Royal Hotel for years to come."

"The menu for the wedding has already been agreed upon," Walter told her. "It cannot be changed."

"But the wedding is not for three weeks yet," protested Grace.

Annabelle gave a teasing laugh. "Surely you have not started preparing the food?"

"It cannot be changed," Walter insisted. "I have already informed the kitchen. The menu is quite final."

"What are you planning to serve?" inquired Amelia curiously.

Walter smiled at the slight, mousy-haired, bespectacled woman seated across from him. She bore no resemblance to her prettier cousins, from her primly arranged hair to her pallid skin and narrow, ashen lips. She was of an indeterminate age, perhaps twenty-seven or more, although there were brief moments where she looked rather younger. Her face was not lined, but there were shadows beneath her eyes, which might have been an important feature for her had they not been obscured behind the gold rims of her scholarly spectacles. Her clothes were tasteful but plain, and he could not decide whether her lack of feminine ornamentation was due to the fact that she still mourned the loss of her husband, or whether she simply disliked personal adornment. What was clear was that she was a woman of considerable poise and energy. She moved with an unhurried grace that spoke of an upbringing of refinement and cultivation, and despite her rather strange American accent, her description of things she had experienced at other hotels and formal affairs indicated that she was both intelligent and well educated.

"We will be serving what has always been popular at wedding dinners," Walter told her. "Stewed trout and cock-a-leekie soup, followed by saddle of lamb, jugged hare, and sheep's haggis, peas and potatoes, then boiled salmon and fried turbot, and finally, date pudding with sticky toffee sauce and cranachan."

"What is cranachan?" asked Amelia.

"It's a traditional Scottish dessert," Charlotte explained. "It's made with toasted oatmeal, heavy cream, soft fruit, honey, and whiskey, all mixed together and left to thicken."

"It sounds wonderful," Amelia said truthfully. "And the rest of the menu also sounds very..." She paused, trying to find the right word. "Hearty."

"None of our guests have ever complained about our wedding menu," Walter assured her.

"And that is to your great credit," Amelia told him. "But I wonder, Mr. Sweeney, if, given the fact that Mrs. MacCulloch has indicated she is hoping for an event that will extend beyond what the people of Inverness have come to know and appreciate from your lovely hotel, you might not consider expanding the menu a little?"

"There will be more than enough food as it is," Walter objected. "I dislike wastage."

"I'm not suggesting you increase the amount of food you serve," Amelia quickly qualified, "just that you might offer a broader variety of choices, so that people could try something a bit different."

"Like what?"

"Well, perhaps you could begin with a choice of a hot or a cold soup," Amelia suggested. "That is particularly nice on summer nights, where people prefer not to indulge in a heavy meat soup to start. The cold soup can be of cucumber, or even some kind of berry, and decorated with a little flower floating in the center, or perhaps a very fine swirl of cream accompanied by a delicate spray of chives."

"You want me to put flowers in the soup?" Walter thought she must be jesting.

"They aren't to eat," Amelia assured him. "They are to make the dishes look inviting."

"The guests will think I'm trying to poison them."

"Actually, many flowers are edible. We would make sure that we selected something that wasn't harmful if someone did decide to taste it."

"I think a flower floating on top of the soup sounds lovely," said Charlotte. "Very creative."

"After the soup you might serve the fish courses, so that the meal gets gradually heavier, instead of going directly to the meats," Amelia continued. "Lobster is very popular these days, either prepared as a curry, or cubed and served with a trickle of lemon butter. Prawns are also very tasty and somewhat special, as is baked trout with slivered almonds. The idea is to offer dishes that are flavorful, attractive, and not something that people would typically prepare in their own homes."

Walter frowned, considering. After a moment, he began to make notes.

"There should be a small spoonful of lemon sorbet served next, in a little crystal glass on a plate, to refresh the palate and give the guests a chance to rest before the next course," Amelia went on. "Then for the meat dishes, it is important to balance the flavors and textures. Lamb and hare are very nice, but you should also offer braised ham, roasted chicken, perhaps some tongue, and a nice, tender cut of rare beef. There must be gravies to accompany each dish, but they should be offered separately, so that each guest can decide for him- or herself whether they want a rich sauce poured over."

"That makes perfect sense," declared Annabelle enthusiastically. "When I was in Paris I found they absolutely drowned everything in heavy cream sauces, and I didn't care for it at all."

"For the vegetables, I think you might want to go beyond peas and potatoes, even though they are common favorites," Amelia suggested. "Why not try lightly steamed asparagus spears, honeyed carrots, thinly sliced beetroot, and buttered green beans? This way there is more color on the plate, especially if some guests wish to try a little of everything.

"In addition to the desserts you have planned, I would suggest a selection of cakes and tarts, at least two ice creams, one strawberry or vanilla, and the other something more exotic, like ginger or melon, perhaps served with thin wafers or candied peel. Finally there should be fruit pyramids constructed of peaches, plums, apricots, nectarines, raspberries, pears and grapes, which are served with cheese and biscuits, and champagne. At the end of the meal everyone should be encouraged to get up and walk around a little, so I would serve coffee, tea, and port in another room, if possible, or if not, at least offer it on tables at the end of the room so that everyone has to walk a bit to get it."

Walter looked up from his writing. "Anything else?"

"Well, I have not yet considered the theme of the room itself, or the decoration of the tables, or the flowers or the linens or the orchestra and what music it should play," Amelia reflected. "Then of course the MacCullochs might want some small token or favor to be given to the guests as they are leaving, and that is also something that the hotel could have a part in creating. You could build a whole new reputation for the hotel based on the intriguing themes you envision for these affairs, and the spectacular way in which they are executed."

"Theme?" Walter crushed his brows together in confusion. "What do you mean?"

"A premise or idea that pulls the affair together in some fun and entertaining way," Amelia explained, "such as turning the room into a tropical paradise with palm and lemon trees, or creating midnight in an English garden, complete with stars and a fountain. Even if the bride's parents prefer to keep the wedding simple, at the very least one must consider the colors and flowers to be used. For that we must consult the bride and find out what she likes, or what is meaningful to her and her betrothed. That way even if the same guests are invited to a dozen weddings and dinners in your hotel over the years, they will always be anxious to attend and see how different and wonderful the event will be. Every guest should be seen as a potential client who may wish to host an event in the future, so we must use every opportunity to impress them with our impeccable service and creativity."

"Yes, of course," agreed Walter, who was feverishly scratching notes again. "Now tell me, Mrs. Chamberlain, what suggestions do you have for the—"

"Oh, my," gasped Annabelle suddenly, rising from her chair, "how the time has flown. I'm afraid we must be off, Mr. Sweeney."

"Off? Off where?"

"We have arranged another interview for Mrs. Chamberlain at the Palm Court Hotel just across the river. It is not as old as the Royal Hotel, of course, but it has all the latest amenities in plumbing and lighting and so forth, and they are anticipating quite a discerning clientele. Come, Mary," she said, gesturing to Amelia, "we really must go or we'll be late."

"Yes, of course." Amelia obediently rose. "It was a pleasure to meet you, Mr. Sweeney," she said, smiling serenely, "and I wish you and your hotel all the best—"

"Can you start today?" demanded Walter. "Now?"

Guarded excitement rippled through her. "Are you saying you wish to hire me?"

"Yes, yes." He waved his pen about impatiently. "I'm most anxious to hear more of your thoughts, so we can set up a meeting with Mrs. MacCulloch and her daughter and discuss our new ideas for her wedding. We haven't much time, you know. Barely three weeks. If we're going to change the menu and create a theme, we must begin making arrangements immediately. Shall we agree to a salary of, say, one hundred pounds a year?"

Amelia regarded him incredulously. She was not terribly well-informed about what people earned, but her father often complained about the enormous bills he received from Mr. Worth's salon in Paris, which generally exceeded twenty thousand dollars a season. Although she did not anticipate needing such an extraordinary wardrobe, how on earth could she be expected to live on a hundred pounds a year?

"A hundred and twenty-five?" Walter suggested, sensing her reluctance to accept.

Amelia looked to Annabelle, Grace, and Charlotte, who in turn looked expectantly at Mr. Sweeney.

"I can go as high as one hundred and fifty, but that is, I'm afraid, my final offer." A tic began to pulse in his cheek.

"I'm sure you're offering as much as you believe you are able," said Amelia, adjusting her gloves, "and I thank you for your consideration—"

"One hundred and seventy-five pounds, and all your meals can be taken in the hotel dining room," Walter interrupted.

"But I shall need to eat the food we make if I am to know how it tastes and what to recommend," Amelia pointed out reasonably. "Therefore eating here is an essential part of my job, and can hardly be negotiated as part of my compensation. If anything, I should be paid extra for the time it will involve."

"Mrs. Marshall, I am in a position to pay you two hundred pounds a year, and that, I'm afraid, is my final offer," Walter said weakly.

"We'll take it," said Grace before Amelia could refuse.

"Very well." Amelia decided she had to trust that Grace must know more about such things than she. "Two hundred pounds will do—"

Walter sighed with relief, feeling as if he had won a battle.

"—to start."

JACK SLOWLY SCANNED THE WRITING ON THE CONtract before him, deciphering the words with effort. Reading had always been a challenge for him, and although Genevieve had worked long hours with him he had never mastered it to a degree that made it easy or pleasurable. There had been times when the infuriating words before him had mocked him with their arrogant superiority, enraging him, until he had been reduced to hurling his books against the wall, and once, into the flames of the fireplace. That had been one of the few times Genevieve had ever been genuinely upset with him. Books were too valuable to be abused or destroyed, she had told him firmly. It was better to channel his frustration into something constructive, like punching Eunice's bread dough or chopping firewood. Jack had marched outside and chopped enough firewood to keep the twenty fireplaces of Haydon's estate burning for two days.

He had never enjoyed working in the kitchen.

"Jack! Jack! Where are you?" Annabelle's voice was bright with excitement. "We're back!"

An unfamiliar swell of anticipation rose within him. He stood and awkwardly straightened his rumpled shirt and waistcoat. He had not seen Amelia since making his unforgivably stupid comment about her abilities the previous day in the kitchen. Although Charlotte had told him he should apologize to her, somehow he had not found an opportunity to do so. Amelia had remained closeted in her chamber that night, and an early meeting had forced him to leave first thing that morning for his Inverness office to discuss his increasingly faltering business. That meant he had missed seeing Amelia before Oliver and his sisters overhauled her appearance and dragged her off to her interview at the Royal Hotel. Feeling strangely uncertain, he went into the corridor, anxious to fix whatever damage he had done and see Amelia smile at him once more.

Annabelle, Charlotte, and Grace stood in the corridor, beaming with satisfaction.

"Where's Amelia?"

"You'll never guess," Annabelle told him teasingly.

"I don't want to guess." Had they just left her somewhere, not realizing how dangerous that could be? "Where is she?"

"She's fine, Jack," Charlotte assured him. "She is still at the Royal Hotel. We've sent Oliver back to collect her once she has finished."

"Finished what?" Eunice appeared through the kitchen doorway, wiping her hands on her apron.

"Did the lass get a position?" Doreen shuffled out behind her.

"Really, Jack, you must let me purchase some decent furniture for you," Annabelle chided as she sailed into his drawing room. "These old, dark pieces are horribly ugly."

"Why did you leave Amelia at the hotel?" he demanded.

"We left her there because she was working. At the very least you should have this old sofa of Genevieve's reupholstered, Jack," Grace suggested, looking at where the fabric had split on the armrest. "It looks positively shabby."

"For God's sake, forget the damn furniture! What have you done with Amelia?"

"We got her a job." Annabelle smiled. "Just like we said we would."

"Actually, Amelia got the job on her own," Charlotte amended. "She didn't really need much help from us."

"Except when it came to the question of her salary." Grace giggled. "She was so stunned when Mr. Sweeney offered her a hundred pounds a year, she nearly refused him!"

Doreen's narrow brow wrinkled in bafflement. "That's more than a fair wage for a young, single lass."

"I'm afraid Amelia is somewhat unfamiliar with what most people earn," explained Charlotte. "Given the luxury she is accustomed to, she thought Mr. Sweeney's offer was most unreasonable."

"But ultimately that worked in her favor—Mr. Sweeney was so afraid of losing her that ultimately he agreed to pay her two hundred pounds instead!" Grace finished triumphantly.

Eunice clapped her hands together with delight. "Sweet saints!"

"What is the lass goin' to be doin' for two hundred pounds?" Doreen demanded, suspicious.

"Oh, Doreen, it's positively brilliant," said Annabelle. "She is going to help the hotel organize its special affairs, from the decoration of the rooms to the setting of the tables and the planning of the menus."

"She's even going to introduce themes to these functions, so that the events will always be different and entertaining and terribly stylish," Charlotte added.

"It's perfect for her," reflected Grace. "No one knows more about what's fashionable and fun at these affairs than Amelia does!"

"She cannot do it." Jack's tone was final.

"Of course she can." Annabelle regarded him with impatience. "Amelia is far more talented than you realize, Jack."

"I don't mean that she is not qualified." In truth, Jack was surprised that Amelia had managed to find employment in something so appropriate to her background. "I meant that it's too dangerous."

"Really, Jack, you must get past this idea that Amelia should simply be shut up in a room and never face the world again," said Grace.

"There is an enormous reward on her head and her family is looking for her." Jack was amazed his family couldn't understand the danger. "She cannot be working at a hotel where she is exposed to dozens of people every day, any one of whom might suddenly recognize her and turn her over to the police."

"No one is going to recognize her," Charlotte assured him gently. "You needn't worry."

"You didn't see her before she left the house today." Grace smiled. "I don't think even you would have known her."

"Certainly no one who is looking for a beautiful young heiress who has turned the heads of noblemen from Paris to London is going to connect her with the plain, sober-looking widow who is now toiling at a hotel in Scotland to support herself," pointed out Annabelle.

"And it isn't as if Mrs. Chamberlain just suddenly appeared out of nowhere on her own," Charlotte added. "By introducing her as a relative, we have given her a background and a connection to Inverness that is credible."

"Besides, most people wouldn't think to find a privileged American heiress working at a hotel," argued Grace. "They think like you do, Jack, that she is spoiled and utterly incapable of doing anything worthwhile."

"I never said that."

"Not in those words, perhaps, but you insinuated it just the same. Amelia was terribly hurt, and I don't blame her."

Charlotte regarded him enquiringly. "You did apologize, Jack, didn't you?"

He shrugged his shoulders uncomfortably. "I will."

"Well, you'd better do so as soon as she comes home," Annabelle advised, "because after that you may not have the chance for a while."

"Why not?"

"Because I have invited Amelia to stay with me, and she has agreed."

Jack regarded his sister incredulously. "You what?"

"Really, it's the most sensible thing for everyone, Jack. Having Amelia around has kept you from your next voyage, and I know you must be terribly anxious to leave. You hate to stay put anywhere for more than a few days."

"Amelia will stay with Annabelle, and that will enable you to get on with your affairs, and let poor Oliver, Eunice, and Doreen finally go home," finished Grace.

"An' who said anythin' about us wanting to go home?" Eunice made it sound as if the idea was ridiculous.

"We like lookin' after Jack and the lass," Doreen added emphatically. "'Tis nae bother."

"You're both very sweet, but I'm sure you must find all the hard work you have to do here very tiring," Annabelle insisted. "At home you don't have to do anything. You can just sit and rest."

"I dinna need to sit and rest," Eunice huffed, planting her sturdy hands on her formidable hips. "I've the strength and the energy of a woman half my age, and the good Lord intended for me to use it."

"An' the same goes for me." Doreen snorted with irritation. "The day I canna scrub a floor or push a rag over the furniture will be the day ye can toss me in my coffin and bang down the lid."

"There, you see?" said Jack. "Eunice and Doreen are fine staying here, and I am in no rush to sail again. As a matter of fact I just gave orders for the *Lightning* to leave tomorrow, without me."

"But now that Amelia is going to stay with me, you needn't inconvenience yourself," Annabelle insisted. "You can sail off to Egypt or Africa or wherever it is you're planning to go, and not worry any more about her."

Jack glared helplessly at his sister. Annabelle's generous offer would free him of the responsibility of looking after Amelia, and enable him to get back to the demands of his life. He could set sail the next day on the *Lightning,* secure in the knowledge that she was being well looked after by his family, who would do everything within their power to see that she was safe. It was a perfectly reasonable solution. He should have felt relieved.

Instead he felt utterly hollow.

"Thank you for your offer, Annabelle," he began stiffly, "but Amelia is going to remain here with me."

"Really, Jack, you're not being reasonable—"

"I'm being perfectly reasonable," he countered. "I'm the one whose carriage she climbed into, and I'm the one who agreed to take her away. Amelia is my responsibility, not yours. She stays with me."

"But what will people think?"

"I don't give a damn what people think."

"You may not, but Amelia does."

"No, she doesn't." Jack thought of Amelia scrabbling down the church wall in her wedding gown, and slapping Percy hard across the face in front of eight hundred people. Those were hardly the actions of a woman who was overly concerned with appearances. "Amelia is American. She does what she wants to do."

"What if she does not want to stay here?"

Charlotte's question took him by surprise. "Did she say she did not want to stay here?"

"Not in those words." Charlotte regarded him steadily. "But she was very upset by the way you spoke about her yesterday."

"If she doesn't want to stay here, then she is free to go wherever she bloody well pleases," he retaliated brusquely. "I don't give a damn."

He turned and stalked angrily from the room, leaving his sisters staring in wonder after him.

A MELIA PUSHED OPEN THE HEAVY DOOR AND WEARILY stepped inside the faintly lit front vestibule. The spicy-sweet scent of baked apples and cinnamon mingled with the lingering aroma of beef-and-onion stew. It was late and she knew the food had already been served and put away, but the memory of it wafted in tantalizing currents upon the air, filling her senses with a warm, comfortable feeling. She sighed and stripped off her gloves.

It was good to be home.

She unpinned her hat as she walked toward the staircase, eager to wash and go to bed. The day had been long and tiring, and while Mr. Sweeney had apologized profusely for keeping her so late, he had asked that she be back to work by eight o'clock the following morning. There were a dozen or more upcoming events he wanted to work on with her, each of which would require meetings with the clients and then the organization of everything necessary to create a unique and scintillating atmosphere. Amelia had no doubt that she could envision ideas for all of them, for she had been to enough balls and luncheons and teas in her life to provide her with inspiration for scores of affairs. Doing the necessary administrative work to bring these events to fruition, however, was another matter entirely. She was expected to draft the letters and place all the necessary orders, then ensure that everything arrived on schedule and more, on budget. She was reasonably adept with figures and believed she would have little trouble keeping track of the expenses she incurred for each event. What would prove more challenging would be setting a budget for each spectacle, and then staying within its limits. Budgets were not something with which she had a great deal of experience.

"You're back," drawled a low, accusing voice.

Jack's towering form was silhouetted against the dim light spilling from his study. It was too dark to make out his face, but she could see he wore no jacket and his badly wrinkled shirt had escaped the confines of his trousers.

"You startled me." She lowered the hand that had flown to her throat.

He slouched against the wall and raised a bottle to his lips. "Did I? How common of me. Not what you're accustomed to, I suppose—being with someone so low and base." He wiped his mouth with the back of his hand.

Amelia frowned, surprised by his obvious hostility. "You're drunk."

"I suppose I am." He shrugged. "Come have a drink and we can be drunk together."

"I'm tired," she informed him with stiff civility. "I believe I shall say good night and retire to my chamber."

"Now those are the words of a proper English duchess if ever I heard any." His voice was laden with contempt. "I'd have thought you braver than that, Amelia. Having slapped one viscount in a ballroom full of aristocrats and left a duke sweating at the altar, I'd not have thought you a girl afraid of indulging in one simple drink with a lowborn sailor like me."

"I'm not afraid."

Even as she spoke the words, she knew they were not precisely true. She remembered when she had inadvertently roused him from his sleep a few nights earlier. He had seized her wrist with bruising strength as he stared at her, his eyes filled with fear and ice-cold fury. In that moment, she had known he was capable of violence. Not toward her, but toward the demons that haunted him. There were ghosts in Jack's past—cruel, vicious memories that still preyed upon a starving, shivering boy who had been forced to survive an unbearable life she could scarcely imagine.

"You're not afraid, are you, my sheltered little American?" He raised his bottle and took another swig before finishing darkly, "You should be."

"Why?" she asked, unable to comprehend what had aroused the resentment he seemed to suddenly have toward her. "What have I done to make you so angry with me, Jack?"

He looked at her a long moment, weighing her question. She seemed different to him somehow, like the beautiful young heiress who had scrambled into his carriage, and yet not like her at all. It was not her dour-looking outfit that accounted for her change, for he had seen her in everything from the most lavish of wedding gowns to the simplest of his own wrinkled shirts. Mere clothes could not begin to diminish her uncommon beauty. No, something more had been done to her. He frowned as he raked her with his gaze, taking in her darkened hair and brows, the matronly spectacles obscuring her eyes, the deftly painted shadows that accentuated the faint wrinkles of her forehead and bruised the skin beneath her lower lashes. Oliver's makeup, he realized, unaccountably annoyed by how effective it was. The old thief and his sisters had said they would transform her so that no one would recognize her. They had taken her and turned her into someone else.

And they had stolen her from Jack in the process.

"Go to bed, Amelia," he snapped. "You'll need your rest for packing in the morning." He turned and staggered back into his study.

Amelia stared after him, stunned. She had defied him by going out and getting work, and he was punishing her by severing the ties of their friendship and casting her out. While she had initially accepted Annabelle's invitation to stay with her and her family, Amelia had discovered that deep down she didn't want to leave Jack and Oliver, Eunice and Doreen. She had intended to graciously thank Annabelle for her kindness the next day, and tell her that she preferred to stay where she was. But now Jack was throwing her out.

You can trust me, he had told her. How eagerly she had grasped those words. She had thought he was her friend. She had believed he was the first man who appreciated her for what she was and what she could become, instead of all that had marked her as a means for gain to every other man she had ever known. But mired within his appreciation of her was the untenable condition that she remain helplessly dependent upon him, like some little lost bird that could never learn to fend for itself. It was more than unacceptable. It was vile and controlling. In his own way, Jack Kent was every bit as dominating as her family, and Percy and Lord Whitcliffe. At one time she would have reluctantly accepted this, would have found a way to silently tolerate it, the way she had tolerated so much else in her life. But she was not the same Amelia Belford who had allowed herself to be used and manipulated by others for so many years. She was changing, and she would be bloody damned if she wouldn't let him know it.

"You lied to me," she hissed, tearing off her spectacles and hurling them down as she marched into the study after him. "You told me I could trust you—that you were my friend. Then the minute I do something of which you don't approve, you throw me onto the street. What did I do that was so wrong, Jack?" Her voice was shaking with fury. "All I did was go out and get a job, so for the first time in my life I could have some degree of independence, instead of always relying on the generosity of others—including you. Why is that so terrible?"

"I don't give a damn about the blasted job," Jack snarled. "Go out and get ten jobs if you want—each one under a different bloody disguise, if it pleases you."

"If you don't care about the job, then why are you so angry?"

"I'm not goddamn angry!"

She stared at him, bewildered. His body was rigid as he glared at her, a terrible mixture of rage and resentment churning through him.

"You *are* angry," she insisted. "Why?"

What could he tell her? he wondered helplessly. That he was angry because she was leaving him? That nothing had been the same since she came into his life, and now he was loathe to be without her? It was as pathetic as it was ridiculous. She couldn't stay with him. He had no right to her, and no hope of ever having any right to her. No matter how faded and dull Oliver and his sisters tried to make her, no matter whether she was gilded with her father's wealth or stripped down to the essential, glorious core of her being, she was as unattainable to him as the moon. Amelia had been reared in a world of overwhelming privilege and protection, and with or without her money she remained what she had always been: hopelessly fine and rare and pure. She was as magnificent as a glittering star, as shimmering and lovely and beyond his reach as the sunlight that played in silvery sparkles upon the ocean.

Such a precious treasure was not meant for him.

Despite all that Haydon and Genevieve had done for him, despite all the hateful lessons and expensive clothes and determined attempts to refine him, he could never escape what he was. The bastard result of some filthy, disease-ridden coupling, a lad who lacked the common birthright of even a proper name or home. If he closed his eyes and tried very hard a faded image of his mother came to mind, all round and soft and ripe with the smell of unwashed wool and cheap perfume and whiskey. But he had not known then that she was cheap and dirty, had not understood that her rouged cheeks and caked powder were the marks of a woman who lifted her skirts for any man who opened his wallet. He had thought her pretty then, had looked forward to the painfully brief visits that she had made to the filthy shack he lived in with that old prick and his wife. His mother had promised to take him away, had promised that it would only be a little longer before she had saved enough to buy a cottage that the two of them could live in. And stupidly, pathetically, he had believed her. He had clung to her tightly corseted form and breathed in the familiar scent of her and listened to her talk as she ruffled her fingers through his hair, pleading with her to stay, begging her not to leave him. But she always did. She left him again and again, almost killing him with despair each time he watched her disappear down the path that led her back to wherever it was from which she came. Until finally she didn't come anymore.

At the time he believed she had merely been delayed, for months and months and ultimately, over a year. And on that day he fought back, when he finally killed that old bastard and ran away, he had felt absolutely certain he would find her. That he would simply go to the nearest village and she would be there, with her rouged lips and her gentle hands, ready to take him in her arms and protect him. At the age of nine, he had no inkling of how very big the world was, and how extraordinarily unimportant and despised his place within it.

He struggled to stifle the sob rising from his chest.

"Jack?"

He stared in confusion at Amelia, wondering how long she had been watching him. Her eyes were wide with concern. It was as if she had seen something, had pierced the layers of his carefully cultivated indifference and caught a glimpse of the pain and loss that lay festering there. He didn't want her pity and concern. He was supposed to be looking after her, not the other way around. He struggled to adopt a cool derision that he hoped cut through whatever she imagined she saw and left her with the impression that he was merely a rude and unfeeling bastard.

"Leave me if you want to," he snarled. "I don't give a shit."

Amelia winced as if he had slapped her.

But something kept her there, kept her from wheeling about and storming from Jack's study, from shouting for Oliver to come down at once so that he could drive her over to Annabelle's house immediately. It was obscured by the shadows of Jack's gaze, but Amelia could see it nonetheless. An emotion so deep and desperate that once she had unveiled it from the rest of his profoundly boorish performance, she was amazed that she had not recognized it earlier. Everything in his manner and stance and words was telling her that she meant nothing to him, and that she should go.

Yet within the smoky gray of his anguished eyes, he was pleading with her to stay.

She moved toward him with steady purpose, her gaze never leaving his. And when she stood so close to him that she could almost feel the powerful beating of his heart against her breast, she raised her hand and laid her palm upon the ragged white scar on his cheek, holding him fast.

"I will not leave you, Jack," she told him simply, "unless you truly wish it."

Jack stared at her, mesmerized by her words, her scent, her touch. She was promising to stay with him. But why? In that brief, frozen moment, it scarcely seemed to matter. He had thought he was losing her, and suddenly he wasn't. His mind was too distorted by rage and need to analyze it further. Wanting to seal her pledge, to bind her to him so that she could not change her mind, he dropped his bottle and wrapped his arms around her, imprisoning her against him.

And then, with a haunting despair that he felt surely was going to destroy him, he sobbed and captured her lips with his.

Amelia released her hold upon Jack's scarred cheek to wrap her arms around his neck, pulling him down as she opened her mouth to him. Her body crushed against his with a frantic cry, feeling the heat and strength and power of him closing around her in an impenetrable shield. Desire pounded through her, heating her blood and setting fire to her flesh until she could think of nothing but the whiskey-sweet taste of his mouth, the rough scrape of his jaw against her cheek, the hard press of his manhood against the melting triangle between her thighs. Somewhere in the faraway reaches of her mind she knew that it was wrong, but a staggering need had obscured all reason, until she was aware of nothing but the hunger to hold him, and touch him, and kiss him, to reach into his soul and make him understand that she would not abandon him, regardless of what others had done in the past. And so she plunged her hands into the dark tangle of his hair and delved his mouth with her tongue, tasting him deeply, passionately, offering herself to him as she made him hers, not caring if it was right or not, not caring about anything except the fact that she wanted him with a desperation that obliterated everything. Nothing was clear except the granite heat of his body as it molded itself to hers, the ravishing caress of his hands as they roamed across her breasts and back and hips, the rigid length of his arousal as it stroked against her, filling her with aching need. She wanted to wash away the pain of whatever was tormenting him so, to cleanse his mind and ease his heart until he no longer needed to lose himself to the hollow respite of alcohol and rage. And so she did not stop him as he fumbled with the buttons on her jacket, did not so much as whimper a feeble protest when he finally growled in frustration and tore the offending garment open. The linen of her blouse disintegrated next, but all she could do was tilt her head back as he buried his face against the soft swell of her breasts, a low, feline cry rippling from her throat as his hands gripped the cool silk of her corset.

Jack dragged his tongue over Amelia's breasts, his senses drowning in heat and taste and touch. A claret nipple blossomed from the lacy edge of her corset and he hungrily closed his mouth over it, sucking upon it long and hard, swirling his tongue over the tender peak until the pressure of Amelia's fingers biting into his shoulders told him she could bear no more. And so he moved to the other, drawing it from its fabric and whalebone nest and suckling it between his lips and teeth until it sprang sweetly ardent against his tongue. He ran impatient fingers down the intricate webbing at her back and found the clasp of her skirt, which he released with a practiced hand. Her hooped petticoats fell next, an elaborate confection of lace and bands of silk-covered steel, which pooled round her ankles in an ivory puddle. All that remained beyond her corset now were her stockings and drawers, a flimsy affair of frills and rosettes that he found maddeningly arousing. He slipped one hand inside the fabric opening between her legs and fondled the satiny mound beneath, holding her fast with one arm as he kissed her deeply, assaulting her with a storm of caresses and sensations as he drew her to him, feeling the brief tension of her resistance erode as he slipped his fingers into the slick petals of her. Sweet, wet heat poured over his hand and he growled with satisfaction, arrogantly pleased that he could arouse her so.

He eased his fingers into her, exploring the intimate folds and pleats, stroking her and stretching her as his mouth tasted the delectable ripeness of her lips. He placed his knee between her legs and pushed her thighs wider, opening her to his gentle touch as he began to rain starving kisses upon her naked shoulders, her slender arms, down the flat plane of her corseted belly, until finally he was kneeling before her. She gasped with shock but it was too late, for he grasped her wrists and pinned them hard against the wall as he flicked his tongue into her hot coral cleft. Her thighs clamped together and she mewled a desperate protest, but he only tasted her more, his tongue slipping in sensual circles across the delicate sleek flesh. He alternated his caresses, first light and teasing, then harder and more demanding, patiently stoking the flames of her until she released the breath she had been holding and the iron clasp of her thighs relaxed.

Amelia leaned against the wall and fought for the strength to stand, overwhelmed by the exquisitely forbidden sensations tearing through her. The sight of Jack on his knees lapping at the dark wet pool of her woman-hood sent shivers of excitement through her. She was most certainly wanton and depraved, she realized, to take pleasure in such a decadently indecent assault. And yet she could not stop herself from enduring his glorious torture, no, instead she stood frozen and breathless, appalled by what he was doing, but even more terrified that he would stop. She could have moved away if she wanted to, for he had released one hand to probe her innermost passage with his finger, thrusting in and out of her as his mouth tasted her with an insistent, steady rhythm. Instead she pulled him closer as she opened herself, shifting and arching against him as he continued to ravish her with his mouth. Sheer, undiluted pleasure was building within her in ever intensifying waves, stretching and rippling, while her breath was reduced to tiny, desperate sips. It was excruciating to be tormented so, to be hovering on the threshold of ecstasy and yet unable to leap over it, excruciating and agonizing and exquisite. A hollow ache was blooming inside her, making her feel restless and desperate, and so she reached for more, suddenly rigid except for the ragged flutter of her chest as she fought to fill her lungs and somehow withstand the unbearable torment of Jack's caresses. Reached and gasped and reached, until finally there was no more breath to be had, nothing except the tiny sob that spilled from the back of her throat as she arched suddenly against him.

And then she was exploding into a thousand fiery pieces, quivering and trembling as she disintegrated into a silvery shower.

Jack caught Amelia as she collapsed against him, holding her close as he lowered her to the floor. He shrugged off his shirt, then tore open the fastenings of his trousers and peeled away the layers of wool, kicking off his shoes and stockings. He wanted her with a staggering desperation, a need so awesome and consuming that he did not think he could bear it. She was his, he told himself desperately. She had given herself to him, had kissed him and opened herself to him and wrapped her arms around him, willingly offering him her heat and tenderness and trust. If that did not make her his, then what did? He was wrong for her, he knew that, just as he knew that she was wrong for him. No woman of Amelia's birthright and grace and tender romanticism could ever survive a life with a baseborn, despised criminal like him. And yet in that moment nothing mattered beyond the apricot flicker of firelight as it played against her heated cheeks, and the soft pants gusting from her throat as she lay before him, staring at him with smoldering eyes. *I will not leave you,* she had told him, the words filled with innocent, fervent promise. But she would leave him, and the realization was like a dirk plunging into his chest, leaving him empty and bleeding and torn. She was already leaving him, although she didn't know it, with her growing independence and her burgeoning discovery of her own strengths and abilities. She no longer needed him, and with every day that passed, she would need him even less. *Stay with me,* he pleaded silently as he stretched over her, cupping her face with his hands and lowering his mouth to hers. *Do not leave me,* he begged feverishly, his hardness poised against the wet heat of her, feeling as if he were about to cry. *I need you,* he confessed brokenly, wanting her to understand even though he did not understand it himself. All this he wanted to say to her and more, certain that if he could but make her realize the depths of his need for her, then she would never be able to go. He inhaled a ragged, steadying breath, staring at her in despair, determined to make her his and knowing that it could never be.

And then he whispered her name and drove himself

deep inside her, losing himself forever as he crushed his mouth to hers.

He felt her freeze beneath him, her body locked in a startled spasm of pain and fear. He cursed silently, hating himself for being so selfish and lacking in control that he did not remember that she was a virgin and needed special care.

"It's all right, Amelia," he managed roughly. "Hold fast to me—the pain will pass soon."

In truth he had no idea whether it would or not, for he had never lain with an inexperienced woman before. It was torture to be so tightly sheathed within her velvet heat and not be able to move, but he held himself steady nonetheless, vowing that he would rather die than cause her any further pain. To ease her anxiety he began to rain tender kisses upon her eyes, her cheeks, along the elegant curve of her jaw, and down into the fluttering hollow at the base of her throat. He stroked the silky fall of her darkened hair, which had escaped its pins and spilled in shimmering waves across the intricately woven carpet. And just as he began to fear that she would never experience the pleasure he so wanted to give her, she sighed and shifted slightly, wrapping her arms around him as the tension seeped from her like sand spilling from a sack.

He started to move slowly within her, gently easing himself in and out of her tight heat, stretching her, filling her, binding her to him with every aching thrust. And then he slipped his hand between them and stroked the pearly center of her, rousing her once more with his kisses and caresses and gentle thrusting, making his own pleasure even more intense as she began to twist and pant beneath him. *Stay with me,* he pleaded as she gripped him ever tighter and began to suckle upon his lips and jaw and neck. *I will keep you safe,* he vowed, moving faster and deeper within her, wanting to lose himself in the glorious depths of her. He would stay that way forever, buried within Amelia's magnificent body, with her softness flexing against him and her fragrance and tiny gasps intoxicating his senses. Faster and harder and deeper he thrust, trying to bind her to him, wanting to be a part of her, not just in that moment but forever. In and out he moved, taking her, possessing her, giving himself to her until finally they moved with one flesh, one breath, one heart. He wanted to slow himself, to make it last forever, but his body was treacherous and moved faster instead. And suddenly he was falling into an abyss, and he cried out in wonder and in anguish, crushing his mouth to hers as he spilled himself inside her. Again and again he drove into her, fighting to keep her, until finally he could endure no more. He gathered her into his arms and rolled onto his side, kissing her with shattered hope as he cradled her body with his own.

Do not leave me, he pleaded, wondering how he would bear it when she did.

He broke the kiss and closed his eyes, unable to look at her for fear that she might see the painful tearing of his soul.

Amelia lay her cheek against Jack's chest, feeling the rapid pounding of his heart. Nothing had prepared her for what had just passed between them. Nothing. She lay perfectly still, listening to him breathe, wondering if he were experiencing emotions nearly as intense and confusing as those that were coursing through her. She wanted him to say something, to tell her what must happen between them now.

He said nothing.

A quiet forlornness seized her, vanquishing the overwhelming joy that had been there moments earlier. Jack would never want to marry her, she realized. To him she was little more than a spoiled heiress, who was incapable of understanding the world from which he came or the dreadful life he had been forced to endure. That was why he had not shared the truth of his past with her. For the first time in her life, her birthright actually discredited her. Perhaps if she still had a dowry, she might have had more appeal for him, for at least then she would have been able to offer him some assistance with the building of his shipping line. As it was, however, she had nothing. Nothing except herself and a pitifully inadequate income of two hundred pounds a year, providing she didn't do something to get herself fired while she charted the unfamiliar waters of being an employee.

If that had been enough, surely this was the moment for him to say so.

He said nothing.

Her tear-blurred gaze fell upon the portrait of Charlotte hanging above the fireplace. When Amelia had first seen it she had not known that the girl seated in the chair was Jack's sister—the namesake of his precious clipper ship. Now that Amelia had met Charlotte, the painting held greater meaning. If Charlotte attempted to pick up the rose at her feet she would injure herself on its thorns, but if she left it where it was, the flower would die. In her life, if Charlotte attempted to walk then everyone would judge her for her affliction—with pity, of course, but also with the conviction that there were many things she could not do. Yet if Charlotte did not try to walk, her life would be cloistered and small. Amelia thought of how lovely Charlotte was as she awkwardly moved about, how she had insisted upon accompanying Amelia to her interview, even though that had necessitated that she climb many steps and endure the stares of others. Yet Charlotte had smiled at each stranger she passed, trying to put them at ease. Although she lacked the vivaciousness of Annabelle and the practical confidence of Grace, Charlotte had overcome her considerable challenges and created a fulfilling life for herself.

Perhaps, Amelia reflected shakily, she could do the same.

Loud, long snores cracked the quiet of the small study. Jack's hold upon her had eased, enabling Amelia to extract herself from the warm cocoon of his body. Feeling cold and ashamed, she quickly gathered up her discarded clothing and dressed. The combination of liquor and exhaustion had put Jack in a deep slumber. Moving carefully so as not to waken him, Amelia gently covered him with his wrinkled shirt and trousers, then bent to brush a dark lock of hair from his forehead.

She left the room and quietly closed the door, destroyed by the realization that she had to leave him, before he completely shattered her heart.

Chapter Eleven

S HE'S GONE."

The old man tapped a bent, chalky finger thought-fully against his chin. "Gone where?"

Neil Dempsey shifted uneasily on his blistered, aching feet. He dreaded it when Lord Hutton asked him a question to which he had no answer. Furious with himself for failing to comprehend the potential importance of the mysterious young woman who had suddenly appeared in Jack Kent's life, he flipped back to the previous day's entries in his leather-bound journal of notes.

"She went off by carriage early yesterday mornin', and to my knowledge, has not returned. The old driver, Oliver, came back without her at around a quarter past nine in the morning. At about a quarter of ten he came out again, strugglin' to carry some boxes, which looked to be the same ladies' garment boxes the old maid, Doreen, had brought into the house a few nights earlier. He placed them inside the carriage afore drivin' off, and returned again about an hour later. At ten after eleven, Oliver came out of the house with Mr. Kent and drove him down to his office, where he stayed until just after two in the mornin'. When Mr. Kent finally emerged, he required assistance to walk, which Oliver provided with some difficulty, Mr. Kent bein' a very large man."

"What was wrong with him?" demanded Lord Hutton, struggling to raise himself off his pillows. "Was he sick?"

"He did lose his supper on the side of the road—"

"Was he rushed home? Was a doctor sent for?"

"—after which Oliver made him stumble beside the carriage a mile or so in the cool night air, in an attempt to sober him up."

The earl huffed impatiently, annoyed. "Go on."

"He left the house at noon today, and went to the offices of the Royal Bank of Scotland, where he met for nearly two hours with a Mr. Stoddart, the bank's manager. After that he went down to the docks, where he supervised the final loading of the *Lightning,* which set sail for Ceylon at precisely five-thirty."

Lord Hutton sighed. "With him aboard, I presume."

"No. He returned home shortly after, and was still there when I left at eleven o'clock." Neil closed his journal. "It seems he changed his plans."

"Indeed." Edward sank back against the damp linens of his bed and steepled his hands together, thinking. He knew that Jack was typically desperate to be at sea, and rarely stayed in either Inverness or London longer than a week or so. He also knew that Jack's shipping company was suffering dire financial consequences as a result of the recent loss of the *Liberty* in London. Had the urgent need to secure more financial assistance prevented Jack from sailing on the *Lightning*? Did he feel that he could be of greater use to his ailing company if he remained in Inverness, negotiating further loans with the bank and perhaps endeavoring to secure more contracts? Or had he forfeited his trip for more personal reasons? Edward had the power to make some enquiries as to the nature of Jack's negotiations with the bank, but to do so was dangerous. It would only invite curiosity and gossip, and that was something he was determined to avoid.

"Fine, then," he said, suddenly weary. "Tomorrow you will watch him again."

"If the girl returns, do you want me to follow her as well?" asked Neil. "Find out where she went?"

"If you follow her, then you cannot follow Kent."

"I could get someone else—"

"No."

"I've a friend who's very reliable, yer lordship. Very discreet. He wouldna say a word—"

"If I have to say no again, our association is finished."

"Aye, yer lordship," Neil returned swiftly, anxious to appease the old bugger. "I'll nae let Kent out of my sight."

"See that you don't."

The door swung open with a bang, and the bounteous form of Mrs. Quigley marched into the room.

"Here now, what's he doin' here?" she demanded, casting a glacial look at Neil. "I told ye there were nae visitors today."

"And I told you to bloody well knock on my goddamn door before entering my chamber!" Edward glared at her, but whatever air of menace he might have achieved disintegrated beneath the sudden streak of pain that coursed through his belly. Feeling as if a dirk had been plunged into his gut, he gripped his stomach with his emaciated hands and clamped his mouth shut, fighting to smother the cry that had escaped the back of his throat.

"All right, then, bide a wee bit, 'tis nearly past." Mrs. Quigley's voice softened slightly as she swiftly mixed water and laudanum in a glass and brought it to his melded lips. "Here now, drink this." She threaded her well-padded arm underneath his shoulders and pulled him up a little, until his gaunt cheek was pressed like a child's against the plump pillow of her bosom. "Drink it down and then have a sleep, and ye'll be feelin' much better, I promise."

Edward choked the bitter elixir down. It did not ease the pain, but the possibility that it might dull it eventually, or at least make him groggy enough to sleep, was enough. When the glass was empty he pressed his lips together once more, still fighting the grip of pain that had seized his bloated, rotting belly. He allowed Mrs. Quigley to lay him back against his pillows like a bairn, too weak to protest. He wished Dempsey had not been there to witness his frailty. He wanted Mrs. Quigley to order the young fool out, before his treacherous innards did something else to humiliate him.

"Ye should go now," Mrs. Quigley informed Neil as she briskly adjusted the covers over Edward. "His lordship needs to rest."

Neil regarded Lord Hutton with uncertainty, afraid to leave without his dismissal. "If there's anythin' else, yer lordship . . ."

A loud eruption of gas escaped Edward's body.

"Get out!" he bellowed, mortified to the depths of his being. *"Now!"*

Neil raced out the door as fast as his feet would carry him, nearly knocking over an elaborate porcelain vase in the process.

"You go, too, Mrs. Quigley." If his bowels were about to do anything more, he was determined to endure it alone.

"I hope ye're nae thinkin' I'm bothered by a wee bit o' wind," Mrs. Quigley said sternly as she opened the windows. "We all have to relieve ourselves when the body tells us 'tis time—that's the way the good Lord made us. Even I've been known to use the privy on occasion." She went to the washbasin and wrung out a cloth.

"At least you can still get to the bloody privy," Edward grumbled.

"Aye, and so could you if ye'd rest when I told ye to and stopped drinkin' those spirits ye keep tucked beneath yer pillow," she told him, gently sponging the perspiration from his face. "I've half a mind to tell that maid she's out on her ear if she brings them to ye again."

"Those spirits are the only thing that keep me relatively civilized," Edward said warningly. "You don't want to find out what I'm like without them."

"Dinna be thinkin' ye can chase me off with yer ranting and threats when things dinna go yer way," she countered, washing his hands. "Ye may be nae so swack as ye used to be, but there's more than a breath or two left in ye yet. As long as there is, I'm fixin' to stay with ye."

"If you think I find that reassuring, I don't."

"If ye think I feel sorry for ye, I don't," she retaliated evenly. "Rest now," she ordered, rinsing out her cloth in the washbasin. "I'll be back in a wee bit with somethin' for ye to eat."

"I'm not hungry."

"Ye will be after ye've slept a little."

"No, I won't."

"Well, that's a pity, then, since I was thinkin' to bring ye a nice glass of port with it, just to help yer digestion."

"You can bring the port and leave the rest."

"Ye can eat yer supper and then have the port."

Edward sighed and closed his eyes, too exhausted to joust anymore. "Fine," he muttered, his senses veiled beneath the dizzying mantle of his medication. "Now leave me."

She left the room in a swish of righteous satisfaction.

He lay there despondently, waiting for sleep to overtake him. In all the months she had tended him, Mrs. Quigley had never permitted him to have a drink.

Either she was becoming more indulgent, or he had even less time than he thought.

AMELIA STUFFED A HALF DOZEN PAGES OF NOTES into her reticule as she hurried down the steps of the Royal Hotel. It was already half past six o'clock, and she knew Oliver would have been waiting for her at least an hour. She still had much work to do on the arrangements for the MacCulloch wedding, but she would have to do it later that night, after dinner.

In the week since she had moved into the home of Annabelle and her husband, Oliver had very kindly offered to drive her both to and from her work at the hotel every day. At first Amelia had protested that this was far too much of an inconvenience for him, but Oliver had been adamant. Ultimately Annabelle convinced Amelia that she might as well resign herself to it, since Oliver was not likely to change his mind. It also made things easier in Annabelle's household, as she and her husband had four children, and between all of them their coachman was already well occupied. It had the added benefit of keeping Amelia in touch with Jack's household, so that every day she was able to enquire about Eunice and Doreen. After she had been well versed as to what the two elderly women were busy cooking, cleaning, or complaining about, she would be silent for a moment. And then, feigning only the mildest of interest, she would ask about Jack, her expression bland as she hungrily devoured whatever scraps of information Oliver might have for her.

She had left Jack's home the morning after their shocking intimacy without seeing him to say good-bye.

She had attempted to write him a letter in which she explained her hasty departure, but an overwhelming sense of shame and confusion had left her unable to find the necessary words. And so ultimately she had left saying nothing to him whatsoever. While Eunice, Doreen and Oliver had been openly disappointed that she was leaving, they seemed to accept her explanation that it was simply more fitting for her to stay with Annabelle and her husband. Amelia had pointed out that her departure freed Jack of his responsibility for her, which meant that he could now sail with his ships wherever it was that he needed to go, while Oliver, Eunice and Doreen could return home to Haydon and Genevieve's estate.

Strangely, Jack had remained at his home, and consequently so did the elderly trio. Amelia could not imagine what was keeping Jack in Inverness when he had made it so clear that his business required him to travel immediately, but she tried not to dwell on it. She had liberated him from his role as her protector. By doing so, she was now learning to cope with a wholly foreign measure of freedom and responsibility. Of course Annabelle and her husband were providing Amelia with a place to live, but in her role as Mrs. Marshall Chamberlain she was experiencing an autonomy unlike anything she had ever known.

She rose each day to carefully apply her makeup and arrange her darkened hair as Oliver, Eunice, Annabelle, and Grace had painstakingly taught her, before going to work at the Royal Hotel. Although the hours were long and her work challenging, she was finding her fledgling career very rewarding. Mrs. MacCulloch was extremely pleased with Amelia's tastefully innovative suggestions for her daughter's wedding, which was now promising to be one of the greatest social events of the year in Inverness. The wedding itself was still two weeks away, but already Mrs. MacCulloch had been praising Amelia's style and vision to friends and associates, who were eagerly booking dinners and events well into the following year—on the condition that Amelia be in charge of organizing them. Mr. Sweeney was so thrilled with the escalation in new business that he had given Amelia a raise of an additional twenty pounds a year. Amelia did not think twenty pounds was very much, but Annabelle had told her that two hundred and twenty pounds a year was an exceptionally generous salary for a young woman, and Amelia realized she had to trust her on that. She was a long way from her coddled existence as Amelia Belford, the bride-to-be of the Duke of Whitcliffe. For the first time she felt as if she exercised some control over the course of her life, and more, she felt like she was doing something challenging and useful, in which she was renowned not merely for her wealth, but for her own singular abilities.

It was a wonderful feeling.

"Evenin', Mrs. Chamberlain," said Oliver, for the benefit of anyone who might have been near as he opened the carriage door for her.

"Good evening, Oliver. I'm so sorry to have kept you waiting—"

Her words disintegrated into a startled gasp as her reticule was suddenly jerked off her wrist.

"My notes!" Amelia cried in horror as a small figure raced down the street. "Stop, thief!" She gathered her skirts and ran after the child as best as she could, given the cumbersome burden of her petticoats.

"Here, now—come back!" Realizing he couldn't run after the two of them, Oliver climbed back onto his seat and snapped his reins, sending the carriage clattering forward.

A heavyset gentleman grabbed the lad as he sped by. "Got you, you wee ruffian!" he proclaimed triumphantly, gripping the boy by his filthy coat.

"Let go, ye pissin' bugger!" The lad kneed the man hard in his groin.

"Sweet Jesus!" Looking as though he might faint, the man released his hold. "You goddamn little—"

The lad was off and running again, cleverly scooting back and forth as he avoided the outstretched hands of the other men who now only halfheartedly tried to capture him. Amelia watched in defeat as the boy zipped down a narrow alley. She would never be able to catch up to him, she realized hopelessly. All her precious notes were lost, which meant hours of work would have to be done again.

A shriek of outrage burst from the alley, followed by a foul streak of child-pitched cursing. Praying that this captor was better able to protect himself than the last, Amelia began to run once again. Her breathing was labored and her ribs flexed painfully against the constriction of her corset as she hurried down the narrow laneway and turned a corner.

"Let go, ye stinkin' old bastard!" swore the boy, struggling wildly.

He twisted and turned in a desperate attempt to land a blow, but Oliver was having none of it. With one gnarled hand holding fast to a tangled hank of hair and the other wrenching the boy's arm behind his back, the old man appeared to have the outraged thief firmly under control.

"Ye may as well stop yer thrashin' about, because I'm nae lettin' ye go until ye've returned the lady's reticule and said ye're sorry," Oliver sternly informed the youth. "I'm nae goin' to turn ye over to the police—do ye hear?"

"Soddin' liar!"

"I truly just want my bag back," Amelia assured the boy. "It's no good to you anyway—there's no money or jewels or anything of that kind in it."

The lad stopped struggling suddenly and flashed Amelia a look of pure disgust. "There ain't?"

"I'm afraid not."

He looked thoroughly annoyed, as if Amelia had totally wasted his time. "Fine, then," he relented, glaring at Oliver. "Let me go, ye old bag o' bones, so I can pull it from my coat."

"I'll get it," said Oliver, who knew better than to trust the little wretch. He released his hold on the boy's hair while keeping his skinny arm held securely behind his back. "An' if ye try to kick me, I swear I'll blister yer backside so ye'll nae be able to sit for a week." With that improbable threat hanging between them, Oliver reached into the boy's coat and retrieved the reticule from where he had stuffed it.

"There." He passed the silk-and-velvet bag to Amelia. "Now apologize to the lass."

The boy snorted with contempt. "Why? She's probably got a hundred of them bags at home. She wasn't goin' to miss one o' them."

"Apologize, ye wee ruffian, afore I change my mind and hand ye to the bobbies."

The lad glowered, but it was clear that Oliver's threat had at least some affect. He shifted his glare to Amelia. "Sorry," he bit out succinctly, the word dripping scorn.

"There now, was that so hard? Ye young thieves today have nae honor or tact," Oliver complained, still holding the lad by his wrist. "Now, when I was a lad—"

"If we're finished, I'm goin'," the lad interrupted rudely.

"Where are you going?" asked Amelia as Oliver reluctantly released him.

The boy stared at her with naked hostility. "Why? So ye can send the bobbies to nab me once ye're off in yer fancy carriage?"

The loathing oozing from him was so intense it took Amelia by surprise. His eyes were a dark, clear green, and the only part of him that wasn't utterly coated in filth. Was this how Jack and his brothers and sisters had been when Genevieve rescued them from prison? she wondered. Had they been so hungry and desperate and hardened by their horrible existence that they immediately hated everyone who had more than they did?

"I was just wondering if you would like to come home and have dinner with me."

Both the lad and Oliver looked at her in astonishment.

The lad recovered first, snorting with derision. "Ye must think I've piss for brains, to think a lady like you would have me in her home. Or were ye plannin' to feed me some old, greasy scraps in the yard, like a dog?" He spat on the ground, making it clear what he thought of that idea.

"I'm inviting you to eat a nice hot dinner at the table with me and the rest of the family," Amelia told him.

"Course ye are," drawled the boy sarcastically. "Ye're thinkin' what a fine thing it is to have me sharin' a plate with yer brats. Sort of a lesson in life, like. Sod it. I dinna need them lookin' down their noses at me."

"Actually, I don't have any children," Amelia told him, but it suddenly occurred to her that Annabelle did. How would her hosts feel if Amelia showed up with this extremely belligerent young thief and asked that he be welcomed in their beautiful home? Would Annabelle think this was a noble and generous thing to do? Or would she worry that the boy might curse and swear in front of her children, frightening and confusing them?

"There's nae lads or lasses at Jack's," Oliver pointed out, attuned to her concern. "We could take him there."

Amelia bit her lip, uncertain. "I wouldn't want to disturb Jack." In truth, she didn't want to even see him, but she could hardly tell Oliver that.

"Ye wouldn't," Oliver assured her. "He's taken to workin' late each night. I'm nae supposed to fetch him this evening 'til after midnight, and I'm certain between you, Eunice and Doreen, ye could have this lad well fed and even cleaned up a wee bit by then."

"Here now, what are ye blatherin' about?" demanded the boy. "I'm nae cleanin' up nothin'. Ye can take me as I am," he declared forcefully, "or bugger off. I've other places to go where they don't give a piss what I look like."

"That's because the people there look and smell even worse than ye," Oliver said impatiently. "If ye want to enjoy what I'm sure will be the best meal ye've ever had in yer life, ye'll shut yer filthy mouth and let us scour some o' that dirt off ye."

The boy folded his arms defiantly across his lean chest. "Piss off."

"You needn't decide so hastily," said Amelia. "Why don't we go home and see what Eunice and Doreen have made for dinner, and then you can decide whether or not it is worth it? Eunice does make a wonderful roast lamb with garlic and herbs," she continued, "and a delicious date pudding with a warm sticky toffee sauce. She also bakes the best bannocks you've ever tasted—all soft and tender, which she serves with lots of fresh butter and cheese. I'm quite certain you would enjoy it."

The boy's eyes widened as she described this veritable feast. "Nae tricks?" he demanded, suspicious. "I can just eat and leave?"

"No tricks," Amelia assured him, her expression solemn. "All I ask is that you permit us to clean you up a bit before you come to the table. I don't think Eunice or Doreen will permit you to touch anything without at least washing your hands and face."

"Fine, then," he sniffed, making it sound as if this was an extraordinary sacrifice on his part. He stalked toward the carriage, jerked the door open and climbed inside.

"Do you think Eunice and Doreen will mind?" Amelia asked Oliver, suddenly worried that she might be imposing upon them by appearing with this foul-smelling urchin.

Oliver chuckled. "They'll be so pleased to see ye, they'll nae care who ye've brought with ye," he predicted. "An' they're well accustomed to dealin' with crabbit lads like this."

"I hope you're right." Amelia accepted Oliver's hand as he assisted her up the step of the carriage.

"What's your name?" she asked brightly of her hostile young dinner guest.

"Alex."

"That's a very handsome name," Amelia commented, trying to put him at ease. "Is it short for Alexander?"

The boy regarded her contemptuously. "Where are ye from, that ye talk so strange?" he demanded, ignoring her question.

"I'm from America," Amelia explained, not bothered by his rudeness. "From a lovely city called New York."

"An' is that where ye got yer spectacles from?" he asked sarcastically. "New York?"

"Why do you ask?"

"I'm thinkin' ye was cheated when ye bought them," he ground out acidly, "since any bloody fool can see I'm a lass."

With that Amelia's guest folded her arms across her

flat chest and glared sullenly out the window, filling the carriage with awkward silence.

Y E NEEDN'T BE DROPPIN' FOOD FROM THE TABLE INTO yer lap," Eunice said, carving another slice of lamb for Alex.

"I'm not," she protested innocently.

"Give it over." Doreen held an empty plate in front of her.

"There's nae to give," Alex insisted, scowling.

"Ye'll nae win against these two," Oliver speculated, mopping up the last of his gravy with a thick chunk of dark bread. "Ye'd best give up now and save yerself a bit o' peace."

"There's nocht in my lap."

Eunice shook her head in wonder, marveling that so many years after Genevieve started bringing home wayward orphans, children could have changed so little.

"I'm fixin' to pack ye a grand basket filled with all yer favorite treats that ye can take with ye when ye go," she told Alex. "So there's nae need to be stealin' food from the table and makin' a mess o' Doreen's lovely linen cloth."

"If the grease sets, I'll be settin' ye to work scrubbin' it out after supper," Doreen warned sternly. "And there'll be nae puddin' with toffee sauce till it's all out, nice and clean."

Amelia watched as Alex glowered at the three elders, looking for all the world as if she were being most unfairly victimized. Just when Amelia was about to come to her rescue and suggest that perhaps Eunice was mistaken, Alex snorted with irritation and shoved her chair back, revealing the sloppy mess of food she was hoarding in her linen napkin.

"Thank ye." Doreen matter-of-factly plopped the greasy bundle onto the bare plate, then took it to the sink.

"Here now, have a wee bit more lamb," cooed Eunice, laying a thick slab onto Alex's plate. "And more tatties and peas as well." She spooned a generous pile of each beside the meat.

"Mind ye dinna eat too fast, or yer belly will heave it up," warned Oliver.

"I'm not," Alex protested, cramming the food into her mouth.

Amelia watched the girl eat as if she was afraid someone might suddenly steal her food away from her, pausing only for an occasional gulp of water and a quick wipe of her mouth against her grimy sleeve. It was obvious Alex was unaccustomed to having so much food offered to her at once, and she was determined to ingest as much as she possibly could before she found herself on the streets once again.

"Where do you live, Alex?" Amelia was concerned about what was to become of her.

"Wherever I please." The words were muffled beneath her chewing and swallowing.

"Then I take it you don't have any parents or relatives looking after you?"

"I can take care of myself," Alex assured her fiercely.

"Yes, you made that quite clear today. But what I'm wondering is, do you have some place where you normally go to spend the night?"

"I have my places." She eyed Amelia warily, unwilling to give her any further details.

"How old are you?"

Alex snorted with contempt. "How old are you?"

"I'm nineteen," Amelia told her, ignoring her impertinence.

Alex regarded her doubtfully. "Are ye sure? Ye look forty."

" 'Tis those spectacles of yers, lass," Oliver explained, amused. "They add a few years to yer face." He regarded her meaningfully, reminding her that she was in disguise.

"Ye should toss 'em," Alex advised, scooping up another creamy spoonful of mashed potatoes. "They make ye look all crabbit and old. And ye should think on changin' yer hair as well," she continued, evaluating Amelia with a critical eye. "There's nae ye can do about that ugly color, o' course, but ye could arrange it so ye dinna look like such an old hen."

"Thank you for your advice," Amelia managed. "How is it that you are such an authority on revising one's appearance?"

"I like to watch people."

"Aye, I'm sure ye do." Doreen's narrow mouth twisted with disapproval. "Ye watch folk by the hour when ye're decidin' who's worth fleecin' and who isn't."

"That's part o' the work." Alex's tone was heavily superior, as if she thought Doreen was too ignorant to understand such matters.

"But ye didna do such a good job when ye snatched Mrs. Chamberlain's reticule here, did ye?" observed Oliver. "Thought it would be full o' brass, and all she had was some papers worth nothin' to ye."

Alex shrugged her shoulders. "I thought it was bonny."

Amelia stared at the girl in surprise. In her filthy, tattered trousers, shirt, and jacket, Alex could not possibly have any use for Amelia's dove gray silk-and-velvet bag, with its ivory tassel and soft wrist cord. The idea of this little urchin girl actually carrying it and using it was ludicrous.

"If you like it, I'll give it to you, Alex," she said. "It's yours."

Alex adopted an air of scornful indifference, barely raising her head from her plate.

"Fine. I know a place where I can sell it."

"Ye'll nae be sellin' any gifts that Mrs. Chamberlain might be givin' ye," objected Eunice firmly. "If it's brass ye're needin', we can find ye a bit and pack it with yer food and yer clothes."

"Once I give the bag to Alex, it is hers to do with as she likes." Amelia was fascinated by the girl's attempt to make it seem like she honestly didn't care about the reticule. "Only she can decide whether she wants to keep it or not."

Alex's expression was shuttered as she continued to stuff food into her mouth. When she finally could not manage another bite, she shoved her plate away, gave her mouth a final smear upon her sleeve, and belched loudly.

"Here now, we'll have none of that at the table," scolded Doreen, wagging a blue-veined finger. "And if ye come to our table again I expect ye to use yer napkin on yer mouth, instead of fillin' it full o' food when ye think no one is looking."

"Where's the pudding?" demanded Alex.

"It's coming." Eunice smiled, always pleased to feed someone with a good appetite. "A fine date pudding with sticky toffee sauce—one of Jack's favorites."

Alex looked at Amelia. "Is he yer husband?"

"No."

"Then who is?"

"I'm not married."

"Then why are ye wearin' that ring?"

Amelia glanced at the thin gold band Annabelle had given her to wear to complete her costume as Mrs. Marshall Chamberlain.

"I'm a widow." She felt unaccountably guilty at

having to lie. "My husband died recently and I left America and came here to make a new life for myself."

Alex regarded her skeptically. Living on the streets had given her a keen perceptiveness, and she sensed Amelia was lying. "How do ye come to be livin' here?"

"Actually, I'm not staying here," Amelia admitted. "But I was staying here until a week ago, and that is why it was fine to come back and have a nice visit with Oliver, Eunice, and Doreen."

Alex rolled her eyes, as if she thought the visit had been anything but nice. "So who's Jack?" She buried her spoon into the steaming bowl of pudding Eunice had placed before her.

"Mr. Kent is Mrs. Chamberlain's cousin," Oliver interjected, deciding that Amelia had probably done as much lying as she could for one day.

Alex began to shovel pudding into her mouth, momentarily arresting her questions. When she was finished she opened her mouth to belch, then thought better of it and snapped it shut.

"There now, did ye enjoy that?" asked Eunice, removing the bowl.

"Is there more?"

"Aye, but I think ye should give yer belly a wee rest. We dinna want ye to be sick—"

"Can I take it with me?"

"Of course ye can," Eunice assured her. "I'll just pack it up with the rest."

Alex pushed her chair from the table and stood. "Guess I'll be goin', then."

Dark shadows pressed gloomily against the kitchen windows. Although Alex had managed to avoid revealing her age, Amelia did not think she could be more than ten years old. How could she possibly survive living on the streets with no one to care for her but herself? Amelia wondered. That day Alex had avoided being arrested and put in prison because neither Amelia nor Oliver would ever do such a thing to a young child. But what would happen tomorrow, when Alex was forced to steal again? Would her next victim forgive her and invite her home for supper? Or would they insist that she be sent to prison, where she would undoubtedly suffer the most appalling abuse before she was finally released, unskilled and unwanted, back to the streets again?

"Alex," she began slowly, "what would you think of—"

Before she could finish, Alex grabbed the back of her chair and doubled over, moaning in pain.

"What's wrong?" Amelia sprang to her side. "Are you ill?"

"My belly," Alex gasped, her eyes shut tight.

"Take her into the drawing room," instructed Doreen, "so we can lay her on the sofa."

"Put your arm around my neck, Alex," directed Amelia.

Groaning in agony, Alex threw a thin arm around Amelia and staggered weakly down the hallway, while Oliver and Doreen went into the drawing room to light the lamps. Amelia helped Alex onto the sofa, and Eunice covered her with a soft plaid.

"She ate too much," Oliver reflected. "Stuffed herself fatter than a Christmas goose, and her belly is nae used to it."

"The date pudding and sauce was too rich for her, most like," agreed Doreen.

"I'll give her a teaspoonful of my stomach cordial," Eunice decided. "The opium is sure to dull the pain and make her sleep."

Alex's eyes flew open.

"What she needs is a good, strong laxative from syrup of violets," suggested Doreen. "Purge her bowels. Of course it causes a fair bit of bloatin' and cramping, and then there's the mess, but afterward ye feel as if ye've been scoured from the inside out."

Miraculously, Alex sat up. "I'm feelin' much better—"

Eunice, Doreen, and Oliver exchanged knowing glances.

"Now Alex, you must lie back," Amelia said soothingly.

"I'm nae takin' any laxative." Alex stubbornly folded her arms across her chest. "Ye canna force me."

"No, of course not." Amelia was surprised by how well the girl suddenly looked. Understanding began to dawn on her. "But even though you're starting to feel better, I think it would be best if you slept here tonight, just so we can be sure there is nothing seriously wrong."

Alex snorted. "Sleep here?" She made it sound as if Amelia had suggested she curl up in the coal bin.

Amelia turned to the three elders. She knew what she was suggesting was an imposition, but she didn't know what else to do. Amelia didn't want Alex to spend the night on the streets, and if Alex's feigned stomach attack was any indication, neither did she. But Amelia couldn't just show up at Annabelle's home with this reeking, insolent urchin in tow, insisting that she was going to spend the night. Although Annabelle might have understood, there was a possibility she might not, given the fact that she had her own children to consider. In Amelia's mind, Jack's home was really the only option.

She was fairly certain that when he returned she would be able to make him see that.

"She can sleep in the spare room we set up for Jack when you were stayin' here," suggested Oliver.

"'Tis nae fancy, but it's clean and warm and dry, which is more than ye could say about wherever ye planned to sleep tonight," Eunice told Alex.

"That will be fine," Amelia said. "Won't it, Alex?"

Alex shrugged her shoulders.

"All right then, up the stairs with ye." Doreen shepherded Alex toward the staircase. "Let's fix ye a nice bath and find some decent clothes for ye—"

Alex stopped. "I'm nae takin' a bath," she informed Doreen adamantly.

"Aye, ye are." Doreen fisted her thin hands on her bony hips. "Ye're nae sleepin' on my clean, pressed sheets with all yer filth and yer greasy hair crawlin' with vermin. Ye'll be havin' a hot bath with soap and lavender water, and scrubbin' yer teeth with tooth wash, and filin' yer nails 'til they're neat, and puttin' on a clean, decent nightgown for sleepin', and gettin' on yer knees to say yer prayers. If any part of that doesna agree with ye, then Oliver will take ye back to wherever he found ye, where ye can be as dirty and foul-mannered as ye wish."

Alex cursed and marched toward the front door.

"But then you'll miss breakfast," blurted out Amelia.

The girl stopped and regarded her sullenly. "What's for breakfast?"

"The usual things," Eunice replied. "Oatmeal, eggs, toast and ham, grilled kippers, tongue, hot rolls, marmalade, coffee, tea and chocolate."

"Makes me hungry just thinkin' about it," said Oliver. "How about it, lass?"

Alex was silent a moment. "Nae lavender water. It stinks."

"Fine, then." Doreen understood it was important that the lass feel she had won at least one small victory. "Nae lavender water."

Looking as if she were marching to her execution, Alex turned and stalked reluctantly up the stairs.

NIGHT HAD RIPENED TO BLACK BY THE TIME JACK mounted the steps to his home. He had told Oliver to fetch him from his office sometime after midnight, but hunger had forced him from the decrepit old building by nine o'clock. He had gone to a tavern in search of a meal and a drink, only to find that one drink quickly turned into two, then three. After four drinks he had lost count. Didn't matter, he told himself. With Amelia gone, he was again accountable to no one except himself.

He fumbled through his pockets for his key, and with some effort managed to open the front door. He lurched through it and clumsily slammed it shut. Assuring himself that everyone was asleep, he shrugged out of his coat and dropped it unceremoniously on the floor. The only person he was in danger of bumping into in his current state was Oliver, who would be annoyed, but at least lacked the means to force Jack to walk home, given that he was already there. Smugly pleased with himself for having managed to outwit the old man on that point, Jack staggered toward the stairs.

"What in the name of Saint Columba are ye doin' home when I was just about to fetch ye?" demanded Oliver, appearing suddenly from the passage leading to the kitchen. He sounded as if he had been inconvenienced by not having to go out.

"I finished early and hired a carriage on the street. Thought I'd save you the trouble of goin' out again tonight."

Oliver's eyes narrowed. "Did ye, now? And how many drinks did ye have afore ye decided to grace us with yer presence?"

He shrugged. "One or two."

"Smells more like five or six."

"What if it was? I'm a grown man, Oliver, not a lad. It's no one's business but my own if I want to get completely guttered."

"Is this what ye do as ye sail to all yer fancy, far-off

places like Egypt and Greece?" demanded the old man in disgust. "Drink every night 'til ye can barely stand? 'Tis nae wonder ye canna manage to come home and make a decent life for yerself. If Miss Genevieve could see the way ye've been carryin' on, she'd box yer ears and tell ye to start actin' like the grown man ye claim to be."

"Genevieve has never hit me," Jack countered.

"Well, maybe she should have," Oliver shot back. "'Tis clear all her patience and gentle ways have nae helped ye learn some wee measure of controllin' yerself."

Jack regarded him warily. Did Oliver know about how he had ruined Amelia the night before she left? Or was the old man talking about the fact that Jack had been drunk every night since, as he tried to come to terms with the fact that he had stolen her virginity and irrevocably destroyed his relationship with her?

"I wish ye'd managed to keep yerself from the bottle tonight, what with Miss Amelia waitin' to speak with ye." Oliver knew there was no use chastising Jack when he was already drunk.

Jack's eyes widened. "Amelia is here?"

"Aye, and she's wantin' to speak with ye, but—"

"Where is she?"

"Upstairs, in the spare bedroom, but ye canna—"

Jack tore past Oliver up the stairs. Amelia was back. After an agonizing week of believing he would never see her radiant smile again, or inhale her summery fragrance, or feel the softness of her palm as she tenderly laid it against his scarred cheek, she had returned. Feeling as if a brilliant wash of sunlight was pouring over him, he charged into the spare bedroom.

And stared in confusion at the strange young girl sleeping on the small cot.

"Shhh." Amelia laid her forefinger against her lips as she rose from a chair in the corner.

She adjusted the plaid she had draped over Alex, then motioned for Jack to follow her into the hallway. Silently closing the bedroom door, she slowly turned to him.

His face was harshly cut against the soft amber light. She searched the silvery depths of his eyes, but found only wariness and brittle anticipation. Given the way she had quit his house without so much as a farewell, it was understandable that he be guarded in his reaction to her. Nevertheless, she was wounded by his coolness. How was it, she wondered, that two people could experience such incredible passion, sharing the deepest intimacies of their bodies and their emotions, and then find themselves staring at one another in such awkward, circumspect silence?

"I'm sorry," she finally murmured, realizing she was going to have to be the one to break the tension between them. "I didn't mean to impose upon you by bringing Alex here, but Oliver didn't think you would object."

Jack nodded, searching his whiskey-drenched mind for some memory of a girl named Alex. He found nothing. In that tautly strained moment, it scarcely seemed to matter. Somehow the girl lying in what Eunice now laughingly referred to as "the guest chamber" had brought Amelia back to him. That much he understood.

"I met Alex today after she tried to steal my reticule," Amelia continued. "Oliver very cleverly managed to catch her, and when I saw how filthy and hungry and desperate she was, I knew I couldn't just drive away and leave her. So I invited her to join me for dinner, thinking that she would enjoy a proper meal, but forgetting that I am merely a guest in Annabelle's home. While I don't think Annabelle would oppose my inviting someone to dinner, it seemed doubtful she would be overly pleased with my bringing home someone like Alex, even though I understand that Annabelle and the rest of you came from rather simple beginnings as well."

She made it sound as if they had all come from some tidy, charming little cottage in the country, where they had spent their days fishing in the lochs and playing with wooden toys. *Yes,* Jack thought, suddenly concerned about how much his family had told her, *I come from rather simple beginnings.*

"There was also the issue of Annabelle's children to be considered." Amelia desperately wished Jack would say something. "Alex's understanding of appropriate behavior is limited, and I was worried that Annabelle might not want her children exposed to that. So bringing her here was really the only option. Oliver said you have been working late these last few days and he didn't think you would mind. I did so fully intending that we would eat and then Oliver and I would take Alex to wherever it was that she usually spends the night, and not inconvenience you at all. But Alex doesn't have any place where she normally stays—although she is most adamant that she can take care of herself. She's very strong-willed and independent."

Of course she is. The wounds of Jack's past began to open. *She has to be or she won't survive.*

"Well, even though I knew I had no right to, I was going to invite her to spend the night here, so she would be warm and safe." Amelia regarded Jack uncertainly. "Before I could she collapsed with stomach pains. So Eunice and Doreen said they would give her a laxative, but then Alex insisted she felt better, which suggested she had feigned being ill so she wouldn't have to leave. So I asked her to stay the night and she agreed—and that's how she came to be sleeping here.

"Of course I don't expect you to let her stay here

more than one night." Amelia decided he was displeased with her intrusion into his home. "I mean, you can't possibly take responsibility for a young orphan girl—I understand that. But I can't just let Alex return to her life in the streets, either, where she might end up in prison, or worse. So tomorrow I'm going to take her to Annabelle's, and ask her if she wouldn't mind letting Alex share my room with me, until I have enough money saved that I can rent a place in which we both can live. Now that she's been bathed she actually looks quite presentable, and I think if I just explain some basic rules of appropriate behavior to her—like not belching at the table and refraining from cursing—she won't be too much of a disruption to Annabelle's household."

She was leaving him, Jack realized. What could he do to make her stay? What could he possibly say that would make her forgive him for the appalling way he had taken advantage of her? His mind began to race. Amelia was here because she cared about this urchin named Alex. It was incredible that in her current situation, in which there was a reward on her head and she was trying to adjust to a new life and learn how to take care of herself, Amelia was also bringing home stray orphans. But she was nothing like the spoiled, self-indulgent heiress he had assumed she was as he sat impatiently waiting for her to appear at her own wedding. Bringing home a little thief who tried to snatch her reticule was only logical for a woman who had insisted on feeding and clothing an entire community of homeless people with her precious emerald earrings.

He didn't want her to go to Annabelle's. He didn't want her to go anywhere. That was all he could focus on as he stared at her, filled with longing and despair and a kind of tentative hope, that maybe, just maybe, she could come to forgive him for who he was and what he had done to her.

"She can stay here."

Amelia frowned in confusion. "You mean for to-night?"

"For as long as you need a place for her."

Surprise drifted across her lovely face, but it was quickly usurped by resignation. "That's very kind of you, Jack, but I don't think it will work. You have to travel a great deal, and I don't see how you could possibly look after a young child on your own."

"I didn't mean that I would look after her," Jack clarified. "I meant that you both could stay here—until you felt you were ready to find a place of your own. I expect to be leaving shortly for several months," he added, lest she fear that he might force himself upon her again. "But I would arrange for Oliver, Eunice, and Doreen to stay on, to help you look after Alex. You will need their help—especially since you will be working at the hotel during the day, and can't take her with you."

He was right, Amelia realized.

"I'm sure Annabelle would want to assist you with Alex, but she already has a husband and four children of her own, in addition to her writing," he continued. "With so many demands upon her already, is it really fair to ask her to take on even more?" In fact he was quite certain that any of his sisters or brothers would have happily opened their homes to both Amelia and her young charge, but he was not about to tell her that.

"I suppose not," Amelia conceded. "But what about Oliver, Eunice, and Doreen? Don't you think they are anxious to go home?"

"If they were, they would have left by now and given me some peace," he muttered. "I think they are having a wonderful time staying here, cooking and cleaning and nagging me. Genevieve and Haydon have so many other younger servants, those three don't have much to do anymore. Having you and Alex around will only make them feel useful—and deflect some of their attention from me."

"They did seem to enjoy feeding Alex this evening." Amelia smiled. "And they knew all her tricks—like when she was hiding food in her napkin, and pretending to be sick so she wouldn't have to leave."

"They know how children think." *Especially urchins who have been forced to steal and lie in order to survive.*

Amelia studied Jack a long moment. He returned her gaze with weary resignation, as if it did not matter to him what she decided. But his jaw was clenched and his hands were fisted at his sides, indicating to her that it did, in fact, matter.

"Stay, Amelia," Jack urged in a low voice, afraid that she was about to refuse him. "Let me at least do this for you."

The words hung in the air, an awkward, inadequate apology. *Forgive me,* was what he had meant to say. *For everything.*

Given the way he had taken advantage of her, he knew she had every right to refuse him. But something had brought her back to him that night, and he did not believe it was simply that an urchin had been in need of a good meal. No, Amelia had returned to his home because she believed it was safe to do so. On some level he couldn't begin to understand, she still trusted him, despite all he had done to destroy that trust.

Amelia stared at him in silence, as helplessly drawn to him in that moment as she had been a week earlier. But she was not the same uncertain, inexperienced girl she had been on that night. Only a week had passed, and yet she had changed. She had assumed the role of an older, independent woman, with responsibilities, deadlines, and a salary, and incredibly, people actually thought she was good at what she did. If she continued to work hard, she could carve out a successful career for herself, which would enable her to make her own decisions about her life. Although Jack had not been supportive of her working, she realized she had him to thank for her new life. But for him, she would have been married to Whitcliffe, crying herself into a state of hysteria every night as she agonized over her fate. Jack had helped her escape that. He had done something that no one else had ever done: He had asked her what she wanted.

And then he had tried to give it to her.

"Very well. We'll stay—but only until I have managed to put aside enough money to rent a place of our own." She did not want Jack to think that she was going to impose upon his generosity indefinitely.

Relief poured through him. "You are both welcome to stay as long as you like. Alex can stay in this room, and you will have my chamber again." He walked down the corridor and opened his bedroom door for her. "I'll send Oliver to get your things from Annabelle's in the morning."

"But where will you sleep?"

"I'll take the sofa in the drawing room."

"But that won't be comfortable."

"I can sleep anywhere, Amelia," he assured her, shrugging. "I'm used to it. Besides, it will only be for a few nights. Then I'll be leaving again."

Of course. A shadow of longing fell across her heart. "Well, then," she said, suddenly feeling awkward, "good night."

"Good night, Amelia." He watched as she closed the door. Then he leaned against the wall and exhaled.

She was back. And they were still friends.

Beyond that, he refused to contemplate.

Chapter Twelve

I T BEGAN AS AN UNEASY SENSATION.

He had been jerking his head around to see if he was being followed from the moment Amelia first hurtled into his life. In the nearly two weeks since she had returned with Alex, the habit had become so acute he was developing stiffness in his neck. He stared suspiciously at every man, woman and child, to the point where he was certain his neighbors had decided he was probably touched in the head.

He had never felt welcome on his tidy little street of elegantly restored homes, occupied by respectable families complete with doughy-faced children and haughty servants. He had no doubt they preferred it when he was away, so long as his three odd servants came in once a week to keep the vermin out of his home. When he was absent, he posed no threat to his neighbors' staid lives. Now that he was in residence with an American widow and a sullen little girl who was rumored to be an urchin and a thief, his neighbors had taken to staring at him with disdain. Although he tried to ignore it, they made him feel the same way he always had whenever he tried to exist in the privileged world Genevieve had brought him into.

Despised and unworthy.

"I think we're being followed," he said tersely, staring out the back window of the carriage.

Oliver rolled his eyes. "Ye always think we're bein' followed," he scoffed. "Yesterday I had to stop ye from accostin' old Mr. Anderson because ye were certain ye'd nae seen him on yer street afore, when the old sod's been livin' here thirty-five years."

"He looked different," Jack pointed out, defensive. "He shaved off his beard."

"Aye—three years ago."

Jack scowled.

"The day afore ye wanted to question that new maid of Mrs. Ingram, because ye were sure ye'd seen her walkin' near ye in London, and wanted to know what coincidence could have brought her all the way to Inverness—"

"She looked familiar—"

"When 'twas just her new hat ye were recallin', on another woman's head."

"They shouldn't make them look the same."

"An' let's nae forget the day ye scared that Rafferty lad so bad, his mother had to give him a tonic and put him to bed."

"That wasn't my fault," Jack objected. "He came charging down the street toward Amelia with a rope in his hand—"

"He was chasin' after his wee puppy." Oliver snorted in disgust. "Ended up flat on his arse with you standin' over him, threatenin' bloody murder."

"He shouldn't have let the damn thing escape in the first place. How was I to know that he wasn't a threat?"

"He's scarcely twelve years old."

"He's very tall for his age."

"He's shorter than Doreen."

"He seemed taller at the time."

"I dinna know how ye'd ken, given how quick ye had him sprawled on his backside."

"Just turn left down the next street," Jack instructed. "Then left again. I want to see what the carriage behind us does."

"An' what will ye do if the driver makes the same turns?" asked Oliver. "Will ye accuse him of followin' ye all the way from London?"

"I don't know how you can be so relaxed about Amelia's safety. The newspapers report sightings of her every day. Just this morning, someone said they had seen her in Inverness."

"Aye—while others have seen her in Paris, Rome, Athens, and New York. Miss Amelia read it to us as she took her tea afore she went to work. She said she didna realize steamships had become so wonderful quick, and maybe this Saturday she'd take a trip to China, as she's always fancied seein' it." He chuckled.

"It isn't funny, Oliver," Jack said flatly. "The reward her family has offered is enormous. All of Europe is searching for a woman matching her description in the hopes of making themselves rich."

"Well, thanks to me, Miss Amelia doesna look like herself anymore," Oliver pointed out, turning the carriage for the second time. "So ye needn't be so—"

"He's turning."

The old man clacked his tongue in exasperation. "Aye—an' so did that carriage in front of us. Next thing ye know, they'll be accusin' us of followin' them."

"Just drive to the end of the street and head west, beyond the edge of the city. If he isn't following us, it would be strange for him to suddenly decide he had to head toward the countryside as well."

"If we're late for dinner, Eunice will be sorely mad."

"Just do it, Oliver."

Oliver huffed in frustration and snapped his reins.

The day was fading as the carriage rolled beyond the busy streets of Inverness. Jack refrained from twisting around to look out the back window as Oliver steered the vehicle onto the road that led to and from the city. *Give it a few minutes.* Just because a carriage was traveling the same routes as his didn't mean it was following him. There had been numerous times in the past few weeks when instinct had told him he was being watched, but he never could be entirely sure, as the offending vehicle or person always disappeared at the last moment.

"There's a small road running south after that clump of trees ahead. Speed up and take it, then stop the carriage after we pass the crest of the first hill."

"When Eunice is blatherin' about how her roast is ruined, I'm nae takin' the blame," Oliver grumbled, cracking his whip.

Jack waited until they had disappeared into the valley beyond the first hill. The moment Oliver brought the vehicle to a stop, he leapt out.

"Wait here—I'm going to the top of the hill to watch."

"Call me if ye need me to come save ye," Oliver joked.

Ignoring the old man's sarcasm, Jack raced back through the deepening darkness to the top of the hill, where he concealed himself amidst the shadowy spires of the pine trees looming at the side of the road.

Long moments passed. Finally Jack caught sight of the same carriage he had seen in Inverness, moving briskly along the deserted country route. It barreled past the turnoff he and Oliver had taken.

Oliver was right. He was becoming completely paranoid. He turned, annoyed. Now he would have to suffer Oliver's infernal mocking all the way home.

The sound of a horse's hooves made him stop.

It had turned back, Jack realized, watching as the carriage sped along the narrow ribbon of road. The driver must have realized he had lost his quarry and was now racing to find it. Jack's jaw tightened as the carriage sped past the turnoff, which was not obvious in the waning light. After a moment the carriage stopped again.

Come on. I'm over here.

The carriage slowly moved forward again, heading toward the pale glow of Inverness.

Shit.

The carriage stopped once more, hesitating in the darkness.

At last it turned and began to move carefully down the westerly road, searching for a place to turn.

"What's happenin'?" demanded Oliver, who had grown bored waiting and decided to hike up the hill to Jack. "Any sign of it?"

"The driver has found the road," Jack replied. "Stay here—I'm going to the other side. As soon as he slows on the crest, I'll grab the horse's reins while you make a lot of noise and open the carriage door. We don't know how many are inside, so make it seem like there are more than just two of us."

"Dinna worry, lad." Oliver's aged eyes sparkled with anticipation. "I'll fill them so full o' fear, they'll think they're about to take their dyin' breath."

Jack sprinted across the road and stood in the shadows, waiting.

Finally the carriage rounded the hill.

Jack leapt out and grabbed the horse's reins, causing the startled animal to rear.

"Jesus Christ—*what the hell are ye doin'?*" roared the stunned driver.

"Keep still an' yer mouths shut, an' maybe we'll nae

slit yer throats," bellowed Oliver dramatically as he flung open the carriage door, his dirk flashing in his withered fist. Blinking against the darkness, he peered inside. "'Tis empty," he informed Jack, clearly disappointed.

Jack hauled down the driver. Before the astonished man could do more than gasp Jack had jerked his arm painfully behind him.

"I'm going to ask you some questions," Jack drawled, "and you're going to answer them truthfully."

"Bugger yourself!"

"Take a moment to think about it," he advised, pressing the point of his dirk into the driver's throat. "Because I don't want there to be any confusion about what I mean by truthfully. What I mean is, if I discover you have lied to me about any detail, no matter how small or insignificant, my men and I will find you and we will smash every bone in your skinny, quivering little body. Is that clear?"

The man regarded him in hostile silence.

"If you need a demonstration to understand what a broken bone feels like, I shall be happy to oblige." He grabbed hold of the man's little finger and began to bend it back.

"All right!" shrieked the man. "I'll tell ye what ye want to know!"

"Your cooperation is appreciated." Jack released his finger. "What is your name?"

"It's Neil. Neil Dempsey."

"And just what are you doing out here, Mr. Dempsey?"

"I was followin' you."

"Why?"

Neil's mind began to race.

"Why?" Jack repeated, sharply twisting his arm.

"Because I've been hired to watch ye!" he squealed.

Jack was careful to conceal his surprise. Watch *him?*

Why the hell would anyone be watching him? It had to have something to do with Amelia.

"Who hired you?"

Neil whimpered. "Please—I canna say—"

"You can say," Jack assured him, wrenching his arm a little further up his back. "But if you would like me to help you remember by tearing your shoulder from its socket, I will be happy to oblige you—"

"Lord Hutton!" he shrieked.

Jack eased his punishing grip. "Who?"

"The Earl of Hutton," Neil explained, his voice quaking.

"And just what does the Earl of Hutton want with me?"

"I dinna know—I swear it!" he screeched as Jack tightened his hold. "All I know is, he hired me to follow ye while ye're here, and let him know everythin' ye do."

Jesus Christ. "And how long have you been following me?"

"Nearly four weeks, now. Ever since ye come back to Inverness."

"I imagine that has kept you quite busy, hasn't it?" Jack didn't know who the Earl of Hutton was, but if he had hired someone to watch him, it was obvious he also knew about Amelia. Why then hadn't he taken her to claim his reward? What sort of game was he playing?

"Where does Hutton live?"

"On an estate about twelve miles from here."

"How convenient. You'll take us there now."

"Dinna make me do that," pleaded Neil. "If I take ye there his lordship will be boilin' mad—"

"Do you think he will kill you?" enquired Jack blandly.

Neil looked shocked. "Of course not—"

"Then you have less to fear by taking us there than

you do by refusing. Is that clear?" He scraped his dirk across the soft flesh of Neil's wildly pulsing neck.

Neil whimpered and nodded.

T HERE NOW, YE JUST FILL THAT UP AND I'LL BE BACK in a moment to take it away," instructed Mrs. Quigley, handing him his chamber pot. "Are ye sure ye dinna need me to help ye?"

"I can still piss by myself," Edward assured her sourly.

"Well, then, that's somethin' ye should be grateful for." She pulled down his richly embroidered covers so he wouldn't have to struggle with them.

"I shall try to remember to thank the good Lord for that particular boon when I say my prayers tonight." His tone was dripping sarcasm.

"Ye might also thank him for grantin' me the patience to put up with ye," she suggested, carefully arranging the sheets over his bare, skeletal feet so they wouldn't get chilled while he relieved himself. "I know that's somethin' I pray for every night."

"Let me know when you think he has given you some."

Mrs. Quigley fisted her hands on her hips and shook her head. "Ye'd think a man with yer brains and station in life would know better than to insult the woman who's in charge of his medicine."

Edward shrugged. "If you don't give it to me, I'll die. And if you do give it to me, I'll die. The only appealing possibility is that you'll give me too much one day, which might make me die sooner."

"Dinna be countin' on that any day soon," she said breezily, opening the door. "I'll be workin' hard at keepin' ye here as long as I can, because I know the good Lord needs all the rest he can get afore ye show up to make his life a misery." She banged the door behind her.

His mood foul, Edward pulled up his nightshirt and waited impatiently for his swollen body to cooperate. He hated pissing into a chamber pot while lying in bed. There was something insufferably demeaning about performing one's bodily functions in such a manner. He closed his eyes and inhaled a deep breath, trying to force himself to relax and forget about how narrow and pathetic his life had become.

There were many days he heartily wished that Mrs. Quigley would give him far more of the laudanum his doctor had prescribed for the pain than his shriveling, faltering body could tolerate. It would be wonderful to just close his eyes, never to waken again. But he could not be sure the medicine would be so kind. There was the possibility that instead it would make him grotesquely ill, with vomiting and shivering and convulsions, and then not kill him after all, but render him more damaged and helpless than he already was.

Such a fate was unthinkable.

"Here now," Mrs. Quigley shouted suddenly from somewhere down the corridor, "stop at once or I'll send for the police!"

"Go ahead," snarled a contemptuous voice.

"You can't go in there!" Edward's butler sounded far more frightened than resolute. "Stop!"

His bedroom door burst open as he grabbed his blankets and hastily tried to cover himself. The empty chamber pot rolled off the bed and smashed upon the floor.

"Forgive me, yer lordship," whined Neil Dempsey, who was being held prisoner with a dirk to his throat by a tall, lean young man with coffee-colored hair and eyes of gray ice. "He's gone completely mad!"

"Sorry to disturb you so late, Lord Hutton," bit out

Jack sarcastically, "but I thought I would save you the trouble and expense of having Mr. Dempsey follow me and just pay you a visit myself. It seems a far more efficient way of finding out whatever it is you want to know, don't you think?"

Edward stared at Jack in shock.

"Drop yer dirk or I'll blast yer bloody head off!"

Edward's gaze snapped to the doorway, where his stable master stood pointing a rifle at Jack, with Mrs. Quigley, his butler, and a dozen or more vaguely familiar members of his staff huddled in fear behind him.

"Get out," Edward commanded, glaring at them. "Now!"

The stable master looked at him in stupefaction, wondering if his employer had lost his mind. "Forgive me, yer lordship, but ye're in grave danger—"

"Get the hell out, I say!" he roared, "*before I fire the whole goddamn lot of you!*"

The bevy of servants hastily withdrew.

"You go, too, Dempsey. He doesn't need you any more." Edward regarded Jack calmly.

Jack's eyes narrowed as he studied the shriveled old man lying helplessly on the bed before him. It was clear that Lord Hutton did not fear him. If anything, there seemed to be an air of anticipation to him, as if he had long expected this moment would come.

Abruptly, Jack released Neil Dempsey, who yelped with relief and dashed into the corridor.

"Close the door." Edward steepled his fingers together as he studied Jack. "I don't want us to be disturbed."

Jack sheathed his dirk in his boot and crossed the enormous bedchamber to slam the door shut.

"Sit down." Lord Hutton indicated a gold-and-silk-covered chair beside his bed.

"I'll stand."

Edward nodded. Feeling in need of fortification, he groped around behind his pillow to retrieve his silver flask.

"Brandy?" His hand trembled slightly as he held the flask out.

"No."

He struggled with the top, unwilling to betray his feebleness by putting the damn thing in his mouth and twisting it off. After a moment of fruitless effort he paused, debating whether he should just shove the recalcitrant vessel back under the pillows, before he humiliated himself even further.

Jack strode over to the bed, removed the cap, and handed the flask back to him.

"Thank you." Duly fortified after a couple of swallows, Edward lowered his drink and regarded Jack with interest. "So, you finally realized you were being watched, did you? I always knew Dempsey was too much of a fool not to be discovered eventually."

Jack said nothing. Everything about Lord Hutton, from his sickly-smelling, garishly ornate bedchamber to his wan, brittle body huddled amidst the stifling crimson covers and draperies of his bed, bothered him. He had no desire to be in his company a second longer than necessary. As he dragged Dempsey through Lord Hutton's ancestral home, he had noted that it seemed opulent enough. Judging by the flock of servants who had scurried to his rescue, it seemed the old man was not wanting for help, either. Even so, Jack knew that somehow Hutton had made the connection between the missing Amelia Belford and the young American widow who had taken up residence in Jack's home.

Ten thousand pounds was a great deal of money to an impoverished aristocrat, as Percy Baring had made abundantly clear.

"What do you want from me, Hutton?"

The aged earl studied him a long moment. Jack had the distinct feeling that he was analyzing him. It was as if he were trying to see beneath Jack's clothes and stance and manner, beneath the years of education and polish. Jack glared back at him with naked contempt. He was heartily sick of being scrutinized by the men and women of Lord Hutton's class. If the old man lying before him thought he was in any way Jack's superior, if he dared to make even one disparaging comment—

"You've got your mother's eyes."

"Is that supposed to be a joke?"

"I never make jokes," Lord Hutton informed him. "I'm too tired and too close to death for such nonsense. I'm telling you that you have your mother's eyes because I believe you do."

"You must have me confused with someone else."

"Actually, I don't," Lord Hutton retaliated, unperturbed by the intense hostility emanating from his guest. "You're Jack Kent, raised from the age of fourteen by the Marquess and Marchioness of Redmond. Lady Redmond discovered you when she was still Miss Genevieve MacPhail, in a squalid little prison cell in the town of Inveraray, where you had been jailed for stealing. While in prison you established a friendship with Lord Redmond, who at the time had been convicted of murder—"

"I don't have time for this," Jack snarled, marching toward the door.

"Your mother was Sally Moffat, who worked as a lady's maid in the home of the Earl of Ramsay."

He froze.

"Ye're Jack Moffat, my sweet lad," his mother would tell him, ruffling her fingers through his hair. *"An' when ye grow up all braw and fine, they'll be callin' ye Mr. Jack Moffat, and treatin' ye with respect, like the gentleman ye are."*

"You do remember her, don't you?" persisted Lord Hutton. "At least a little?"

Slowly, Jack turned to face him.

"Yes, I can see that you do," Edward decided. "Perhaps not well, given how infrequent her visits to you were once she placed you with that foul couple after you were born. But well enough, I suspect, to have at least some memory of her before she died of syphilis."

Outrage jerked him to the brink of violence. If not for Lord Hutton's frail condition, he would have hauled him up by his shoulders and thrown him across the room.

"Why?" Jack clenched his hands as he fought to control his fury. "Why are you doing this?"

Lord Hutton stared at him a long moment, taking in his anger and his pain. Then he shifted his gaze to stare at his portrait, which hung on the wall behind his enraged young guest.

"There was a time," he began, his tone almost wistful, "when I was something like you. Young. Strong. Reasonably handsome. I had my whole life ahead of me. Somehow, in the arrogant idiocy of my youth, I thought that all I should do was enjoy myself as much as I possibly could. In the course of my relentless pursuit of pleasure I spent many a fortnight at the country estate of Lord Ramsay. Do you know him?"

"No."

"A pity," said Lord Hutton, shaking his head. "Ramsay was almost as much of an idiot as I was, but he did know how to throw the most glorious house parties."

"How nice for you," ground out Jack acridly.

"It was, actually," Edward retaliated, suddenly weary of Jack's sneering attitude. "For it was at one of those parties, some thirty-seven years ago, that I met your mother."

A sick sense of foreboding surged through Jack.

Jesus Christ, he thought, as a maelstrom of dark emotions began to churn within him.

"She worked as a lady's maid to Ramsay's young wife," Edward continued. "As I recall Miss Moffat was exceptionally pretty, and in spite of, or perhaps because of, her relative lack of education and worldliness, I found her very charming as well." He regarded Jack steadily, his expression unapologetic, silently letting the import of that statement sink in.

Jack didn't want to hear any more. He was sure of it. And yet he remained where he was, his legs cemented to the floor, his hands coiled into helpless fists.

Shut up. Shut up before I smash my fist into your god-damn lying mouth.

"A few months later, your mother came to see me at my home," Lord Hutton continued. "She had been dismissed from her position as Lady Ramsay's maid, because by then it was evident that Miss Moffat was with child. She claimed that I was the father, and asked me if I would help her. Of course there was no way of knowing whether I was actually the father of her unborn child or not," he quickly pointed out. "That is both the advantage and the disadvantage we males have when it comes to the business of procreation. What is amazing, really, is how willing we are to indulge in pleasure when it suits us, but how reluctant we are to accept responsibility for the consequences. It is, I regret to say, one of the less admirable qualities of our sex."

Jack had heard enough. He didn't know what Lord Hutton's motive was for making up this fantastic story, and he didn't care. He had to leave, before the urge to strangle the old bastard for delving into his past and playing these vile games with him was overwhelming.

"I don't know why you think any of this is of interest to me," he snarled, desperate to escape the suffocating chamber and Lord Hutton's insane ramblings. "I don't give a damn about your sordid little affairs, Hutton. If you ever hire that weasel Dempsey or anyone else to follow me around again, I'll come back here and make you sorry you ever heard of me—is that clear?"

Without waiting for an answer, he spun toward the door.

And froze.

"As I said," murmured Lord Hutton with quiet, almost melancholy resignation, "I believe you have your mother's eyes."

Jack stared at the portrait in mesmerized horror, unable to speak. But for the eyes and the hair, which the young man in the painting wore in the longer, forward-brushed styling of some decades earlier, he might well have been looking at a picture of himself. The roughly chiseled features of the nose, jaw and chin were virtually identical, as was the fullness of the lips. In his youth Lord Hutton had been heavier-set than Jack, the result of a lifetime of rich food and taking exercise only when he wished it for pleasure. Beyond that, there was a smug self-satisfaction to his smiling expression with which Jack could not identify. In his own way Jack supposed he was arrogant, but it was a superiority born of a lifetime of being treated with disdain, except by the family Genevieve had so lovingly brought him into. Lord Hutton's conceit was the result of being born an earl, and therefore raised to believe that he was vastly superior to most of the population.

"Even though I couldn't be sure that I had been the cause of her condition, I decided I would help Miss Moffat," Lord Hutton finally continued, breaking the strained silence. "I gave her sixty-five pounds, thinking that should keep her well enough for a year or so, and I advised her to go back to her parents' home and live with them. I was shockingly naive, of course. I imagined that she would return to some quaint and loving mother and father in the countryside, who would welcome her and agree to take on the responsibility of raising the child, should it survive, while Sally went and found work again at some comfortable estate. She was a bonny lass, and I thought she would eventually find some fine young man to marry her, and care for the child as his own. I assured myself that I had done all that could reasonably be expected of me, given that there was no way of knowing if the bairn was actually mine. I believed that it would all turn out well enough. After all, housemaids have been known to start swelling beneath their skirts for hundreds of years. I imagined that somehow they managed to get on."

Of course they do, thought Jack bitterly. *They turn to stealing and end up in prison, the way Jamie's mother did, or they sell the one thing they have left to sell. Either way, their lives are destroyed.*

"So that was it?" He fought hard to keep his voice stripped of emotion. "Sixty-five pounds and you wished her well?"

"Actually, not quite. My wife had heard our voices, so she came to my study to see who had come to visit at such a late hour. When she saw Sally, she instantly recognized her condition." His expression was appropriately discomfited as he added, "My wife was also expecting at the time."

Jack did not bother to hide his disgust. "What did she do?"

"In a gesture that was completely in keeping with my wife's guileless nature, she accepted my explanation that Miss Moffat had been relieved of her position in Lord Ramsay's household, and had merely come to me for money so she could return home, where the father of her child was anxiously waiting to marry her. My wife was horrified by Ramsay's poor treatment of Sally, and insisted upon giving her a trunk full of clothes, including numerous outfits and blankets for her baby. All of this was packed up while Sally took tea in the kitchen. When it was ready it was loaded into one of my carriages, whereupon my wife instructed our coachman to take Sally to her parents' home, which was in the countryside south of here, about twenty-five miles from Inveraray. He returned a few days later, and assured us that she had arrived safely."

Jack waited.

"I never heard from Sally Moffat again after that. I never knew whether the child she was carrying was born alive or dead, or whether she survived the ordeal of birth." Lord Hutton's eyes became distant as he turned to look at the blackness of the summer night beyond his window. "Bringing a child into the world can be unspeakably difficult for some women," he reflected quietly. "But at the time I didn't know that. It would be fair to say, upon reflection, that I didn't know much of anything at all."

His remorseful attitude surprised Jack. Although he refused to acknowledge that any part of Lord Hutton's tale had anything to do with him, he asked, out of interest for the one person who evidently had taken pity on his mother, "Did Lady Hutton survive giving birth?"

"She barely survived." The earl's expression was grim. "But the ordeal was excruciating. Unfortunately, her labor was brought on early, by an argument we had over her discovery of my infidelities. And when it was all over, I had a wife who despised me beyond measure, and would never be able to carry a bairn again."

Jack didn't care about the child who was born. Didn't care if it was alive or dead. And yet his mouth was strangely dry as he asked, "And the bairn?"

"A girl. Who grew to be as beautiful as her mother, and to hate me with equal passion."

So that was it. Lord Hutton lay dying, with but one

child—a daughter who hated him. This woman was his half sister, but given how much he loathed Hutton, that was hardly a laudable connection. And now the earl was seeking out the progeny of his past affairs, in the hopes of—what, exactly? Jack was well enough versed on the laws governing the aristocracy to know that a bastard son could not inherit a title or an estate. Even so, he wanted to make it clear that he needed nothing from the earl.

"I don't want anything from you."

Lord Hutton permitted himself a resigned smile. "Of course you don't. You despise me, just as you have grown to despise every member of the aristocracy—except for Lord and Lady Redmond, of course. They are the only ones who have never judged you for your unfortunate past. What they have done is commendable. However much you may be angry with Dempsey for his prying, his reports these past few months have made it clear that you are quite a remarkable young man."

Jack gave him a scathing look. He was utterly uninterested in Lord Hutton's opinion of him.

"I don't really give a damn what you think about me or how I have lived my life," Lord Hutton added, inadvertently mirroring Jack's sentiments. "I don't need your friendship at this late stage, and I'm not so much of a fool as to believe that I could ever have your respect. Obviously I failed both you and your mother horribly, and that is something for which I can never make amends. I know that."

Jack said nothing.

"I also don't give a damn about the fact that my wife did not provide me with a male heir," he continued, "in case you're thinking that is why I went to such lengths to find out about your existence. My title and this estate and its lands will all be passed to my brother's eldest son—your cousin, if you choose to think of him so. He is a sniveling little cur who has spent most of his life fearing that my late wife might suddenly become pregnant, or worse, that after her death I might actually marry again. I don't doubt that he will be barely adequate in his role as earl. So be it. None of this," he said, waving a shrunken hand at the lavish chamber surrounding him, "matters to me anymore."

Spoken like a true aristocrat, Jack reflected contemptuously. Only someone who had never known what it was like to be filthy and cold and starving could be so cavalier about the obvious benefits of wealth and privilege.

"Then what do you want from me?"

Edward regarded the hostile young man before him with deliberate calm. "At first, all I wanted was to find out if you had survived, and if so, what had become of you. I had thought about your mother and her unborn child for years, and had assured myself that whatever happened, she had likely survived well enough. But after I became ill, I suppose I grew more reflective about how little I actually accomplished in the course of my life. There is nothing to show for my time here."

"You have this estate," Jack noted scornfully.

"I cannot take credit for something that existed long before I was born," Lord Hutton told him. "I added a few things to the art collection and maintained the estate, but that is hardly noteworthy. Our assets are actually worth less today than they were when I was born, given the depreciated value of farmland and my constant battle against falling revenues. My nephew will have a hard time keeping the estate going, and the fight is one I do not envy. All I have been, really, is the keeper of a title and lands that I neither created nor earned. I had a wife who might have loved me, had I not crushed her tender feelings before I understood how precious they were. And I fathered two children. A daughter who absorbed all of her mother's vitriol, and now refuses to visit me even though I am in the final grotesque stage of my life. And a son who was forced to endure the most appalling of childhoods, and who up until a moment ago was wholly unaware of my existence, because I was too ignorant to take proper responsibility for my actions." His expression was bitter as he finished, "It is hardly an estimable list of accomplishments."

Jack regarded him evenly. If the old bastard expected him to argue, he was wrong.

"All I wanted was to find out what happened to you," Edward continued. "Just to learn if you had survived, and if you had, to know who you had become. It wasn't easy tracking you down. One of my investigators finally found old Dodds, the scum your mother paid to look after you. He was a nasty piece of work, who had nothing good to say about you—"

"You're mistaken." Jack's voice was cold. "Dodds is dead."

"No, he isn't," Lord Hutton countered, "but if there were any justice in the world, he would be. He lives in a filthy shack just outside of Inveraray, and my investigator said he was a drunken, foul-mouthed pig, who spoke of you as if..."

A deafening roar filled Jack's ears, making it impossible to hear what Lord Hutton was saying. Dodds was alive. After years of believing that he had killed him on the day he ran away, the knowledge that he had survived was overwhelming. He took a deep breath, releasing the sick, childhood terror that had gripped his chest at the mention of his name.

After twenty-seven years, he had finally learned he was not a murderer.

"...so I hired Dempsey to watch you when you returned, not certain if you truly were the son of Sally Moffat or not," Lord Hutton finished. "I took great interest in everything you did, including all of your business affairs. I believe the North Star Shipping Company has the potential to be a great enterprise one day, if you can rise above the disasters that have been plaguing your ships and get your finances in order." He paused a moment. "That is an area in which I believe I can be of some assistance, if you will permit me," he offered hesitantly. "Although I cannot grant you a title or any part of this estate, I can give you some financial assistance, which I would very much like to do."

"No."

"Pride and anger are keeping you from being reasonable," observed Lord Hutton. "You need help with your business, which I am in a position to provide. Moreover, it is my duty as your father to help you, and beyond that, I want to help you. Surely those factors must bear some weight in your decision."

"They don't," Jack informed him brusquely. "If you are trying to ease your guilt over what you did to my mother and to me, don't bother. She came to you desperate for assistance, and you gave her exactly what you thought she was due for whatever pleasure you got from her—sixty-five pounds. You felt with that she should be able to survive, and she did. She survived long enough to give birth to me and find a place to put me. Long enough to look for some kind of decent work that might support a young unmarried woman and her child, and quickly discover that there wasn't any. Long enough to turn to whoring, out of what I can only assume was the most hideous desperation, because if she couldn't come up with the funds to pay Dodds and his wife, they would have thrown me out. Long enough for me to watch her become defeated and drunk and old, even though she couldn't have been more than in her early twenties. Long enough for her to have all that you found so pretty and charming when you first met her beaten out of her, by the ugliness of her life and the violent, disease-ridden bastards who paid to use her. So keep your goddamn money, Hutton. I don't need it and I don't need you."

"I'm your father," Lord Hutton objected, torn between anger and an agonizing need to make amends.

"No," Jack informed him flatly, "you're not. You're the man who impregnated my mother and abandoned her. My father is Haydon Kent, Marquess of Redmond, who was nearly beaten to death one day as he tried to save me from being lashed in jail. And my mother is Genevieve MacPhail Kent, who pulled me from my miserable existence on the streets and gave me my family."

"I have no wish to come between you and any member of your new family," Lord Hutton quickly assured him. "I just want to—"

"They are not my *new* family, Lord Hutton," Jack interrupted. "They are my *only* family."

Edward glowered at his son, hiding his pain beneath a mask of fury. The angry young man before him may have shared the same handsome features he had enjoyed in his own youth, but beyond that, it seemed, the similarities ended. Had Edward been in the same position, he would have readily accepted his offer of money. He might have despised his sire, but money was money, and he would have felt that whatever he received was his rightful due. But Jack Kent had been molded by forces unlike anything Edward had ever known. His son had suffered the most appalling abuse and deprivation as a lad, never knowing when he would eat, or what he would have to risk in order to find a place to sleep. Edward could not imagine how horrific those early years had been. But it seemed that having known what it was to have absolutely nothing, Jack had gained incredible strength and determination.

Which would keep Edward out of his life, without any hope of forgiveness.

"I'm sorry," he managed tautly, knowing that Jack would never understand how much that simple admission cost him. Suddenly fearing that the stinging in his eyes might actually turn to tears, he coughed and looked away.

Jack shifted uncomfortably on his feet.

It was too much to absorb at once. Everything had changed in the split second in which he had seen his features so clearly rendered in the portrait of Lord Hutton. Suddenly he had an identity he didn't want, and information about a past he had fought his entire life to bury. None of this had anything to do with the life Genevieve had given him—the life he had fought so hard to make worthy and successful. Lord Hutton wanted forgiveness, he realized helplessly.

Only Sally Moffat could have granted him that, and she was dead.

"I don't want your money, Hutton." Jack paused, unsure how to make him understand. "Not because I want to punish you, but because I don't take money I haven't earned. Do you understand?"

Edward turned to look at him. "Not completely," he admitted. "But I'm not so much of a fool that I don't realize that there is a great deal about the world that I still don't know. Unfortunately, I no longer have the luxury of time that I once had." He studied Jack a long moment, considering. "If you won't accept my offer of money, perhaps you will permit me to give you something else. A gift."

"That depends on what it is."

"Information regarding the attempts to sabotage your shipping business."

Jack's expression hardened. "How would you know about that?"

"I have spent the last six months trying to learn everything about you," Edward explained. "When mysterious accidents suddenly started happening to your ships, I took great interest."

"Not even the police have been able to determine who is responsible for the attacks on my ships."

"The police suffer from the delusion of being more righteous than most of the population, which leaves them indifferent to helping someone with your criminal background," Edward summarized with a dismissive flutter of his hand. "And the men you hired to guard your ships were hopeless. They watched your ships less than half the time they were supposed to, and when they did deign to actually work, they countered their boredom and discomfort with vast amounts of alcohol, rendering them virtually oblivious to everything around them."

"I thought you were only having me followed."

"The investigators I hired were paid to report on everything that concerned you. It was my desire to learn as much as I could."

Which included Amelia, Jack reflected uneasily. Although Lord Hutton had not yet mentioned her, it was obvious he had to be aware of her presence in Jack's house.

What remained to be seen was whether or not he knew who she really was.

"Will you accept this one thing from me, then?" Lord Hutton's expression was guardedly hopeful. "Will you let me at least help you to save your business from destruction?"

Jack hesitated.

Pride and anger kept him from wanting to accept anything from the dying old man before him. But he was acutely aware that his company was swiftly bleeding to death. If he couldn't stanch the flow soon, he would be forced to declare bankruptcy. His failure would effectively destroy any hope of his ever creating his own wealth. He would be labeled a business pariah, and the associates whom Haydon had so enthusiastically convinced to invest in North Star Shipping would refuse to ever touch anything with Jack's name on it again. He would be failing everyone, from the sailors who depended upon him for their livelihoods, to the clients whose contracts he could no longer honor, to his investors and his family.

Finally, he would be failing Amelia, who depended upon him for a safe place to live as she worked to build a new life for herself and Alex.

"Very well," he relented finally. "I am interested in any information you have regarding the attacks on my ships."

Edward nodded, immensely pleased to be able to offer him something. "No doubt you have heard of the Great Atlantic Steamship Company?"

Jack regarded him incredulously. "You're not suggesting that they are responsible?"

"Why do you find the possibility so remote?"

"Great Atlantic is one of the most highly regarded shipping companies in England," Jack told him. "They have been in business for over a hundred years, and they have contracts for shipping all over the world. They can't possibly be so threatened by my company that they would actually try to destroy my ships. The amount of business I do relative to theirs is inconsequential."

"You are thinking only in terms of the present," Edward countered. "Most of the great shipping lines of this decade began with equally modest origins. In 1815, Brodie McGhee Wilcox started business as a mere ship broker in London. Within thirty years he and his former office boy had formed the Peninsula and Oriental Steam Navigation Company, and were sailing to India, Ceylon, Singapore, and Hong Kong at barely half the rates of the great East India Company, which made them the superior choice for government contracts. Anyone can see the remarkable speed with which your company has grown. Until these unfortunate incidents began, you were building an estimable reputation for yourself for providing fast, reliable service at far more competitive rates than the industry average. A number of your contracts had previously been awarded to Great Atlantic, and given their precarious financial situation, they cannot afford to lose any more—particularly since their stock has fallen so dramatically. If you continue to expand and undermine their rates, within a few years you will be a formidable rival for much of the business Great Atlantic now enjoys. They are not so shortsighted that they cannot see that, and their investors are starting to panic. Many have put their entire fortunes into the company in the hopes of salvaging their dwindling wealth. Lord Philmore is widely known to be hopelessly in debt despite his upcoming marriage to some American heiress, while Lord Spalding is—"

"Viscount Philmore is one of the investors?"

"Do you know him?"

Jack's mouth tightened as he thought of Percy cradling his hand on the floor of the Wilkinsons' ball. "We've met."

"Then you know what an idiot he is." Edward scowled. "They're all idiots, really. Which is why you have the advantage."

"How can you be certain Great Atlantic is responsible for the damage to my ships?"

"Take the key from this drawer beside my bed, and unlock the door to that cabinet," Edward directed. "In it you will find the reports from my investigators who were hired to watch your ships while they were docked in London and Edinburgh during the past few months. It's all in there."

Jack retrieved the key and opened the cabinet. A quick perusal of the first of four leather-bound books within confirmed that they contained a wealth of information. Page after page of carefully written notes described the status of Jack's ships during their time docked, including arrival and departure times and dates, details concerning the movements of the crew members, itemized lists of the cargo loaded and unloaded, maintenance work performed, and special entries when Jack went aboard. There were also notes detailing any unusual or suspicious activities regarding the ships.

It was obvious the men Lord Hutton had hired to report on Jack's vessels had taken their jobs seriously.

"On the night of the damage to the *Shooting Star* my man reported that three men who were not part of the crew boarded the ship unnoticed at approximately two o'clock in the morning," Edward told him. "He did not follow them when they disembarked, because it was his job to report on the ship. After that incident I doubled the watch on the ships. That way if there were any further mysterious visitors, one man could track them while the other remained with the ship. That was how we were finally able to make the connection to Great Atlantic. They were careful, but not quite careful enough."

Anger surged through Jack as he flipped through the second journal.

"On the lower shelf of the cabinet you will find another report that you may also find interesting," continued Edward. "It details Great Atlantic's extremely tenuous financial situation—which they have gone to great lengths to conceal. I had to pay a rather substantial sum to secure it." He regarded Jack meaningfully. "I have no doubt you will be able to make good use of the information."

Intrigued, Jack picked up the dark ledger on the lower shelf and began to scan the pages within. The initial section of the ledger detailed Great Atlantic's fleet and its assets, which at first glance appeared significant. But Jack quickly realized that many of the company's ships were well over twenty years old, which meant they were slower and in constant need of repair. At least a dozen of them were ready to be scrapped, but the company could not afford the cost of replacing them.

"The company has tried to strengthen itself by focusing on luxury passenger services, which has necessitated the acquisition of a series of larger, faster, more elegantly appointed ships," Edward continued. "Unfortunately, they have done this by mortgaging their assets, becoming dangerously in debt to both national and private banks and to private investors. Last year one of those banks failed, resulting in their loans to Great Atlantic being called. Another is on the brink of failure, which will prove disastrous for Great Atlantic. They are about to take delivery of a magnificent new passenger ship commissioned over two years ago, but they haven't the funds to pay for it. Which creates a unique opportunity for you."

Jack began to rifle through the pages faster, swiftly analyzing the chaos of Great Atlantic's finances. Lord Hutton was right, he realized. Given the staggering debt the company had amassed, it had no hope of securing the funds needed to pay for its latest ship. It would have to either forfeit its delivery, or sell it immediately.

"Of course it would take time for you to raise the money, assuming you could get the ship for an exceptional price," Edward mused, watching as Jack flipped through the ledger. "However, if you will permit me to help..."

"I'm not interested in buying their ship," Jack interrupted, slamming the ledger shut. "I'm going to buy the whole goddamn company."

Edward stared at him, astonished.

"If your information is correct and that second bank failure is imminent, Great Atlantic will be faced with bankruptcy." Guarded excitement began to build within him. "If I can secure enough investors, I can negotiate a deal to buy the company at a fraction of its value, merge it with my own, sell off or scrap its money-losing ships, and create a smaller, leaner company that provides fast, secure shipping services at half the standard industry rates. That's what I believe the industry is going to demand over the next two decades," he continued. "And to ensure they give my offer serious consideration, I'll inform them I have evidence proving they are responsible for the sabotage of my ships. If word of that gets out, not only will they face public censure, but I'll make it my personal crusade to see that every goddamn last one of them faces a criminal investigation. Somehow I doubt board members like Philmore and Spalding have the stomach to risk going to prison."

Pleasure coursed through Edward, making him feel more exhilarated than he had in months. "If there is anything else I can do for you—perhaps I could be one of your investors—"

Jack shook his head. "This is enough. Thank you."

Edward tried to conceal his disappointment. It was not enough, and they both knew it. Nothing would ever make amends for the way he had failed his son and Sally Moffat.

"Will I see you again?" Edward tried to sound as if he didn't particularly care one way or the other.

"Somehow I doubt you want people gossiping about how I suddenly started to visit you. I'm sure I created enough of a disturbance by forcing my way in here this evening with a dirk to a man's throat."

"I don't give a damn about people," Edward growled. "They can talk all they like. If you would consider visiting me again, I would be honored."

"We'll see."

Edward nodded. He understood that he would receive no firmer commitment than that. "Tell me something." He regarded Jack intently. "Is she really that missing heiress?"

Jack kept his expression neutral. "Who?"

"Don't play games with me. I'm old and sick and I probably won't last the night. I give you my word that your secret is safe with me. Is she Amelia Belford?"

Jack hesitated. He did not know Hutton well enough to trust him. Even if he did, he couldn't be sure that some curious servant wasn't listening with an ear pressed against the door. Yet somehow he could not bring himself to lie to him, either.

"Never mind." Edward settled back against his pillows and wearily closed his eyes. "Tell my servants not to kill you on your way out, or I'll be most displeased."

He was being dismissed. Realizing there was nothing more to say, Jack collected the journals Lord Hutton had given to him and moved to the door. He grasped the latch, then paused. "Good night, Lord Hutton."

Edward nodded curtly, pretending to be too tired to watch as Jack left the room.

Only when he heard the door shut and he was certain that he was alone did he finally open his eyes, releasing the painful fall of tears that had kept him from bidding his son good-bye.

AMELIA SAT UPRIGHT, HER CHEST POUNDING. She was lying on top of Jack's bed, fully clothed. A

soft glow radiated from the oil lamp beside her, thinly illuminating the confines of the chamber. Sadness clutched
her in a suffocating grip as her gaze fell upon the pile of
trunks stacked in the corner.

The soft click of the front door closing told her that
Jack was finally home. A quick glance at the clock on
the mantel revealed that it was nearly three o'clock in
the morning. The lateness of the hour surprised her.
Since Jack had invited her and Alex to stay with him, he
had made every effort to come home at a reasonable
time each evening. This enabled him to eat dinner with
everyone and then spend some time with Alex and
Amelia before they retired for the night.

True to his word, Jack had tried to make the little
thief Amelia had brought into his home feel welcome
and safe. He had even volunteered to help teach Alex her
numbers. The poor girl had sullenly endured Amelia's attempts to teach her to script the letters of the alphabet,
and her progress was slow. But when it came to her numbers, Jack actually managed to keep Alex amused. He and
Oliver would put on loose overcoats, the pockets of
which were stuffed with various treasures. Then they
would stroll up and down the drawing room, whistling
and pretending to be distracted while Alex deftly picked
their pockets. At the end Alex had to count the articles
she had collected, which were then placed back into the
coats' pockets. Then Alex wore the garment while Jack
and Oliver worked together to steal the items back, each
time asking her how many things she had left as they
showed her what they had managed to lift.

Although Amelia was not entirely convinced that a
game of pickpocket was the most appropriate way to
teach a child the rudiments of addition and subtraction,
it was clear that Alex enjoyed the game immensely.
There was no question she was mastering her arithmetic

skills at a much swifter rate than she was reading and writing.

She was also becoming better at picking pockets, which Oliver seemed to think was wonderful.

Smoothing her hands over her gown Amelia hurried to the door, anxious to speak to Jack before he disappeared into the small bedchamber at the end of the corridor. With Alex occupying the guest room and Amelia still in Jack's chamber, Eunice and Doreen had insisted that another bedroom be prepared so that Jack would stop sleeping on the sofa in the drawing room. A chamber that had previously been used for storage was subsequently cleaned out and a modest bed and wardrobe were purchased. While Amelia felt guilty that she had put Jack out of his handsomely furnished room, Jack assured her that he didn't care in the least about his surroundings.

She peered into the corridor.

"What's wrong?" Jack demanded the moment he saw her.

His gaze was steady and his demeanor serious, suggesting that he had not consumed a drop of alcohol. He stood just inches away from her, his powerful presence filling the shifting shadows around them with heat and strength. Suddenly feeling small and lost, tears welled in her eyes as the façade of calm that she had somehow managed to maintain throughout the day began to crumble.

The silvery fall of Amelia's tears tore into Jack's heart. Forgetting his vow never to touch her again, he opened his arms and pulled her against him, forming a protective shield around her as dread tightened his belly. "Tell me, Amelia."

"My mother is dying," she wept, her face buried against his chest. "She's dying, and it's all my fault."

"How do you know she is dying?" he asked quietly. "And how could it possibly be your fault?"

She reluctantly broke free from his embrace to retrieve the newspaper that lay strewn across the bed. "I was reading the newspaper with Eunice and Doreen, because they like to hear about all the places where I have recently been seen, and even Alex finds it funny now that we've told her who I really am. Suddenly I noticed this headline: '*American Railway Magnate's Wife Critically Ill.*'" She lifted the paper closer to the lamp and read: "'Mrs. John Henry Belford is gravely ill after suffering a heart attack, reputedly caused by the trauma of her only daughter's recent disappearance. A statement released by Mr. John Henry Belford late last night said that while Mrs. Belford's condition is serious, the family remains hopeful that she may survive. Mr. Belford is pleading with the kidnappers of his daughter to demonstrate compassion in light of his wife's illness and release his child, so that she may see her mother for what may be a final time. Miss Amelia Belford was mysteriously abducted from her wedding to the Duke of Whitcliffe in late August, and has yet to be released. Mr. Belford has offered a reward for any information leading to the whereabouts of his daughter, which he recently increased to twenty-five thousand pounds...'"

"You're not thinking of going back to London?" Jack demanded, suddenly noticing the trunks in the corner.

"Of course I am. I'm leaving on the first train tomorrow morning. I only hope I won't be too late."

"Amelia, listen to me," he urged, his unease growing. "We don't know anything about your mother's condition except what has been written here, and newspapers are not the most reliable source of information. Just look at all the reports of people who have claimed to have seen you in the past few weeks in every major city from Paris to Cape Town."

"This article refers to a statement made by my father. Are you suggesting that he is lying in order to trick me into coming home?"

"I'm just saying we should take a day or two to determine what the facts are."

"My mother may not have a day or two," she countered vehemently. "I cannot believe you hold my family in such low regard that you think they would resort to such a cruel ploy in order to bring me home."

"I'm not suggesting your mother isn't ill." Jack realized he was treading a fragile path. "But your family has been desperate to find you for weeks now. This may be a trick to bring you to them. If you give me a couple of days, I can have someone in London investigate—"

"Don't trouble yourself." Her voice was cold. "My mother needs me and I'm going to her. There is nothing more to discuss."

Anger reared within him. "If you return to London, your family will never let you go," he said with absolute certainty. "They will force you to marry Whitcliffe or whatever other pompous little prick they have bought for you, so that the scandal of your disappearance and the shame you have brought them these past weeks will be neatly swept beneath the sanctity of marriage."

"I have no intention of marrying anyone," Amelia assured him flatly. "All I want to do is see my mother and relieve the unbearable anxiety she must be suffering, not knowing what has become of me. I want her and my father to know I am well, and that I have managed to take care of myself. I want them to see that I actually have some talent which has enabled me to earn a living, modest though it may be."

"Do you really think once they have heard about how you have been working in a third-rate hotel and living in a small, badly furnished house in Inverness with a collection of former thieves and pickpockets, they will simply wish you well and let you return? That you will just get on a train and come back?" His voice was harsh as he finished, "Do you honestly believe you will even want to come back?"

The chiseled line of his jaw was set and his brow was furrowed with anger. But it was his eyes that captured Amelia's attention. For in their steely gray depths she saw a flash of something she had not seen since the night she had so willingly given herself to him.

The night he had thought she was leaving him.

"What are you afraid of, Jack?" she enquired softly.

What could he tell her? Jack wondered helplessly. That he was afraid she would leave him and never return? That even if her parents didn't try to force her to marry Whitcliffe, Amelia would probably decide on her own that her little dalliance with what she must have considered virtual poverty was over? The allure of London, with its brilliant balls and parties, would seem glorious compared to the drudgery of her life in Inverness. Once she returned to her parents' home and started wearing three Parisian gowns a day while servants dashed about bringing her everything she could possibly desire, the novelty of rising at six o'clock each morning to don her plain outfits so she could toil long hours as a lowly employee at the Royal Hotel would swiftly fade. She would become the beautiful, pampered Amelia Belford once again.

And he would lose her forever.

Amelia watched as he struggled with his answer. Jack Kent was not the kind of man who would admit to being afraid of anything. A childhood spent on the streets fighting to survive, coupled with years of enduring the scorn of others, made it impossible for him to show weakness—even to her. And what did she expect?

That he would profess his undying love and beg her to
stay? His world was the sea and his ships, and building
the wealth he believed he needed in order to secure his
place in society and earn the respect of others, however
grudging it may be. He had helped her escape a life she
despised, and had generously opened his home to both
her and Alex. But he had never promised to make her
his wife, despite the incredible passion that had flared
between them.

She swallowed and looked away.

Jack clenched his fists in frustration. "I'm asking you
to trust me, Amelia. If in two days I can confirm that
your mother is indeed ill, I will take you to London myself."

"In two days my mother could be dead. If you truly
feel you must protect me, then come with me to London tomorrow."

He thought of Great Atlantic and their plan to destroy his company. The *Shooting Star* was due to set sail
in four days, which meant its cargo was currently being
loaded. Any sabotage to the ship now would result in
staggering losses and the cancellation of his contract,
which he simply could not afford. He had to spend the
next few days arranging for the security of his ships, before Great Atlantic struck again. At the same time he
needed to start implementing his strategies to knock the
company off its brittle financial pedestal and send it scur-
rying to stay viable.

"I cannot leave right now," he told her. "I have
some important business matters to attend to."

"Then we have nothing more to discuss. Good
night." She turned away, not wanting him to see how
much he had wounded her.

Jack stood frozen, staring at the proud, straight line
of Amelia's back. The back that had been forced to grow
ramrod straight through the use of some torturous de-

vice she had been strapped into as a child. He was losing her, he realized. It did not seem to matter that he didn't deserve her, and couldn't possibly give her the life to which she had been born. Didn't matter that he was the bastard of a poor maid turned whore and an irresponsible earl who could never publicly acknowledge him. Didn't matter that he had lived a life of such filth and violence and desperation that if Amelia ever learned the truth of it, she would shrink from him in horror and disgust. Nothing mattered except for the fact that she was leaving him.

She was leaving him, and he didn't think he could bear it.

A terrible desperation gripped him, stripping away the flimsy mantle of control he had maintained since she had returned. He grabbed her by her shoulders and spun her around, forcing her to look at him.

And then he crushed his lips to hers, driving his tongue into the dark heat of her startled mouth.

A cry of outrage escaped her throat as she lurched against him, beating him with her small fists as she struggled to free herself from his savage grip. But he only kissed her more deeply as he hauled her up and carried her to the bed. His hands tore at the buttons of her simply tailored outfit, which was so unlike the sumptuous gowns she had worn as Amelia Belford. She was better than he, there was no question of that, yet the realization only made him more determined to have her. Away came the mountainous layers of her gown, petticoats and corset, until finally she lay naked beneath him, her wrists pinned into the softness of the plaid beneath her and her breasts heaving with fury against his chest. She said nothing, but only looked at him with those magnificent eyes that reminded him of a summer storm, now glittering with fire and challenge.

I will make you mine, Jack vowed feverishly as he

lowered his head to suck hard upon the wine-stained peak of her breast. A moan of reluctant pleasure spilled from her lips and she closed her eyes. He growled and moved lower, roughly kissing the creamy flat of her belly before flicking his tongue deep into the hot rosy petals between her thighs. She gasped and went still, her body hovering between outrage and swiftly blooming need. He tasted her again, tormenting her with pleasure as he slowly dragged his tongue across the apricot-sweet folds of her in a long, hungry caress. He would touch her and taste her and fill her until she was lost, he vowed darkly. He would bring her to the brink of the most exquisite ecstasy she had ever known, until she was quivering and pleading with him for release. And then he would carry her over it, irretrievably binding her to him, and utterly ruining her for any other man.

Amelia held her breath, frozen, the last vestiges of her control snapping like taut silken threads. Her body was melting beneath Jack's erotic assault like a wisp of snow upon fire. Blood surged hotly through her flesh, pooling in her lips and breasts and into the slick wetness between her thighs, making her restless with need. She wanted Jack with a desperation that stunned her, obliterating the ragged traces of whatever virginal propriety she might once have had. And so she surrendered herself to his tender assault, enjoying the rough feel of his cheeks grazing the insides of her thighs while his tongue delved and probed and his hands roamed with rough determination across the hills and valleys of her body. Her flesh grew hotter and more liquid, until finally she could bear no more. She grabbed Jack by his shoulders and pulled him up, then began to claw in frustration at the fastenings of his trousers. He rose above her and wrenched off his clothes, hurling them to the floor. Finally he stretched naked over her, a sleek hard wall of bronzed muscle, covering her with his strength and heat.

Jack cradled his hands against Amelia's cheeks, studying her. She returned his gaze steadily, the magnificent turquoise of her eyes shimmering with desire and an emotion he did not recognize. There was so much he wanted to tell her, yet he feared that whatever he said would be wrong, for he had never been adept at articulating his feelings. Only bitterness and anger flowed easily from him. But in that moment his heart was filled with a tenderness and fear so excruciating he felt as if he were being torn apart.

"Do not leave me," he ventured, his voice caught somewhere between a command and a plea. And then, because he knew in the pit of his soul that she would, he added with almost shattered desperation, "Please."

Amelia wrapped her arms around his neck and covered his lips with hers. She felt him hesitate, as if he were unsure of her answer. Her hands slid down the muscled expanse of his back to grip the tightly molded contours of his hips. Then she pulled down upon him as she raised herself, sheathing him deep within.

Jack kissed her hard as he began to move inside her. *I love you*, he confessed silently, trying to bind her to him with every aching thrust. *I will take care of you*, he pledged, hoping that she could feel the enormity of his feelings for her in the hunger of his kiss, the yearning of his caress, the relentless rhythm of his body moving inside her. *I will try to make you happy*, he promised, even though he did not believe he had ever made anyone happy in his entire life. In and out he moved, faster and farther and deeper, filling her and stretching her and reaching within her, until their flesh and bone and skin were melded and it was impossible to know where his life ended and hers began. He wanted to stay like that forever, buried deep within the strength and sweetness and light that was Amelia. He tried to slow himself, to fight the rising crest of passion, but her breath was coming in shallow gasps and her body was tightening as she writhed against him. Again and again he drove himself into her, feeling as if he were losing part of his soul to her that he could never reclaim.

Suddenly she cried out and wrapped herself around him, kissing him feverishly as pleasure stripped away the last shreds of her restraint. Fighting the sob rising from his chest he drove himself into her, filling her with every fragment of his strength and need and fear. He gave himself wholly to her as he tried to take some small part of her for himself, so that when she finally left him, he just might be able to endure it.

When their breathing had slowed and their bodies began to cool, he raised himself onto his elbows and brushed a soft strand of hair off her forehead. He was acutely aware that she had not answered his plea. It did not matter.

Whatever promises she made, she would never be able to keep.

He lowered his head and captured her lips with his, kissing her with aching tenderness as his hands began to rouse her once more. When she was shifting and flexing beneath him he joined himself to her once again.

And for one brief moment he felt as if she actually loved him, and his soul was filled with glorious light.

Chapter Thirteen

AMELIA RAISED HER HANDKERCHIEF TO HER NOSE and inhaled a few shallow breaths. The comforting scent of Eunice's plain laundry soap and Scottish sunlight filled her nostrils, temporarily quelling the nausea churning within her.

From the moment her train had chugged into the city of London she had felt as if she couldn't breathe. She had assumed that as she approached the more fashionable West End and Mayfair, the air would be more pleasant. To her surprise, the suffocating stench of coal fires, manure, sewage, and insufficiently washed bodies persisted even into the most elegant district of the city. In Inverness the air was always cool and clean as it blew off the Moray Firth and the pristine mountains of the Highlands. When she had first arrived there she had thought the small Scottish town unbearably remote and provincial. Yet as she drove through the noisy, polluted streets of London, she wondered how she had ever enjoyed living in such a crowded, dirty place.

"We're here, Mrs. Chamberlain," announced the driver, opening the carriage door.

Amelia slowly stepped down from the carriage and faced the imposing stone façade of her parents' rented town house. The windows were not covered, which would have meant there had been a recent death in the house. Her mother was still alive.

Desperate to see her, she raced up the stairs and through the front door.

"Here now—what do you think you're doing?" demanded a shocked butler who was puttering with an enormous vase of flowers in the entrance hall. "You cannot simply charge in here—"

"I'm Amelia Belford. Where is my mother?" Amelia was not surprised that the former butler was gone. Few servants managed to survive her mother's exacting standards for long. "Is she in her bedroom?"

The man stared at her, stunned. "You're Miss Belford?"

"Yes—where is she?"

"Mrs. Belford is in the dining room," he began, valiantly trying to recover his composure. "If you'll just follow me . . ."

Amelia sped past him along the hallway and burst into the dining room.

"Good God, Amelia—is that really you?" Her father was startled as he looked up from his newspaper.

Rosalind Belford was seated at the breakfast table, dressed in a magnificent gown of coral-and-gold brocade, with several ropes of pearls draped around her neck. A massive diamond pin gleamed from her left shoulder, and she wore huge ruby and diamond earrings that were far too extravagant for day wear. Her gray-threaded hair was elegantly coiffed and her lips were carefully rouged.

She appeared the epitome of robust health.

"Thank heaven you're back." Relief had flooded her face, softening her features as she stared at Amelia.

"You cannot imagine how worried we have been about you—are you all right?"

"I thought you were ill." Amelia was unable to believe her family had gone to such lengths to deceive her. Her voice nearly broke as she finished, "It said in the newspaper that you were dying, Mother."

Rosalind carefully set down her teacup, averting her eyes from her daughter's accusing gaze. "Unfortunately, Amelia, we couldn't think of any other way to get you to come home."

"Amy! You're back!"

Amelia turned to see Freddy hurrying toward her, a glass of port in one hand. She turned her back on the rest of her family to wrap her arms tightly around him.

"Dearest Freddy," she murmured, fighting the tears threatening to spill down her cheeks, "tell me you weren't part of this awful deception."

"You know me better than that, Amy," her brother chided, gently lifting her chin with his finger. "I told them not to do it—I knew you would be horribly distressed by the thought of Mother dying."

"We never wanted to have to resort to trickery to lure you home, Amelia," her father assured her. "At first we thought you would quickly come to your senses and return home on your own. But as the weeks dragged on and it became evident that you wouldn't, your mother and I decided it was time to take more drastic measures. After all, we couldn't just let you stay in hiding forever."

"Where the devil have you been, anyway?" William regarded her curiously. "There have been sightings of you all over the world, and you wouldn't believe the parade of scum that has shown up trying to claim your reward."

"I've also received more than a dozen letters from blackguards who claimed to have kidnapped you," added her father, scowling. "If not for Freddy's assurance that you left with that scraggly old fellow at the ball of your own free will, I'd have damn well paid out my entire fortune by now trying to get you back." His expression was angry, but there was an unmistakable thread of anguish in his voice as he gruffly demanded, "Have you any idea how worried we have been, Amelia?"

"I'm sorry to have put all of you through that, Papa." Feeling genuinely guilty, Amelia bent and kissed his cheek. "But as you can see, I'm fine." She squeezed his hand.

"You don't look fine." Rosalind rose from the table and moved toward her daughter, needing a closer look to be sure she was truly well. "You look dreadful. Pale and exhausted and—dear Lord, whatever have you done to your beautiful hair?"

"It's just a temporary color." Amelia self-consciously tucked a stray dark hair under her hat. "It washes out."

"You look older." Her father's brow was furrowed with concern. "Were you ill?"

"I'm wearing cosmetics, Papa, to make me look older so people won't recognize me."

Holding fast to her hand, John continued to study her. "It's more than that, Amelia—there's something different about you."

"I *am* different, Papa," Amelia told him earnestly. "I've learned so much while I've been away—things I never knew about. I've even been learning how to cook."

"Wonderful." William put down his knife and fork and shoved his plate away, unable to fathom his sister's extraordinary behavior. "I can see the headlines now: '*American Heiress Reduced to Scullery Maid.*' God, Amelia, haven't you dragged our name low enough already?"

"Don't worry, William," said Freddy cheerfully. "You'll get your turn soon enough."

"If anyone is going to further embarrass the family,

it will be you, Freddy," William retaliated. "All of London knows you're a drunk—"

"That's enough out of both of you!" commanded his father. "By God, I've grown sick of you two and your constant sniping. If you can't be civil to one another, then keep your mouths shut, do you hear?"

William glared at Freddy.

Freddy raised his glass ever so slightly to William in a mocking toast, then downed his port in a single swallow.

John Belford shook his head, unable to fathom how he had sired two such sons, both of whom were complete enigmas to him. Freddy was pleasant enough, but he was utterly lacking in the discipline and ambition that had driven John his entire life. While William was ambitious, he was also humorless and intolerant, characteristics that kept him from enjoying the life his father had worked so hard to give him. Sighing, he turned to study his lovely daughter, trying to understand the changes he sensed in her. "Where have you been, Amelia?"

"I've been staying with friends," she replied evasively. "And they have helped me and taken good care of me, but I've also been learning to take care of myself." Her voice was filled with pride as she solemnly announced, "I've even got a job."

Rosalind gasped, horrified.

"Really?" Freddy regarded her with fascination. "Doing what?"

"Organizing some special affairs." Amelia knew she had to be careful about how much she revealed to her family. "It's actually very satisfying, and I've found I'm quite good at it."

"Oh, wonderful," drawled William. "If Whitcliffe finds out he'll think you've gone mad and want nothing more to do with you."

"There is no shame in working to support oneself,"

countered John sternly. "I've worked my entire life, and it wasn't always by sitting in some damned office all day the way you do, William. When I was barely more than a boy I was loading and unloading fish and produce in New York harbor. Even your mother worked when she was young, selling produce in her father's grocery store. Her fingers were stained from stacking all that damned fruit."

"John, please!" Rosalind nervously fingered her pearls, terrified that one of the servants might have overheard him. She abhorred any reference to her working-class background. She had fought long and hard to achieve a modicum of respectability in society, but she wasn't so naive that she didn't realize that everyone who knew of her humble beginnings secretly despised her for them. In the eyes of both servants and society, she was nothing more than a lower-class shop girl dressed in expensive clothes.

"Amelia shouldn't feel ashamed for working while she was off on her little adventure," John insisted. "She showed great resourcefulness, putting on a disguise and getting herself a job. She demonstrated what she's made of, and I, for one, am damned proud that my daughter was willing to work. That's the Belford spirit."

"Unless you look at Freddy," sneered William.

"At least I know how to enjoy myself with my friends," Freddy retaliated. "You are such a snob, you don't have any friends."

"Your friends are all bought," William shot back. "If you didn't have money, they'd have nothing to do with you."

"For God's sake, stop it both of you!" thundered John.

"Lord Whitcliffe must never find out about Amelia working," Rosalind insisted. "The wife of a duke does not work—not even before they are married."

Amelia regarded her mother in amazement. "Surely

you don't think I am still going to wed Lord Whitcliffe?"

"Of course you are." Her mother's tone was gently patronizing, as if any thought to the contrary was ludicrous. "And don't think for a moment that it was easy getting him to agree. Although your father and I have insisted to everyone that you were abducted, Lord Whitcliffe was thoroughly mortified by the disgrace of having his bride disappear from his own wedding. Then of course there is your bizarre behavior at the Wilkinsons' ball to be contended with, and the question of where and with whom you have been these past weeks..."

"Where have you been, Amelia?" asked Freddy.

"I've been staying with some very kind people outside of London."

"They weren't kind in the least if they put a young, inexperienced girl of your breeding and station to work," objected Rosalind, "and permitted you to hide from your family, who care about you and only want what is best for you. Who were they?"

"It doesn't matter, Mother." Amelia had no intention of telling anyone about Jack and his family. "You wouldn't know them."

Rosalind blinked, taken aback that her daughter was actually refusing to answer her question. "Well, I can only pray that you have not done anything further while you were away that will put us to shame. Your father had to increase your dowry by another fifty thousand pounds to get Lord Whitcliffe to consent to honor his betrothal when you finally returned."

"I'm surprised he didn't ask for stock in father's company as well, given all that I have put him through," Amelia reflected sarcastically.

"He did." Her father scowled. "But I told him any stock that I granted would have to be in your name. He didn't like that, but he finally accepted. Told me that under English law what's yours is his anyway—the lazy swine."

"We're just grateful that he didn't break the betrothal altogether, which he certainly might have, given the circumstances." Rosalind wanted to make Amelia understand how perilously close she had come to destroying her future.

"It would have been better for him if he had," Amelia told her. "Because I have no intention of marrying him."

Rosalind stared at her in shock. "Have you gone absolutely mad, Amelia?"

"I never wanted to marry Lord Whitcliffe, Mother. He was your choice, not mine."

"Don't be ridiculous." Rosalind could not understand what had come over Amelia. "You have always understood that a young girl of your station cannot possibly expect to make her own choice when it comes to her husband. You're a Belford, and every man who has offered for you has done so expecting to profit handsomely from that."

"Including that damned fool, Philmore." Her father snorted with contempt. "Filled your head with all kinds of foolish rubbish, and the next minute he was off chasing every other heiress in London."

"Your father and I want what is best for you, and we have to protect you from being taken advantage of," Rosalind continued. "Lord Whitcliffe is the only man who has offered for you who has something substantial to give in return—the title of duchess, a magnificent estate, and titles which will be passed on to your children and grandchildren. Your marriage to him will also open many business possibilities for your father both here and on the Continent. It is a perfect union."

"It isn't perfect at all," Amelia protested. "I don't love him. I don't even *like* him."

"That is because you don't know him very well. He is a man of impeccable breeding with a solid education. I'm certain that after you are married and have had an opportunity to spend some time together, you will find that you are extremely well suited."

"I'm sure we won't be well suited at all," Amelia countered vehemently. "And the fact that we both come from privileged backgrounds is not the basis for a happy marriage."

"Really, Amelia, what has come over you? For years we have told you that you would one day marry an aristocrat, and the idea always pleased you."

"But I always believed I would meet someone wonderful—someone whom I cared about." She regarded her mother imploringly. "Didn't you care about Papa when you married him?"

Rosalind was momentarily disconcerted by such a personal question. "Things were very different for us," she began, trying to construct a careful answer. "I could see that your father was hardworking and ambitious, and your father knew I wasn't afraid of work, either. We had come from similar backgrounds, and we both wanted the same thing—to make a better life for our children. That is what you should want as well."

"But did you care about each other?"

Rosalind cast a desperate glance at John, trying to find a way to respond without defeating her own argument.

"Our courtship was entirely different, Amelia," he pointed out. "Your wealth makes you extremely enticing to every unmarried man who meets you. You cannot be expected to marry someone poor, as I was when your mother and I met, and you can't marry just any rogue who fills your head with lies, the way Philmore did."

"But Lord Whitcliffe only wants to marry me because of my dowry," Amelia argued, trying to appeal to him.

"I'm afraid that's true of every man who offered for you, Amelia." His voice gentled a little. He took no pleasure in revealing the unfairness of life to his idealistic young daughter. "And would be true of every man who ever did show an interest in you. Like it or not, there is no escaping who you are and what you represent. Your mother and I can only try to give you a husband who can offer you the most in terms of your status and opportunities for your children."

"And that man is Lord Whitcliffe," Rosalind finished emphatically. She studied Amelia a moment, pained by her obvious unhappiness, yet absolutely certain that she and John were doing the right thing. "You will want for nothing, Amelia—your father and I will make certain of that."

"What I want is to go back to the life I have made for myself," Amelia pleaded. "I have friends there—people who care about me—and you can't make me stay here..."

"Anyone who would help to keep a confused, impressionable young girl from returning to her family and honoring her betrothal to a duke while putting her to work is not a friend, nor are they suitable company for you." Realizing she and John were getting nowhere with their attempts at rational persuasion, Rosalind decided it was time to take a firmer approach. "If you ever try to return to them, I will have you followed." Determined to eradicate any thoughts Amelia might have of running away again, she continued, "When I find out who they are, I promise you that your father and I will see to it that they are destroyed both financially and socially—is that clear?" Her expression softened. "Now then, I suggest we arrange for a bath so we can get you out of those clothes and wash that atrocious color out of your hair. I have ordered another wedding gown for you, and it will need to be fitted immediately if it is to be ready in two days. That will give me just enough time to arrange for the church and a small reception here afterward. Once you are married and settled at Lord Whitcliffe's estate, we can plan a more lavish celebration." She rang for the butler.

"I'm sorry to disappoint you, Mother, but I will not be marrying Lord Whitcliffe." Amelia inhaled a steadying breath, fighting to keep her voice resolute as she defied her parents. "I don't know how to say it more plainly than that. I came here to see you because I thought you were dying and might take comfort in seeing me. Now that I know you are well, I intend to leave on the first train possible."

"You're not going anywhere, Amelia Belford." Rosalind could not understand her daughter's behavior, but she had no intention of permitting her to ruin her life. "I forbid it."

"You cannot keep me here against my will."

"Of course I can. You're my daughter, and your father and I will decide what is best for you and this family, even if that means locking you in your room until your wedding."

"Then I'll just run away again."

"Really, Amelia, you have no more sense than a child." William regarded her in exasperation. "Do you really believe you can just walk out of here and go back to wherever it is you have been hiding these past few weeks? As we speak, the news that Amelia Belford has returned home is spreading like fire throughout this neighborhood."

She looked at William in confusion. "No one knows I am here..."

"Perkins, the butler, knows, and he would have marched straight downstairs to the kitchen to announce it to all the servants. By now they have told the neighbors' servants, the delivery boys, and everyone in the shops the maids have run off to. A pack of journalists are probably on their way over this very moment to get the story. By early this evening all of London will know of your return, and by tomorrow so will the rest of the world. Within five minutes you won't be able to step outside without being mobbed. You have become even more famous since your disappearance than you were before, and everyone is going to want to see you to make certain that you are truly safe."

William was right, Amelia realized helplessly. In her desperation to see her mother, she had not considered the attention her return would instigate.

"You cannot be permitted to leave this house," Rosalind decided. Recalling Amelia's embarrassing escape at the church, she continued, "I will instruct the servants to have someone keep watch out front and back, in case you decide to do something ridiculous like climb out of a window."

Amelia regarded her father imploringly. "Please, Papa..."

"I'm afraid your mother is right." It wounded him to see Amelia so unhappy, but John had no doubt that he and Rosalind were doing the right thing. His innocent young daughter might have enjoyed running away and having her little adventure, but ultimately he had to protect her from making a decision that she would certainly come to regret. "One day you will see that, Amelia."

Amelia cast one last desperate look at Freddy.

"Don't even think about involving your brother in another one of your mad schemes, Amelia," Rosalind warned. "I know all about how he assisted you the last time. If he dares to do anything so foolish again, or if you try to run away or do anything to avoid your marriage to Lord Whitcliffe, both of you will be cut off. Given Freddy's expensive tastes and the extensive bills he has accumulated here in London, I doubt he will find that agreeable."

Anger clouded Freddy's face. "Maybe I'll just find a job like Amelia did."

"Unless there are jobs which allow you to be drunk by noon, I'm not sure what it is you are fit to do," William reflected.

"If either of you dare to defy me, Frederick, you will have to find out," warned Rosalind. "Is that clear?"

Freddy regarded Amelia helplessly.

"It's all right, Freddy." Amelia adored her sweetly aimless brother, and could not bear the thought of him being punished because of her. "Don't worry—everything is going to be fine."

"Perkins, kindly escort Miss Belford to her room and see that her new maid is sent to her at once," Rosalind instructed as the butler entered the dining room. "She requires a hot bath, and her new wedding gown must be fetched from the dressmaker's so that it can be fitted. Tell my maid I require her assistance immediately in making a list of everything that needs to be done and preparing invitations for this afternoon's mail. That way they will be received in tomorrow's first post."

"Yes, Mrs. Belford," said Perkins. "There is a group of gentlemen from the newspapers outside who wish to know if Mr. Belford would be willing to speak to them regarding the safe return of Miss Belford. They would also like to see Miss Belford, if possible."

"Tell them Amelia is resting and preparing for her upcoming marriage to Lord Whitcliffe," Rosalind instructed John, "which will take place the day after tomorrow. It's short notice, but at least we should be able to get some coverage in the society pages. If they want to see her, they will have to wait patiently outside until she is sufficiently recovered from her ordeal, and at this time we don't know when that will be."

Her mother had effectively invited the journalists to stay camped outside their doorstep waiting for her to make an appearance, Amelia realized despondently. The last tenuous possibility that she might somehow be able to secretly escape the house and return to the life she had made in Inverness was shattered.

She was Amelia Belford once again, and she was trapped.

By THE TOES OF SAINT ANDREW, JUST HOW MUCH did ye drink?" demanded Oliver, throwing open the curtains.

Jack cracked open a bleary eye, then winced at the blast of sunlight pouring into the study.

"Not much," he mumbled, feeling as if his head were about to explode. "I was working late," he added, noticing that his cheek was pillowed against a mountain of papers and journals on his desk.

"Is that what ye call it? Gettin' yerself completely guttered is more how I see it."

"I'm not guttered," Jack insisted, cautiously raising his head.

"Then ye'll nae mind a few visitors, will ye?"

"I don't want to see anyone." He wondered if it were possible for a skull to actually split open from pain. "Tell whoever it is to come back tomorrow."

"He says ye're to come back tomorrow," Oliver informed the group standing in the doorway.

"I can see why," observed Haydon wryly.

Genevieve regarded Jack with concern. "Perhaps we should have sent a note letting him know that we were coming."

"I've seen him look worse." Jamie marched in, took

a quick look at Jack and frowned. "On second thought, maybe not."

"Really, Jack, this is no way to behave when you have guests staying in your home," chided Annabelle. "You look *dreadful*."

"Maybe he's not feeling well," protested Charlotte, limping into the study behind her.

"I don't think I'd feel well after drinking all that whiskey, either," Grace reflected, sniffing the air.

"He needs something to eat." Simon's expression was bright as he joined his parents and siblings. "Do you think Eunice has lunch ready?"

"Beggin' yer pardon." Alex brushed against Haydon as she squeezed her way through the crowded study. "Sorry—I just need to see Jack," she apologized, bumping into Jamie.

Wondering when, exactly, his study was declared a public meeting place, Jack gingerly forced himself to sit up. His eyes narrowed as he looked at Alex, who was standing before him with a satisfied smile on her face.

"Give it back," he ordered.

She regarded him innocently. "What do ye mean?"

"You know exactly what I mean. Give it back. Now."

She huffed with annoyance. "Can't we at least count it first?"

"No. You give it back now, Alex, or you'll have no dessert tonight."

Looking thoroughly irritated, she reached into the sleeve of her new dress and pulled out a dark leather coin purse. "Here," she said, tossing it to Haydon. "I only wanted to count what's inside."

Haydon caught the purse in surprise. "Thank you."

"There." Alex glowered at Jack. "Are ye happy?"

"Not quite."

She huffed mightily again. "Let's wait 'til he notices."

"No."

"Ye're nae fun today," she complained.

"Don't throw it," Jack warned.

"I wasn't goin' to," she protested, pulling a gold watch and chain from her other sleeve. "I was only borrowin' it," she told Jamie, handing the watch back to him.

"You're good," said Jamie, impressed. "I didn't feel a thing."

"Is that everything?" Jack eyed Alex suspiciously.

She shrugged her shoulders. "If ye was watchin' me, ye should know."

"Alex..." he began warningly.

"That's all she pinched in here," Oliver told him. "I was keepin' an eye on her."

"Well, it seems I have a great deal of catching up to do," said Genevieve, pulling off her gloves. "Since you don't seem to want to come out to the house for dinner, Jack, and you've obviously been too busy to extend an invitation to us, Haydon and I decided that we would come by for a visit today. We're most anxious to meet your houseguest, Miss Belford. We have heard a great deal about her from your brothers and sisters. Is she still at work at the hotel?"

"She's gone," Jack said abruptly.

Annabelle regarded him in surprise. "Gone where?"

"Back to her family in London. She left on the train yesterday, and would have arrived there this morning."

"But she'll be back." Alex frowned at Jack for making it sound so final. "She told me so afore she left—while ye was still sleepin'."

"Maybe." He shrugged. He did not want to dash Alex's hopes too soon. Despite her indifferent demeanor, Jack knew she had actually grown extremely fond of Amelia.

"Oh, Jack, how could you possibly let her return alone?" wondered Charlotte, looking at him with concern. "She must have wanted to go home because she heard her mother was ill—why on earth didn't you go with her?"

"I couldn't," he snapped, defensive. "She insisted on leaving immediately, and unfortunately, I had business matters to attend to, and could not simply..."

"Jack." Her voice was filled with gentle reprimand.

"I couldn't go with her, Charlotte."

"Then you should have asked one of us to go," said Annabelle. "I could have gone, or Jamie, or Simon..."

"He didn't want anyone to go with her." Charlotte's gaze was fixed sympathetically upon her brother. "He was hoping that she would choose to stay with him."

"Amelia is free to do whatever she likes," he said brusquely. "I don't really give a damn one way or the other. I asked her not to go, and she did. I assume that if she wants to return, she will."

"She won't be able to," Grace countered. "Her parents will never allow it. You know how desperate they are for Amelia to marry Lord Whitcliffe. Her disappearance these past few weeks has been profoundly embarrassing for them. I'm quite sure that once Amelia is back in their grasp, they'll not be so careless as to let her escape again."

"Maybe she won't want to escape again," Jack retaliated. "Maybe once she has returned to living in luxury, she'll come to her senses and realize what she was missing."

Alex looked at him in confusion. "What was she missin'? She had everythin' she needed here."

"Amelia isn't the one who needs to come to her senses, Jack," said Charlotte. "You are."

"What is that supposed to mean?"

"I mean it's about time you stopped feeling sorry for yourself," she told him. "It's time you put your past where it belongs—in the past. And realized that you aren't condemned to spend the rest of your life alone, feeling bitter and angry at the world."

"I don't."

"You do," Charlotte insisted. "And if you don't stop now, then you may indeed have to spend the rest of your life alone. But it won't be because of Amelia. It will be because of you."

"You can forget whatever romantic notions you may have in your head, Charlotte." Jack was infuriated at having his life dissected in front of his entire family. "There is nothing between me and Amelia. She was a friend, and I helped her escape from a marriage she claimed to not want, and gave her a place to stay for a while. Nothing more."

"Oh, Jack." Charlotte's eyes were filled with sadness. "How can you lie to me?"

There was a moment of strained silence.

"If all of you would kindly leave us for a moment," Genevieve began quietly, "I would like to speak with Jack, alone."

"Come on then," said Oliver, rousing the little group into action. "Let's see if we canna get Eunice to fix us some nice tea and biscuits."

Genevieve waited until the room had cleared and the door shut before seating herself on the sofa. "I've always loved that painting of Charlotte," she remarked, studying the portrait she had created so many years earlier. "When I gave it to you, I sensed that you loved it just as much as I did."

"It's a beautiful painting," Jack said shortly.

"I suppose it is. But that isn't what first drew you to it. You liked it simply because it was a painting of Charlotte."

He did not deny it.

"Before you went away to university, I used to worry about you and Charlotte. I could see that there was a powerful bond between the two of you, and I was afraid you might confuse your feelings for each other for something else. I knew that no matter how deeply you and Charlotte cared for each other, it would be wrong for you to marry her. Do you know why?"

"You thought I wouldn't be gentle enough with her," Jack replied bluntly. "You knew I had a violent past and a temper, and you thought Charlotte deserved better than that, after all that she had been through—and she did."

"No, that wasn't it at all, Jack. I knew you and Charlotte were wrong for each other, because you would always see Charlotte as a victim. After being an older brother to her for so many years and thinking of her as a shy, frightened, abused little girl who needed protection, you would spend your life trying to shield her from the rest of the world, and even from yourself. You would never come to treat her as an equal. By loving her so much and wanting to keep her safe, you would have locked her into a narrow, stifling role that would have kept her from challenging herself, and ultimately discovering all that she could be.

"And Charlotte would have suffocated you," Genevieve continued, "although not intentionally. As her husband, you would have felt guilty every time you left her to go on one of your lengthy voyages, even though you needed so desperately to escape Scotland and see the world. Ultimately, you would have resented that. She also would have inadvertently forced you to suppress your emotions and your temper, because you would have been afraid that she was too fragile to deal with them. You needed a woman who could accept your moods and your passions, and not be afraid to match them. Finally, had you married Charlotte your contempt and anger toward the world would have grown unchecked. You would have always believed she was being judged for her own unfortunate beginnings, and you both would have suffered because of it."

"I don't see how any of this matters now." Jack's voice was clipped. "Charlotte married Harrison, and I was damn happy for her when she did, once I knew what sort of man he was."

"You were also relieved, because you no longer felt responsible for her happiness."

He said nothing.

"So my question to you is, who do you think is responsible for your happiness?"

"No one."

"Wrong. You are. Only you can decide what will make you truly happy, Jack."

"I am happy."

"You're the most miserable I have ever seen you."

"I'm not miserable."

"Then why do I feel as if your heart is breaking?"

"I suppose because you've been listening to Charlotte, and she seems to think I'm unhappy."

There was a long moment of silence before Genevieve finally asked, "Do you love Amelia Belford, Jack?"

A harsh laugh escaped him. "It wouldn't matter if I did. She would never marry a man like me."

"And what kind of a man is that?"

"A bastard," he said ruefully. "An urchin. A thief. A street fighter. A prisoner. A struggling, barely successful entrepreneur. Take your pick. None of those things are what she has in mind for a husband."

"What does she have in mind?"

"Someone rich. Preferably an aristocrat, with a huge estate and lots of money. Someone who has the time and inclination to take her to lots of fancy balls and dance with her and play all those bloody games of society."

"It seems to me she already had that in Lord Whitcliffe. Yet she gave it up to run away with you."

"She didn't run away with me," Jack objected. "She

ran away, and because she just happened to climb into my carriage, I helped her. She thought she was going off to marry Viscount Philmore, but it turned out the sniveling little fop was already betrothed to someone else." He snorted with contempt.

"And so she stayed with you. She came to Inverness, and from what I understand from your brothers and sisters, she created a new identity for herself, and got herself a job, and even brought that little Alex here to live. Those hardly sound like the actions of a spoiled heiress who is pining to go home."

"It doesn't matter," Jack argued. "Now that she has gone home, she'll see everything that she was missing. This is a woman who was born to a wealth you and I can barely imagine, Genevieve—far greater than anything Haydon inherited or earned in his lifetime. She has lived a life of unbelievable privilege and protection—she doesn't understand the real world. She thinks all criminals are like Oliver and Alex, for God's sake." He turned to look out the window before finishing in a raw voice, "And she doesn't know the truth about me."

"What truth?"

"About my past," he replied shortly.

"Actually, I believe she does—in quite some detail. Annabelle told me that she and Amelia talked about your childhood at length while Amelia was staying with her. Annabelle wasn't the first to mention it, either. Apparently Oliver, Eunice and Doreen had already told her about it."

Jack stared at her, dumbfounded. "She knows?"

"Why does that surprise you?"

"Because she never acted like she knew."

"How do you think she should have acted?"

Like she was better than me. Like I was not worthy of her.

But Amelia had never acted like she thought she was better than him—or anybody else, for that matter. For all her privilege and breeding, for all her travel and education and jewels and gowns and the expectation that she would marry someone of either staggering wealth or nobility, Amelia had always treated him exactly the same.

As an equal.

"When I first fell in love with Haydon, I believed he would never want to marry someone like me," Genevieve reflected softly. "He was a marquess, and I was a poor, outcast spinster whom society thought was mad because I had given up a life of privilege and respectability to take care of urchin children no one else wanted. How could a wealthy, handsome, titled man like Haydon possibly want to marry a woman like that?"

"You were strong, and kind, and generous." Jack felt his old fury stir as he remembered how society had denigrated Genevieve. "He was lucky to find you."

"We were lucky to find each other," Genevieve amended, smiling. "But all the while I was thinking that I was not worthy of Haydon, he believed that he was not worthy of me, because of the mistakes he had made in his past. So there we were, each of us too consumed with self-doubt and guilt to realize how the other felt. If we had just walked away without telling each other, we would never have known the incredible love and happiness that we have shared these past twenty-two years."

Jack shook his head. "Amelia Belford is not in love with me, Genevieve."

"How do you know?"

Because a woman as magnificent as she could never love a selfish bastard like me.

"Everything I've heard about her suggests to me that she is quite special," Genevieve continued, watching him. "I'm your mother, so of course I think that any young woman with an ounce of sense would be foolish not to love you. But the only question that matters at this moment is, do you care for her enough to find out? Because if your brothers and sisters are right, she is trapped now. She is a prisoner of her family's ambition, while you are a prisoner of your unwillingness to put your past aside and look at her purely with your heart."

He went to the window and stared outside, weighing Genevieve's words.

He had let Amelia go. He had always known that eventually she would leave him. Yet for a brief moment he had allowed himself to think that he had managed to bind her to him—that he had made her understand with his touch what he couldn't seem to articulate with words. He had been so furious when he discovered the note she had left him, he had barely flinched when Oliver returned home later that evening to say that she had not been at the hotel when he went to pick her up. Walter Sweeney, the manager, had seemed surprised that Oliver didn't know she had taken the train to London earlier that day, saying she had some urgent family matter to attend to. Jack had retired to his study to pore over the journals Lord Hutton had given him, angrily telling himself that he didn't give a damn what she did. He would just immerse himself in his work the way he always had. He would devote himself to bringing down Great Atlantic and building North Star Shipping into the successful company he knew it could be. But he couldn't.

Amelia was gone, and suddenly nothing else seemed to matter.

"Oliver!" he called suddenly. He strode across the room and jerked the door open, only to find his entire family crowded around the doorway.

"Were you listening?" he demanded.

"Of course not." Alex managed much better than the rest to look thoroughly affronted by his suggestion. "We was just comin' to ask ye if ye wanted yer tea brought to ye."

"I don't have time for tea," Jack told her. "I need my bags brought up to my room, Oliver. I'm taking the next train to London."

"Good." Alex nodded with satisfaction. "I've always wanted to see London."

"You're not coming, Alex."

"Ye canna stop me from goin'," she told him bluntly. "If ye willna buy me a ticket, then I'll just pinch one, or nick the money to buy one. Either way, I'm goin'."

"I'll pay your fare, Alex," offered Jamie. "That will save you the trouble of lifting my wallet. We can sit together on the train," he suggested brightly, "and you can tell me how you would go about fleecing the other passengers."

"Oh, Jamie, that's a lovely idea," agreed Annabelle. "I was just thinking a trip to London would be very nice. I could meet with my publisher, and we might even take in a play while we're there."

"I'm going, too," Simon decided. "I can use the time on the train to work on my drawings for my latest invention."

"I've been meaning to get to London to see the new fashions for autumn," reflected Grace.

"I would like to visit the National Gallery and the British Museum," Charlotte added.

"And I really must check on the house, and see how Lizzie and Beaton are getting along." Genevieve looked at Haydon expectantly.

He sighed. "I'm sure I have some business matters in London to attend to," he said, wrapping an arm around her waist.

"Well, I'm nae leavin' ye to be driven around London by that old drunk, Beaton." Oliver scowled. "He's liable to forget where he left ye."

"You're not coming with me." Jack's tone was final.

Simon regarded him with feigned confusion. "Who said anything about going with you?"

"We're just taking a trip—that's all," Grace assured him.

"Are we now?" Eunice entered the room carrying an enormous platter of ginger biscuits. "I've been thinkin' of takin' a wee trip myself, lately."

"London seems as good a place as any to go," reflected Doreen. "Besides, I doubt poor Lizzie can feed and tend to all o' ye by herself."

"Surely you can't object to us traveling on the same train with you," Annabelle said sweetly.

"You won't even know we're there," Charlotte promised.

Jack's expression was dark. "I doubt that."

"You can't expect to just march into Amelia's home and walk out with her, Jack," pointed out Simon, munching on a biscuit. "Even if she wants to go with you, her parents are liable to make a fuss."

"Think about what happened at the Wilkinsons' ball," said Annabelle.

"If things get sticky, you're going to need us," Jamie added.

Grace nodded in agreement. "The more distractions we can create, the better."

They were right, Jack realized, moved by his family's desire to help.

"Fine, then," he relented. "But you do exactly as I say—is that clear?"

The little band of former thieves solemnly nodded.

Chapter Fourteen

AMELIA LIFTED AN EDGE OF HEAVY VELVET CURtain to peer at the drunken, cheering mob jostling each other on the street below.

They had started to assemble from the moment word of her return had raced through the streets of London, some two days earlier. At first the crowd had consisted mainly of journalists, photographers, and the idle curious, who had nothing better to do than languish about all day hoping to catch a glimpse of the famous Amelia Belford, runaway American heiress. Despite her mother's attempts to control the details of both her disappearance and her return, which the abundantly bribed newspapers dutifully reported as an abduction, the popular consensus was that Amelia had run away.

The stories of what had happened to her during her disappearance were wildly fanciful. They ranged from her falling madly in love with some Arabian prince who had made her the favorite of his harem, to her giving away all of her jewels to the poor on the London docks one night and then retreating to a convent in Italy to live a life of poverty and seclusion. Whatever her adventures had been, all of London was thrilled that she had returned to her family and the welcoming arms of her betrothed. When her father informed the newspapers that Amelia's much-anticipated wedding to the Duke of Whitcliffe would take place after all, the throng crowding their elegant neighborhood swelled into the thousands. An army of policemen had to be hired for her wedding day to maintain some semblance of order amidst the shouting, pushing hoards, just to ensure that Amelia's bridal carriage would be able to travel the short distance to the church and home again, where a hastily arranged reception for some one hundred and fifty guests would be held.

She let the curtain drop and moved slowly back to her bed. Lying down atop the intricately embroidered silk coverlet, she pressed the heels of her hands against her aching eyes. *I will not cry anymore,* she told herself fiercely. *I will not.* She squeezed her eyes tight and inhaled a ragged breath, fighting the wave of despair that was threatening to engulf her.

At first she had been able to control her tears, even as her mother flitted about giving orders and worrying about every detail of Amelia's hastily arranged nuptials. A seemingly endless contingent of unfamiliar maids, dressmakers, florists, cooks, footmen and delivery people had descended upon the house, whipping every room into a frenzy of activity as preparations were made for the lavish reception that was to follow the ceremony. Through it all Amelia somehow managed to act as if everything was all right. Nineteen years of being trained to endure in stoic silence was too ingrained to permit her to do otherwise.

Her mother had been most effective in thwarting any attempt Amelia might have made to run away. More daunting than the servants watching her and the crowd camped outside was the formidable assertion that if

Amelia did anything to avoid her marriage to Whitcliffe, both she and Freddy would be cut off. While Amelia had learned she could survive without her parents' support, she was absolutely certain Freddy could not.

From the time he was born, not one droplet of either her father's discipline or her mother's ambition had made itself apparent in Freddy's sunny, carefree personality. Her beloved brother was content to live the life of the millionaire's idle son, who didn't need to trouble himself with the tiresome details of earning a living. Bewildered by his youngest son's lack of motivation, John Belford had put all his efforts into grooming William for one day taking over the management of his railway company. As Rosalind was preoccupied with raising Amelia to marry an aristocrat, Freddy had been permitted to carry on however he liked. The result was a handsome, charming, fun-loving young man, who found rising by noon rather taxing, given that he regularly stayed out drinking and carousing until dawn.

Freddy could never survive being cut off by his family.

There was also the threat of what Amelia's parents would do to anyone who dared help her in her new life. With several thousand well-wishers flocked outside her door, as well as scores of policemen and journalists, Amelia had no hope of escaping unnoticed. She would be followed wherever she went, which meant her parents would easily find her in her new life in Inverness. Rosalind had promised to destroy anyone who helped her, and Amelia was painfully aware that her father's wealth and influence made this a powerful threat. Jack and his family would fall victim to an assault in which none of them would be spared, either financially or in the media onslaught that would follow. Once her parents discovered she was working at the Royal Hotel, her mother would simply ask her father to buy it and have her dismissed, along with dear Mr. Sweeney. All the people who had been so kind and generous to Amelia would suffer for befriending her.

She would not let that happen.

She could endure being married to Whitcliffe, she told herself, fighting the sick revulsion that churned through her when she thought about sharing her body with him the way she had with Jack. She could endure anything if it meant protecting those she loved. She would learn to live her life as a prisoner, incarcerated on a remote estate, married to an elderly man who openly disliked her, and whom she very nearly despised. She would not have love, but she would have the memory of love.

And the remembrance of an exquisite passion that for one brief moment had flamed so gloriously hot and bright, she had felt as if she would know joy forever.

It was far more than most women of her station ever had, she reflected, brushing away the tear leaking down her cheek. She wrapped her arms around herself and turned onto her side, muffling her sobs in her pillow.

It was far more than most women of any station ever had.

Excuse me, madam," said Perkins, ushering two pretty, crisply starched maids into the dining room. "Miss Belford's new maids have arrived to assist her in getting ready—Miss MacGinty and Mademoiselle Colbert."

"You're twenty minutes late," fretted Rosalind.

One of the maids was tall and slender, with elegantly arranged blond hair that reflected her ability with a brush and hairpins. The other maid was dark-haired and velvet-eyed, with a slightly lusher figure. Both women had a fan of fine laugh lines beneath their eyes, suggesting that they were past the bloom of their twenties.

"You, there," Rosalind called out to one of the scrawny men dragging the leased tables into the dining room, "can't you see you're scratching the floorboards? Kindly lift the table!"

"Pardonnez-moi," said the blond maid, regarding Rosalind with the haughtiness for which French maids were renowned, "but eet was most *difficile* to reach dis house through that ugly mob. If madame no longer wishes for our assistance..."

"Of course I wish for your assistance," Rosalind hastily assured her.

The last thing she needed was to have the maids she had hired to arrange Amelia's hair and dress her quit in a fit of pique. There were one hundred and fifty people arriving that afternoon for an extravagant reception that had yet to be cooked, to be served on rented china, linens, and crystal that had not yet arrived, on the ugly, badly scratched tables that were currently being crammed into the dining room, drawing room and entrance hall. The flowers that had been delivered earlier were red and yellow, when Rosalind had expressly ordered ivory and peach; the only musicians she had been able to engage on such short notice consisted of a violinist and a bagpiper, the sound of which she could scarcely imagine; the ice sculptures were already half melted by the uncommon heat of the day; and something was burning in the kitchen and filling the house with a disgusting smell. The preparations were going abominably, and Rosalind was acutely aware that if anything was found lacking at Amelia's wedding reception, all of London society would take great delight in gossiping about it for months after.

"Perkins will take you up to Miss Belford's chamber," she told the maids. "Miss Belford is to be dressed and ready to leave for the church at precisely two o'clock. I have left a picture on her bureau of how I would like her hair to be arranged, which I hope you will be able to duplicate. Try to lace her corset as tightly as possible, to show her gown to the best possible effect. Did you bring your implements for dressing her hair?"

"But of course." Mlle. Colbert, the French maid, sounded insulted by the suggestion that she might have forgotten something so vital.

"I also brought some of my own special cosmetics with me," said Miss MacGinty, indicating the leather case she carried, "in case you would like me to make her even more beautiful on this very special day."

"I do not want her wearing rouge or heavy powder," Rosalind told her, "but you'll have to do something about the dark circles under her eyes. Just try to make her look as naturally lovely as possible."

"Very good, madame." Maintaining a superior air even as she curtsied, Mlle. Colbert finished, "It shall be exactly as you say."

Amelia ROSE FROM THE BED WHEN SHE HEARD THE knocking upon her door and went to the washstand, where she hastily pressed a wet cloth against her swollen eyes. Whoever it was, she did not want them to find her weeping. "Come in."

"Forgive me for disturbing you, Miss Belford," apologized Perkins, squinting into the dark chamber's gloom. "Your maids have arrived to help you get ready. Miss MacGinty and Mademoiselle Colbert."

"Thank you, Perkins." Amelia barely glanced at the two women.

He began to leave, then hesitated. "Do you need anything, Miss Belford?" he asked with uncharacteristic gentleness.

Yes, Amelia thought, feeling on the verge of hysteria. *I need to go home.* "No, thank you."

He nodded and left the room, closing the door behind him.

"Well, I think you need some light," Annabelle said, abandoning her French accent as she went to the window and threw open the dark velvet curtains. "It's positively dreary in here, Amelia. I swear I've played death scenes in more light."

"I was thinking the same thing." Grace opened the curtains of a second window and a bright wash of sunlight streamed into the room. "That's much better, don't you think?"

Amelia stared at the two women in shock. "Annabelle—Grace—what on earth are you doing here?"

"We heard you were in London and came by to see how you were faring," said Annabelle breezily.

"We were worried about you." Grace regarded her with concern. "How are you, Amelia?"

"I'm fine." She fought to control the waver in her voice. "I'm getting married, you know."

"Yes, we had heard that," Annabelle told her. "It was in all the newspapers."

"Does Jack know?"

"Yes."

Amelia swallowed thickly. She could well imagine how betrayed Jack would feel. "I don't want him to know that you found me crying. You won't tell him, will you?"

"Of course not," Grace soothed. "Not if you don't want us to."

"I know he would be upset if he thought I was being forced into this marriage. It's better that he thinks I just changed my mind. That once I came home I realized how much I missed my old life, and decided I wanted to marry Lord Whitcliffe after all."

Grace went to her and gently brushed a tangled lock of hair off her face. "Do you want to marry Lord Whitcliffe, Amelia?"

"It doesn't matter what I want," Amelia told her, despondent. "It never has."

"Of course it matters," countered Annabelle. "Do you want to marry Whitcliffe or not?"

"I have no choice," Annabelle told her. "My mother has vowed to cut both me and my brother off completely if I don't go through with this wedding. I can survive without my family's money, but poor Freddy can't."

"Does he suffer from some sort of terrible ailment?" wondered Grace.

"No, nothing like that. It's just that Freddy isn't accustomed to working, and I'm afraid he isn't trained to do very much."

"You said the same thing about yourself," pointed out Annabelle, "and then you went out and got yourself a job."

"I was able to get that job because your family helped me."

"We would help Freddy too, if we had to," Grace assured her. "You mustn't let your concern for him force you into a marriage you don't want."

"It isn't just Freddy I'm worried about. My mother has threatened to destroy anyone who tries to help me escape this marriage and begin a new life elsewhere. If she finds out about you and Jack and your family, she will have my father see to it that all of you are ruined, both financially and socially."

Annabelle laughed, amused. "He doesn't have the power to do that."

"He is terribly rich, Annabelle," Amelia argued. "He can buy almost anything."

"Wealth doesn't buy everything in England and Scotland," Grace told her. "Your father is American, and does not have the benefit of the loyalties and associations that come from being born here, or having a title."

"Which is part of the reason your parents are so anxious for you to acquire one for the family," Annabelle added. "Even if it means sacrificing their only daughter's happiness."

"They believe that eventually I will come to be happy, once I am settled into my life as a duchess. Mother thinks that love isn't necessary for a successful marriage." Amelia fought to keep her voice steady. "She believes that as long as a husband and wife have similar interests and are civilized with one another, that is enough."

"I suppose for some people, that is enough." Grace regarded her intently. "But those are people who have never known what it is to really be in love, Amelia."

A painful fist of emotion squeezed Amelia's heart.

"If you want to marry Lord Whitcliffe, then Grace and I will arrange your hair and help you into your gown and make sure that you look positively beautiful for your wedding." Annabelle took Amelia's hand. "But if you don't want to marry Whitcliffe, Amelia, you must tell us now so we can make alternate arrangements."

"If I returned to Jack, my parents would do everything within their power to ruin him and his shipping company," Amelia reflected despondently. "You're wrong if you think my father doesn't have the means to do that—he does. I can't let that happen. I don't want Jack to be hurt because he tried to help me. I could never live with the knowledge that I had been the cause of North Star Shipping's failing—not when I know how terribly important it is to him."

"Maybe you should let Jack decide whether or not he is willing to take that risk."

Her eyes widened. "Jack is here?"

"The whole family is, actually. Jack was most upset

to learn that you had gone to London without him. I think he wants to talk to you about that."

"I don't think he is particularly happy about the fact that you're getting married, either," reflected Grace, glancing down at the enormous crowd filling the street below.

"But how can I possibly see him?" wondered Amelia. "I can't leave the house, and my mother will never let him in to speak to me."

"If you want to see him, Amelia, then you shall— but we have to work quickly. Just tell us."

Amelia hesitated. Jack had never promised her his undying love or marriage. He had never filled her head with flowery pledges and romantic vows that ultimately meant nothing, the way Percy had. But Jack had been the first person in her life to genuinely care about what it was that she wanted, which was the freedom to make her own life. And to the best of his ability, he had tried to give that to her.

Do not leave me, he had pleaded with her on that final night, as he filled her heart and her soul with agonizing tenderness. In those final hours together, she had felt his need for her, as surely as if he had given her a piece of himself to her. But she had left him. She had ignored his raw, desperate appeal and sneaked away, telling herself that when it suited her she would simply return. Instead she had become trapped in the web of her family's deceit.

And Jack had come after her.

"Yes, I want to see him." Whatever was to happen that day, she had to see Jack first.

Even if it was only to ask for his forgiveness before she said good-bye.

"WHY, LORD WHITCLIFFE, WHAT A SURPRISE." FREDDY moodily eyed his sister's betrothed over the rim of his glass. "Did you come by to see if you could chisel a little more money out of us before you finally say the vows and bring this whole sordid merger to a close? Or have you had a sudden attack of conscience, which is forcing you to call the despicable affair off?"

"Really, Freddy, it's much too early to be celebrating with drink and making silly jokes," scolded Rosalind.

She wore an artificially bright smile as she swept into the drawing room, where her sons and husband had gathered to wait until it was time to depart for the church. A swarm of servants was buzzing around them, setting tables and polishing silver and arranging vases overflowing with flowers. Rosalind was dressed in a gown of lavender satin trimmed with sable which was proving to be uncomfortably hot, and her head was adorned with an enormous hat so copiously piled with ribbons and silk flowers she feared people might think she was wearing the wedding cake.

"He isn't accustomed to being up this early, Mother," William joked from behind his newspaper. "He needs the drink to stay awake."

"More like I need it to stomach the sight of you," Freddy retorted.

"Shut your mouths." John Belford glared at his two sons, looking as if he might suddenly reach out and cuff them on the back of their heads. "I'm tired of listening to both of you."

"Do forgive us, Lord Whitcliffe," apologized Rosalind, mortified that the duke had been witness to her family's coarse behavior. She did not want him to think that he was marrying into a family of ill-mannered Americans, as she feared most of the English aristocracy sniped behind their backs. "As you can see, we are rather preoccupied with getting ready for the reception today. Whatever brings you here before the ceremony?"

Lord Whitcliffe looked at her as if he thought she must be demented. "You do—and it had better be bloody important, to drag me through that disgusting crowd of drunken filth on the morning of my own wedding. I damn near had my carriage turned over by ruffians as we drove down the street."

Rosalind frowned, confused. "I'm sorry, I don't understand what you mean. How is it that I brought you here?"

"You sent me a note, madam, asking that I call upon you at once to discuss a matter of profound importance prior to the wedding. The rude little urchin who brought it was quite adamant that you had instructed him to deliver it into my hand alone. He then had the gall to turn his back on me before he was dismissed, and when I criticized him for it, he belched. That is what comes from hiring a filthy little guttersnipe to perform the duties of a footman."

Lord Whitcliffe spat the words at her like annoying seeds. He disliked the Belfords generally, but he held particular contempt for Rosalind, who he saw as nothing more than a garishly dressed, social-climbing shop girl. John Belford was less pretentious but a complete boor, who continually succeeded in stunning London society by telling them tales of his impoverished background, as if it were something of which to be proud. Freddy was a complete drunk, but at least he was more tolerable than William, who simply oozed arrogance toward everyone he met. If not for their extraordinary wealth, Lord Whitcliffe would have nothing to do with them whatsoever. Once he had married their silly fool of a daughter and planted her firmly upon his estate, he hoped the rest of her atrocious family returned to America for good.

"If you're thinking to amend the amount we agreed upon as restitution for the humiliation your daughter has caused me these last weeks, do not waste your breath," he continued curtly. "Fifty thousand pounds is damned cheap when one considers the disgrace she has brought to the Whitcliffe name."

"And an illustrious name it is, too." Freddy raised his drink in a mocking toast. "I can't wait to start telling everyone that I'm your brother-in-law, Whitcliffe. You won't mind if I visit you and Amelia on your estate, and bring along a few friends?"

Lord Whitcliffe winced.

"Forgive me, Lord Whitcliffe, but I'm afraid I don't know what you are talking about," Rosalind said, growing flustered. "I sent no—"

"*Pardonnez-moi, madame,*" interrupted Annabelle, summoning all of her dramatic abilities as she burst into the room, anxiously wringing her hands, "but mademoiselle is very sick."

"What do you mean, sick?" demanded Lord Whitcliffe, glaring at her. "This had better not be another one of her tricks..."

"I'm sure what the girl means is that Amelia is merely suffering from an attack of nerves," interjected Rosalind, trying to defuse Lord Whitcliffe's anger. "All brides get a little stomach upset on the day of their wedding—it's perfectly normal..."

"*Non, non,* it is not the stomach." Annabelle shook her head vehemently. "She has the spots."

"The spots?" John Belford straightened in his chair, concerned. "What the devil do you mean, the spots?"

"She means that Amelia's complexion has become a little mottled as a result of her nerves," Rosalind assured him, unwilling to consider the possibility that Amelia might actually be ill. "Very well, then," she said, turning to Annabelle, "just cover them up with cosmetics."

"It is not nerves," Annabelle countered firmly. "She has the hot skin, she has the weakness, she has the spots. You must send for a doctor *immédiatement.*" Deciding she needed to kindle a little more fear in her audience, she added gravely, "I have seen this before—with the pox."

"Good God!" Lord Whitcliffe's wrinkled little eyes bulged in horror. "Do you mean to say she has smallpox?"

Annabelle raised a hand to her heart and regarded him sympathetically, as if she believed that he must love his betrothed dearly. "I'm so sorry, monsieur."

"We must send for a doctor at once," said Freddy, alarmed. He rose to ring for the butler.

"Wait a moment." Rosalind was acutely aware that the servants were stealing nervous glances at each other. The last thing she wanted was for panic to sweep through the house, or for word to get out that Amelia might be ill. "I will see Amelia first to determine how ill she is. This is probably nothing more than a mild rash brought on by nerves, which can quickly be remedied with some cool water and a light application of ointment. Do not do *anything*," she instructed firmly, "until I have returned."

Freddy set down his drink. "I want to see her, too."

"So do I," said Lord Whitcliffe, although he did not sound entirely certain.

"Now, Lord Whitcliffe, everyone knows that it is bad luck for a groom to see his bride on their wedding day before they are married," Rosalind chimed gaily, trying to reinforce her assertion that there was nothing seriously wrong with Amelia. "Besides, she may not be dressed appropriately to receive you."

Relief spread across his face. "Very well, then."

"I'll be back in a few minutes," she chirped, as if she were going off on some trivial errand.

She swept through the house and up the staircase, a resolute gust of satin and sable as Annabelle and Freddy hurried along behind her.

"Now then, Amelia," she began, pushing open the bedroom door, "what's all this nonsense about a rash?"

Freddy's face paled in horror. "My God."

Amelia lay on the bed covered by a single damp sheet, while Grace worriedly pressed a cool cloth against her forehead. The curtains had been closed once more, plunging the hot chamber into a stifling dreariness.

When playing a deathly-ill scene, Annabelle had told Amelia as she deftly painted her face, throat and chest with pink spots, *lighting and ambience are extremely important.*

"It's all right, Freddy," Amelia murmured. "I'm fine." She slowly turned her head to stare vacantly at her mother.

"What's wrong with you, Amelia?" Rosalind demanded, startled. "When did you become ill?"

When playing someone who is very ill, Annabelle had instructed, *first you should deny the illness. That is more convincing than moaning and complaining.*

"I'm not ill," Amelia assured her weakly. "I just need to rest a little, and then I'll get into my gown." She sighed and closed her eyes.

"But—how did this happen?" Rosalind looked at Grace and Annabelle in confusion.

"Mademoiselle told us she was not feeling well when we came in," Annabelle replied in a low voice. "She said she had been aching and hot for all of yesterday. Did she not tell you?"

"No—she stayed in her room for most of yesterday, and I was extremely busy. I assumed she was just a little tired." Rosalind felt a little defensive.

"When we opened the curtains to let in the light, we noticed the spots starting to appear," Grace said quietly, still pressing a cloth to Amelia's forehead.

"What spots?" Amelia did not bother to open her eyes.

"It's nothing, Amy," Freddy assured her. "Just a little rash from the heat. You rest and don't worry about a thing."

"But I have to get dressed... my wedding..."

"You have time, Amelia," Freddy told her. "It's still early."

Rosalind ventured closer to the bed, staring in dismay at the feverish, spotted specter of her daughter. "You'll be fine, Amelia," she murmured gently, trying to convince herself that was true. "Just rest a while." She adjusted the sheet, then turned abruptly and left the room.

"You've got to send for a doctor now, Mother," Freddy insisted, joining her in the corridor. "Immediately."

"But the wedding." Rosalind felt as if she was in shock.

"To hell with the goddamn wedding!" Freddy's voice was shaking with fury. "Amelia could be dying, and you're worried about your precious wedding? If she dies, you'll never be able to marry her off to *anyone*!"

"*C'est possible* the doctor will give her something to make her better, madame," Annabelle interjected. "Then the wedding will only be delayed a little."

Rosalind regarded her hopefully. "Do you think so?"

"Only the doctor will know what can be done."

"We have not had need for a doctor while we've been in London," Rosalind reflected. "Do you suppose Perkins will be able to suggest one?"

"You must send only for Dr. Chadwick," Annabelle told her adamantly. "He is doctor to all the most esteemed households in London. He is very reputable— very discreet. That is *très important*."

"Yes, of course." Rosalind was thankful that the maid was being so helpful. "Do you know if he lives far from here?"

"It is not far," Annabelle assured her.

"You'll have to go and fetch him, Frederick," Rosalind decided. "Until we know for certain what is ailing Amelia, I don't want any of the servants to know that she is sick."

"If I step out of that front door, I'll be mobbed by the journalists," Freddy pointed out. "And my carriage is certain to be followed to the doctor's house, which will only arouse suspicion and panic."

"Monsieur is right." Annabelle assumed an air of great purpose. "If madame will permit me, I would be pleased to fetch the doctor myself. I can go on foot, which will be faster than trying to take a carriage through these blocked streets. No one is going to follow a maid."

Rosalind was relieved by the suggestion. "Thank you, Mademoiselle Colbert. You will, of course, be compensated handsomely for your trouble."

"Ce n'est pas nécessaire," Annabelle informed her, telling her it wasn't necessary. She turned toward the stairs so Rosalind would not see her smile as she finished sweetly, "I do it for Mademoiselle Amelia."

Chapter Fifteen

THE CROWD OUTSIDE THE BELFORDS' LONDON MAN-
sion was growing restless.

According to the newspapers, the wedding between
Miss Amelia Belford and His Grace, the Duke of Whitcliffe, was scheduled to take place at St. George's Church
in Hanover at precisely half after two o'clock. Yet here
it was, already past two o'clock, and still no sign of either the bride or any member of her family. Even more
peculiar, the Duke of Whitcliffe himself had arrived in
his own carriage earlier that morning, reputedly looking
flustered and angry. What was the groom doing there?
everyone wondered. Had there been some last-minute
change to the marriage contract? Was His Grace asking
for more money? Or was that rich American, John
Henry Belford, demanding more than a title in exchange for his only daughter? Perhaps the foolish girl
had run away again. Or been abducted. Or attempted
suicide by throwing herself down the stairs, or slashing
her wrists, or eating poison. Maybe she had lost her
virginity during her so-called abduction, and Lord
Whitcliffe was refusing to marry her. No, that was not

reasonable, everyone swiftly agreed. After all, the dowry attached to Miss Belford was rumored to be in excess of some five hundred thousand pounds.

No man would refuse to marry such a staggering fortune, even if the bride carried a bastard in her belly.

Suddenly a dark carriage turned down the street and came to a stop in front of the house. The crowd drew a suspenseful breath as the old driver climbed down from his seat and opened the passenger door. Out stepped the pretty, honey-haired maid who had been seen leaving from the servants' entrance shortly before. Surprise rippled through the crowd. Who or what could this young woman have been sent to fetch that would have necessitated a return in a carriage? Before they could reflect on this a nurse appeared, her face obscured by the plain gray wool of her hooded cloak. She was evidently ill at ease before the enormous, gawking crowd, for she kept her head bent and her face hidden as she turned to offer assistance to the next passenger.

An elderly, spectacled man with a wiry bush of snowy hair seeping from beneath the brim of his tall hat climbed slowly from the vehicle. He was dressed entirely in black, which might have meant only that he had an aversion to colorful clothing, but everyone interpreted it as a bad sign. When the nurse reached into the carriage to retrieve his heavy leather bag, the crowd gasped. A doctor, just as everyone had suspected. It could only mean one thing.

Someone was dying.

The journalists shouted at him: What was his name? Who had fallen ill? What was wrong with them and did he expect them to live? as if they believed he should be able to render a diagnosis without actually seeing the patient. The old fellow ignored them as he mounted the steps, accompanied by the maid and the nurse, who apparently suffered from a limp. The front door swung open and the trio was whisked inside by Belford's dour-looking butler, who cast the mob a look of acute disgust before slamming the door shut once more. Undeterred, the journalists surged toward the carriage driver, demanding to know the names of his passengers and what he knew about their visit. The old driver raised his whip and flicked it menacingly over their heads, telling them to stand back, and saying if they so much as dared breathe on either his carriage or his horses he would make the whole blithering lot of them bloody sorry for it. At that point the police intervened, but the journalists were already retreating, madly scribbling notes into their journals. Two things they knew with absolute certainty:

The driver was bad-tempered.

And Scottish.

D<small>R. CHADWICK, THANK YOU SO MUCH FOR COMING</small> on such short notice," said Rosalind, greeting him in the entrance hall.

"I was in surgery," the old man snapped, crushing his white brows together with irritation. "Cutting out an abscess in the liver. Ghastly sight. The whole organ was green with bile. The moment I sliced into it, it burst and sprayed all over my assistant. I expect he's still trying to clean up the mess. Of course it didn't help with him vomiting all over the bloody place. That's the way it is sometimes, with surgery," he continued, scowling now at Freddy and William. "A damned messy business. I told the young fool he should wear a cap, but we can't tell you young people anything these days, can we now? Your grandfather here knows what I am talking about—don't you, sir?" he shouted, having decided that Lord Whitcliffe was deaf. "You don't get to be eighty years of age without learning a thing or two, do you?"

"I'm not eighty," protested Lord Whitcliffe, out-raged. "I'm only sixty."

"Of course you are." The doctor winked at him, amused. "And you look damned fine for your age, as your grandsons will attest."

"They are *not* my grandsons." Lord Whitcliffe's face was turning purple.

"Don't worry, your father's episodes of dementia are quite common in someone his age," the doctor told Amelia's father. "Best to just humor him, and keep him away from strong spirits. Next thing you know, he'll be telling me he's the bridegroom!" He barked with laughter.

"Actually, he is the bridegroom," William informed him tautly.

Dr. Chadwick blinked in amazement. "Really? Well, then, sir," he shouted, "aren't you the lucky one? Let's see what we can do about getting your lovely bride feeling better, shall we?" He turned to Rosalind. "Tell me, madam, how was your last bowel movement?"

"I beg your pardon!" Rosalind managed, shocked.

"How was your last bowel movement?" he bellowed. "Seems your father's bride has a little trouble hearing also," he told Amelia's father. He shifted his attention back to Rosalind and yelled, "Was it loose or formed?"

"Frederick," she began, struggling to maintain a dignified composure, "would you kindly show Dr. Chadwick upstairs to Amelia's chamber?"

"This way, Doctor." Freddy gestured for the elderly man to follow. "I'll take you to see my sister—she is the one who is ill."

"Well, then, what the devil are we doing blathering about here?" the doctor demanded impatiently. "Don't worry about your granddaughter," he shouted at Lord Whitcliffe. "I'll have her ready to watch you marry this grand old lady in no time." He tilted his head at Rosalind.

Rosalind gasped.

"What you need, madam, is a good purgative to clean you out," Dr. Chadwick advised. "Damned messy, but well worth the trouble. Remind me to give you one before I go."

He shuffled after Freddy up the staircase, oblivious to the outrage he had caused.

"I'll need plenty of hot water, soap, towels, a glass, and a good bottle of whiskey, Sister Cuthbert," he told his nurse as Freddy opened the door to Amelia's chamber. "Perhaps these two ladies will be good enough to assist you," he suggested, drafting Annabelle and Grace into service. "You go on downstairs, young man, and help to keep your grandfather calm," he added to Freddy. "Poor old chap seemed rather agitated. Be a damned shame for him to drop dead of a heart attack before his wedding night. Of course, given his considerable age and his weight, I wouldn't be at all surprised if he dropped dead after."

"One can only hope." Freddy cast a concerned look at Amelia, who was lying utterly limp upon her bed. "You will do everything you possibly can for her, Doctor, won't you?"

"She will have all the benefits of modern medicine," Dr. Chadwick assured him, setting down his enormous black bag. "Leeches, blood transfusions, surgery—whatever she needs. Just keep everyone out of my way while I'm with my patient." He closed the door.

Then he turned.

The room was dark and his disguise extraordinary, but it didn't matter. Amelia could feel his powerful presence filling the chamber, as surely as she could feel the anxious beating of her own heart. She sat up on the bed and stared at him.

"Hello, Jack," she said quietly.

Jack stayed by the door, suddenly uncertain. There was so much he wanted to say to Amelia, and yet he had no idea where to begin. And so he said nothing. He merely stood there, studying her through the darkness. She was dressed in an ivory nightgown trimmed with yards of delicately wrought lace and satin ribbon. The neckline was low and the sleeves barely skimmed her elbows, revealing the soft paleness of her skin, which was generously dotted with alarming pink spots. Annabelle and Grace had done a fine job of making her look deathly ill, with her feverishly damp hair curling around her and dozens of small, ugly lesions rising upon her flesh. Even a real doctor would have been fooled, at least from a distance. He wanted to wrap his arms around her and bury his face against the velvet cream of her throat, to breathe in the honey-sweet fragrance of her as he held her close. But a crippling insecurity froze him. He had begged her not to leave him, and she had.

He could not bear losing her a second time.

"I'm sorry." His voice was low and filled with regret.

Amelia regarded him in surprise. "For what?"

"For everything." He shrugged helplessly, knowing that was not an answer. Inhaling a deep breath, he struggled to find the words to make her understand.

"That day I found you trying to steal my carriage, you asked me if I knew what it was to be desperate enough to risk everything for the chance to find another life. And the truth was, Amelia, I did know. But I wouldn't admit it—not to you. Because you thought I was like the other guests at your wedding: people from privileged, decent backgrounds, who haven't had to live on the streets and wear filth and fight to survive. You didn't know who I was. Of course I knew it was just a matter of time before you found out. I was sure you suspected something the night I grabbed your wrist so roughly in my study. But every day I found some reason to keep the truth from you. Because I thought you would look at me differently once you knew. And I didn't want that. I wanted you to look at me the way you always did."

"How did I look at you?" asked Amelia softly.

He shook his head, unsure how to put it into words. "Not like you thought I was beneath you. And not like you thought I might be dangerous—even when I was drunk and gave you reason to."

"How, then?"

He shrugged and looked away. "Most of the time you looked at me as if you actually liked me. As if I was your friend. And sometimes..." He stopped.

"Yes?"

"You made me want to be the man I thought you were seeing," he finished awkwardly, wishing he could explain it better than that. "You made me want to be better than what I was."

Amelia regarded him intently. "I've always seen you for what you are, Jack. Caring, and brave, and generous. I needed your help and you gave it, just as you gave it to Charlie the night he was trapped aboard the *Liberty,* and to Alex when she needed a place to stay. You're strong, and you're not afraid to let others rely on that strength. You're honorable, and whatever you were forced to do as a child in order to survive takes nothing away from that. You're disciplined and hardworking, because you have had to fight to make the life you want. And you care about others, because you know what it is to be alone and afraid and desperate. I see you for the man you are, Jack." Her words were measured and emphatic. "Not for what you were as a boy, although I realize that is an important part of who you are today. And not for what I think you might be. I see you exactly as you are."

"I'm a bastard," he confessed ruefully, desperately wishing it were otherwise. "My mother was a poor maid who fell into bed with one of her employer's guests, and later was forced to whore in order to support herself— and me." His expression was dark with self-loathing as he continued, "And when I was a lad, I had to do things to survive—terrible things—"

"I don't care," she interrupted fiercely, rising from the bed. "Do you hear me, Jack? You can tell me about all this if you want to, or keep it buried in your past. It doesn't matter. I won't pretend that I can understand all that you have been through, but I'll promise you one thing. Nothing will ever change the way I'm looking at you now. Nothing."

Feeling as if his heart was being torn from his chest, he forced himself to meet her gaze.

And suddenly he understood what she was trying to tell him.

"I love you, Amelia," he managed in a raw whisper. "If you let me, I'll spend the rest of my life trying to make you happy. And I'll love you. Always." He clenched his fists and waited, wondering how he would bear it when she refused him.

She moved toward him in silence. "Would you do something for me?"

He nodded.

She reached out and took his hand, which was strong and warm against her own. Slowly, she raised it to her lips, kissing it tenderly before she pressed it hard against her heart. "Would you please take me home?"

Her eyes were glittering with tears.

"Yes." Jack's voice was rough with emotion. "I will take you home, Amelia."

He pulled her tightly against him and crushed his

mouth to hers. His hands roamed possessively over her, feeling the softness of her shoulders and breasts and hips, fingers threading into the warm damp weight of her hair. He did not deserve her. He understood that. She was much too fine and elegant and rare for him to ever be worthy of her. But in that feverish, desperate moment, he no longer gave a damn. He loved her. He had not meant to fall in love with her, but he had. And she wanted him to take her home. That was how she had come to think of his dilapidated little house, with its worn furnishings and its second-rate paintings of ships and rusted old swords hanging upon the walls. He would take her there. He would take her anywhere she wanted to go. It didn't matter to him anymore.

For him, home was wherever he could be with Amelia.

"Dr. Chadwick," called Rosalind, suddenly rapping upon the door. "May I come in?"

Abruptly, Jack released his hold upon Amelia. "Quick—get back into bed!"

Amelia scrambled across the room and dove back under the covers. "Jack—straighten your wig!"

Jack made a quick adjustment to his snowy cap, then fixed a grave expression upon his face and slowly opened the door. Amelia's family stood crowded outside, anxiously awaiting a report.

"I'm sorry, Dr. Chadwick," apologized Freddy, "but they refused to stay downstairs."

"Of course I'm not going to stay downstairs," Rosalind objected, fighting to maintain a semblance of calm. "I want to know how my daughter is, and if she will be able to get married today." She peered anxiously over Jack's shoulder into the gloom of the chamber. "Is she better?"

"Don't be idiotic," he snapped. "I'm a physician, madam, not some damned miracle worker. Your daughter is very ill."

Lord Whitcliffe looked thoroughly disgruntled by this unwelcome news. "What the devil is wrong with her?"

"She has the pox," Jack bellowed at him, cupping his hands around his mouth.

"Mon Dieu!" cried Annabelle, who was climbing the staircase with Grace and Charlotte, carrying a jug of hot water.

"May God have mercy upon us." Grace set down her tray and made the sign of the cross.

"Shall I fetch a quarantine sign for the front door, Dr. Chadwick?" asked Charlotte.

"I'm afraid so, Sister Cuthbert." Jack's expression was grim. "Those of you who have been exposed to the young lady may already have been infected and not know it. This disease is highly contagious, as I'm sure you are all aware."

"Quarantine?" Rosalind blinked in confusion, oblivious to the breathless hush that had gripped the entire house. "What do you mean, quarantine?" Her voice was shrill.

There was a paralyzed moment of utter silence.

And then a stampede erupted on the floors below. Abandoning their posts in terrified droves, dozens of servants raced for the doors. They knocked over vases, furniture and each other in their desperate attempt to escape the disease-ridden mansion, startling the curious crowd outside as they spewed forth in a monumental tidal wave of panic.

"It's the pox!" they shouted, sending a palpable surge of terror through the crowd. *"Amelia Belford has the pox!"*

An explosion of drunken humanity instantly discharged in every direction, sweeping up the police officers who until that moment had been trying valiantly to maintain some semblance of order. Even the journalists were jolted into action by this appalling development.

Driven by a heady dose of self-preservation, they started to run with the river of fleeing onlookers, forfeiting any attempt to stay and interview the family. Amelia Belford had the pox. That was story enough in itself.

"Oh, dear God," wailed Rosalind. "How on earth could this have happened?"

"She probably picked it up while she was running around these past few weeks." William's face was filled with disgust. "God only knows what sort of scum she was consorting with."

"Where are you going, Lord Whitcliffe?" demanded Freddy sharply.

The duke hesitated guiltily at the top of the stairs. "There's no real need for me to stay here," he explained, his hand gripping the banister. "After all, I've barely had any contact with the girl—I've not seen her at all since her return—and I'm afraid my being quarantined here is out of the question..."

"She's your bride," John pointed out, furious. "I would expect that you would at least feel some desire to stay close to my daughter and see how she is faring, since she was about to become your wife."

Jack's white eyebrows shot up in feigned astonishment. "That young lass is your bride? Well, then, sir," he bellowed, "by all means, you must see her. I'm certain a visit from her beloved groom will help to calm her considerable distress, but I must warn you to steady yourself. The pox is not a pretty sight, even in one as lovely as she. It can be damned messy, in fact. Best to look at her now, as tomorrow she will only be worse. Once the lesions become pustular and burst, the patient looks perfectly dreadful."

His eyes bulging with dread, Lord Whitcliffe forced himself over to Amelia's chamber door and looked inside.

"Is that you, Lord Whitcliffe?" she whispered weakly, extending a clawlike hand to him. "Please come and hold my hand—I'm not feeling very well." Amelia raised herself onto one elbow so he could fully appreciate the grotesque blotches dotting her face, chest and arms.

Lord Whitcliffe stood frozen, his spider-veined face drained of blood.

And then he bolted for the staircase, nearly knocking over his prospective in-laws in the process.

"I'm sorry, but I really cannot stay!" he yelped, racing down the stairs as fast as his considerable girth would allow. "I cannot!"

Jack restrained the urge to smile as he peered over the banister and watched the old duke skating across the freshly polished marble floor of the entrance hall. The front door closed with a bang, officially terminating Amelia's betrothal to the illustrious Duke of Whitcliffe.

"Excitable fellow, that one." He scratched his head.

"Good riddance," snorted John in disgust. "I never liked the pompous old prick anyway."

"This is a disaster!" Rosalind felt as if she was on the brink of hysterics. "The servants are gone, the wedding is off, and we are trapped while Amelia lies deathly ill— whatever shall we do?"

"I suggest you go down to the kitchen and see what needs to be done to preserve the food that was being prepared for today's reception," Jack suggested pragmatically. "You're likely to be in here a few weeks. Sister Cuthbert is experienced with tending to patients with infectious diseases," he continued, indicating Charlotte. "She and I have already had chicken pox; therefore, we will be the only ones permitted to enter and leave the house. We will see that the young lady is kept clean and comfortable, and I'll give her medication for the pain and an ointment for her itching. The rest of you should keep your visits with her brief so as not to tire her and to minimize your own exposure."

"I'm sorry," began Freddy, not certain he had heard correctly, "but did you say my sister has *chicken* pox?"

"Why—have you had it?"

"No." He tried not to laugh. "But I believe when you said that she had 'the pox,' everyone thought that you meant she had *smallpox*."

"Damned difficult to tell the difference between the two, especially in the first two to three days of the rash," Jack told him. "I've seen hundreds of cases, however, and I'm almost positive this is a case of chicken pox. We'll know for certain in a few days—perhaps as long as a week. Until then, this house is quarantined, just in case I'm wrong."

"That is impossible!" protested William. "I can't stay locked in here for a week. I've a business to run!"

"Actually, it's *my* business," John pointed out. "And as long as I can send and receive mail, I can bloody well run it."

"Come, *messieurs,*" said Annabelle, smiling at William and Freddy. "Let us go down to the kitchen and see about organizing the food. Perhaps we can prepare a nice lunch, *non?*"

Freddy flashed his most charming smile at Annabelle. "I don't know much about cooking, but under your tutelage, mademoiselle, I'm sure I can learn."

"I will help, too," offered Grace.

"And so will I."

Everyone looked at Rosalind in surprise.

"I do know how to cook," she informed them briskly. "Although I'll admit, it has been a number of years since I have had to do so. I'll just go to my room first and change out of this ridiculously hot outfit."

"Let me know when lunch is served," William muttered, heading for the staircase.

"You're coming too, William," Rosalind informed her eldest son. "This is a time of crisis, and in such times, we all have to work together. We certainly cannot expect Mademoiselle Colbert and Miss MacGinty to cook and wait on all of us, when they are lady's maids who only came here to help Amelia dress for her wedding. As it is, we are indebted to them for their kindness."

"I can't work in the kitchen." William looked stunned by his mother's suggestion. "I've never even been in the kitchen."

"That was rather negligent on my part," Rosalind decided. "There is no reason why a reasonably intelligent young man like yourself shouldn't know how to prepare a simple meal. Why, even your father knew how to fry eggs and bake a pan of biscuits when I met him."

"Damn right," said John. "And they were the best biscuits your mother ever tasted. I wasn't born with all of this nonsense, Dr. Chadwick," he informed Jack, gesturing impatiently at the lavish surroundings. "I was raised on a small farm with eight brothers. We couldn't afford servants, so my mother insisted we all work in the kitchen, just as we had to work in the barn or the fields. If we didn't cook, we didn't eat—it was as simple as that."

"A sound philosophy," Jack mused.

"As a boy, I never had shoes that fit me properly," John continued, sensing he was impressing the doctor with his impoverished beginnings. "If you look at my feet, you'll see that my toes are completely bent—"

"Really, John, Dr. Chadwick has greater things to worry about at the moment than your feet," Rosalind interjected.

"I think it's damned interesting," Jack assured her, feeling a slender thread of solidarity with Amelia's father. He had also spent most of his youth wearing ill-fitting shoes, generally stolen, and most often too big. Under different circumstances, he and John Belford might have shared a mutual respect. As it was, he was about to steal the man's daughter out from under his nose.

Somehow he doubted the wealthy railway magnate would ever have warm feelings for him after that.

"Sister Cuthbert, I need you to assist me with the patient," he told Charlotte.

"Of course, Dr. Chadwick." Charlotte limped dutifully into Amelia's chamber.

"Here is your soap, towels, and whiskey," said Grace, carrying her tray into the bedroom.

"And here is your water," Annabelle added, taking in her jug. "Do you need anything else?" She regarded Jack meaningfully.

"After Sister Cuthbert and I have tended to the patient, I'll let you know if there is anything more. Then I must get back to the hospital to see if my liver patient is still alive. Damned unlikely, after all that mess."

"But surely you're going to stay to look after my daughter?" Rosalind wanted to ensure that Amelia received the best possible care.

"Sister Cuthbert will be back later to check on her," Jack promised. "And I will visit each day, to assess her fever and see how her lesions are progressing. For the moment she requires rest, food, and drink, and sufficient medication to keep her comfortable." He disappeared into Amelia's chamber and closed the door.

"Very well then," said Rosalind. "Since there is nothing more we can do for Amelia at the moment, let us go to the kitchen and see about preparing lunch."

With that she shepherded her family, Annabelle, and Grace down to the unknown territory of the kitchen, leaving Amelia in the tender care of Dr. Chadwick and his quietly capable nurse.

WHERE ARE YOU GOING?" DEMANDED WILLIAM ABRUPTLY.
Startled, Charlotte managed an innocent smile. "Dr.

Chadwick asked me to fetch some supplies from the carriage."

"Let me get them for you."

"Thank you, but that isn't necessary." She sensed it wasn't gallantry that motivated him, but a nagging suspicion that something about his sister's sudden illness wasn't quite right. "I am perfectly capable of walking to the carriage and back by myself, Mr. Belford."

"I didn't mean to imply that you couldn't," William assured her, realizing the gray little creature had obviously taken offense. "I only thought given the extreme heat of the day, you might appreciate not having to climb up and down all those stairs."

"I find the exercise is good for me."

"Indeed." He took a deep swallow of brandy.

Charlotte laid her palm upon the door handle and hesitated. She and Jack had thought all of Amelia's family was occupied in the kitchen downstairs with Annabelle and Grace. Apparently, William had found a way to escape the drudgery of the kitchen after all.

"That's a remarkable cloak you're wearing," he observed. "Most people would not wear such a heavy garment on a hot day—especially with the hood up."

"The cloak is part of my uniform when I am outside. I wear the hood up to protect my face from the sun and the dust that fills the air."

"Sister Cuthbert, what the devil is keeping you?" barked Dr. Chadwick from the floors above. "We haven't got time for you to stand about blathering all day about fashion."

"I'll be right there," Charlotte told him.

"Well, hurry up—and ask those maids to make some tea, will you? I want to see Miss Belford drink something before I go."

"Would you be kind enough to go down to the kitchen and ask Miss MacGinty to make some tea?"

Charlotte asked William sweetly. "That will permit me to retrieve what I need from the carriage and take it up to Doctor Chadwick faster."

It would be ungentlemanly to refuse, but William had hoped to avoid the kitchen so he could keep from being conscripted into service again by his mother. "Very well." Depositing his empty glass on one of the rented tables that had been abandoned as the servants fled the house, he ambled downstairs.

"Dr. Chadwick wants you to make my sister some tea," he told Annabelle.

"Can't you see that Mademoiselle Colbert is busy, William?" Rosalind was hot and somewhat exasperated as she poked a fork into a pot of overcooked potatoes. The servants had rushed out of the kitchen leaving everything a mess, and she was having difficulty deciding what to do with all the abandoned food. "I'm sure you can manage to boil some water and make tea yourself."

"Now that I would like to see," said Freddy, who was awkwardly hacking away at an enormous fruitcake while Grace arranged the crudely chopped pieces upon a tray.

"*Non,* it will be quicker for me to do it." Annabelle abandoned the pink medallions of beef she was dropping into a frying pan. "Perhaps, Monsieur Belford, you would not mind watching this meat for me as it cooks. You must turn it just as it browns, carefully, without piercing the meat." She handed him a long fork, wiped her hands on a cloth, and disappeared into the pantry to search for the tea canister containing a mixture of sugar and potassium nitrate that Simon and Jamie had placed there earlier that day.

"One thing is certain—we won't be going hungry." Amelia's father found he was actually enjoying himself with his jacket off and his sleeves rolled up, carving an enormous leg of lamb. "When I was a boy, a roast like this would be made to feed us for a week."

"Really, John, how you exaggerate," scolded Rosalind, still jabbing uncertainly at her soggy potatoes. "How on earth could a single roast feed a family of fourteen for a week?"

"We never ate it as sliced meat," he explained, expertly carving another piece. "We had it chopped up in stew, or served in chunks over potatoes, or boiled and shredded in a soup—"

"Fire!" cried Annabelle, racing out of the pantry amidst a cloud of dense gray smoke.

"Throw some water on it!" shrieked Grace.

Freddy obligingly grabbed Rosalind's pot of potatoes, ran to the pantry door, and flung them in. Smoke continued to spew merrily from the little room.

"We need to smother it!" John snatched up an enormous bowl of flour and charged into the gray fog.

"John!" screamed Rosalind. "Come out of there at once, do you hear?"

He answered with a violent fit of coughing.

"Go in there, William, and bring out your father, before he has a heart attack!"

William reluctantly followed his father into the blinding haze.

"What the devil are you doing?" shouted John furiously as William grabbed him. "Let me go!"

"Mother told me to get you," William insisted. "Come on—oh, for God's sake!"

Both men stumbled out, covered in flour.

"What the devil are you people burning down there?" barked Dr. Chadwick crossly. "The air up here is foul!"

"The smoke must be drifting upstairs," said Grace. "Mademoiselle Colbert and I will open the windows to clear the house."

The two women hurried up the stairs, leaving Amelia's family to deal with the problem of the acrid smoke still pouring from the pantry.

"I think it's starting to die down," mused Freddy, heaving another pot of water into the pantry. He cautiously entered the little chamber, blinking against the gradually thinning haze.

"That's strange," he remarked, spying the smoldering tea canister. "Do you suppose Mademoiselle Colbert accidentally set the tea afire?"

John, Rosalind, and William crowded into the pantry to stare in confusion at the thin plume of gray gusting from the splendidly painted tin.

"Tea could never make that much smoke." Puzzled, John moved closer to examine the canister. "Whatever is burning smells odd—like saltpeter." He frowned at the twist of burnt rag protruding from the top of the container. "What the devil is that—a fuse?"

Understanding hit William with the force of a hard slap. "Jesus Christ!" His face contorted with fury, he raced out of the kitchen and up the stairs.

"Did you get that foul stink under control?" demanded Dr. Chadwick, who was cramming his hat onto his head by the front door. "It's not good for the lungs, you know. Turns them black. Looks perfectly ghastly when you cut them open." He frowned. "What the devil is that white mess all over you?"

"Where is my sister?" demanded William, convinced that the smoke in the kitchen was part of a scheme to help Amelia escape.

Dr. Chadwick looked at him as if he had taken leave of his senses. "Have you been drinking, young man?"

"Don't play games with me, you old fool—where is she?"

"Your sister is upstairs in her chamber, resting quietly." Dr. Chadwick's tone was mild, as if he was speaking to someone who suffered from bouts of paranoia. "She's sick with the pox, as I'm sure I have mentioned. As soon as I have finished examining my other patients, I will send Sister Cuthbert back to check on her."

William glanced through the open door at Dr. Chadwick's carriage. An ancient driver was helping Sister Cuthbert as she slowly climbed inside, taking care to avoid the sun beneath the hood of her cloak. "Where are those two maids? Miss MacGinty and Miss Colbert?"

"They are upstairs, opening the windows." Dr. Chadwick's gray eyes narrowed. "Have you been taking opium?"

"Of course not!"

"Very well, then." He picked up his bag. "I suggest you get some rest, young man. Experiencing sudden, irrational fears indicates the onset of brain fever, which is a most unpleasant affliction, I can assure you. The brain boils in its own juices, resulting in madness before a slow and agonizing death. Ghastly business. Sometimes I drill a hole in the skull to drain off the liquid, but that has unfavorable side effects, including idiocy. Hard to know how deep to drill before the brain comes squirting out. Best to lie down now."

"I don't have brain fever!"

"You may be right." Dr. Chadwick shrugged. "You could just be suffering from the onset of the pox." He shuffled out the door.

William loosened his necktie, suddenly feeling unaccountably hot. That's because it was bloody hot, he told himself crossly. The whole house was suffocating, thanks to the blistering heat and the choking stink of smoke. He began to slowly mount the stairs. Perhaps he should lie down, just for a minute.

By the time he reached the next floor, he felt as if he were melting. He tore off his jacket and opened his shirt, which was sodden with sweat. Was it too much to hope for a breeze in this smoky, pox-laden house? he wondered furiously. He walked toward the windows, desperate for a gasp of cooler air.

They were closed.

"Miss Colbert!" he shouted. "Miss MacGinty!"

No one answered.

He strode along the corridor toward Amelia's chamber. He supposed the two maids had gone there to see to her needs. That was understandable, but surely one of them could have dealt with the windows. He rapped on the door and waited. He preferred to speak to them in the corridor rather than venturing into the stifling, disease-ridden air of Amelia's room. No point in taking any chances. After a moment, he rapped again.

Silence.

A strange sense of foreboding gripped him. Forcing aside his considerable fear of Amelia's condition, he slowly opened the door.

And stared incredulously into the gloomy shadows of the empty chamber, and the hastily abandoned nightgown puddled in the middle of the floor.

Chapter Sixteen

"...THEN THE LAD CLIMBS INTO THE CARRIAGE SLOW as molasses, lookin' more dead than old if ye ask me, and I shut the door and we drive away, just like that." Oliver chortled, thoroughly pleased with his latest escapade.

"Jack made Oliver drive around for over an hour, just to be certain that no one was following us," continued Charlotte.

"But the streets of Mayfair were deserted after the servants ran from the house screaming that Amelia had smallpox. Obviously Jamie and Simon were very convincing when they started the charge for the door." Grace looked at her brothers with amusement.

"As soon as I heard Mrs. Belford yell 'quarantine,' I started screaming and used my most terrified expression, just the way Annabelle taught me." Jamie bulged his eyes and stretched his mouth as wide as it could go.

"When I came upstairs after hiding my smoking canister in the pantry, I didn't know if the servants were running from the pox or from him," quipped Simon.

"I never taught you to look like that, Jamie," Annabelle protested.

"Ye look as if yer head is about to explode," added Alex, frowning.

Doreen snorted with amusement. "'Tis that or he needs a good laxative!"

"Finally, Charlotte, Grace, and I were able to convince Jack that Amelia was safe and he let us come home," Annabelle finished.

"An' a good thing ye finally showed up when ye did," said Eunice, serving a plate of shortbread. "We was ready to march over to Miss Amelia's house and fetch her ourselves when we thought ye was takin' too long."

"If I'd been there, I'd have given old Whitcliffe a thrashing." Beaton puffed up with outrage as he poured coffee into little china cups. "Imagine runnin' off like that, when poor Miss Amelia was lyin' on her deathbed."

"But she wanted the greedy old codger to run off, Beaton." Lizzie looked at Amelia fondly. "The poor lamb just wanted to come home."

Genevieve leaned against Haydon and squeezed his hand, profoundly relieved that her children were safe. Her little band of orphans was grown, but that did not make her worry any less about their safety or their happiness. She glanced across the crowded drawing room at Amelia, wondering just how this profoundly privileged American heiress was going to adapt to living amidst such a colorful family.

"Jack has always been very concerned about my being followed," Amelia reflected, smiling. "He constantly imagined that whoever happened to be traveling behind us in Inverness was actually someone trying to come after me—but of course it never was. Poor Oliver had a terrible time trying to keep him from leaping out of the carriage and accosting people."

"Aye, that's true," Oliver agreed. "But one night, it seemed we were bein' followed, didn't it, lad?"

Jack stood slouched against the wall, his arms folded

across his chest. He knew Oliver suspected something important had been revealed to Jack during his visit to Lord Hutton. Jack had downplayed the matter, saying only that it had to do with information regarding the attacks on his ships. Oliver had regarded him skeptically, but had not pressed the matter further. One day Jack would tell his family about his relationship to the earl, but only when he had come to terms with it himself. While they would be pleased he had solved the mystery of his sire, nothing about Jack or his life would change. His family would still be the people around him, each of whom would do anything to help him, just as he would do anything for them.

Including Amelia.

"I don't remember." He shrugged.

"Now that Amelia has left her family once again, I expect her father will increase the reward for her return," speculated Haydon. "We will still have to be careful about her being followed—even in Inverness."

"I'm not so sure," Jack countered. "Her father seemed fairly disgusted by Whitcliffe when he went flying out the door. Now that he's gone, I think Amelia's parents will finally give up on trying to force her into a marriage she doesn't want."

"They won't get the chance again," Amelia stated flatly. "You and I will be married and my parents will no longer have any control over me."

Everyone's gaze shifted with amusement to Jack, who had suddenly lost his ability to speak.

"What's the matter?" Amelia regarded Jack expectantly. "You are going to marry me, aren't you?"

"Best answer her quick, laddie," advised Oliver.

"Lassies dinna like their men to dither on matters o' the heart," Eunice added.

"Just ask any of yer sisters," finished Doreen.

"If Jack won't marry you, Amelia, I will," Jamie offered, trying to be helpful. "I'm sure we would get on fine."

"She doesn't want to be married to a doctor who is always running off to see some sick person," objected Simon. "She'll be much happier married to me. We can work on new inventions together."

"Really, you two, stop teasing." Annabelle feigned vexation. "If Jack won't marry Amelia, then she and Alex can live with me. We could work together on a new book—*The Orphans of Argyll and the Runaway Heiress.*"

"I think Amelia and Alex should stay with me," said Grace. "Amelia knows a great deal about fashion, and we could come up with some wonderful new designs for next spring."

Charlotte looked at Jack with a mixture of sympathy and amusement. "I don't think Jack cares for those suggestions."

"Then why doesn't he say somethin'?" Alex scowled at him. "Are ye goin' to marry her or no?"

Jack flashed a look of pure exasperation at his family. "I thought I would actually ask her first," he managed tautly, "when we were finally alone."

Alex snorted with impatience. "Why do ye need to ask her, when she's already asked you?"

"The lass has a point," agreed Oliver merrily.

"Miss Amelia asked first because she's American," Lizzie explained to everyone with great authority. "American girls are very direct in their way of speakin', on account of the way they've been raised."

"I've always liked the way Miss Amelia speaks." Beaton gazed at her adoringly. "She's a real spanker."

"Perhaps we should all say good night to Jack and Amelia," Genevieve suggested, realizing the two might appreciate a little privacy.

"I think that's a good idea." Haydon offered his arm

to his wife and drew her close. "It has been a long day. Good night, everyone."

"I'm hungry," protested Alex, who was reluctant to go to bed.

"Of course ye are, ye poor wee duck," clucked Eunice. "Come down to the kitchen then, and I'll fix ye a nice plate of oatcakes and cheese."

"I'm hungry too," Simon told her.

"That's all right, lad, there's plenty for ye as well."

"I was actually thinking a few of your scones with marmalade would be nice." He regarded her hopefully.

"Do you have any of that clapshot left?" wondered Jamie.

Annabelle's eyes lit up. "With butter and pepper?"

"Maybe we could warm up some of the salmon hash to go with it," Grace suggested.

"Sweet Saint Columba, did I nae just feed ye supper?" Eunice fisted her hands upon her plump hips and glared at the little group with mock severity.

"Aye, ye did—and I've never tasted date puddin' so fine." Alex's expression was angelic. "No one makes puddin' like ye do, Eunice."

"Well, there's nae denyin' that," Eunice agreed, thoroughly flattered. "Come on then, duckies," she said, shepherding them out of the drawing room with the rest of the servants following. "Let's see what we can do about fillin' yer bellies until mornin'."

"Good night, Amelia." Charlotte bent down and kissed her cheek. "I'm so glad you're finally here," she said softly. "We've been waiting for you a long time."

Jack waited impatiently for the last of his family to leave the drawing room. When he and Amelia were finally alone he closed the doors. Slowly, he turned to her.

"I'm sorry if I embarrassed you in front of your family." Amelia realized she probably shouldn't have demanded if he was going to marry her in front of everyone. "Lizzie is right—I do have a way of just blurting out whatever comes into my head. It's just that I thought everything between us was settled, and I assumed that after everything you said—after what you told me . . ." She stopped, suddenly uncertain. "It was true, Jack," she began hesitantly, afraid that she had misunderstood. "Wasn't it?"

"I meant every word of what I said, Amelia. But I want to be sure you understand what you are giving up." He began to pace the room, feeling a need to have some distance from her as he tried to explain.

"I can't give you all the things you are accustomed to," he informed her bluntly. "North Star Shipping is a small, struggling company. While I believe eventually I can build it into something profitable, I can't guarantee I will ever have the extraordinary success your father has achieved. Of course I would make sure you had everything you needed, but you wouldn't be able to spend thousands of pounds on art and furniture, or gowns and hats from Paris—"

"I don't want those things," she assured him. "They aren't important to me."

"There is also the matter of where we would live," Jack continued, unconvinced. "With almost all of my money tied up in my business, I can't afford to buy you a bigger house—"

"We don't need a bigger house, Jack," Amelia objected. "There's more than enough room for you and me and Alex to live in your home quite comfortably, and if Oliver, Eunice, and Doreen choose to stay here with us, there is room for them as well."

"You're not used to living in such small quarters."

"You're right, I'm not. Freddy and I used to ride our bicycles in the corridors of our mansion in New York—much to the servants' horror. One day we were having a race and I had to swerve to avoid running down a maid, and I ended up crashing and breaking my arm." Her voice was teasing as she finished, "I promise not to try that at your house."

"I'm serious, Amelia." He resumed his pacing, convinced she did not comprehend the enormity of what she was doing. "My shipping business requires me to travel. I wouldn't travel as much as I do now, and I would try to limit myself to voyages that wouldn't take more than a week or two, but there would be times when you would be without me."

"I'm sure that between Alex, Oliver, Eunice, Doreen, and the rest of your family, I won't be lonely, if that is concerning you. I'll also have my work at the hotel to keep me occupied."

"You wouldn't have to continue working at the hotel. I may not be rich, but I can provide a comfortable enough life for you that that wouldn't be necessary."

"But I want to work," Amelia told him earnestly. "I enjoy my work, Jack. It gives me a sense of accomplishment and independence. Of course I realize Mr. Sweeney and everyone else will be shocked when they discover I'm actually Amelia Belford, but I expect that once they get beyond that, I'll be able to continue much the same as before. I have all kinds of wonderful ideas to make the next few events at the Royal Hotel really lovely and exciting—"

"You don't have to do this, Amelia." He had to give her the chance to leave him before she made a decision that she would undoubtedly regret. "You don't have to give up everything you have ever known to live with me in a shabby little house, surrounded by aging thieves and a family that society barely pretends to accept, and a husband they openly hold in contempt. You don't have to condemn yourself or your children to a life of always being looked down on, of never really belonging..."

"You're right, I don't." She rose from the sofa and

took his hands, forcing him to look at her. "I have a choice, Jack. And I choose with all my heart to spend my life with you. It doesn't matter how much money we have. Of course I want North Star Shipping to do well, but only because I know how important that is to you. I don't need an enormous house or hundreds of gowns—surely you must realize that by now. As for what society says about us, I honestly don't care. You forget that British society looked down upon me long before I met you. They despised me for being rich and American before I even set foot upon English soil. And our children will be fortunate to have a father as wonderfully strong and brave and caring as you. That matters far more than wealth or titles or pedigrees." She stared into the shadowed gray depths of his eyes, trying to cast light upon his fear.

"I love you, Jack," she told him fervently. "And I always will. You can believe me now, or spend the next fifty years letting me prove it to you." Her voice was teasing as she finished primly, "I really do think you ought to marry me, though, if you are at all concerned about protecting what little is left of my reputation."

Jack stared down at her in wonder, unable to believe that something so glorious could actually be within his grasp. A tentative joy seeped through him, slowly at first, like water trickling out from beneath the melting shield of a frozen pond. Amelia loved him. And she wanted to share her life with him.

It was as simple, and as incredible, as that.

"Marry me, Amelia." He drew her close and lowered his head until his lips barely grazed the velvet of her mouth. Then he whispered with aching, humble tenderness, "Please."

Amelia wrapped her arms around his neck and pressed herself against him, surrounding him with her gentleness and strength and love.

"Yes," she said, that single, earnest word encapsulating the exquisite joy she felt as she pledged herself to him. She kissed him deeply, eradicating the last remnants of his uncertainty and his fear. And when she felt his body harden and his powerful muscles begin to shift and clench beneath her touch, she laid her hand firmly against his heart, feeling it beat strong and whole and sure against her palm. "Yes."

About the Author

KARYN MONK has been writing since she was a girl. In university she discovered a love for history. After several years working in the highly charged world of advertising, she turned to writing historical romance. She is married to a wonderfully romantic husband, Philip, who she allows to believe is the model for her heroes.

Be sure to look for
Karyn Monk's next enchanting
romance, on sale in spring 2004

Read on for a preview...

HE HOISTED HIS LEG OVER THE WINDOW SASH AND dropped heavily into the dark chamber, barely stifling a groan.

I am getting too goddamn old for this.

Cursing silently, he rubbed the muscle spasm gripping his shoulder. He should have known better than to climb that tree. Since when had they started growing with so few bloody branches? He had thought he would ascend it with the agility of an acrobat, easily shifting from branch to branch. Instead he had dangled from it like a frantic puppy, legs swinging and scrambling, arms quivering. At one point he had lost his grip and nearly crashed to the ground. That would have been fine entertainment for the ladies and gentlemen attending Lord and Lady Chadwick's dinner party on the main floor, he reflected darkly. Nothing like having a masked man plummet from the sky just outside your dining room window as the servants are heaping your plate with stringy mutton and greasy peas.

He stood unmoving, giving his eyes a chance to adjust to the dark. It was quickly apparent that Lady Chadwick liked gold. Everything within her bedchamber fairly shimmered, from the heavy brocade coverlet upon her gilded bed to the garishly carved commode that towered like a throne beside it. No doubt in her private moments she imagined herself the consort of a magnificent prince or duke, instead of the bloated, sniveling fop she had elected to marry. He supposed every woman was entitled to some fantasy in her life. His gaze shifted to the bureau at the opposite end of the chamber, which boasted a profusion of richly decorated bottles and jars. Stealing silently across the shadows, he reached for the jewelry chest rising amidst the clutter.

Locked.

He eased open the uppermost drawer of the bureau and rifled through the layers of undergarments folded within. The key lay nestled amidst the armor of Lady Chadwick's formidable corsets. Why did women always assume thieves would never think to look there? he wondered. He supposed it was based on the assumption that most men were either too modest or too gentlemanly to rummage through a woman's lingerie.

As it happened, he was neither.

Carefully inserting the key into the jewelry case's tiny lock, he turned it once, then raised the lid.

A glittering collection of precious stones lay gleaming upon the dark velvet within. In addition to her penchant for gold, Lady Chadwick also enjoyed the sensation of large diamonds, rubies and emeralds against her skin. He supposed that was fair compensation for enduring the tedium of marriage to Lord Chadwick for so many years. He lifted a magnificent emerald necklace to the thin moonbeam filtering through the window, watching in fascination as its color shifted from near-black to the clear green hue of the river he had played in for so many years as a lad.

The chamber door opened suddenly, flooding him in a wash of light.

"Oh, I beg your pardon," the young woman standing in the threshold quickly apologized. "I didn't realize anyone was in here—"

Harrison watched with grim resignation as understanding swept through her. Ultimately, he had no choice. Even so, guilt weighed heavy in his chest as he grabbed the girl and jerked her toward him. She stumbled forward and he caught her, then kicked the door shut. He clamped a gloved hand against her mouth and twisted her around, imprisoning her slender form against him. Her fear was palpable, he could feel it in the rapid pounding of her heart against his arm, could hear it in her soft, desperate little pants of breath. Self-loathing welled within him.

For God's sake, focus.

"If you scream, I will kill you," he whispered harshly into her ear. "Do you understand?"

Her body stiffened. He was acutely aware of the scent of her as he held her close. Not roses or lavender, or any of the other sickly-sweet perfumes he was accustomed to women wearing. The girl pinned against him had an unusually light, clean fragrance, like the essence of a meadow just after a summer rain.

"I'm going to take my hand away from your mouth now. If you swear to me that you won't scream or try to run away, I give you my word that you won't be harmed. Do I have your promise?"

She nodded.

Harrison warily removed his hand from the girl's lips. He didn't know whether he could trust her. Her evening gown suggested she was one of Lady Chadwick's dinner guests. Whatever her reasons for quitting the dining room, it likely wouldn't be long before some dutiful maid was sent to find out what was detaining her. The girl's delicate ribcage continued to rise and fall against his arm. Her breathing had slowed a little, and he was grateful for that, even though he supposed it would have been better for both of them had she swooned. Then he could have simply laid her on the bed and climbed back out the window. As it was, he was going to have to tie her up so she couldn't go screaming out of the room the moment he left, compromising his escape.

"Please." Her voice was small, hesitant. "You're holding me so tight I can't breathe."

She was Scottish, he realized, the sweetly refined cadence of her voice pleasing to him.

"Forgive me." He instantly released her.

She faltered slightly, as if she had not expected him to free her quite so abruptly. He instinctively reached out to catch her, but this time his hold was gentle. She glanced at him over her shoulder, surprised.

"Thank you."

Moonlight spilled across her face, illuminating her features. She was not as young as he had thought, for there were fine lines around her enormous dark eyes and across the paleness of her forehead, suggesting her age to be at least twenty-five years or more. Her cheekbones were high and pronounced, emphasizing the elegant fragility that seemed to surround her. Her finely shaped brows were drawn together and her mouth was set in a sober line as she studied him, her expression hovering somewhere between fear and something else, an emotion that looked almost like empathy. That was ridiculous, he told himself impatiently.

No woman of gentle breeding would sympathize with a common jewel thief—especially one who had just threatened to kill her.

"You dropped your necklace." She pointed to the sparkling pool of emeralds and diamonds upon the carpet.

Harrison regarded her incredulously.

"It might be better to leave that one, and take a few smaller pieces instead," she suggested. "Lady Chadwick is sure to notice that her precious emerald necklace is missing the minute she goes to put her jewelry away tonight. If you take some of her less important pieces, she is unlikely to realize that they are gone right away, which means you will have an easier time selling them. Once their theft has been reported to the police and the newspapers, your sources might be reluctant to buy them."

He raised a bemused brow. "Are you always this helpful during a robbery?"

She colored slightly, embarrassed. "I just thought you might consider the advantages of selecting quality pieces which are more modest in appearance. The larger, more opulent stones are not always the most valuable—they can be flawed within."

"I realize that."

"Forgive me—of course you do." Her gaze became curious. "You're the Dark Shadow, aren't you?"

Harrison stalked over to the bureau and began to ransack Lady Chadwick's intimate apparel, searching for something with which he could tie up his quizzical young guest.

"When do you think you will have stolen enough?"

He paused to look at her. "I beg your pardon?"

"The newspapers have been filled with stories of your robberies for months now," she explained. "I'm wondering when you think you will have stolen enough that you will be able to resign from a life of crime and apply your talents toward a more law-abiding profession. Ultimately, sir, I'm sure you will find the rewards are much greater in leading a respectable, productive life."

Anger pulsed through him. In his experience, women who spewed sanctimonious advice about the path of righteousness had invariably lived sheltered lives. They didn't know the first goddamn thing about life beyond their own smug existence.

"It is something you should consider," she continued seriously. "If you are caught you will be sent to prison. I can assure you that is not a very pleasant place to be."

"I'll bear that in mind." He yanked a stocking from the drawer. "I regret having to do this, but I'm going to have to bind you to that chair over there. I'll try not to make the bindings too tight—"

"Miss Kent?" There was a cursory rap upon the chamber door before it swung open.

"*Help!*" shrieked a horrified maid, appalled by the sight of Harrison in his dark clothes and mask stalking toward the girl with a twisted stocking in his hands. "*Murder!*" She tore down the corridor, screaming loud enough to wake the dead.

"Quick—go out the window!" exclaimed the girl. "Hurry!"

Swearing furiously, Harrison threw down the stocking and sprinted toward the window. Shouting and screaming split the night air, causing the coachmen and the curious on the previously sedate street to surge toward the house. He was relatively certain he could scrabble down that godforsaken tree in less than a minute without breaking any significant bones.

The distinct possibility that some earnest champion from the mob might shoot him down from the branches like a giant, hapless bird gave him pause.

"What are you waiting for—go!" The girl waved her arms at him as if she were shooing an errant child out the door.

Realizing he had little choice, he heaved one leg over the window sash and stretched his aching arms toward the tree.

A shot streaked through the darkness, clipping the branch where his fingers had brushed.

"I got him!" roared an excited voice from below. "Stop, thief!"

"Come back!" hissed the girl, grabbing him by his coat. "You can't go that way!"

"I realize that," Harrison agreed tautly.

"You'll have to leave from Lord Chadwick's chamber across the hall—hopefully there won't be anyone waiting for you on the other side of the house." She went to the doorway and peered into the corridor.

"Come out with your hands in the air!"

Harrison joined the girl at the doorway to see a scrawny young groomsman trudging warily up the stairs, balancing a battered old rifle unsteadily before him.

"I warn you," he bleated nervously, "I've killed before an' I ain't afraid to do it again."

Harrison thought that unlikely, unless the lad was referring to killing rodents in the stable. At that moment, however, the prospect of being shot by a terrified youth with an ancient firearm struck him as highly undesirable—especially given that the boy might miss and hit the pretty young stranger who was so gallantly trying to assist him instead. With no hope of racing across the hallway to another chamber, his only chance for escape had disintegrated. How ironic, he reflected bitterly, to be caught and arrested for his crimes at this late stage.

He exhaled in disgust and raised his hands.

"He has a pistol!" screamed the girl suddenly at the groomsman. "Don't shoot or he'll kill me!"

Harrison stared at her in disbelief. "What in the name of God are you doing?"

"We have no choice," she whispered fiercely. "You've got to use me to get out of here!"

"Let her go!" The groomsman sounded as if he was going to be sick. "I told you, I ain't afraid to shoot!"

"For Christ's sake, Dick, don't threaten him!" barked a footman, venturing up the stairs behind him.

"He's liable to murder the whole bloody lot of us!" added the butler, joining them.

"Fine then!" squealed the groomsman, thoroughly agitated. "Maybe you'd like to have this instead!" He shoved his weapon at him.

"Don't give it to me, you idiot," snapped the butler, pushing it back. "I don't know how to fire it!"

"Silence, all of you!" Breathless and sweating profusely, Lord Chadwick struggled to affect an air of dignified authority as he reached the top of the staircase. "This is Lord Chadwick speaking." He paused to dab his brow with a linen handkerchief, letting the import of his presence sink in.

"Lord Chadwick, thank goodness you're here." The girl pretended to sound relieved. "Please tell everyone to clear the staircase and let us come down—he won't shoot anyone as long as no one tries to stop him—"

"Everyone in the house has exactly two minutes to go down to the kitchen and lock the door behind them," snapped Harrison. Since this girl had just added abduction to his litany of crimes, he supposed he might as well play some actual part in it.

"Go into the kitchen?" Lord Chadwick sounded outraged by the idea. "Look here, sir, I don't know who you are or what you mean by breaking into my home, but I assure you that I am not moving from this spot until you release my guest safely into my custody, do you hear? Miss Kent's well-being is my responsibility, and I have no intention of abandoning her to your foul, despicable ways—"

"The first person I see upon leaving this room will be shot dead, Lord Chadwick," Harrison vowed darkly, "and that includes you. Now *move* before I—"

A deafening blast suddenly tore through the house, cutting short Harrison's threat.

"Run for your lives!" His bulging eyes nearly bursting from their tiny sockets, Lord Chadwick knocked his startled servants aside as he fought to beat them down the stairs. *"Run before he murders all of us!!"*

The entire household instantly exploded into a maelstrom of fleeing bodies, the distinctions of sex and class obliterated as servants and aristocrats crashed into one another in their desperate bid for safety.

"I told them to go into the kitchen," muttered Harrison, exasperated. "Now I've got an even bigger crowd to contend with once I get outside."

"If you keep me in front of you, they won't shoot," the girl suggested.

"I'm not taking you with me—that idiot groomsman is liable to kill you in his attempt to save you."

"I think he dropped his rifle." She glanced around the door and saw the clumsy firearm lying abandoned on the carpet. "There, you see? He must have thrown it down after it went off."

"It's Miss Kent, is it?" Harrison's tone was bland.

"It's Charlotte, actually. Miss Kent always sounds so terribly formal—"

"It may surprise you to learn, Miss Kent, that I'm not in the habit of abducting helpless women and using them as a shield. I don't intend to start now." A dull throbbing started to pound at the base of Harrison's skull. He was beginning to wish he had stayed home that night.

"You're not actually abducting me—I'm offering to

help you," Charlotte pointed out. "Unless you are prepared to be arrested and spend the rest of your days in a prison cell, you have to let me help you get out of here."

Her eyes were large and earnest. It was impossible to determine their color in the soft veil of light spilling into the room, but it struck Harrison that they were unlike any he had ever seen. There was a singular strength emanating from the strange young woman standing before him, a unique resolve that was as bewildering as it was captivating.

"Are you carrying a pistol?" she demanded.

"No."

She frowned. "What about a dirk?"

Reluctantly, he nodded. "I have a dagger in my boot."

"A dagger is fine for threatening to cut my throat," she allowed matter-of-factly, "but if someone decides to try to wrestle it from your hand, we're going to have a problem."

He didn't know what to make of her. Any normal gentle-born woman would have been drowning in tears by now, begging him to release her unharmed. Instead this strange girl was scanning the room, apparently trying to come up with another weapon for him. He went to the window and glanced at the crowd still gathered on the street below. The hammering in his head was spreading now, sending deep tentacles of pain streaking across his forehead and into his temples.

"I know!" she exclaimed suddenly. "You can hold Lady Chadwick's hairbrush in your pocket and press it against my ribs as we go out, giving everyone the impression that you have a firearm."

She grabbed a heavy silver brush from the bureau and held it out to him. As if she actually believed he was a man of great daring, who was easily capable of outwitting an irate mob on the strength of a mere hairbrush. For some strange reason, he was loath to disillusion her. When was the last time a woman had looked at him with such pure, untainted trust in her eyes? he wondered bleakly. The pain in his head was getting worse now. He knew in a few minutes it would be excruciating, and then he would be unable to think at all. If there was any chance of escape, however small, this was his only moment to grasp it.

"And what do we do when we get outside?" he asked.

"Don't you have a carriage waiting for you?"

"No."

She frowned again, as if she found it incomprehensible that a thief could attempt a robbery so poorly prepared. "Then we'll have to take mine," she decided, moving toward the doorway.

"Are you hurt?"

She regarded him in confusion. "No—why?"

"Your leg—you seem to be having trouble walking."

"It's nothing," she assured him shortly. "I'm fine."

Shoving Lady Chadwick's hairbrush into his coat, he wrapped his arm around her.

"I don't need your help to walk," she protested, trying to push him away. "I'm quite capable of—"

"I'm only doing as you suggested and pretending that I am using you as a shield."

"Oh." She stopped fighting him, but her body was rigid beneath his arm. It was obvious he had touched a raw nerve when he mentioned her leg.

"Once we are outside, if anyone decides to overtake me, I want you to get the hell away from me so you are out of harm's way." Harrison regarded her seriously. "Is that clear?"

She shook her head. "No one is going to attack you as long as I stay in front—"

"Is that clear?"

"If I move away from you, someone might shoot you."

"We're not leaving, Miss Kent, until you say yes."

She sighed, reluctant. "Yes."

"Fine then. Let's go."

They moved awkwardly down the staircase together.

By the time they had reached the main floor, his accomplice was breathing heavily, and despite her assurances that she was fine, Harrison knew her gait was painfully stiff. He had little time to reflect upon this, however, as they stepped up to the front door and into the view of the crowd awaiting them outside.

"Everyone move back," Harrison commanded, holding fast to his partner, "and send Miss Kent's carriage over."

The terrified horde obediently took a few steps backward. The carriage, however, was not forthcoming.

"Send Miss Kent's carriage over," repeated Harrison heatedly. "*Now!*"

"I heard ye the first time, ye soddin' piece o' scum," barked a furious voice. "An' if ye so much as bend a wee hair on the lass's head while I'm bringin' it to ye, I'll be scapin' yer cowardly flesh from yer thievin' bones and choppin' it fine afore I grind ye into haggis!"

Harrison watched in astonishment as an ancient little man scuttled as fast as his skinny legs would carry him toward the line of carriages on the street. Displaying a remarkable agility for his advanced years, he hauled himself up into the driver's seat of one vehicle, snapped his reins against the horse's hindquarters and sent it lurching forward.

"That's Oliver," Charlotte whispered to Harrison as the carriage barreled toward them. "He is very protective of me."

"Wonderful," drawled Harrison.

The carriage clattered to a stop directly in front of the entrance. Oliver cast Harrison a murderous look before regarding Charlotte with concern. "Are ye hurt, lass?"

"No, Oliver," Charlotte assured him gently. "I'm fine."

"Ye'd best make sure she stays that way, ye spineless cur," he warned Harrison, "if ye're thinkin' ye'd like to keep yerself in one fine piece."

The idea of the wiry little Scotsman fighting him was

preposterous. But Harrison recognized the old man's overwhelming fear for the girl pinned against him, and he knew better than to trifle with the elder's emotions.

He had learned that strength born of fear and frustration could be far more dangerous than that of mere youth and muscle.

"I give you my word that Miss Kent will not come to any harm as long as you do exactly as I say," he told him.

Oliver snorted in disgust. "Canna trust the word of a rogue who'd snatch a helpless young lass an' push a pistol to her ribs," he spat contemptuously. "Ye thieves today have nae honor, an' that's the sad truth o' the matter. Now in my day, ye'd nae see me wavin' a gun about—"

"Please, Oliver," interrupted Charlotte. "We have to go *now*."

Oliver glowered at Harrison. "All right then, ye wicked rascal, see if ye've enough manners in ye to help Miss Charlotte into the carriage, an' we'll be off."

Relaxing his hold upon her slightly, Harrison reached up to open the carriage door.

"*No!*" cried Charlotte suddenly.

Harrison turned just in time to see a nattily attired gentleman clutching a pistol in front of the doorway from which he and Miss Kent had just emerged. One of Lord Chadwick's guests had not abandoned the house after all, he realized numbly. Instead he had hidden inside, waiting for the perfect moment to race out and shoot the infamous Dark Shadow in the back. The man's beefy hands were trembling visibly, his brow jeweled with perspiration as he leveled the pistol at Harrison.

Harrison wrapped himself around Charlotte, enveloping her in the hard shield of his body just as the weapon exploded. Fire ripped into him, burning a path through flesh and bone. Holding Charlotte fast, he jerked open the carriage door.

"Stop, thief!" roared his assailant. "I have another pistol!"

Harrison whipped around, shoving Charlotte behind

his back. He brandished Lady Chadwick's hairbrush menacingly through the fabric of his coat. "Throw it down or I'll shoot your bloody—"

Another shot exploded through the darkness.

Harrison froze, knowing if he flinched the bullet would strike his prospective young charge instead.

For a moment no one moved, anxiously waiting to see if the infamous Dark Shadow had been killed.

"Thomas!" screamed a woman suddenly. "Oh, dear God—Thomas!"

Confused, Harrison raised his gaze to the front doorway.

The fashionably attired guest lay sprawled upon the stairs, his arms and legs spread out upon the polished stone steps. At first it looked as if he had merely slipped and fallen. But something was leaking across the pale surface of the step beneath him and weeping onto the next in a grotesque river of crimson.

"Saint Columba—ye've killed him, ye filthy swine!" blazed Oliver, appalled.

Harrison stared in bewilderment at the limp, bleeding form of the man on the stairs, his hand still gripping Lady Chadwick's hairbrush.

"Get in the carriage!" hissed Charlotte. "Now!"

"I'm nae takin' him anywhere," Oliver raged, "the bastartin devil! He can bloody well hang—"

"He didn't do it!" Charlotte was trying desperately to get Harrison to move. "He couldn't have, Oliver—he doesn't have a pistol!"

Oliver scowled, confused. "He doesn't?"

"Please, you can't stay here!" Charlotte pulled hard on Harrison's arm, trying to get him into the carriage.

The night was filled with screams now. Men and women were running away, disappearing down laneways and into neighboring mansions, wildly trying to escape the murdering Dark Shadow. There was nothing he could do for the poor bastard bleeding on Lord Chadwick's steps, Harrison realized bleakly. Surrendering to Miss Kent's pleas, he helped her into the carriage. Then he hauled himself up and banged the door shut as the vehicle flew forward.

Pain was everywhere now—blinding in ferocity. Its talons had sunk deep into his brain and eyes and ears, while the fire streaking through his shoulder was radiating to the tips of his fingers. His coat sleeve was sodden with blood, and his mouth was nauseatingly dry. He was alive, and so was the strange young woman who had interrupted his disastrous escapade.

Everything else was lost.